Joe Haldeman puts his own stamp on the seventeenth Nebula collection by selecting almost all fiction and including, as he writes in his introduction, those "watershed stories that mark the emergence of new talents." Here, then, is the "stuff of wonder" — the fullest and most exciting Nebula annual yet.

Ace Science Fiction Books by Joe Haldeman

NEBULA AWARD STORIES 17
WORLDS APART

NEBULA AWARD
STORIES 17

Edited by
JOE HALDEMAN

ACE SCIENCE FICTION BOOKS
NEW YORK

NEBULA AWARD STORIES 17

An Ace Science Fiction Book / published by arrangement with
Holt, Rinehart and Winston

PRINTING HISTORY
Holt, Rinehart and Winston edition published 1983
First Ace edition / June 1985

ISBN: 0-441-56797-5

Ace Science Fiction Books are published by
The Berkley Publishing Group,
200 Madison Avenue, New York, New York 10016.
PRINTED IN THE UNITED STATES OF AMERICA

For
Damon Knight and Kate Wilhelm

Contents

Introduction

Joe Haldeman

This is the only foreign story in this anthology. I'm pretty sure it's the only one whose writing began on a cramped little tray hemmed in by smoked reindeer meat and cold Finnish beer. Seven miles over the Arctic Ocean, I'm writing in the warm belly of a Finnair DC-10, while below me unrolls a thoroughly hostile chiaroscuro of black water lanes crazing through blinding snow, as the icepack shivers apart in concession to spring. If we were exposed down there, we would die in minutes if not seconds, and the only thing keeping us alive is a complex smorgasbord of loud machinery that gives disconcerting shudders and lurches every now and then. Yet for the first time in a couple of weeks I feel quite safe and comfortable: I've been two weeks in the Soviet Union.

Which is true but not fair. Intourist and the Soviet Writer's Union, in the process of shuffling our group of science fiction writers and fans from Moscow to Kiev to Leningrad, went out of their way to make us feel wanted and important. And some warm times, as you sat digesting your fifth shot of vodka, as you smoothed yet another incredible pile of caviar onto fine-grained black bread—as you tested cultures by trading jokes and photographs—some warm times you felt almost at home. But then there would be a look. There would be a word said or, more often, not said. And the look or the word was a wall.

You are the aliens here.

We want your understanding, yes. But don't try to make us understand you. We already know what you are.

Part of this feeling was certainly projection on my part. No American my age, born at the end of World War II and growing up in the Cold one, can look at the hammer and sickle and see simply a warm symbol of workers' solidarity. No one whose main exposure to the Russian language has been the scary, inflexible rhetoric of Stalin and Khrushchev and Brezhnev can hear its musical lilt with simple pleasure. And those of us who carry Russian lead in our bodies, mementos of the late unpleasantness, might be excused for finding uncomfortable the sight of thousands of Soviet soldiers massed for May Day celebration.

But it wasn't only projection of my own generation's fears and prejudice and memories; the others felt it too, with birthdates from 1901 to 1964, black and white, VFW to NOW. It was not just culture shock or linguistic isolation. It was real. It was a wall.

And despite all of my preparation, it took me by surprise, which I think is the point of this essay.

I have been not quite around the world in the service of science fiction, which is to say in self-service to my own career. (I hope next year to complete the circle with China.) With and without interpreters, I've sat with foreign cohorts and tried to penetrate the barriers of Serbo-Croatian, Japanese, Hungarian, and every common European tongue. By and large we have been able to communicate, because we share the meta-language of science fiction. Let me give you some rules of its grammar:

All things change.

There is no thought that cannot be challenged.

Philosophy does not change reality.

The past is a closed and dusty volume. The future is real but malleable.

Die Gedanken sind frei: thoughts are free.

Soviet science fiction can be good, but it applies a different grammar. Some things do not change. Some truths are not to be questioned. Phenomena inconsistent with Marxism do not exist. The past is our guide to the future; its essential character was predetermined by the wisdom of Marx and Lenin. And your thoughts are only free so long as you keep them to yourself.

Not all Soviet writers feel this way, of course. Just the ones who get published.

I found out that not much of my own work is publishable in the Soviet Union, even though it is generally critical of American values and often sympathetic to socialism. It sometimes treats things that don't exist, though, such as homosexuality,* and it is often negative if not downright seedy.

The one word that kept cropping up when we discussed science fiction with Soviet critics, editors, and publishers was *kind.* This was emphasized in every formal meeting, and also came up when we were just sitting around our hotel rooms, speaking clearly into the television set. A work of art must be *kind.* I finally objected, while meeting with a children's publisher in Leningrad. I asked the translator what they meant by *kind*—in English, I explained, it is a rather broad word, encompassing shades of *accommodating, empathetic, polite, benevolent, considerate, merciful.* She said, "Yes, of course," which was an answer we got to a great variety of questions, and told me the Russian word: *dobreya,* amplifying the translation by saying it meant "good will." My Russian dictionary at home adds the helpful definition "nice."

---

* In one of the books I read preparatory to visiting Russia, the author tells of being shown a classroom full of third-graders who were diligently practicing their handwriting. Something about the sight bothered him, and after a moment he caught it: Where were all the left-handers? he asked the teacher. "Oh," she said with a smile, "we have no left-handed children."

Most science fiction in the Soviet Union seems to be published under the rubric of "children's literature." When we asked whether that meant it was relegated to a second-class status, we got the same protestation everywhere (indeed it sometimes felt as if an approved script had preceded us from city to city)—children's literature must be *good* literature; its standards must be even higher than those imposed on literature for adults. I'd never deny that this can be true—if I've ever invented a character half as good as Long John Silver or Huck Finn, I'm not aware of it—but it doesn't really answer the question. A better answer was provided by the often-repeated assertion that one of the most valuable functions of science fiction is to instill an enthusiasm for science in the young, and prepare them for careers in science and engineering. Also repeated was the pleasant term "moral guidance."

People familiar with the history of American science fiction will hear the ghost of Hugo Gernsback in those two statements of purpose, but it's not the old-fashionedness of the attitude that is disturbing. Gernsback was just one brilliant, cranky man, and the only power he had to enforce his attitudes was the rejection slip. A Soviet writer's manuscript is judged not only by an editorial board, but by committees of people whose primary interest in the work is not literary. If *they* reject your manuscript, you can't just mail it out to another publisher. If they reject it with enough force, you may find yourself in a place where the postage rates are rather high.

Politics aside (as much as possible), this root assumption, that the moral content of a story has to be consistent with a predetermined formal dialectic, seems absolutely antithetical to the spirit of science fiction. A lot of good science fiction—I would like to think *most* of it—makes its philosophical points obliquely and even outrageously. There is strong moral content in Delany's *Dhalgren*; in Ballard's *Crash*; in Wolfe's *The Claw of the Conciliator*—and if the truths we find in such works are not very comfortable, if they are unkind, they are no less true.

To mitigate that a little, it has to be conceded that any writer—any artist—creates his work within a framework of approved values characterizing the moral and ethical consensus of the most powerful stratum of his society, and all of his work is at least unconsciously affected by that consensus. You might even go so far as to say that most serious work is centrally concerned with such conventions, either reinforcing them or questioning them. Limiting the artist's universe to reinforcement, then, doesn't in theory prevent him from doing serious work. I would chafe under the restriction—probably find another way of making a living—and so would most of the writers I know. But we didn't grow up in so tightly controlled a society. It could be that a Soviet writer accepts political conformity as a condition of employment just as easily as I accept the condition that my work must be entertaining (when in my heart I would rather that it be important), with neither of us thinking too much about it in the day-to-day production of work. A cage can be made of exceedingly fine mesh.

I wish I could have talked freely with a Soviet writer. That was "not possible," another phrase we got used to. We met them only in very public circumstances, with translators and others monitoring what was said. The people we talked to in private were publishers, critics, and copyright-office people who spoke good English, had traveled to foreign countries, and were allowed to come up to our rooms unaccompanied. They didn't earn such privileges by voting Republican. If any writers were similarly privileged, they either weren't interested in talking to us or their English wasn't up to the job.*

It seems to me that a Soviet fiction writer must have a hell of a job in front of him, serving three masters at once. The work has to be ideologically correct, of course, but if the writer

---

* We were told that English was virtually the second language of the Soviet Union, with some 70 percent studying it in school. But outside of Intourist control, I made better use of German; very few people could, or would, answer the simplest question in English. This is not necessarily sinister. Foreign language is a use-it-or-lose-it proposition, and there aren't many opportunities for an ordinary Russian citizen to practice English.

is a serious one, he has to juggle that with the obscure yet
compelling demands of an artist's sensibility and conscience.
While those two balls are in the air, he has to add a third one,
a crumpled-up balance sheet, because—sad shade of capitalism—if a writer's books don't sell, he stops getting published.
If he doesn't publish for a few years, the State compels him to
take a useful job somewhere.

The State has some compassion, though; it does make
allowances for illness, family problems, and age. In terms of
material comfort and security, at least according to the picture
the Writer's Union painted for us, a Soviet fiction writer is
better off than his average American counterpart. He gets paid
according to a simple formula that takes into account the
length of the book and what type of book it is, and he gets
paid again promptly for each subsequent edition. This has to
make his financial life a lot more manageable than an American writer's. He may never become a millionaire, but neither
will he ever spend months bickering over the size of an advance, and then more months waiting for the publisher to
come through. He has no worries about health care, insur-
ance, libel laws. His union maintains large, comfortable clubs
in all the major cities, and vacation retreats at the seashores,
spas, and mountains. In many ways, it sounds like a good life.

I would love to compare notes with one of them, talk
honestly about the tensions and compromises that lie between
the thought and the book, compare the satisfactions and trou-
bles that each of our systems offers its servants. The formal
differences seem profound, but I suspect that in the most important parts of our lives, in the business of properly ordering
thoughts and putting them down in just the right sequence of
words—and then living with the rest of the human race, away
from our typewriters—we go down the same tortuous road.

There are several annual "Best SF of the Year" anthologies,
but this is the only one that throws a sop to democracy. Most
of the stories contained herein were chosen by the six hun-

dred–odd (yes, *odd*) members of the Science Fiction Writers of America, rather than by one eccentric editor.

Any member of the SFWA can nominate a story, and the stories with the most nominations go on a final ballot. A five-member Nebula Jury (of which I was a part this year) can add at most one entry to each category on the final ballot. This is to give a chance to deserving stories that appeared in expensive hardcovers or obscure journals.

This book contains an excerpt from the novel that won the Nebula Award, the novelette and novella winners, and most of the short stories that made it to the final ballot.*

This volume is somewhat reactionary in that it's almost all fiction. In recent years, the Nebula anthology has become (in my humble yet temporarily all-powerful opinion) somewhat top-heavy with essays. My own feeling is that the Nebula volume has an important archival function, not just for the prizewinning stories but, perhaps more important, for those watershed stories that mark the emergence of new talents—

---

* Unfortunately, it doesn't include the winning short story, "The Bone Flute," by Lisa Tuttle. Ms. Tuttle refused the award in protest against some members' campaign practices: they or their editors mailed out copies of their stories to the membership, which from Ms. Tuttle's viewpoint amounts to discrimination against members who can't afford the Xerox bill, or don't have accommodating editors. Under the circumstances, she couldn't allow her story to be in this volume. (Please do find it somewhere else, though; it's quite good.)

I'm not unsympathetic with her stance—if I were, this footnote wouldn't be here—but feel that the practice is a self-correcting one, since members who receive these copies are aware of the element of *de facto* discrimination, and react to it. I tend to turn the copies over and use them as scratch paper.

Normal campaign practices for the Nebula, for those interested in such gossip, don't go beyond making sure your friends know you have a story on the ballot that's the best damned thing since Heinlein was a pup. Of course this does give an element of "popularity contest" to the Nebulas, but that's also true of Emmys and Oscars and school-board elections. All you can do is grumble, and make sure your vote is based on merit alone. Except, of course, when your own story is on the ballot. Then you don't even have to read the others.

stories that drew the attention of fellow writers and stayed in their memories, whether the authors were well known or obscure. I've included survey articles by two experts as well as this obligatory essay, but the rest of the book is the real stuff, the stuff of wonder.

Be glad, with me, that we have it. I don't think there will be a Soviet edition.

1981 and Counting

Algis Budrys

Some people say Algis Budrys is the only real science fiction critic in America, where there are a lot of book reviewers. He is the son of diplomats who were unable to return home after World War II, and he has lived here ever since.

Budrys is best known for his novel Rogue Moon, *though the recent* Michaelmas *was also well received. His most recent book is* Some Will Not Die *(Starblaze), a revised version of the earlier* False Night. *He reviews books for the* Washington Post *and other newspapers, and his criticism appears regularly in* The Magazine of Fantasy and Science Fiction.

Many of the major novels of 1981 were stages in larger works—Julian May's *The Many-Colored Land*, Gene Wolfe's *The Claw of the Conciliator*, to name two that we may be sure have been taken permanently into the SF literature. 1981 was the year in which it was announced that Arthur C. Clarke had not, after all, retired, and that Isaac Asimov was working on another book in the Foundation series. Frank Herbert produced another Dune book, not quite a sequel to its predecessors, yet what else but a sequel? In the fantasy domain of SF, there was the announcement of Terry Brooks's sequel to *The Sword of Shanarra*, and the news of more volumes in the Chronicles of Thomas Covenant.

In a literature that is increasingly discussed as if it contained nothing but novels, 1981 will undoubtedly be looked back on as a year indissolubly tied to other years. May's novel is a major event; inventive, rich, the work of an author so long absent from the field that she was little more than a legend to the present generation. But it won't be 1981 that's recalled in connection with this occurrence; the Saga of the Pliocene Exile will be said to have appeared "in the early 1980s," as will Wolfe's *The Book of the New Sun*. What we have here is a year that for one reason or another will not carve its particular niche in the traditions of our field, despite the fact that a great deal of good and sometimes superb work appeared in it.

Or so it might be said. But we haven't talked about the short stories, of which this anthology will give you what I think is the best possible sampling. I commend them to you without much further comment; you'll see for yourself that inventiveness and freshness have not vanished from the field, and that the media for shorter work are obviously alive and well.

What I would like to talk to you about is this instance of the difference between what is perceived and what happened. I think this is a difference that has been widening. Not dangerously, alas for dramatic propositions. But enough so that we might do well to consider it, and rein it in a little.

One can hardly blame publishers of novels for pretending that novels are all that are important. And since it's largely the book publishers who command the advertising and public-relations means to communicate the sense of what's going on in the field, the reader even of many magazines is apt to feel that anything not a novel is somehow less considerable. Again, that's not hard to understand—the magazines carry the ads and the book review columns that subtly reinforce this impression. And should a magazine carry a biographical sketch of, or an interview with an author, what is usually mentioned is the work published in books. Some of the fiction in the magazines is labeled part of "a novel in progress," or an excerpt from "a forthcoming novel." It all goes to make the free-standing short story, novelette, or novella appear to be some sort of by-the-way thing.

And yet the major influential works in American SF have almost always been of less than novel length; most of them have been outright short stories, little packages of utter revolution.

This is not invariably true. But this would be an utterly different field without John Campbell's "Twilight," Fritz Leiber's "Coming Attraction," Cordwainer Smith's "Scanners Live in Vain," Walter M. Miller, Jr.'s "A Canticle for Leibowitz," or James Tiptree, Jr.'s "Houston, Houston, Do You Read?" It would be different as well without *Stranger in a Strange Land*, *The Space Merchants*, or *The Left Hand of Darkness*, but again and again it has been the short work that left ripples spreading through the field in general, whereas even the greatest novels—the aforementioned three, plus *The Demolished Man*, *Slan*, *Dune*, *Childhood's End*, to add some others—have signaled not so much a general change as a milestone in a particular writer's career. And no career, no matter how mighty, is ultimately as important as a shift in the direction of an entire literature.

How can a short story do this, when a novel has so much more scope? Well, a novel—particularly the recent SF novel, where the fashion is for the epic—is about many things, for all that it may have a strong unifying theme. A short story—an ideal short story—is about some one thing, and in the right hands can be about some one thing that doesn't ordinarily occur but occurs with great force. And it occurs in one swift moment of crystallization, with an almost audible pang, whereas the usual novel grows and flowers in a more majestic manner. The truly effective short story is harder to write than a novel of equivalent worth.

This is a fact that professionals have long recognized, and for that reason, when they instituted the Nebula Awards, they were careful to see to it that short work would be properly rewarded. And whereas the novel Nebula is usually won by an established name in the field, the short-work Nebulas have been quick to recognize the uncommon newcomer.

In a sense, this is a reflection of the fact that the major novelists come from the ingenious young short-story writers, by and large. By and large, there would be a natural tendency to seek out the newer names, to let the established writer wait for his novel Nebula or to rest content in Nebulas past, although that tendency does not express itself as clearly when one looks down the lists over the years. But whatever the actual factors are, the short-work awards represent a consciousness for the future, while the novel Nebulas honor the present.

And so I've verged on giving the impression that the short work is, after all, recognized as much for what it promises as for what it is. But this is not true in any common manner. It is possible to believe, when a new writer appears with short work of Nebula quality, that he or she will probably be a major novelist of the future. In that sense, there is a promise. But it is a promise that exists in addition to the independent merit of the work. If it is not fulfilled, if the author never does produce a major novel, he or she may still have a great influence on the field.

As "Don A. Stuart," author of "Twilight" and usherer-in of the Golden Age of 1940s SF, John Campbell never wrote a novel. Ray Bradbury's "novels" of the 1950s are short-story collections gathered from the 1940s. Theodore Sturgeon's reputation rests not so much on his novels, proficient as they are, as on works such as "Microcosmic God," "Killdozer," and countless other novelettes and novellas, including "Baby Is Three," the core of his best-known novel, *More Than Human*. The novel of *A Canticle for Leibowitz* is not as important as the original short story. The novel of Lester del Rey's "Nerves" or of James Blish's "A Case of Conscience" did not strike with the impact of the original novellas. And this pattern, laid down in a time that may be little more than misty legend for most of today's readers, persists.

If Damon Knight, for all his good books, is still a man remembered almost exclusively for his short stories, and if few recall that *Fahrenheit 451* was originally "The Fireman" but quite properly consider Bradbury essentially a writer in short forms, there is still Harlan Ellison, and there is still the fact that John Varley, James Tiptree/Alice Sheldon, George R. R. Martin, Lisa Tuttle, Tom Reamy, and, yes, even Joe Haldeman and Joanna Russ, would occupy almost precisely the same places in this field if they had never written a novel. And their names form only part of what could easily be a much longer list. We want to remember that the new Foundation novel is the first Foundation *novel* Asimov ever wrote; the longest previous piece was a two-part serial, and even so was unique for length.

The fact is that the history of this field would be much what it actually is if *all* its books were dovetailed short stories or expanded shorter works; although the percentage of free-standing novels has risen sharply over the past twenty and particularly the last ten years, still a large proportion of what we see in the libraries and on the "new books" table at the store continues the historic tendency to assembled work. It is not possible to go on from this to a statement that people buy these books out of a nostalgia for the original short stories; that wouldn't account for the multigenerational popularity of the Foundation series or *The Martian Chronicles*.

No, the conclusion one comes to is that SF readers, unlike the readers of general fiction or of any of the "category" fictions of which SF is mistakenly adduced to be one, on some level recognize that the short-story form is the essential SF form. We like our books with multiple climaxes, casts of characters who may come and go in midstream, events that come in series rather than develop in parallel. We don't like them to the exclusion of all other possible forms available in long formats, but we do like them, very much, and in that way we differ from most other readers.

What this seems to reflect is some version of the old saw that in SF, the idea is the hero. I would rather argue that in SF a demonstration of what can be done with the idea is the hero—i.e., the thing to which the reader thrills. But however complex you want to make the concept, it remains true that in a literature of ideas, the tendency would be toward the best vehicle for defined ideas, and thus toward the short story. The problem with the short story in a commercial literature, which SF obviously is, is that the short story doesn't pay very much. Therefore, the prudent writer is motivated toward the novel.

Behold, then, this book full of the work of imprudent writers? That hardly seems a fair description. Let us think again:

For one thing, it's possible for a type of writing to be an obvious commercial property without being a thoroughgoingly commercial literature. SF is aggressively marketed by publishing houses that turn it to account, and I think we can safely presume that those houses would as lief publish something else, if they could find a type of product that brought in a higher return on the investment. From that end of the business, the transaction is a simple profit-and-loss event.

A book is a package, marketed like package goods. And although in SF—almost uniquely in SF—the magazines verge on being cottage industries, directed by what amount to family-held small corporations and in at least one case produced, all but the printing and binding, in the publisher's own exurban home, it is nevertheless possible to see the magazines, too, from an accountant's point of view. That this cold view does not represent the paramount truth—that even the glossy *Omni* owes its existence to a publisher's personal preference for and heavy involvement in it—does not dispel the fact that the cold view exists, or that the casual observer may readily see it as the only view. But the writer sees it all from a different standpoint, and has sufficient evidence that the reader, too, does not share the corporate comptroller's simple criteria.

Every writer of SF, from novice to Grand Master, is well aware that there is more than enough money available for work whose essential quality need be no different from what it was in the days when all rights in perpetuity for a novel were going for three hundred dollars. (Admittedly, six hundred dollars was more usual, but being totally swindled by an evanescent corporation was also not unheard of.) Every writer in the field over the age of fifty has worked under those conditions, which now make for amusing anecdotes at the table, and there are plenty of them. An awareness of money thus saturates the field, and in most cases is restimulated with some poignancy when the first of the month rolls around or the favorite child elects for an Ivy League education. But that is the writer as business manager; it is not the writer alone at midnight with a blank piece of paper, self-assigned to the task of making something come to life that has never been seen before.

The buck stops there. Some writers are content to produce work not particularly new, or not new at all except in unessential details, but you won't find any of that work here. Most writers, when writing, are hindered by the thought of money; any thought not concentrated on the task at hand is an intrusion and tends to get itself thrown out.

Whether the finished work will be good, bad, or indifferent, according to the writer's talent and circumstances, while it is happening it is an exquisitely personal process, dependent on inner rearrangements of everything that the writer's entire life of thought has made of every piece of information ever presented to the mind by the senses. It is something that has never happened to anyone else in the same way, and never will happen to anyone else in that way, throughout the history of human self-awareness. The writer writing is situated at a unique moment in the history of the universe, and knows it. The writer writing a novel has moments of respite. The writer doing shorter work does not.

Lest we lose ourselves in the grandeur of this romantic vision, let us remember that while this condition is noble, it is not elective, and furthermore not unique to writing or even to the recognized arts. It comes with the territory. It can be described in simple Pavlovian pleasure/pain terms, and can be made to seem little just as readily as it can be made to seem transcendent. But what it does mean in any case is that the inner sensation of writing finds its purest, most intense form in short writing.

This does not mean that any given short story is "better" than any given novel. The sensation of writing has nothing to do with the quality or nature of the finished work. But it does have to do with how the writer feels at midnight. And I think, in truth, that top-flight writers *feel* more intensely. Therefore I am suspicious of the writer who has stopped doing short stories, and if you look around you will notice that very few of the writers who do more than entertain you as before have stopped doing short stories even when it makes no economic sense to continue. And this is just as true outside SF, except that it so happens SF offers a deeper and broader range of media for short fiction than any other field.

Obviously, I don't think it does just so happen; it is inherent in the nature of the field, reinforcing the nature of writing, that makes it happen. And when we speak of the nature of the field, we speak of the reader.

Obviously, nothing would happen without the reader. Not so obviously, no one concerned with the process of creating, editing, publishing, marketing, and critically evaluating writing can have an exact idea of what goes on in the reader. We do not read the same way; there is a glass wall between what we are and what we were—readers moved by reading to a desire to write or at least shape writing. And it is the central irony of our present estate that even the attempt, let alone the successful attempt, has forever removed us from being able to read simply. We all try to remember what that was like, and we all try to guess; we can identify an "audience" (although we do not know precisely which given individual might be a member of it unless he or she steps forward and tells us), but we cannot identify a reader.

So, like the marketers, we tend to speak of markets. There is no other rational approach. But we practice the irrational; what will pass through the glass wall is intuition, and this unquantifiable but very real sense of reader presence informs our midnights. I don't think any two of us could agree on what that presence is, exactly. Fortunately, we avoid making comparisons. I know who you are; my colleague, over there, probably has some different picture of you, but I would not care to disturb his equanimity by correcting it, and I appreciate her showing me the same courtesy. Nevertheless, there are some objective evidences, and these tend to point toward the idea that the SF reader, too, tends to favor short work in the sense that it seems to be more readily discussible.

Writers very rarely meet readers in an innocent situation. One party or the other—probably both—is aware that whatever is said will be conditioned by something with more overtones than the usual one-to-one interaction. So I can't be sure. But it seems to me, over a span of thirty years, that while you cannot generally expect readers to recall the titles or even the authors of stories read some time ago—barring a few cherished favorites—what readers remember about a novel *is* the title, and what they remember about a short story is the central statement. What, for instance, is *Stranger in a Strange Land* about? Well, it's about a fellow, raised by Martians, who comes home to Earth with a new and effective slant on religion. But what is that slant, exactly? Ah, well, that takes several paragraphs of rumination and discussion—not a bad thing in itself, but inherently fuzzy—whereas Isaac Asimov's "Nightfall" says that people who have never seen the stars will go crazy with fear at their first glimpse of the open night sky, no matter how glorious; period, sharp edge.

A defined packet of readily retrievable information, tagged by an emotional response, has been stored forever in the reader's mind. It is a clear-cut piece of personal experience. Together with similar experiences stored nearby, it can be used to build up an ongoing picture of what SF is, and what good SF is, and what sort of SF the reader would like to see more of.

It can do more than that—it can provide the reader with checkpoints along the road he has come. I can tell you exactly where I was when I first read "Nightfall"—curled up on a surplus U.S. Marine bunk at the freshman campus of the University of Miami, in the Everglades, turning the pages of a brand-new copy of the first edition of *Adventures in Time and Space*, in early 1948. I can tell you where I was when I read "Twilight," and I can do the same for you in re "Coming Attraction." But although I am very fond of *Pebble in the Sky*, have read *The Moon Is Hell* with admiration and fascination, and have read and admired a great many Fritz Leiber novels, the experience of reading and assimilating a novel has its own rewards but does not usually have that moment of crystallization.

And I think it's through those moments that a reader places himself in context as a reader of SF; such moments define for her, in a sense, what SF is; they help to form the impulses that will lead to buying a proffered book or not buying it, to support a magazine or regard it with boredom, and thus to encourage the field to trend in some particular direction in preference to other possible directions. It is also through those moments, of course, that the impulse to become a writer is coalesced.

So 1981, despite the many good novels that appeared in it, is by circumstance a year in which the role of the shorter work emerges with particular clarity; it is for the work in this volume, very likely, that 1981 will be remembered specifically, by readers and by readers-turning-writers, and it is because of outstanding short work that any number of SF futures will be dated from it.

And now I leave you to it.

Venice Drowned

Kim Stanley Robinson

I remember Kim Stanley Robinson as one of the best writers in quite an impressive group of students I taught at the Clarion science fiction writing workshop in the mid-seventies. He was not the one who dismantled the ceiling, though, nor the one who carried around a small bale of marijuana and a glazed expression, nor the one who supposedly had shacked up with one of the instructors, nor the one who liberated the fire hose . . . unfortunately for me, Stan was just a pleasant, hardworking guy who was mainly there to write, and write well. Which makes it difficult to do a racy introduction for him. Doubly difficult because he pleads modesty and will only reveal the following information:

1. *He did his Ph.D. thesis on the novels of Philip K. Dick (whether in the department of English, theology, philosophy, or pharmacy, he does not say).*
2. *He teaches at the University of California at Davis.*
3. *His first novel,* The Wild Shore, *came out from Ace in 1984.*

"Venice Drowned" is a nearly flawless exemplar of a kind of writing that can only be done in science fiction. I don't know if it has a name—in academic jargon I suppose it would be something like "refractive mimesis"—but it's that creepy kind of double-vision writing where an imagined world, similar to ours but different in some dramatic particular, is described with such painstaking authority that it becomes absolutely real, to such an extent that the world ceases to be simply background for the story; in a curious way, it becomes the story. Philip Dick was the master of this kind of invention, of course, which doesn't detract from Stan's achievement. Rereading it gives me goosebumps.

By the time Carlo Tafur struggled out of sleep, the baby was squalling, the teapot whistled, the smell of stove smoke filled the air. Wavelets slapped the walls of the floor below. It was just dawn. Reluctantly he untangled himself from the bedsheets and got up. He padded through the other room of his home, ignoring his wife and child, and walked out the door onto the roof.

Venice looked best at dawn, Carlo thought as he pissed into the canal. In the dim mauve light it was possible to imagine that the city was just as it always had been, that hordes of visitors would come flooding down the Grand Canal on this fine summer morning. . . . Of course, one had to ignore the patchwork constructions built on the roofs of the neighborhood to indulge the fancy. Around the church—San Giacomo du Rialto—all the buildings had even their top floors awash, and so it had been necessary to break up the tile roofs, and erect shacks on the roofbeams made of materials fished up from below: wood, brick lath, stone, metal, glass. Carlo's home was one of these shacks, made of a crazy combination of wood beams, stained glass from San Giacometta, and drain pipes beaten flat. He looked back at it and sighed. It was best to look off over the Rialto, where the red sun blazed over the bulbous domes of San Marco.

"You have to meet those Japanese today," Carlo's wife, Luisa, said from inside.

"I know." Visitors still came to Venice, that was certain.

"And don't go insulting them and rowing off without your pay," she went on, her voice sounding clearly out of the doorway, "like you did with those Hungarians. It really doesn't matter what they take from under the water, you know. That's the past. That old stuff isn't doing anyone any good under there, anyway."

"Shut up," he said wearily. "I know."

"I have to buy stovewood and vegetables and toilet paper and socks for the baby," she said. "The Japanese are the best customers you've got; you'd better treat them well."

Carlo reentered the shack and walked into the bedroom to dress. Between putting on one boot and the next he stopped to smoke a cigarette, the last one in the house. While smoking he stared at his pile of books on the floor, his library as Luisa sardonically called the collection; all books about Venice. They were tattered, dog-eared, mildewed, so warped by the damp that none of them would close properly, and each moldy page was as wavy as the Lagoon on a windy day. They were a miserable sight, and Carlo gave the closest stack a light kick with his cold boot as he returned to the other room.

"I'm off," he said, giving his baby and then Luisa a kiss. "I'll be back late; they want to go to Torcello."

"What could they want up there?"

He shrugged. "Maybe just to see it." He ducked out the door.

Below the roof was a small square where the boats of the neighborhood were moored. Carlo slipped off the tile onto the narrow floating dock he and the neighbors had built, and crossed to his boat, a wide-beamed sailboat with a canvas deck. He stepped in, unmoored it, and rowed out of the square onto the Grand Canal.

Once on the Grand Canal he tipped the oars out of the water and let the boat drift downstream. The big canal had

always been the natural course of the channel through the
mudflats of the Lagoon; for a while it had been tamed, but
now it was a river again, its banks made of tile rooftops and
stone palaces, with hundreds of tributaries flowing into it.
Men were working on roof-houses in the early-morning light;
those who knew Carlo waved, hammers or rope in hand, and
shouted hello. Carlo wiggled an oar perfunctorily before he
was swept past. It was foolish to build so close to the Grand
Canal, which now had the strength to knock the old structures
down, and often did. But that was their business. In Venice
they were all fools, if one thought about it.

Then he was in the Basin of San Marco, and he rowed
through the Piazzetta beside the Doge's Palace, which was still
imposing at two stories high, to the Piazza. Traffic was heavy
as usual. It was the only place in Venice that still had the
crowds of old, and Carlo enjoyed it for that reason, though he
shouted curses as loudly as anyone when gondolas streaked in
front of him. He jockeyed his way to the Basilica window and
rowed in.

Under the brilliant blue and gold of the domes it was
noisy. Most of the water in the rooms had been covered with a
floating dock. Carlo moored his boat to it, heaved his four
scuba tanks on, and clambered up after them. Carrying two
tanks in each hand he crossed the dock, on which the fish
market was in full swing. Displayed for sale were flats of mul-
let, lagoon sharks, tunny, skates, and flatfish. Clams were piled
in trays, their shells gleaming in the shaft of sunlight from the
stained-glass east window; men and women pulled live crabs
out of holes in the dock, risking fingers in the crab-jammed
traps below; octopuses inked their buckets of water, sponges
oozed foam; fishermen bawled out prices, and insulted the
freshness of their neighbors' product.

In the middle of the fish market, Ludovico Salerno, one
of Carlo's best friends, had his stalls of scuba gear. Carlo's two
Japanese customers were there. He greeted them and handed
his tanks to Salerno, who began refilling them from his ma-

chine. They conversed in quick, slangy Italian while the tanks filled. When they were done, Carlo paid him and led the Japanese back to his boat. They got in and stowed their backpacks under the canvas decking, while Carlo pulled the scuba tanks on board.

"We are ready to voyage at Torcello?" one asked, and the other smiled and repeated the question. Their names were Hamada and Taku. They had made a few jokes concerning the latter name's similarity to Carlo's own, but Taku was the one with less Italian, so the sallies hadn't gone on for long. They had hired him four days before, at Salerno's stall.

"Yes," Carlo said. He rowed out of the Piazza and up back canals past Campo San Maria Formosa, which was nearly as crowded as the Piazza. Beyond that the canals were empty, and only an occasional roof-house marred the look of flooded tranquillity.

"That part of city Venice here not many people live," Hamada observed. "Not houses on houses."

"That's true," Carlo replied. As he rowed past San Zanipolo and the hospital, he explained, "It's too close to the hospital here, where many diseases were contained. Sicknesses, you know."

"Ah, the hospital!" Hamada nodded, as did Taku. "We have swam hospital in our Venice voyage previous to that one here. Salvage many fine statues from lowest rooms."

"Stone lions," Taku added. "Many stone lions with wings in room below Twenty-forty waterline."

"Is that right," Carlo said. Stone lions, he thought, set up in the entryway of some Japanese businessman's expensive home around the world. . . . He tried to divert his thoughts by watching the brilliantly healthy, masklike faces of his two passengers as they laughed over their reminiscences.

Then they were over the Fondamente Nuova, the northern limit of the city, and on the Lagoon. There was a small swell from the north. Carlo rowed out a way and then stepped forward to raise the boat's single sail. The wind was from the east, so they would make good time north to Torcello. Behind them, Venice looked beautiful in the morning light, as if they were miles away, and a watery horizon blocked their full view of it.

The two Japanese had stopped talking and were looking over the side. They were over the cemetery of San Michele, Carlo realized. Below them lay the island that had been the city's chief cemetery for centuries; they sailed over a field of tombs, mausoleums, gravestones, obelisks, that at low tide could be a navigational hazard. . . . Just enough of the bizarre white blocks could be seen to convince one that they were indeed the result of the architectural thinking of fishes. Carlo crossed himself quickly to impress his customers, and sat back down at the tiller. He pulled the sail tight and they heeled over slightly, slapped into the waves.

In no more than twenty minutes they were east of Murano, skirting its edge. Murano, like Venice an island city crossed with canals, had been a quaint little town before the flood. But it didn't have as many tall buildings as Venice, and it was said that an underwater river had undercut its islands; in any case, it was a wreck. The two Japanese chattered with excitement.

"Can we visit to that city here, Carlo?" asked Hamada.

"It's too dangerous," Carlo answered. "Buildings have fallen into the canals."

They nodded, smiling. "Are people live here?" Taku asked.

"A few, yes. They live in the highest buildings on the floors still above water, and work in Venice. That way they avoid having to build a roof-house in the city."

The faces of his two companions expressed incomprehension.

"They avoid the housing shortage in Venice," Carlo said. "There's a certain housing shortage in Venice, as you may have noticed." His listeners caught the joke this time and laughed uproariously.

"Could live on floors below if owning scuba such as that

here," Hamada said, gesturing at Carlo's equipment.

"Yes," he replied. "Or we could grow gills." He bugged his eyes out and waved his fingers at his neck to indicate gills. The Japanese loved it.

Past Murano, the Lagoon was clear for a few miles, a sunbeaten blue covered with choppy waves. The boat tipped up and down, the wind tugged at the sail cord in Carlo's hand. He began to enjoy himself. "Storm coming," he volunteered to the others and pointed at the black line over the horizon to the north. It was a common sight; short, violent storms swept over Brenner Pass from the Austrian Alps, dumping on the Po Valley and the Lagoon before dissipating in the Adriatic . . . once a week, or more, even in the summer. That was one reason the fish market was held under the domes of San Marco; everyone had gotten sick of trading in the rain.

Even the Japanese recognized the clouds. "Many rain fall soon here," Taku said.

Hamada grinned and said, "Taku and Tafur, weather prophets no doubt, make big company!"

They laughed. "Does he do this in Japan, too?" Carlo asked.

"Yes indeed, surely. In Japan rains every day—Taku says, 'It rains tomorrow for surely.' Weather prophet!"

After the laughter receded, Carlo said, "Hasn't all the rain drowned some of your cities too?"

"What's that here?"

"Don't you have some Venices in Japan?"

But they didn't want to talk about that. "I don't understand. . . . No, no Venice in Japan," Hamada said easily, but neither laughed as they had before. They sailed on. Venice was out of sight under the horizon, as was Murano. Soon they would reach Burano. Carlo guided the boat over the waves and listened to his companions converse in their improbable language, or mangle Italian in a way that alternately made him want to burst with hilarity or bite the gunwale with frustration.

Gradually, Burano bounced over the horizon, the cam-

panile first, followed by the few buildings still above water.
Murano still had inhabitants, a tiny market, even a midsummer festival; Burano was empty. Its campanile stood at a distinct angle, like the mast of a foundered ship. It had been an
island town, before 2040; now it had "canals" between every
rooftop. Carlo disliked the town intensely and gave it a wide
berth. His companions discussed it quietly in Japanese.

A mile beyond it was Torcello, another island ghost town.
The campanile could be seen from Burano, tall and white
against the black clouds to the north. They approached in
silence. Carlo took down the sail, set Taku in the bow to look
for snags, and rowed cautiously to the edge of town. They
moved between rooftops and walls that stuck up like reefs or
like old foundations out of the earth. Many of the roof tiles
and beams had been taken for use in construction back in
Venice. This happened to Torcello before; during the Renais-
sance it had been a little rival of Venice, boasting a population
of twenty thousand, but during the sixteenth and seventeenth
centuries it had been entirely deserted. Builders from Venice
had come looking in the ruins for good marble or a staircase
of the right dimensions. . . . Briefly a tiny population had
returned, to make lace and host those tourists who wanted to
be melancholy; but the waters rose, and Torcello died for
good. Carlo pushed off a wall with his oar, and a big section of
it tilted over and sank. He tried not to notice.

He rowed them to the open patch of water that had been
the Piazza. Around them stood a few intact rooftops, no taller
than the mast of their boat; broken walls of stone or rounded
brick; the shadowy suggestion of walls just underwater. It was
hard to tell what the street plan of the town would have been.
On one side of the Piazza was the cathedral of Santa Maria
Ascunta, however, still holding fast, still supporting the white
campanile that stood square and solid, as if over a living
community.

"That here is the church we desire to dive," Hamada said.

Carlo nodded. The amusement he had felt during the sail

was entirely gone. He rowed around the Piazza looking for a flat spot where they could stand and put the scuba gear on. The church outbuildings—it had been an extensive structure—were all underwater. At one point the boat's keel scraped the ridge of a roof. They rowed down the length of the barnlike nave, looked in the high windows: floored with water. No surprise. One of the small windows in the side of the campanile had been widened with sledgehammers; directly inside it was the stone staircase and, a few steps up, a stone floor. They hooked the boat to the wall and moved their gear up to the floor. In the dim midday light the stone of the interior was pocked with shadows. It had a rough-hewn look. The citizens of Torcello had built the campanile in a hurry, thinking that the world would end at the millennium, the year 1000. Carlo smiled to think how much longer they had had than that. They climbed the steps of the staircase, up to the sudden sunlight of the bell chamber, to look around; viewed Burano, Venice in the distance . . . to the north, the shallows of the Lagoon, and the coast of Italy. Beyond that, the black line of clouds was like a wall nearly submerged under the horizon, but it was rising; the storm would come.

They descended, put on the scuba gear, and flopped into the water beside the campanile. They were above the complex of church buildings, and it was dark; Carlo slowly led the two Japanese back into the Piazza and swam down. The ground was silted, and Carlo was careful not to step on it. His charges saw the great stone chair in the center of the Piazza (it had been called the Throne of Attila, Carlo remembered from one of his moldy books, and no one had known why), and waving to each other they swam to it. One of them made ludicrous attempts to stand on the bottom and walk around in his fins; he threw up clouds of silt. The other joined him. They each sat in the stone chair, columns of bubbles rising from them, and snapped pictures of each other with their underwater cameras. The silt would ruin the shots, Carlo thought. While they cavorted, he wondered sourly what they wanted in the church.

Eventually, Hamada swam up to him and gestured at the church. Behind the mask his eyes were excited. Carlo pumped his fins up and down slowly and led them around to the big entrance at the front. The doors were gone. They swam into the church.

Inside it was dark, and all three of them unhooked their big flashlights and turned them on. Cones of murky water turned to crystal as the beams swept about. The interior of the church was undistinguished, the floor thick with mud. Carlo watched his two customers swim about and let his flashlight beam rove the walls. Some of the underwater windows were still intact, an odd sight. Occasionally the beam caught a column of bubbles, transmuting them to silver.

Quickly enough the Japanese went to the picture at the west end of the nave, a tile mosaic. Taku (Carlo guessed) rubbed the slime off the tiles, vastly improving their color. They had gone to the big one first, the one portraying the Crucifixion, the Resurrection of the Dead, and the Day of Judgment: a busy mural. Carlo swam over to have a better look. But no sooner had the Japanese wiped the wall clean than they were off to the other end of the church, where above the stalls of the apse was another mosaic. Carlo followed.

It didn't take long to rub this one clean; and when the water had cleared, the three of them floated there, their flashlight beams converged on the picture revealed.

It was the Teotaca Madonna, the God-bearer. She stood against a dull gold background, holding the Child in her arms, staring out at the world with a sad and knowing gaze. Carlo pumped his legs to get above the Japanese, holding his light steady on the Madonna's face. She looked as though she could see all of the future, up to this moment and beyond; all of her child's short life, all the terror and calamity after that. . . . There were mosaic tears on her cheeks. At the sight of them, Carlo could barely check tears of his own from joining the general wetness on his face. He felt that he had suddenly been transposed to a church on the deepest floor of the ocean; the pressure of his feelings threatened to implode him, he could

scarcely hold them off. The water was freezing, he was shivering, sending up a thick, nearly continuous column of bubbles
. . . and the Madonna watched. With a kick he turned and
swam away. Like startled fish his two companions followed
him. Carlo led them out of the church into murky light, then
up to the surface, to the boat and the window casement.

Fins off, Carlo sat on the staircase and dripped. Taku and
Hamada scrambled through the window and joined him.
They conversed for a moment in Japanese, clearly excited.
Carlo stared at them blackly.

Hamada turned to him. "That here is the picture we desire," he said. "The Madonna with child."

"What?" Carlo cried.

Hamada raised his eyebrows. "We desire taking home
that here picture to Japan."

"But it's impossible! The picture is made of little tiles
stuck to the wall—there's no way to get them off!"

"Italy government permits," Taku said, but Hamada si-
lenced him with a gesture:

"Mosaic, yes. We use instruments we take here—water
torch. Archaeology method, you understand. Cut blocks out
of wall, bricks, number them—construct on new place in
Japan. Above water." He flashed his pearly smile.

"You can't do that," Carlo stated, deeply affronted.

"I don't understand?" Hamada said. But he did: "Italian
government permits us that."

"This isn't Italy," Carlo said savagely, and in his anger
stood up. What good would a Madonna do in Japan, anyway?
They weren't even Christian. "Italy is over there," he said, in
his excitement mistakenly waving to the southeast, no doubt
confusing his listeners even more. "This has never been Italy!
This is Venice! The Republic!"

"I don't understand." He had that phrase down pat. "Italian government has giving permit us."

"Christ," Carlo said. After a disgusted pause: "Just how
long will this take?"

"Time? We work that afternoon, tomorrow; place the

bricks here, go hire Venice barge to carry bricks to Venice—"

"Stay here overnight? I'm not going to stay here overnight, God damn it!"

"We bring sleeping bag for you—"

"No!" Carlo was furious. "I'm not staying, you miserable heathen hyenas—" He pulled off his scuba gear.

"I don't understand."

Carlo dried off, got dressed. "I'll let you keep your scuba tanks, and I'll be back for you tomorrow afternoon, late. *Understand?*"

"Yes," Hamada said, staring at him steadily, without expression. "Bring barge?"

"What?—yes, yes, I'll bring your barge, you miserable slime-eating catfish. Vultures . . ." He went on for a while, getting the boat out of the window.

"Storm coming!" Taku said brightly, pointing to the north.

"To hell with you!" Carlo said, pushing off and beginning to row. "Understand?"

He rowed out of Torcello and back into the Lagoon. Indeed, a storm was coming; he would have to hurry. He put up the sail and pulled the canvas decking back until it covered everything but the seat he was sitting on. The wind was from the north now, strong but fitful. It pulled the sail taut; the boat bucked over the choppy waves, leaving behind a wake that was bright white against the black of the sky. The clouds were drawing over the sky like a curtain, covering half of it: half black, half colorless blue, and the line of the edge was solid. It resembled that first great storm of 2040, Carlo guessed, that had pulled over Venice like a black wool blanket and dumped water for forty days. And it had never been the same again, not anywhere in the world. . . .

Now he was beside the wreck of Burano. Against the black sky he could see only the drunken campanile, and suddenly he realized why he hated the sight of this abandoned town: it was a vision of the Venice to come, a cruel model of the future. If the water level rose even three meters, Venice would become nothing but a big Burano. Even if the water didn't rise, more people were leaving Venice every year. . . . One day it would be empty. Once again the sadness he had felt looking at the Teotaca filled him, a sadness become a bottomless despair. "God damn it," he said, staring at the crippled campanile; but that wasn't enough. He didn't know words that were enough. "God *damn* it."

Just beyond Burano the squall hit. It almost blew the sail out of his hand; he had to hold on with a fierce clench, tie it to the stern, tie the tiller in place, and scramble over the pitching canvas deck to lower the sail, cursing all the while. He brought the sail down to its last reefing, which left a handkerchief-sized patch exposed to the wind. Even so, the boat yanked over the waves and the mast creaked as if it would tear loose. . . . The choppy waves had become whitecaps; in the screaming wind their tops were tearing loose and flying through the air, white foam in the blackness. . . .

Best to head for Murano for refuge, Carlo thought. Then the rain started. It was colder than the Lagoon water and fell almost horizontally. The wind was still picking up; his hand-kerchief sail was going to pull the mast out. . . . "Jesus," he said. He got onto the decking again, slid up to the mast, took down the sail with cold and disobedient fingers. He crawled back to his hole in the deck, hanging on desperately as the boat yawed. It was almost broadside to the waves and hastily he grabbed the tiller and pulled it around, just in time to meet a large wave stern-on. He shuddered with relief. Each wave seemed bigger than the last; they picked up quickly on the Lagoon. Well, he thought, what now? Get out the oars? No, that wouldn't do; he had to keep stern-on to the waves, and besides, he couldn't row effectively in this chop. He had to go where the waves were going, he realized; and if they missed Murano and Venice, that meant the Adriatic.

As the waves lifted and dropped him, he grimly contem-plated the thought. His mast alone acted like a sail in a wind

of this force; and the wind seemed to be blowing from a bit to
the west of north. The waves—the biggest he had ever seen on
the Lagoon, perhaps the biggest *ever* on the Lagoon—pushed
in about the same direction as the wind, naturally. Well, that
meant he would miss Venice, which was directly south, maybe
even a touch west of south. Damn, he thought. And all because he had been angered by those two Japanese and the
Teotaca. What did he care what happened to a sunken mosaic
from Torcello? He had helped foreigners find and cart off the
one bronze horse of San Marco that had fallen . . . more than
one of the stone lions of Venice, symbol of the city . . . the
entire Bridge of Sighs, for Christ's sake! What had come over
him? Why should he have cared about a forgotten mosaic?

Well, he had done it; and here he was. No altering it.
Each wave lifted his boat stern first and slid under it until he
could look down in the trough, if he cared to, and see his mast
nearly horizontal, until he rose over the broken, foaming crest,
each one of which seemed to want to break down his little
hole in the decking and swamp him—for a second he was in
midair, the tiller free and useless until he crashed into the next
trough. Every time at the top he thought, this wave will catch
us, and so even though he was wet and the wind and rain were
cold, the repeated spurts of fear adrenaline and his thick wool
coat kept him warm. A hundred waves or so served to convince him that the next one would probably slide under him
as safely as the last, and he relaxed a bit. Nothing to do but
wait it out, keep the boat exactly stern-on to the swell . . . and
he would be all right. Sure, he thought, he would just ride
these waves across the Adriatic to Trieste or Rijeka, one of
those two tawdry towns that had replaced Venice as Queen of
the Adriatic . . . the princesses of the Adriatic, so to speak, and
two little sluts they were, too. . . . Or ride the storm out, turn
around, and sail back in, better yet. . . .

On the other hand, the Lido had become a sort of reef, in
most places, and waves of this size would break over it, capsiz-
ing him for sure. And, to be realistic, the top of the Adriatic

was wide; just one mistake on the top of these waves (and he couldn't go on forever) and he would be broached, capsized, and rolled down to join all the other Venetians who had ended up on the bottom of the Adriatic. And all because of that damn Madonna. Carlo sat crouched in the stern, adjusting the tiller for the particulars of each wave, ignoring all else in the howling, black, horizonless chaos of water and air around him, pleased in a grim way that he was sailing to his death with such perfect seamanship. But he kept the Lido out of mind.

And so he sailed on, losing track of time as one does when there is no spatial referent. Wave after wave after wave. A little water collected at the bottom of his boat, and his spirits sank; that was no way to go, to have the boat sink by degrees under him. . . .

Then the high-pitched, airy howl of the wind was joined by a low booming, a bass roar. He looked behind him in the direction he was being driven and saw a white line, stretching from left to right; his heart jumped, fear exploded through him. This was it. The Lido, now a barrier reef tripping the waves. They were smashing down on it; he could see white sheets bouncing skyward and blowing to nothing. He was terrifically frightened. It would have been so much easier to founder at sea.

But there—among the white breakers, off to the right—a gray finger pointing up at the black—

A campanile. Carlo was forced to look back at the wave he was under, to straighten the boat; but when he looked back it was still there. A campanile, standing there like a dead lighthouse. "Jesus," he said aloud. It looked as if the waves were pushing him a couple hundred meters to the north of it. As each wave lifted him he had a moment when the boat was sliding down the face of the wave as fast as it was moving under him; during these moments he shifted the tiller a bit and the boat turned and surfed across the face, to the south, until the wave rose up under him to the crest, and he had to straighten it out. He repeated the delicate operation time after time, sometimes nearly broaching the boat in his impatience. But that wouldn't do—just take as much from each wave as it will give you, he thought. And pray it will add up to enough.

The Lido got closer, and it looked as if he was directly upwind of the campanile. It was the one at the Lido channel entrance or perhaps the one at Pellestrina, farther south; he had no way of knowing and couldn't have cared less. He was just happy that his ancestors had seen fit to construct such solid bell towers. In between waves he reached under the decking and by touch found his boathook and the length of rope he carried. It was going to be a problem, actually, when he got to the campanile—it would not do to pass it helplessly by a few meters; on the other hand he couldn't smash into it and expect to survive either, not in these waves. In fact the more he considered it, the more exact and difficult he realized the approach would have to be, and fearfully he stopped thinking about it and concentrated on the waves.

The last one was the biggest. As the boat slid down its face, the face got steeper until it seemed they would be swept on by this wave forever. The campanile loomed ahead, big and black. Around it, waves pitched over and broke with sharp, deadly booms; from behind, Carlo could see the water sucked over the breaks, as if over short but infinitely broad waterfalls. The noise was tremendous. At the top of the wave it appeared he could jump in the campanile's top windows— he got out the boathook, shifted the tiller a touch, took three deep breaths. Amid the roaring, the wave swept him just past the stone tower, smacking against it and splashing him; he pulled the tiller over hard, the boat shot into the wake of the campanile—he stood and swung the boathook over a window casement above him. It caught, and he held on hard.

He was in the lee of the tower; broken water rose and dropped under the boat, hissing, but without violence, and he held. Onehanded, he wrapped the end of his rope around the sailcord bolt in the stern, tied the other end to the boathook.

The hook held pretty well; he took a risk and reached down to tie the rope firmly to the bolt. Then another risk: when the boiling soupy water of another broken wave raised the boat, he leaped off his seat, grabbed the stone windowsill, which was too thick to get his fingers over—for a moment he hung by his fingertips. With desperate strength he pulled himself up, reached in with one hand and got a grasp on the inside of the sill, and pulled himself in and over. The stone floor was about four feet below the window. Quickly he pulled the boat-hook in and put it on the floor, and took up the slack in the rope.

He looked out the window. His boat rose and fell, rose and fell. Well, it would sink or it wouldn't. Meanwhile, he was safe. Realizing this, he breathed deeply, let out a shout. He remembered shooting past the side of the tower, face no more than two meters from it—getting drenched by the wave slapping the front of it—why, he had done it perfectly! He couldn't do it again like that in a million tries. Triumphant laughs burst out of him, short and sharp: "Ha! Ha! Ha! Jesus Christ! Wow!"

"Whoooo's theeeerre?" called a high scratchy voice, floating down the staircase from the floor above. "Whoooooo's there? . . ."

Carlo froze. He stepped lightly to the base of the stone staircase and peered up; through the hole to the next floor flickered a faint light. To put it better, it was less dark up there than anywhere else. More surprised than fearful (though he was afraid), Carlo opened his eyes as wide as he could—

"Whooooooo's theeeeeerrrrrrrre? . . ."

Quickly he went to the boathook, untied the rope, felt around on the wet floor until he found a block of stone that would serve as anchor for his boat. He looked out the window: boat still there; on both sides, white breakers crashed over the Lido. Taking up the boathook, Carlo stepped slowly up the stairs, feeling that after what he had been through he could slash any ghost in the ether to ribbons.

It was a candle lantern, flickering in the disturbed air—a room filled with junk—

"Eeek! Eeek!"

"Jesus!"

"Devil! Death, away!" A small black shape rushed at him, brandishing sharp metal points.

"Jesus!" Carlo repeated, holding the boathook out to defend himself. The figure stopped.

"Death comes for me at last," it said. It was an old woman, he saw, holding lace needles in each hand.

"Not at all," Carlo said, feeling his pulse slow back down. "Swear to God, Grandmother, I'm just a sailor, blown here by the storm."

The woman pulled back the hood of her black cape, revealing braided white hair, and squinted at him.

"You've got the scythe," she said suspiciously. A few wrinkles left her face as she unfocused her gaze.

"A boathook only," Carlo said, holding it out for her inspection. She stepped back and raised the lace needles threateningly. "Just a boathook, I swear to God. To God and Mary and Jesus and all the saints, Grandmother. I'm just a sailor, blown here by the storm from Venice." Part of him felt like laughing.

"Aye?" she said. "Aye, well then, you've found shelter. I don't see so well anymore, you know. Come in, sit down, then." She turned around and led him into the room. "I was just doing some lace for penance, you see . . . though there's scarcely enough light." She lifted a tomboli with the lace pinned to it; Carlo noticed big gaps in the pattern, as in the webs of an injured spider. "A little more light," she said and, picking up a candle, held it to the lit one. When it was fired, she carried it around the chamber and lit three more candles in lanterns that stood on tables, boxes, a wardrobe. She motioned for him to sit in a heavy chair by her table, and he did so.

As she sat down across from him, he looked around the ⸢

chamber. A bed piled high with blankets, boxes and tables covered with objects . . . the stone walls around, and another staircase leading up to the next floor of the campanile. There was a draft. "Take off your coat," the woman said. She arranged the little pillow on the arm of her chair and began to poke a needle in and out of it, pulling the thread slowly.

Carlo sat back and watched her. "Do you live here alone?"

"Always alone," she replied. "I don't want it otherwise." With the candle before her face, she resembled Carlo's mother or someone else he knew. It seemed very peaceful in the room after the storm. The old woman bent in her chair until her face was just above her tomboli; still, Carlo couldn't help noticing that her needle hit far outside the apparent pattern of lace, striking here and there randomly. She might as well have been blind. At regular intervals Carlo shuddered with excitement and tension; it was hard to believe he was out of danger. More infrequently they broke the silence with a short burst of conversation, then sat in the candlelight absorbed in their own thoughts, as if they were old friends.

"How do you get food?" Carlo asked, after one of these silences had stretched out. "Or candles?"

"I trap lobsters down below. And fishermen come by and trade food for lace. They get a good bargain, never fear. I've never given less, despite what he said—" Anguish twisted her face as the squinting had, and she stopped. She needled furiously, and Carlo looked away. Despite the draft, he was warming up (he hadn't removed his coat, which was wool, after all), and he was beginning to feel drowsy. . . .

"He was my spirit's mate, do you comprehend me?"

Carlo jerked upright. The old woman was still looking at her tomboli.

"And—and he left me here, here in this desolation when the floods began, with words that I'll remember forever and ever and ever. Until death comes. . . . I wish you *had* been death!" she cried. "I wish you had."

Carlo remembered her brandishing the needles. "What is this place?" he asked gently.

"What?"

"Is this Pellestrina? San Lazzaro?"

"This is Venice," she said.

Carlo shivered convulsively, stood up.

"I'm the last of them," the woman said. "The waters rise, the heavens howl, love's pledges crack and lead to misery. I—I live to show what a person can bear and not die. I'll live till the deluge drowns the world as Venice is drowned, I'll live till all else living is dead; I'll live . . ." Her voice trailed off; she looked up at Carlo curiously. "Who are you, really? Oh, I know. I know. A sailor."

"Are there floors above?" he asked, to change the subject.

She squinted at him. Finally she spoke. "Words are vain. I thought I'd never speak again, not even to my own heart, and here I am, doing it again. Yes, there's a floor above intact; but above that, ruins. Lightning blasted the bell chamber apart, while I lay in that very bed." She pointed at her bed, stood up. "Come on, I'll show you." Under her cape she was tiny.

She picked up the candle lantern beside her, and Carlo followed her up the stairs, stepping carefully in the shifting shadows.

On the floor above, the wind swirled, and through the stairway to the floor above that, he could distinguish black clouds. The woman put the lantern on the floor, started up the stairs. "Come up and see," she said.

Once through the hole they were in the wind, out under the sky. The rain had stopped. Great blocks of stone lay about the floor, and the walls broke off unevenly.

"I thought the whole campanile would fall," she shouted at him over the whistle of the wind. He nodded, and walked over to the west wall, which stood chest high. Looking over it, he could see the waves approaching, rising up, smashing against the stone below, spraying back and up at him. He could feel the blows in his feet. Their force frightened him; it was hard to believe he had survived them and was now out of danger. He shook his head violently. To his right and left, the white lines of crumbled waves marked the Lido, a broad swath of them against the black. The old woman was speaking, he could see; he walked back to her side to listen.

"The waters yet rise," she shouted. "See? And the lightning . . . you can see the lightning breaking the Alps to dust. It's the end, child. Every island fled away, and the mountains were not found . . . the second angel poured out his vial upon the sea, and it became as the blood of a dead man: and every living thing died in the sea." On and on she spoke, her voice mingling with the sound of the gale and the boom of the waves, just carrying over it all . . . until Carlo, cold and tired, filled with pity and a black anguish like the clouds rolling over them, put his arm around her thin shoulders and turned her around. They descended to the floor below, picked up the extinguished lantern, and descended to her chamber, which was still lit. It seemed warm, a refuge. He could hear her still speaking. He was shivering without pause.

"You must be cold," she said in a practical tone. She pulled a few blankets from her bed. "Here, take these." He sat down in the big heavy chair, put the blankets around his legs, put his head back. He was tired. The old woman sat in her chair and wound thread onto a spool. After a few minutes of silence she began talking again; and as Carlo dozed and shifted position and nodded off again, she talked and talked, of storms, and drownings, and the world's end, and lost love. . . .

In the morning when he woke up, she wasn't there. Her room stood revealed in the dim morning light: shabby, the furniture battered, the blankets worn, the knickknacks of Venetian glass ugly, as Venetian glass always was . . . but it was clean. Carlo got up and stretched his stiff muscles. He went up to the roof; she wasn't there. It was a sunny morning. Over the east wall he saw that his boat was still there, still floating. He grinned—the first one in a few days; he could feel that in his face.

The woman was not in the floors below, either. The lowest one served as her boathouse, he could see. In it were a pair of decrepit rowboats and some lobster pots. The biggest "boatslip" was empty; she was probably out checking pots. Or perhaps she hadn't wanted to talk with him in the light of day.

From the boathouse he could walk around to his craft, through water only knee deep. He sat in the stern, reliving the previous afternoon, and grinned again at being alive.

He took off the decking and bailed out the water on the keel with his bailing can, keeping an eye out for the old woman. Then he remembered the boathook and went back upstairs for it. When he returned there was still no sight of her. He shrugged; he'd come back and say good-bye another time. He rowed around the campanile and off the Lido, pulled up the sail, and headed northwest, where he presumed Venice was.

The Lagoon was as flat as a pond this morning, the sky cloudless, like the blue dome of a great basilica. It was amazing, but Carlo was not surprised. The weather was like that these days. Last night's storm, however, had been something else. There was the mother of all squalls; those were the biggest waves in the Lagoon ever, without a doubt. He began rehearsing his tale in his mind, for wife and friends.

Venice appeared over the horizon right off his bow, just where he thought it would be: first the great campanile, then San Marco and the other spires. The campanile . . . Thank God his ancestors had wanted to get up there so close to God—or so far off the water—the urge had saved his life. In the rain-washed air, the sea approach to the city was more beautiful than ever, and it didn't even bother him as it usually did that no matter how close you got to it, it still seemed to be over the horizon. That was just the way it was, now. The Serenissima. He was happy to see it.

He was hungry, and still very tired. When he pulled into

the Grand Canal and took down the sail, he found he could barely row. The rain was pouring off the land into the Lagoon, and the Grand Canal was running like a mountain river. It was tough going. At the fire station where the canal bent back, some of his friends working on a new roof-house waved at him, looking surprised to see him going upstream so early in the morning. "You're going the wrong way!" one shouted.

Carlo waved an oar weakly before plopping it back in. "Don't I know it!" he replied.

Over the Rialto, back into the little courtyard of San Giacometta. Onto the sturdy dock he and his neighbors had built, staggering a bit—careful there, Carlo.

"Carlo!" his wife shrieked from above. "Carlo, Carlo, Carlo!" She flew down the ladder from the roof.

He stood on the dock. He was home.

"Carlo, Carlo, Carlo!" his wife cried as she ran onto the dock.

"Jesus," he pleaded, "shut up." And pulled her into a rough hug.

"Where have you been, I was so worried about you because of the storm, you said you'd be back yesterday, oh, Carlo, I'm so glad to see you. . . ." She tried to help him up the ladder. The baby was crying. Carlo sat down in the kitchen chair and looked around the little makeshift room with satisfaction. In between chewing down bites of a loaf of bread, he told Luisa of his adventure: the two Japanese and their vandalism, the wild ride across the Lagoon, the madwoman on the campanile. When he had finished the story and the loaf of bread, he began to fall asleep.

"But, Carlo, you have to go back and pick up those Japanese."

"To hell with them," he said slurrily. "Creepy little bastards. . . . They're tearing the Madonna apart, didn't I tell you? They'll take everything in Venice, every last painting and statue and carving and mosaic and all. . . . I can't stand it."

"Oh, Carlo . . . it's all right. They take those things all

over the world and put them up and say this is from Venice, the greatest city in the world."

"They should be here."

"Here, here, come in and lie down for a few hours. I'll go see if Giuseppe will go to Torcello with you to bring back those bricks." She arranged him on their bed. "Let them have what's under the water, Carlo. Let them have it." He slept.

He sat up struggling, his arm shaken by his wife.

"Wake up, it's late. You've got to go to Torcello to get those men. Besides, they've got your scuba gear."

Carlo groaned.

"Maria says Giuseppe will go with you; he'll meet you with his boat on the Fondamente."

"Damn."

"Come on, Carlo, we need that money."

"All right, all right." The baby was squalling. He collapsed back on the bed. "I'll do it; don't pester me."

He got up and drank her soup. Stiffly he descended the ladder, ignoring Luisa's good-byes and warnings, and got back in his boat. He untied it, pushed off, let it float out of the courtyard to the wall of San Giacometta. He stared at the wall.

Once, he remembered, he had put on his scuba gear and swum down into the church. He had sat down in one of the stone pews in front of the altar, adjusting his weight belts and tank to do so, and had tried to pray through his mouthpiece and the facemask. The silver bubbles of his breath had floated up through the water toward heaven; whether his prayers had gone with them, he had no idea. After a while, feeling somewhat foolish—but not entirely—he had swum out the door. Over it he had noticed an inscription and stopped to read it, facemask centimeters from the stone. *Around this Temple Let the Merchant's Law Be Just, His Weight True, and His Covenants Faithful.* It was an admonition to the old usurers of the Rialto, but he could make it his, he thought; the true weight could refer to the diving belts, not to overload his clients and sink them to the bottom. . . .

The memory passed and he was on the surface again, with a job to do. He took in a deep breath and let it out, put the oars in the oarlocks and started to row.

Let them have what was under the water. What lived in Venice was still afloat.

The Quiet

George Florance-Guthridge

*George Florance-Guthridge is the most western, most northern,
and by all odds the coldest writer in this collection. He lives and
teaches in Gambell, an Eskimo village on St. Lawrence Island,
which is about fifty miles from Siberia. He says that this story
(along with some forthcoming work that also combines an-
thropology with near-future science fiction) "was one of the major catalysts for my interest in a teaching position in a remote
location."*

*The one time I met Guthridge, he was an English professor
who had just published his first story, his name not yet hyphen-
ated (the "Florance" in his byline is a tribute to his wife's role
as live-in critic). He pursued the craft of English-professorship
for six or seven years, and then edited a science magazine
from 1980 to 1982.*

*Guthridge has sold about four dozen stories in the past few
years, as well as a truly oddball Western novel,* The Bloodletter,
*featuring the adventures of Joshua .44-40, a fifteen-year-old re-
tarded dwarf.*

Kuara, my son, the Whites have stolen the moon.

Outside the window, the sky is black. A blue-white disc hangs among the stars. It is Earth, says Doctor Stefanko. I wail and beat my fists. Straps bind me to a bed. Doctor Stefanko forces my shoulders down, swabs my arm. "Since you can't keep still, I'm going to have to put you under again," she says, smiling. I lie quietly.

It is not Earth. Earth is brown. Earth is Kalahari.

"You are on the moon," Doctor Stefanko says. It is the second or third time she has told me; I have awakened and slept, awakened and slept, until I am not sure what voices are dream and what are real, if any. Something pricks my skin. "Rest now. You have had a long sleep."

I remember awakening the first time. The white room, white cloth covering me. Outside, blackness and the blue-white disc.

"On the moon," I say. My limbs feel heavy. My head spins. Sleep drags at my flesh. "The moon."

"Isn't it wonderful?"

"And you say my husband, Tuka—dead."

Her lips tighten. She looks at me solemnly. "He did not survive the sleep."

"The moon is hollow," I tell her. "Everyone knows that. The dead sleep there." I stare at the ceiling. "I am alive and on the moon. Tuka is dead but is not here." The words seem to float from my mouth. There are little dots on the ceiling.

"Sleep now. That's a girl. We'll talk more later."

"And Kuara. My son. Alive." The dots are spinning. I close my eyes. The dots keep spinning.

"Yes, but . . ."

The dots. The dots.

"About a hundred years ago a law was formulated to protect endangered species—animals that, unless humankind was careful, might become extinct," Doctor Stefanko says. Her

face, no longer blurry, seems underlain with shadow. She has
dark gray hair, drawn cheeks. I have seen her somewhere—
long before I was brought to this place. I cannot remember
where. The memory slips away. Dread haunts my heart.

Gai, wearing a breechcloth, stands grinning near the window. The disc Doctor Stefanko calls Earth haloes his head.
His huge, pitted tongue sticks out where his front teeth are
missing. His shoulders slope like those of a hartebeest. His
chest, leathery and wrinkled, is tufted with hair beginning to
gray. I am not surprised to see him, after his treachery. He
makes num-power pulse in the pit of my belly. I look away.

"Then the law was broadened to include endangered
peoples. Peoples like the Gwi." Managing to smile, Doctor
Stefanko presses her index finger against my nose. I toss my
head, I don't trust her. She frowns. "Obviously it would be
impossible to save entire tribes. So the founders of the law did
what they thought best. They saved certain representatives.
You. Your family. A few others, such as Gai. These representatives were frozen."

"Frozen?"

"Made cold."

"As during gum, when ice forms inside the ostrich-egg
containers?"

"Much colder."

It was not dream, then. I remember staring through a
blue, crinkled sheen. Like light seen through a snakeskin. I
could not move, though my insides never stopped shivering.
So this is death, I kept thinking.

"In the interim you were brought here to the moon. To
Carnival. It is a fine place. A truly international facility, built
as a testament to the harmony of nations. Here we have tried
to recreate the best of what used to be." She pauses, and her
eyes grow keen. "This will be your new home now, U."

"And Kuara?"

"He will live here with you, in time." Something in her
voice makes fear touch me. Then she says, "Would you like to
see him?" Some of the fear slides away.

"Is it wise, Doctor?" Gai asks. "She has a temper, this one." His eyes grin down at me. He stares at my pelvis.

"Oh, we'll manage. You'll be a good girl, won't you, U?"

My head nods. My heart does not say yes or no.

The straps leap away with a loud click. Doctor Stefanko and Gai help me to my feet. The world wobbles. The Earth-disc tilts and swings. The floor slants one way, another way. Needles tingle in my feet and hands. I am helped into a chair. More clicking. The door hisses open and the chair floats out, Doctor Stefanko leading, Gai lumbering behind. We move down one corridor after another. This is a place of angles. No curves, except the smiles of Whites as we pass. And they curve too much.

Another door hisses. We enter a room full of chill. Blue glass, the inside laced with frost, stretches from floor to ceiling along each wall. Frozen figures stand behind the glass. I remember this place. I remember how sluggish was the hate in my heart.

"Kuara is on the end," Doctor Stefanko says, her breath white.

The chair floats closer. My legs bump the glass; cold shocks my knees. The chair draws back. I lean forward. Through the glass I can see the closed eyes of my son. Ice furs his lashes and brows. His head is tilted to one side. His little arms dangle. I touch the glass in spite of the cold. I hear Gai's sharp intake of breath and he draws back my shoulders, but Doctor Stefanko puts a hand on Gai's wrist and I am released. There is give to the glass. Not like that on the trucks in the tsama patch. My num rises. My heart beats faster. Num enters my arms, floods my fingers. "Kuara," I whisper. Warmth spreads upon the glass. It makes a small, ragged circle.

"He'll be taken from here as soon as you've demonstrated you can adjust to your new home," Doctor Stefanko says.

Kuara. If only I could dance. Num would boil within me. I could kia. I would shoo away the ghosts of the cold. Awakening, you would step through the glass and into my arms.

Though we often lacked water, we were not unhappy. The tsama melons supported us. It was a large patch, and by conserving we could last long periods without journeying to the waterholes. Whites and tame Bushmen had taken over the Gam and Gautscha Pans, and the people there, the Kung, either had run away or had stayed for the water and now worked the Whites' farms and ate mealie meal.

There were eleven of us, though sometimes one or two more. Gai, unmated, was one of those who came and went. Tuka would say, "You can always count us on three hands, but never on two or four hands." He would laugh, then. He was always laughing. I think he laughed because there was so little game near the Akam Pan, our home. The few duiker and steenbok that had once roamed our plain had smelled the coming of the Whites and the fleeing Kung, and had run away. Tuka laughed to fill up the empty spaces.

Sometimes, when he wasn't trapping springhare and porcupine, he helped me gather wood and tubers. We dug xwa roots and koa, the water root buried deep in the earth, until our arms ached. Sometimes we hit na trees with sticks, making the sweet berries fall, and Tuka would chase me round and round, laughing and yelling like a madman. It was times like those when I wondered why I had once hated him so much.

I wondered much about that during kuma, a hot season when starvation stalked us. During the day I would take off my kaross, dig a shallow pit within what little shade an orogu bush offered, then urinate in the sand, cover myself with more sand, and place a leaf over my head. The three of us—Tuka, Kuara, and I—lay side by side like dead people. "My heart is sad from hunger," I sang to myself all day. "Like an old man, sick and slow." I thought of the bad things. My parents marrying me to Tuka before I was ready because, paying bride service, he brought my mother a new kaross. Tuka doing the marrying thing to me before I was ready. Everything before I was ready! Sometimes I prayed into the leaf that a paouw would fly down and think his penis a fat caterpillar.

Then one night Tuka snared a honey badger. A badger, during kuma! Everyone was excited. Tuka said, "Yesterday, when we slept, I told the land that my U was hungry, and I must have meat for her and Kuara." The badger was very tender. Gai ate his share and went begging, though he had never brought meat to the camp. When the meat was gone we roasted ga roots and sang and danced while Tuka played the gwashi. I danced proudly. Not for Tuka but for myself. Num-power uncurled from the pit of my belly and came boiling up my spine. I was afraid, because when num reaches my skull, I kia. Then I see ghosts killing people, and I smell the rotting smell of death, like decaying carcasses.

Tuka took my head in his hands. "You must not kia," he said. "Not now. Your body will suffer too much for the visions." For other people, kia brings healing—of self, of others; for me it only brings pain.

Tuka held me beside the fire and stroked me, and num subsided. "When I lie in the sand during the day, I dream I have climbed the footpegs in a great baobab tree," he said. "I look out from the treetop, and the land is agraze with giraffe and wildebeest and kudu. 'You must kill these animals and bring them to U and Kuara before the Whites kill them,' my dream says."

Then he asked, "What do you think of when you lie there, U?"

I did not answer. I was afraid to tell him; I did not want him to feel angry or sad after his joy from catching the honey badger. He smiled. His eyes, moist, shone with firelight. Perhaps he thought num had stopped my tongue.

The next day the quiet came. Lying beneath the sand, I felt num pulse in my belly. I fought the fear it always brought. I did not cry out to Tuka. The pulsing increased. I began to tremble. Sweat ran down my face. Num boiled within me. It entered my spine and pushed toward my throat. My eyes were wide and I kept staring at the veins of the leaf but seeing dread. I felt myself going rigid and shivering at the same time.

My head throbbed; it was as large as a ga root. I could hear my mouth make sputtery noises, like Kuara used to at my breast. The pressure inside me kept building, building.

And suddenly was gone. It burrowed into the earth, taking my daydreams with it. I went down and down into the sand. I passed ubbee roots and animals long dead, their bones bleached and forgotten. I came to a water hole far beneath the ground. Tuka was in the water. Kuara was too. He looked younger, barely old enough to toddle. Tuka, smiling, looked handsome. *He is not a bad person*, I told myself; *he just wants his way too much. But he has brought meat to our people, I cannot forget that. And someday perhaps he will bring me a new kaross. Perhaps he will bring many things. Important things.*

I took off my kaross, and the three of us held hands and danced, naked, splashing. There was no num to seize me. No marrying-thing urge to seize Tuka. Only quiet, and laughter.

"This will be your new home, U," Doctor Stefanko says as she opens a door. She has given me a new kaross; of *genuine* gemsbok, she tells me, though I am uncertain why she speaks of it that way. When she puts her hand on my back and pushes me forward, the kaross feels soft and smooth against my skin. "We think you'll like it, and if there's anything you need . . ."

I grab the sides of the door and turn my face away. I will not live in or even look at the place. But her push becomes firmer, and I stumble inside. I cover my face with my hands.

"There now," Doctor Stefanko says. I spy through my fingers.

We are in Kalahari.

I turn slowly, for suddenly my heart is shining and singing. No door. No walls. No angles. The sandveld spreads out beneath a cloudless sky. Endless pale gold grass surrounds scattered white-thorn and tsi bushes; in the distance lift several flat-toped acacias and even a mongongo tree. A dassie darts in and out of a rocky kranze.

"Here might be a good place for your tshushi—your shelter," Doctor Stefanko says, pulling me forward. She enters the tall grass, bends, comes up smiling, holding branches in one hand, gui fibers in the other. "You see? We've even cut some of the materials you'll need."

"But how—"

"The moon isn't such a horrible place, now is it?" She strides back through the grass. "And we here at Carnival are dedicated to making your stay as pleasant as possible. Just look here." She moves a rock. A row of buttons gleams. "Turn this knob, and you can control your weather; no more suffering through those terrible hot and cold seasons. Unless you want to, of course." she adds quickly. "And from time to time some nice people will be looking down . . . *in* on you. From up there, within the sky." She makes a sweep of her arm. "They want to watch how you live; you—and other tribal people like you—are quite a sensation, you know." I stare at her without understanding. "Anyway if you want to see them, just turn this knob. And if you want to hear what the monitor's saying about you, turn this one." She looks up, sees my confusion. "Oh, don't worry; the monitor translates everything. It's a wonderful device."

Standing, she takes hold of my arms. Her eyes almost seem warm. "You see, U, there is no more Kalahari on Earth—not as you knew it, anyhow—so we created another. In some ways it won't be as good as what you were used to, in a lot of ways it'll be better." She smiles. "We think you'll like it."

"And Kuara?"

"He's waking now. He'll join you soon, on a trial basis." She takes hold of my hands. "Soon." Then she walks back in the direction we came, quickly fading in the distance. Suddenly she is gone. A veil of heat shimmers above the grass where the door seemed to have been. For a moment I think of following. Finally I shrug. I work at building my tshushi. I work slowly, methodically, my head full of thoughts. I think of Kuara, and something gnaws at me. I drop the fiber I am

holding and begin walking toward the opposite horizon,
where a giraffe is eating from the mongongo tree.

Grasshoppers, kxon ants, dung beetles, hop and crawl
among the grasses. Leguaan lizards scuttle. A mole snake
slithers for a hole beneath a uri bush. I walk quickly, the sand
warm but not hot beneath my feet. The plain is sun-drenched,
the few omirimbi watercourses parched and cracked, yet I feel
little thirst. A steenbok leaps for cover behind a white-thorn.
This is a good place, part of me decides. Here will Kuara
become the hunter Tuka could not be. Kuara will never laugh
to shut out sadness.

The horizon draws no closer.

I measure the giraffe with my thumb, walk a thousand
paces, remeasure, walk another thousand paces, remeasure.

The giraffe does not change size.

I will walk another thousand. Then I will turn back and
finish the tshushi.

A hundred paces farther I bump something hard.

A wall.

Beyond, the giraffe continues feeding.

The Whites with the Land Rovers came during ga, the hottest
season. The trucks bucked and roared across the sand. Tuka
took Kuara and hurried to meet them. I went too, though I
walked behind with the other women. There were several
white men and some Bantu. Gai was standing in the lead
truck, waving and grinning.

A white, blond-haired woman climbed out. She was
wearing white shorts and a light brown shirt with rolled-up
sleeves. I recognized her immediately. Doctor Morse, come to
study us again. Tuka had said the Whites did not wonder
about their own culture, so they liked to study ours.

She talked to us women a long time, asking about our
families and how we felt about SWAPO, the Southwest African People's Army. Everyone spoke at once. She kept waving her hands for quiet. "What do you think, U?" she would

ask. "What's your opinion?" I said she should ask Tuka; he was a man and understood such things. Doctor Morse frowned, so I said SWAPO should not kill people. SWAPO should leave people alone. Doctor Morse nodded and wrote in her notebook as I talked. I was pleased. The other women were very jealous.

Doctor Morse told us the war in South Africa was going badly; soon it would sweep this way. When Tuka finished looking at the engines I asked him what Doctor Morse meant by "badly." Badly for Blacks, or Whites. Badly for those in the south, or for those of us in the north. He did not know. None of us asked Doctor Morse.

Then she said, "We have brought water. Lots of water. We've heard you've been without." Her hair caught the sunlight. She was very beautiful for a white woman.

We smiled but refused her offer. She frowned but did not seem angry. Maybe she thought it was because she was white. If so, she was wrong; accept gifts, and we might forget the ones Kalahari gives us. "Well, at least go for a ride in the trucks," she said, beaming. Tuka laughed and, taking Kuara by the hand, scrambled for the two Land Rovers. I shook my head. "You really should go," Doctor Morse said. "It'll be good for you."

"That is something for men to do," I told her. "Women do not understand such things."

"All they're going to do is ride in the back!"

"Trucks. Hunting. Fire. Those are men's things," I said.

Only one of the trucks came back. Everyone but Tuka, Kuara, and some of the Bantu returned. "The truck's stuck in the sand; the Whites decided to wait until dawn to pull it out," Gai said. "Tuka said he'd sleep beside it. You know how he is about trucks!" Everyone laughed. Except me. An empty space throbbed in my heart; that I wanted him home angered me.

Then rain came. It was ga go—male rain. It poured down strong and sudden, not even and gentle, the female rain that fills the land with water. Rain, during ga! Everyone shouted and danced for joy. Even the Whites danced. A miracle! people said. I thought about the honey badger caught during kuma, and was afraid. I felt alone. In spite of my fear, perhaps because of it, I did a foolish thing. I slept away from the others.

In the night, the quiet again touched me. Num uncurled in my belly. I did not beckon it forth. I swear I didn't. I wasn't even thinking about it. As I slept, I felt my body clench tight. In my dreams I could hear my breathing—shallow and rapid. Fear seized me and shook me like the twig of a ni-ni bush. I sank into the earth. Tuka and Kuara were standing slump-shouldered at the water hole where we had danced. Kuara was wearing the head of a wildebeest; the eyes had been carved out and replaced with smoldering coals. "Run away, Mother," he kept saying.

I awoke to shadows. A fleeting darkness came upon me before I could move. I glimpsed Gai grinning beneath the moon. Then a hand was clapped over my mouth.

Doctor Stefanko returns after I've finished the hut. She and Gai bring warthog and kudu hides, porcupine quills, tortoise shells, ostrich eggs, a sharpening stone, an awl, two assagai blades, pots of Bantu clay. Many things. Gai grins as he sets them down. Doctor Stefanko watches him. "Back on Earth, he might not have remained a bachelor if your people hadn't kept thinking of him as one," she tells me as he walks away. Then she also leaves.

Later, she brings Kuara.

He comes sprinting, gangly, the grass nearly to his chin. "Mama," he shouts, "Mama, Mama," and I take him in my arms, whirling and laughing. I put my hands upon his cheeks; his arms are around my waist. Real. Oh, yes, so very real, my Kuara! Tears roll down my face. He looks hollow-eyed, and his hair has been shaved. But I do not let concern stop my heart. I weep from joy, not pain.

Doctor Stefanko again reminds me he's here on a trial basis only. Then she leaves, and Kuara and I talk. He babbles about a strange sleep, and Doctor Stefanko, and Gai, as I show him the camp. We play with the knobs Doctor Stefanko showed me; one of them makes a line of small windows blink on in the slight angle between wall-sky and ceiling-sky. The windows look like square beads. There, faces pause and peer. Children. Old men. Women with smiles like springhares. People of many races. I tell him not to smile or acknowledge their presence. Not even that of the children. Especially not the children. The faces are surely ghosts, I warn. Ghosts dreaming of becoming Gwi.

We listen to the voice Doctor Stefanko calls the monitor. It is singsong, lulling. A woman's voice, I think. "U and Kuara, the latest additions to Carnival, members of the last Gwi tribal group, will soon become accustomed to our excellent accommodations," the voice says. The voice floats with us as we go to gather roots and wood.

A leguaan pokes its head from the rocky kranze, listening. Silently I put down my wood. Then my hand moves slowly. So slowly it is almost not movement. I grab. Caught! Kuara shrieks and claps his hands. "Notice the scarification across the cheeks and upper legs," the voice is saying. "The same is true of the buttocks, though like any self-respecting Gwi, U will not remove her kaross in the presence of others except during the Eland Dance." I carry the leguaan wiggling to the hut. "Were she to disrobe, you would notice tremendous fatty deposits in the buttocks, a phenomenon known as steatopygia. Unique to Bushmen (or 'Bushwomen,' we should say), this anatomical feature aids in food storage. It was once believed that . . ."

After breaking the leguaan's neck, I take off the kaross of genuine gemsbok and, using gui fiber, tie it in front of my hut. It makes a wonderful door. I have never had a door. Tuka and I slept outside, using the tshushi for storage. Kuara will have a door. A door between him and the watchers.

He will have fire. Fire for warmth and food and U to sing beside. I gather kane and ore sticks and carve male and female, then use galli grass for tinder. Like Tuka did. "The Gwi are marked by a low, flattened skull, tiny mastoid processes, peppercorn hair, a nonprognathous face . . ." I twirl the sticks between my palms. It seems to take forever. My arms grow sore. I am ready to give up when smoke suddenly curls. Gibbering, Kuara leaps about the camp. I gaze at the fire and grin with delight. But it is frightened delight. I will make warmth fires and food fires, I decide as I blow the smoke into flame. Not ritual fires. Not without Tuka.

I roast the leguaan with eru berries and tsha-cucumber, which seems plentiful. But I am not Tuka, quick with fire and laughter; the fire-making has taken too long. Halfway through the cooking, Kuara seizes the lizard and, bouncing it in his hands as though it were hot dough, tears it apart. "Kuara!" I blurt in pretended anger. He giggles as, the intestines dangling, he holds up the lizard to eat. I smile sadly. Kuara's laughing eyes and ostrich legs . . . so much like Tuka!

"The Gwi sing no praises of battles or warriors," the voice sing-says. I help Kuara finish the leguaan. "They have no history of warfare; ironically, it was last century's South African War, in which the Gwi did not take part, that assured their extinction. Petty arguments are common (even a nonviolent society cannot keep husbands and wives from scrapping), but fighting is considered dishonorable. To fight is to have failed to . . ." When I gaze up, my mouth full of lizard, there are no faces in the windows.

At last, dusk dapples the grass. Kuara finds a guinea-fowl feather and a reed; leaning against my legs, he busies himself making a zani. The temperature begins to drop. I decide the door would fit better around my shoulders than across the tshushi.

A figure strides out of the setting sun. I shield my eyes with my arm. Doctor Stefanko. She smiles and nods at Kuara, now tying a nut onto his toy for a weight, and sits on a log. Her smile remains, though it is drained of joy. She looks at me seriously.

"I do hope Kuara's presence will dissuade you from any more *displays* such as you exhibited this afternoon," she tells me. "Surely you realize that if . . . well, if *problems* arise, we may have to take the boy back to the prep rooms until . . . until you become more accustomed to your surroundings." She taps her forefinger against her palm. "This impetuousness of yours has got to cease." Another tap. "And cease now."

Head cocked, I gaze at her, not understanding.

"Taking off your kaross simply because the monitor said you do not." She nods knowingly. "Oh, yes, we're aware when you're listening. And that frightful display with the lizard!" She makes a face and appears to shudder. "Then there's the matter with the fire." She points toward the embers. "You're supposed to be living here like you did back on Earth. At least during the day. Men *always* started the fires."

"Men were always present." I shrug.

"Yes. Well, arrangements are being made. For the time being, stick to foods you don't need to cook. And use the heating system." She goes to the rock and, on hands and knees, turns one of the knobs. A humming sounds. Smiling and rubbing her hands over the fire, she reseats herself on the log, pulls a photograph from her hip pocket, and hands it to me. I turn the picture right side up. Doctor Morse is standing with her arm across Gai's shoulders. His left arm is around her waist. The Land Rovers are in the background.

"Impetuous," Doctor Stefanko says, leaning over and clicking her fingernail against the photograph. "That's exactly what Doctor Morse wrote about you in her notebooks. *She* considered it a virtue." Again she lifts her brow. "We do not." Then she adds proudly, "She was my grandmother, you know. As you can imagine, I have more than simply a professional interest in our Southwest African section here at Carnival."

I start to hand back the photograph. She raises her hand, halting me. "Keep it," she says. "Think of it as a wedding present. The first of many."

That night, wrapped in the kaross, Kuara and I sleep in each other's arms, in the tshushi. He is still clutching the zani, though he has not once thrown it into the air to watch it spin

down. Perhaps he will tomorrow. Tomorrow. An ugly word. I
lie staring at the dark ground, sand clenched in my fists. I
wonder if, somehow using devices to see in the dark, the
ghosts in the sky-windows are watching me sleep. I wonder if
they will watch the night Gai climbs upon my back and grunts
throughout the marrying thing.

Sleep comes. A tortured sleep. I can feel myself hugging
Kuara. He squirms against the embrace but does not awaken.
In my dreams I slide out of myself and, stirring up the fire,
dance the Eland Dance. My body is slick with eland fat. My
eyes stare rigidly into the darkness and my head is held high
and stiff. Chanting, I lift and put down my feet, moving
around and around the fire. Other women clap and sing the
kia-healing songs. Men play the gwashi and musical bows.
The music lifts and lilts and throbs. Rhythm thrums within
me. Each muscle knows the song. Tears squeeze from my eyes.
Pain leadens my legs. And still I dance.

Then, at last, num rises. It uncurls in my belly and
breathes fire-breath up my spine. I fight the fear. I dance
against the dread. I tremble with fire. My eyes slit with agony.
I do not watch the women clapping and singing. My breaths
come in shallow, heated gasps. My breasts bounce. I dance.
Num continues to rise. It tingles against the base of my brain.
It fills my head. My entire body is alive, burning. Thorns are
sticking everywhere in my flesh. My breasts are fiery coals. I
can feel ghosts, hot ghosts, ghosts of the past, crowding into
my skull. I stagger for the hut; Kuara and U, my old self,
await me. I slide into her flesh like someone slipping beneath
the cool, mudslicked waters of a year-round pan. I slide in
among her fear and sorrow and the anguished joy of Kuara
beside her.

She stirs. A movement of a sleeping head. A small groan;
denial. I slide in further. I become her once again. My head is
aflame with num and ghosts. "U," I whisper. "I bring the
ghosts of all your former selves, and of your people." Again
she groans, though weaker; the pleasure-moan of a woman

making love. Her body stretches, stiffens. Her nails rake
Kuara's back. She accepts me, then; accepts her self. I fill
her flesh.

And bring the quiet, for the third time in her life. Down
and down into the sand she seeps, like ga go rain soaking into
parched earth, leaving nothing of her self behind, her hands
around Kuara's wrists as she pulls him after her, the zani's
guinea-fowl feather whipping behind him as if in a wind.
She passes through sand, Carnival's concrete base, moon-
rock, moving ever downward, badger-burrowing. She breaks
through into a darkness streaked with silver light; into the
core of the moon, where live the ancestral dead, the ghosts of
kia. She tumbles downward, crying her dismay and joy, her
kaross fluttering. In the center of the hollow, where water
shines like cold silver, awaits Tuka, arms outstretched. He is
laughing—a shrill, forced cackle. Such is the only laughter a
ghost can know whose sleep has been disturbed. They will
dance this night, the three of them: U, Tuka, Kuara.

Then Tuka will teach her the secret of oa, the poison
squeezed from the female larvae of the dung beetle. Poison
for arrows he will teach her to make. Poison for which Bushmen know no antidote.

She will hunt when she returns to Gai and to Doctor
Stefanko.

She will not hunt animals.

Going Under

Jack Dann

When I first met Jack Dann, he had one arm in a cast and a pretty woman, feebly protesting, slung over the other shoulder, and what can one say? No one else at the party seemed surprised that he should show up that way.

Jack is bawdy and hilarious, irrepressible—a very social and sociable creature invading a profession supposedly full of introverted bookworms. You might expect his writing to be light-hearted, slick; but it's not.

There's a phenomenon, familiar to people who have writers as friends, that I call The Buchwald Paradox. The name comes from an article in the Washington Post Sunday magazine, some years back, about the problems of making up a guest list for an upper-crust Washington party. Never ever invite Art Buchwald, it advised; this man who is so funny on paper is an absolute sea anchor at a party. He sits behind his cigar and mumbles that the world is going to hell. The author of this article found it to be generally true that funny writers were rather morose people. But the converse is also true. If you want to liven up your party, she said, you should invite a writer whose work is unrelentingly serious. And nail down the lampshades.

So it is with Jack. Most of his writing is rather deep and dark, carefully crafted, thoughtful, intense. When he emerges from the chrysalis of work he is quite a different sort of animal. (This paradox also characterizes at least two other contributors to this volume, Gene Wolfe and Gardner Dozois.)

Jack has published four novels, a book of short stories, and a chapbook of poetry; he has edited or co-edited nine anthologies of science fiction. His stories have appeared in most of the science fiction magazines and the more prestigious original anthologies, as well as the occasional slick journal of popular gynecology. This one, from Omni *magazine, takes us oddly forward and back in time, centering around an event that is a modern archetype of helpless terror.*

She was beautiful, huge, as graceful as a racing liner. She was a floating Crystal Palace, as magnificent as anything J. P. Morgan could conceive. Designed by Alexander Carlisle and built by Harland and Wolff, she wore the golden band of the company along all nine hundred feet of her. She rose 175 feet like the side of a cliff, with nine steel decks, four sixty-two foot funnels, over two thousand windows and side-lights to illuminate the luxurious cabins and suites and public rooms. She weighed 46,000 tons, and her reciprocating engines and Parsons-type turbines could generate over fifty thousand horsepower and speed the ship over twenty knots. She had a gymnasium, a Turkish bath, squash and racquet courts, a swimming pool, libraries and lounges and sitting rooms. There were rooms and suites to accommodate 735 first-class passengers, 674 in second class, and over a thousand in steerage.

She was the R.M.S. *Titanic*, and Stephen met Esme on her Promenade Deck as she pulled out of her Southampton dock, bound for New York City on her maiden voyage.

Esme stood beside him, resting what looked to be a cedar box on the rail, and gazed out over the cheering crowds on the docks below. Stephen was struck immediately by how beautiful she was. Actually, she was plain-featured, and quite young.

She had a high forehead, a small, straight nose, wet brown eyes that peeked out from under plucked, arched eyebrows, and a mouth that was a little too full. Her blond hair, though clean, was carelessly brushed and tangled in the back. Yet, to Stephen, she *seemed* beautiful.

"Hello," Stephen said, feeling slightly awkward. But colored ribbons and confetti snakes were coiling through the air, and anything seemed possible.

Esme glanced at him. "Hello, you," she said.

"Pardon?" Stephen asked.

"I said, 'Hello, you.' That's an expression that was in vogue when this boat first sailed, if you'd like to know. It means 'Hello, I think you're interesting and would consider sleeping with you if I were so inclined.' "

"You must call it a ship," Stephen said.

She laughed and for an instant looked at him intently, as if in that second she could see everything about him—that he was taking this voyage because he was bored with his life, that nothing had ever *really* happened to him. He felt his face become hot. "Okay, 'ship,' does that make you feel better?" she asked. "Anyway, I want to pretend that I'm living in the past. I don't ever want to return to the present, do you?"

"Well, I . . ."

"Yes, I suppose you do, want to return, that is."

"What makes you think that?"

"Look how you're dressed. You shouldn't be wearing modern clothes on this ship. You'll have to change later, you know." She was perfectly dressed in a powder-blue walking suit with matching jacket, a pleated, velvet-trimmed front blouse, and an ostrich feather hat. She looked as if she had stepped out of another century, and just now Stephen could believe she had.

"What's your name?" Stephen asked.

"Esme," she answered. Then she turned the box that she was resting on the rail and opened the side facing the dock. "You see," she said to the box, "we really are here."

"What did you say?" Stephen asked.

"I was just talking to Poppa," she said, closing and latching the box.

"Who?"

"I'll show you later, if you like," she promised. Then bells began to ring and the ship's whistles cut the air. There was a cheer from the dock and on board, and the ship moved slowly out to sea. To Stephen it seemed that the land, not the ship, was moving. The whole of England was just floating peacefully away, while the string band on the ship's bridge played Oscar Strauss's *The Chocolate Soldier*.

They watched until the land had dwindled to a thin line on the horizon, then Esme reached naturally for Stephen's hand, squeezed it for a moment, then hurried away. Before Stephen could speak, she had disappeared into the crowd, and he stood looking after her long after she had gone.

Stephen found her again in the Café Parisien, sitting in a large wicker chair beside an ornately trellised wall.

"Well, hello, *you*," Esme said, smiling. She was the very model of a smart, stylish young lady.

"Does that mean you're still interested?" Stephen asked, standing before her. Her smile was infectious, and Stephen felt himself losing his poise, as he couldn't stop grinning.

"But *mais oui*," she said. Then she relaxed in her chair, slumped down as if she could instantly revert to being a child—in fact, the dew was still on her—and she looked around the room as though Stephen had suddenly disappeared.

"I beg your pardon?" he asked.

"That's French, which *no one* uses anymore, but it was *the* language of the world when this ship first sailed."

"I believe it was English," Stephen said smoothly.

"Well," she said, looking up at him, "it means that I might be interested *if* you'd kindly sit down instead of looking down at me from the heights." Stephen sat down beside her and she said, "It took you long enough to find me."

"Well," Stephen said, "I had to dress. Remember? You didn't find my previous attire ac—"

"I agree and I apologize," she said quickly, as if suddenly afraid of hurting his feelings. She folded her hands behind the box that she had centered perfectly on the damask-covered table. Her leg brushed against his; indeed, he did look fine, dressed in gray striped trousers, spats, black morning coat, blue vest, and a silk cravat tied under a butterfly collar. He fiddled with his hat, then placed it on the seat of the empty chair beside him. No doubt he would forget to take it.

"Now," she said, "don't you feel better?"

Stephen was completely taken with her; this had never happened to him before. He found it inexplicable. A tall and very English waiter disturbed him by asking if he wished to order cocktails, but Esme asked for a Narcodrine instead.

"I'm sorry, ma'am, but Narcodrines or inhalors are not publicly sold on the ship," the waiter said dryly.

"Well, that's what I *want*."

"One would have to ask the steward for the more modern refreshments."

"You did say you wanted to live in the past," Stephen said to Esme, and ordered a Campari for her and a Drambuie for himself.

"Right now I would prefer a robot to take my order," Esme said.

"I'm sorry, but we have no robots on the ship either," the waiter said before he turned away.

"Are you going to show me what's inside the box?" Stephen asked.

"I don't like that man," Esme said.

"Esme, the box . . ."

"It might cause a stir if I opened it here."

"I would think you'd like that," Stephen said.

"You see, you know me intimately already." Then she smiled and winked at someone four tables away. "Isn't he cute?"

"Who?"

"The little boy with the black hair parted in the middle."
She waved at him, but he ignored her and made an obscene
gesture at a woman who looked to be his nanny. Then Esme
opened the box, which drew the little boy's attention. She
pulled out a full-sized head of a man and placed it gently
beside the box.

"Jesus," Stephen said.

"Stephen, I'd like you to meet Poppa. Poppa, this is
Stephen."

"I'm pleased to meetcha, Stephen," said the head in a
full, resonant voice.

"Speak properly, Poppa," Esme said. "Meet *you*."

"Don't correct your father." The head rolled his eyes
toward Stephen and then said to Esme, "Turn me a bit, so I
can see your friend without eyestrain." The head had white
hair, which was a bit yellowed on the ends. It was neatly
trimmed at the sides and combed up into a pompadour in the
front. The face was strong, although already gone to seed. It
was the face of a man in his late sixties, lined and suntanned.

"What shall I call, uh, him?" Stephen asked.

"You may speak to me directly, son," said the head. "My
given name is Elliot."

"Pleased to meetcha," Stephen said, recouping. He had
heard of such things, but had never seen one before.

"These are going to be all the rage in the next few
months," Esme said. "They aren't on the mass market yet, but
you can imagine their potential for both adults and children.
They can be programmed to talk and react very realistically."

"So I see," Stephen said.

The head smiled, accepting the compliment.

"He also learns and thinks quite well," Esme continued.

"I should hope so," said the head.

The room was buzzing with conversation. At the other
end, a small dance band was playing a waltz. Only a few
Europeans and Americans openly stared at the head; the

Africans and Asians, who were in the majority, pretended to ignore it. The little boy was staring unabashedly.

"Is your father alive?" Stephen asked.

"I *am* her father," the head said, its face betraying its impatience. "At least give me *some* respect."

"Be civil, or I'll close you up," Esme said, piqued. She looked at Stephen. "Yes, he died recently. That's the reason I'm taking this trip, and that's the reason for this. . . ." She nodded to the head. "He's marvelous, though. He *is* my father in every way." Then, mischievously, she said, "Well, I did make a few changes. Poppa was very demanding, you know."

"You ungrateful—"

"Shut up, Poppa."

And Poppa simply shut his eyes.

"That's all I have to say," Esme said, "and he turns himself off. In case you aren't as perceptive as I think you are, I love Poppa very much."

The little boy, unable to control his curiosity any longer, came over to the table, just as Esme was putting Poppa back in the box. In his rush to get to the table, he knocked over one of the ivy pots along the wall. "Why'd you put him away?" he asked. "I want to talk to him. Take him out, just for a minute."

"No," Esme said firmly, "he's asleep just now. And what's *your* name?"

"Michael, and please don't be condescending."

"I'm sorry, Michael."

"Apology accepted. Now, please, can I see the head, just for a minute?"

"If you like, Michael, you can have a private audience with Poppa tomorrow," Esme said. "How's that?"

"But—"

"Shouldn't you be getting back to your nanny now?" Stephen asked, standing up and nodding to Esme to do the same. They would have no privacy here.

"Stuff it," Michael said. "And she's not my nanny, she's my sister." Then he pulled a face at Stephen; he was able to contort his lips, drawing the right side toward the left and left toward the right, as if they were made of rubber. Michael followed Stephen and Esme out of the cafe and up the staircase to the Boat Deck.

The Boat Deck was not too crowded; it was brisk out, and the breeze had a chill to it. Looking forward, Stephen and Esme could see the ship's four huge smokestacks to their left and a cluster of four lifeboats to their right. The ocean was a smooth, deep green expanse turning to blue toward the horizon. The sky was empty, except for a huge, nuclear-powered airship that floated high over the *Titanic*—the dirigible *Californie*, a French luxury liner capable of carrying two thousand passengers.

"Are you two married?" Michael asked, after pointing out the airship above. He trailed a few steps behind them.

"No, we are not," Esme said impatiently. "Not yet, at least," and Stephen felt exhilarated at the thought of her really wanting him. Actually, it made no sense, for he could have any young woman he wanted. Why Esme? Simply because just now she was perfect.

"You're quite pretty," Michael said to Esme.

"Well, thank you," Esme replied, warming to him. "I like you too."

"Watch it," said the boy. "Are you going to stay on the ship and die when it sinks?"

"No!" Esme said, as if taken aback.

"What about your friend?"

"You mean Poppa?"

Vexed, the boy said, "No, *him*," giving Stephen a nasty look.

"Well, I don't know," Esme said. Her face was flushed. "Have you opted for a lifeboat, Stephen?"

"Yes, of course I have."

"Well, *we're* going to die on the ship," Michael said.

"Don't be silly," Esme said.

"Well, we are."

"Who's 'we'?" Stephen asked.

"My sister and I. We've made a pact to go down with the ship."

"I don't believe it," Esme said. She stopped beside one of the lifeboats, rested the box containing Poppa on the rail, and gazed downward at the ocean spume curling away from the side of the ship.

"He's just baiting us," Stephen said, growing tired of the game. "Anyway, he's too young to make such a decision, and his sister, if she is his sister, could not decide such a thing for him, even if she were his guardian. It would be illegal."

"We're at sea," Michael said in the nagging tone of voice children use. "I'll discuss the ramifications of my demise with Poppa tomorrow. I'm sure *he's* more conversant with such things than you are."

"Shouldn't you be getting back to your sister now?" Stephen asked. Michael responded by making the rubber-lips face at him, and then walked away, tugging at the back of his shorts, as if his undergarments had bunched up beneath. He only turned around to wave good-bye to Esme, who blew him a kiss.

"Intelligent little brat," Stephen said.

But Esme looked as if she had just now forgotten all about Stephen and the little boy. She stared at the box as tears rolled from her eyes.

"Esme?"

"I love him and he's dead," she said, and then she seemed to brighten. She took Stephen's hand and they went inside, down the stairs, through several noisy corridors—stateroom parties were in full swing—to her suite. Stephen was a bit nervous, but all things considered, everything was progressing at a proper pace.

Esme's suite had a parlor and a private promenade deck with Elizabethan half-timbered walls. She led him right into the plush-carpeted, velour-papered bedroom, which contained a huge four-poster bed, an antique night table, and a desk and a stuffed chair beside the door. The ornate, harp-sculpture desk lamp was on, as was the lamp just inside the bed curtains. A porthole gave a view of sea and sky. But to Stephen it seemed that the bed overpowered the room.

Esme pushed the desk lamp aside, and then took Poppa out of the box and placed him carefully in the center of the desk. "There." Then she undressed quickly, looking shyly away from Stephen, who was taking his time. She slipped between the parted curtains of the bed and complained that she could hear the damn engines thrumming right through these itchy pillows—she didn't like silk. After a moment she sat up in bed and asked him if he intended to get undressed or just stand there.

"I'm sorry," Stephen said, "but it's just—" He nodded toward the head.

"Poppa *is* turned off, you know."

Afterward, reaching for an inhalor, taking a long pull, and then finally opening her eyes, she said, "I love you too." Stephen only moved in his sleep.

"That's very nice, dear," Poppa said, opening his eyes and smiling at her from the desk.

Little Michael knocked on Esme's door at seven-thirty the next morning.

"Good morning," Michael said, looking Esme up and down. She had not bothered to put anything on before answering the door. "I came to see Poppa. I won't disturb you."

"Jesus, Mitchell—"

"Michael."

"Jesus, Michael, it's too early for—"

"Early bird gets the worm."

"Oh, right," Esme said. "And what the hell does that mean?"

"I calculated that my best chance of talking with Poppa was if I woke you up. You'll go back to bed and I can talk with him in peace. My chances would be greatly diminished if—"

"Awright, come in."

"The steward in the hall just saw you naked."

"Big deal. Look, why don't you come back later, I'm not ready for this, and I don't know why I let you in the room."

"You see, it worked." Michael looked around the room. "He's in the bedroom, right?"

Esme nodded and followed him into the bedroom. Michael was wearing the same wrinkled shirt and shorts that he had on yesterday; his hair was not combed, just tousled.

"Is *he* with you, too?" Michael asked.

"If you mean Stephen, yes."

"I thought so," said Michael. Then he sat down at the desk and talked to Poppa.

"Can't we have *any* privacy?" Stephen asked when Esme came back to bed. She shrugged and took a pull at her inhalor. Drugged, she looked even softer, more vulnerable. "I thought you told me that Poppa was turned off all night," he continued angrily.

"But he *was* turned off," Esme said. "I just now turned him back on for Michael." Then she cuddled up to Stephen, as intimately as if they had been in love for days. That seemed to mollify him.

"Do you have a spare Narcodrine in there?" Michael shouted.

Stephen looked at Esme and laughed. "No," Esme said, "you're too young for such things." She opened the curtain so they could watch Michael. He made the rubber-lips face at Stephen and then said, "I might as well try everything. I'll be dead soon."

"You know," Esme said to Stephen, "I believe him."

"I'm going to talk to his sister, or whoever she is, about this."

"I heard what you said." Michael turned away from Poppa, who seemed lost in thought. "I have very good hearing, I heard everything you said. Go ahead and talk to her, talk to the captain, if you like. It won't do you any good. I'm an international hero, if you'd like to know. That girl who wears the camera in her hair already did an interview for me for the poll." Then he gave them his back and resumed his hushed conversation with Poppa.

"Who does he mean?" asked Esme.

"The woman reporter from *Interfax*," Stephen said.

"Her job is to guess which passengers will opt to die, and why," interrupted Michael, who turned around in his chair. "She interviews the *most* interesting passengers, then gives her predictions to her viewers—and they are considerable. They respond immediately to a poll taken several times a day. Keeps us in their minds, and everybody loves the smell of death." Michael turned back to Poppa.

"Well, she hasn't tried to interview *me*."

"Do you really want her to?" Stephen asked.

"And why not? I'm for conspicuous consumption, and I want so much for this experience to be a success. Goodness, let the whole world watch us sink, if they want. They might just as well take bets." Then, in a conspiratorial whisper, she said, "None of us really knows who's opted to die. *That's* part of the excitement. Isn't it?"

"I suppose," Stephen said.

"Oh, you're such a prig," Esme said. "One would think you're a doer."

"What?"

"A doer. All of us are either doers or voyeurs, isn't that right? But the doers mean business," and to illustrate she cocked her head, stuck out her tongue, and made gurgling noises as if she were drowning. "The voyeurs, however, are just along for the ride. Are you *sure* you're not a doer?"

Michael, who had been eavesdropping again, said, referring to Stephen, "He's not a doer, you can bet on that! He's a voyeur of the worst sort. *He* takes it all seriously."

"Mitchell, that's not a very nice thing to say. Apologize or I'll turn Poppa off and you can go right—"

"I told you before, it's Michael. M-I-C-H-A—"

"Now that's enough disrespect from both of you," Poppa said. "Michael, stop goading Stephen. Esme says she loves him. Esme, be nice to Michael. He just made my day. And you don't have to threaten to turn me off. I'm turning myself off. I've got some thinking to do." Poppa closed his eyes and nothing Esme said would awaken him.

"Well, he's never done *that* before," Esme said to Michael, who was now standing before the bed and trying to place his feet as wide apart as he could. "What did you say to him?"

"Nothing much."

"Come on, Michael, *I* let you into the room, remember?"

"I remember. Can I come into bed with you?"

"Hell, no," Stephen said.

"He's only a child," Esme said as she moved over to make room for Michael, who climbed in between her and Stephen. "Be a sport. *You're* the man I love."

"Do you believe in transmigration of souls?" Michael asked Esme.

"What?"

"Well, I asked Poppa if he remembered any of his past lives, that is, if he had any. Poppa's conscious, you know, even if he is a machine."

"Did your sister put such ideas in your head?" Esme asked.

"Now you're being condescending." However, Michael made the rubber-lips face at Stephen, rather than at Esme. Stephen made a face back at him, and Michael howled in appreciation, then became quite serious and said, "On the contrary, *I* helped my sister to remember. It wasn't easy, either, because she hasn't lived as many lives as I have. *She's* younger than me. I bet I could help *you* to remember," he said to Esme.

"And what about me?" asked Stephen, playing along, enjoying the game a little now.

"You're a nice man, but you're too filled up with philosophy and rationalizations. You wouldn't grasp any of it; it's too simple. Anyway, you're in love and distracted."

"Well, I'm in love too," Esme said petulantly.

"But you're in love with everything. He's only in love with one thing at a time."

"Am I a thing to you?" Esme asked Stephen.

"Certainly not."

But Michael would not be closed out. "I can teach you how to meditate," he said to Esme. "It's easy, once you know how. You just watch things in a different way."

"Then would I see all my past lives?" Esme asked.

"Maybe."

"Is that what you do?"

"I started when I was six," Michael said. "I don't *do* anything anymore, I just see differently. It's something like dreaming." Then he said to Esme, "You two are like a dream, and I'm outside it. Can I come in?"

Delighted, Esme asked, "You mean, become a family?"

"Until the end," Michael said.

"I think it's wonderful, what do you think, Stephen?"

Stephen lay back against the wall, impatient, ignoring them.

"Come on, be a sport," Michael said. "I'll even teach you how to make the rubber-lips face."

Stephen and Esme finally managed to lose Michael by lunchtime. Esme seemed happy enough to be rid of the boy, and they spent the rest of the day discovering the ship. They took a quick dip in the pool, but the water was too cold and it was chilly outside. If the dirigible was floating above, they did not see it because the sky was covered with heavy gray clouds. They changed clothes, strolled along the glass-enclosed lower Promenade Deck, looked for the occasional flying fish, and spent an interesting half hour being interviewed by the woman from *Interfax*. They they took a snack in the opulent first-class smoking room. Esme loved the mirrors and stained-glass windows. After they explored cabin and tourist class, Esme talked Stephen into a quick game of squash, which he played rather well. By dinnertime they found their way into the garish, blue-tiled Turkish bath. It was empty and hot, and they made gentle but exhausting love on one of the Caesar couches. Then they changed clothes again, danced in the lounge, and took a late supper in the Café.

He spent the night with Esme in her suite. It was about four o'clock in the morning when he was awakened by a hushed conversation. Rather than make himself known, Stephen feigned sleep and listened.

"I can't make a decision," Esme said as she carefully paced back and forth beside the desk upon which Poppa rested.

"You've told me over and over what you know you must do," said Poppa. "And now you change your mind?"

"I think things have changed."

"And how is that?"

"Stephen, he . . ."

"Ah," Poppa said, "so now *love* is the escape. But do you know how long that will last?"

"I didn't expect to meet him, to feel better about everything."

"It will pass."

"But right now I don't want to die."

"You've spent a fortune on this trip, and on me. And now you want to throw it away. Look, the way you feel about Stephen is all for the better, don't you understand? It will make your passing away all the sweeter because you're happy, in love, whatever you want to claim for it. But now you want to throw everything away that we've planned and take your life some other time, probably when you're desperate and unhappy and don't have me around to help you. You wish to die as mindlessly as you were born."

"That's not so, Poppa. But it's up to *me* to choose."

"You've made your choice, now stick to it, or you'll drop dead like I did."

Stephen opened his eyes; he could not stand this any longer. "Esme, what the hell are you talking about?"

She looked startled and then said to Poppa, "You were purposely talking loudly to wake him up, weren't you?"

"*You* had me programmed to help you. I love you and I care about you. You can't undo that!"

"I can do whatever I wish," she said petulantly.

"Then let me help you, as I always have. If I were alive and had my body, I would tell you exactly what I'm telling you now."

"What is going on?" Stephen asked.

"She's fooling you," Poppa said gently to Stephen. "She's using you because she's frightened."

"I am not!"

"She's grasping at anyone she can find."

"I am not!" she shouted.

"What the hell is he telling you?" Stephen asked.

"The truth," Poppa said.

Esme sat down beside Stephen on the bed and began to cry, then, as if sliding easily into a new role, she looked at him and said, "I did program Poppa to help me die."

Disgusted, Stephen drew away from her.

"Poppa and I talked everything over very carefully, we even discussed what to do if something like this came about."

"You mean if you fell in love and wanted to live."

"Yes."

"And she decided that under no circumstances would she undo what she had done," Poppa said. "She has planned the best possible death for herself, a death to be experienced and savored. She's given everything up and spent all her money to do it. She's broke. She can't go back now, isn't that right, Esme?"

Esme looked at Stephen and nodded.

"But you're not sure, I can see that," Stephen insisted.

"I will help her, as I always have," said Poppa.

"Jesus, shut that thing up," Stephen shouted.

"He's not a—"

"Please, at least give us a chance," Stephen said to Esme. "You're the first authentic experience I've ever had, I love you, I don't want it to end. . . ."

Poppa pleaded his case eloquently, but Esme told him to go to sleep.

He obediently closed his eyes.

The great ship hit an iceberg on the fourth night of her voyage, exactly one day earlier than scheduled. It was Saturday, 11:40 P.M. and the air was full of colored lights from tiny splinters of ice floating like motes of dust. "Whiskers 'round the light" they used to be called by sailors. The sky was a panoply of twinkling stars, and it was so cold that one might imagine they were fragments of ice floating in a cold, dark, inverted sea overhead.

Stephen and Esme were again standing by the rail of the Promenade Deck. Both were dressed in the early-twentieth-century accouterments provided by the ship: he in woolen trousers, jacket, motoring cap, and caped overcoat with a long scarf; she in a fur coat, a stylish Merry Widow hat, high-button shoes, and a black velvet, two-piece suit edged with white silk. She looked ravishing, and very young, despite the clothes.

"Throw it away," Stephen said in an authoritative voice. "Now!"

Esme brought the cedar box containing Poppa to her chest, as if she were about to throw it forward, then slowly placed it atop the rail again. "I *can't.*"

"Do you want me to do it?" Stephen asked.

"I don't see why I must throw him away."

"Because we're starting a new life together. We want to live, not—"

Just then someone shouted and, as if in the distance, a bell rang three times.

"Could there be another ship nearby?" Esme asked.

"Esme, throw the box away!" Stephen snapped; and then he saw it. He pulled Esme backward, away from the rail. An iceberg as high as the forecastle deck scraped against the side of the ship; it almost seemed that the bluish, glistening mountain of ice was another ship passing, that the ice rather than the ship was moving. Pieces of ice rained upon the deck, slid across the varnished wood, and then the iceberg was lost in the darkness astern. It must have been at least one hundred feet high.

"Omygod!" Esme screamed, rushing to the rail and leaning over it.

"What it is?"

"Poppa, I dropped him, when you pulled me away from the iceberg. I didn't mean to. . . ."

Stephen put his arms around her, but she pulled away. "If you didn't mean to throw it away—"

"Him, not it!"

"—him away, then why did you bring him up here?"

"To satisfy you, to . . . I don't know, Stephen. I suppose I was going to *try* to do it."

"Well, it's done, and you're going to feel better, I promise. I love you, Esme."

"I love *you*, Stephen," she said distractedly. A noisy crowd gathered on the deck around them. Some were quite drunk and were kicking large chunks of ice about, as if they were playing soccer.

"Come on, then," Stephen said, "let's get heavy coats and blankets, and we'll wait on deck for a lifeboat. We'll take the first one out and watch the ship sink together."

"No, I'll meet you right here in an hour."

"Esme, it's too dangerous, I don't think we should separate." Stephen glimpsed the woman from *Interfax* standing alone on the elevated sun deck, recording this event for her millions of viewers.

"We've got time before *anything* is going to happen."

"We don't know that," Stephen insisted. "Don't you realize that we're off schedule? We were supposed to hit that iceberg *tomorrow*."

But Esme had disappeared into the crowd.

It was bitter cold, and the Boat Deck was filled with people, all rushing about, shouting, scrambling for the lifeboats, and, inevitably, those who had changed their minds at the last moment about going down with the ship were shouting the loudest, trying the hardest to be permitted into the boats, not one of which had been lowered yet. There were sixteen wooden lifeboats and four canvas Englehardts, the collapsibles. But they could not be lowered away until the davits were cleared of the two forward boats. The crew was quiet, each man busy with the boats and davits. All the boats were now swinging free of the ship, hanging just beside the Boat Deck.

"We'll let you know when it's time to board," shouted an officer to the families crowding around him.

The floor was listing. Esme was late, and Stephen wasn't going to wait. At this rate, the ship would be bow-down in the water in no time.

She must be with Michael, he thought. The little bastard must have talked her into dying.

Michael had a stateroom on C Deck.

Stephen knocked, called to Michael and Esme, tried to open the door, and finally kicked the lock free.

Michael was sitting on the bed, which was a Pullman berth. His sister lay beside him, dead.

"Where's Esme?" Stephen demanded, repelled by the sight of Michael sitting so calmly beside his dead sister.

"Not here. Obviously." Michael smiled, then made the rubber-lips face at Stephen.

"Jesus," Stephen said. "Put your coat on, you're coming with me."

Michael laughed and patted his hair down. "I'm already dead, just like my sister, almost. I took a pill too, see?"

and he held up a small brown bottle. "Anyway, they wouldn't let me on a lifeboat. I didn't sign up for one, remember?"

"You're a baby, they—"

"I thought Poppa explained that to you." Michael lay down beside his sister and watched Stephen like a puppy with its head cocked at an odd angle.

"You do know where Esme is, now tell me."

"You never understood her. She came here to die."

"That's all changed," Stephen said, wanting to wring the boy's neck.

"Nothing's changed. Esme loves me, too. And everything else."

"Tell me where she is."

"It's too late for me to teach *you* how to meditate. In a way, you're *already* dead. No memory, or maybe you've just been born. No past lives. A baby." Again, Michael made the rubber-lips face. Then he closed his eyes. He whispered, "She's doing what I'm doing."

An instant later, he stopped breathing.

Stephen searched the ship, level by level, broke in on the parties, where those who had opted for death were having a last fling, looked into the lounges where many old couples sat, waiting for the end. He made his way down to F Deck, where he had made love to Esme in the Turkish bath. The water was up to his knees; it was green and soapy. He was afraid, for the list was becoming worse minute by minute; everything was happening so fast.

The water rose, even as he walked.

He had to get to the stairs, had to get up and out, onto a lifeboat, away from the ship, but on he walked, looking for Esme, unable to stop. He had to find her. She might even be on the Boat Deck right now, he thought, wading as best he could through a corridor.

But he had to satisfy himself that she wasn't down here.

The Turkish bath was filling with water, and the lights

were still on, giving the room a ghostly illumination. Odd-
ments floated in the room: blue slippers, a comb, scraps of
paper, cigarettes, and several seamless plastic packages.

On the farthest couch, Esme sat meditating, her eyes
closed and hands folded on her lap. She wore a simple white
dress. Relieved and overjoyed, he shouted to her. She jerked
awake, looking disoriented, shocked to see him. She stood up
and, without a word, waded toward the other exit, dipping her
hands into the water, as if to speed her on her way.

"Esme, where are you going?" Stephen called, following.
"Don't run away from *me*."

Just then an explosion pitched them both into the water,
and a wall gave way. A solid sheet of water seemed to be
crashing into the room, smashing Stephen, pulling him under
and sweeping him away. He fought to reach the surface and
tried to swim back, to find Esme. A lamp broke away from the
ceiling, just missing him. "Esme!" he shouted, but he couldn't
see her, and then he found himself choking, swimming, as the
water carried him through a corridor and away from her.

Finally, Stephen was able to grab the iron curl of a railing
and pull himself onto a dry step. There was another explosion,
the floor pitched, yet still the lights glowed. He looked down
at the water that filled the corridor, the Turkish bath, the entire deck, and he screamed for Esme.

The ship shuddered, then everything was dead quiet. In
the great rooms, chandeliers hung at angles; tables and chairs
had skidded across the floors and seemed to squat against the
walls like wooden beasts. Still the lights burned, as if all were
quite correct, except gravity, which was misbehaving.

Stephen walked and climbed, followed by the sea, as if in
a dream.

Numbed, he found himself back on the Boat Deck. But
part of the deck was already submerged. Almost everyone had
moved aft, climbing uphill as the bow dipped farther into the
water.

The lifeboats were gone, as were the crew. Even now he

looked for Esme, still hoping that she had somehow survived. Men and women were screaming "I don't want to die," while others clung together in small groups, some crying, others praying, while there were those who were very calm, enjoying the disaster. They stood by the rail, looking out toward the lifeboats or at the dirigible, which floated above. Many had changed their clothes and looked resplendent in their early twentieth-century costumes. One man, dressed in pajama bottoms and a blue and gold smoking jacket, climbed over the rail and just stepped into the frigid water.

But there were a few men and women atop the officers' quarters. They were working hard, trying to launch collapsible lifeboats C and D, their only chance of getting safely away from the ship.

"Hey!" Stephen called to them, just now coming to his senses. "Do you need any help up there?" He realized that he was really going to die unless he did something.

He was ignored by those who were pushing one of the freed collapsibles off the port side of the roof. Someone shouted, "Damn!" The boat had landed upside down in the water.

"It's better than nothing," shouted a woman, and she and her friends jumped after the boat.

Stephen shivered; he was not yet ready to leap into the twenty-eight-degree water, although he knew there wasn't much time left, and he had to get away from the ship before it went down. Everyone on or close to the ship would be sucked under. He crossed to the starboard side, where some other men were trying to push the boat "up" to the edge of the deck. The great ship was listing heavily to port.

This time Stephen didn't ask; he just joined the work. No one complained. They were trying to slide the boat over the edge on planks. All these people looked to be in top physical shape; Stephen noticed that about half of them were women wearing the same warm coats as the men. This was a game to all of them, he suspected, and they were enjoying it. Each one

was going to beat the odds, one way or another; the very thrill
was to outwit fate, opt to die and yet survive.

But then the bridge was underwater.

There was a terrible crashing, and Stephen slid along the
float as everything tilted.

Everyone was shouting; Stephen saw more people than
he thought possible to be left on the ship. People were jumping overboard. They ran before a great wave that washed
along the deck. Water swirled around Stephen and the others
nearby.

"She's going down," someone shouted. Indeed, the stern
of the ship was swinging upward. The lights flickered. There
was a roar as the entrails of the ship broke loose: anchor
chains, the huge engines and boilers. One of the huge black
funnels fell, smashing into the water amid sparks. But still the
ship was brilliantly lit, every porthole afire.

The crow's nest before him was almost submerged, but
Stephen swam for it nevertheless. Then he caught himself and
tried to swim away from the ship, but it was too late. He felt
himself being sucked back, pulled under. He was being
sucked into the ventilator, which was in front of the forward
funnel.

Down into sudden darkness . . .

He gasped, swallowed water, and felt the wire mesh, the
airshaft grating that prevented him from being sucked under.
He held his breath until he thought his lungs would burst; he
called in his mind to Esme and his dead mother. Water was
surging all around him, and then there was another explosion.
Stephen felt warmth on his back, as a blast of hot air pushed
him upward. Then he broke out into the freezing air. He
swam for his life, away from the ship, away from the crashing
and thudding of glass and wood, away from the debris of deck
chairs, planking, and ropes, and especially away from the
other people who were moaning, screaming at him, and trying
to grab him as buoy, trying to pull him down.

Still, he felt the suction of the ship, and he swam, even

though his arms were numb and his head was aching as if it were about to break. He took a last look behind him, and saw the *Titanic* slide into the water, into its own eerie pool of light. Then he swam harder. In the distance were other lifeboats, for he could see lights flashing. But none of the boats would come in to rescue him; that he knew.

He heard voices nearby and saw a dark shape. For a moment it didn't register, then he realized that he was swimming toward an overturned lifeboat, the collapsible he had seen pushed into the water. There were almost thirty men and women standing on it. Stephen tried to climb aboard and someone shouted, "You'll sink us, we've too many already."

"Find somewhere else."

A woman tried to hit Stephen with an oar, just missing his head. Stephen swam around to the other side of the boat. He grabbed hold again, found someone's foot, and was kicked back into the water.

"Come on," a man said, his voice gravelly. "Take my arm and I'll pull you up."

"There's no *room*!" someone else said.

"There's enough room for one more."

"No, there's not."

A fight threatened, and the boat began to rock.

"We'll all be in the water if we don't stop this," shouted the man who was holding Stephen afloat. Then he pulled Stephen aboard.

"But no more, he's the last one!"

Stephen stood with the others; there was barely enough room. Everyone had formed a double line now, facing the bow, and leaned in the opposite direction of the swells. Slowly the boat inched away from the site where the ship had gone down, away from the people in the water, all begging for life, for one last chance. As he looked back to where the ship had once been, Stephen thought of Esme. He couldn't bear to think of her as dead, floating through the corridors of the ship. Desperately he wanted her, wanted to take her in his arms.

Those in the water could easily be heard; in fact, the calls seemed magnified, as if meant to be heard clearly by everyone who was safe, as a punishment for past sins.

"We're all deaders," said a woman standing beside Stephen. "I'm sure no one's coming to get us before dawn, when they have to pick up survivors."

"We'll be the last pickup, that's for sure, that's if they intend to pick us up at all."

"Those in the water have to get their money's worth."

"And since we opted for death . . ."

"I didn't," Stephen said, almost to himself.

"Well, you've got it anyway."

Stephen was numb, but no longer cold. As if from far away, he heard the splash of someone falling from the boat, which was very slowly sinking as air was lost from under the hull. At times the water was up to Stephen's knees, yet he wasn't even shivering. Time distended, or contracted. He measured it by the splashing of his companions as they fell overboard. He heard himself calling Esme, as if to say good-bye, or perhaps to greet her.

By dawn, Stephen was so muddled by the cold that he thought he was on land, for the sea was full of debris: cork, steamer chairs, boxes, pilasters, rugs, carved wood, clothes, and of course the bodies of those unfortunate who could not or would not survive; and the great icebergs and the smaller ones called growlers looked like cliffs and mountainsides. The icebergs were sparkling and many-hued, all brilliant in the light, as if painted by some cheerless Gauguin of the north.

"There," someone said, a woman's hoarse voice. "It's coming down, it's coming down!" The dirigible, looking like a huge white whale, seemed to be descending through its more natural element, water, rather than the thin, cold air. Its electric engines could not even be heard.

In the distance, Stephen could see the other lifeboats.

Soon the airship would begin to rescue those in the boats, which were now tied together in a cluster. As Stephen's thoughts wandered and his eyes watered from the reflected morning sunlight, he saw a piece of carved wood bobbing up and down near the boat, and noticed a familiar face in the debris that seemed to surround the lifeboat.

There, just below the surface, in his box, the lid open, eyes closed, floated Poppa. Poppa opened his eyes then and looked at Stephen, who screamed, lost his balance on the hull, and plunged headlong into the cold black water.

The Laurel Lounge of the dirigible *California* was dark and filled with survivors. Some sat in the flowered, stuffed chairs; others just milled about. But they were all watching the life-like holographic tapes of the sinking of the *Titanic*. The images filled the large room with the ghostly past.

Stephen stood in the back of the room, away from the others, who cheered each time there was a close-up of someone jumping overboard or slipping under the water. He pulled the scratchy woolen blanket around him, and shivered. He had been on the dirigible for more than twenty-four hours, and he was still chilled. A crewman had told him it was because of the injections he had received when he boarded the airship.

There was another cheer and, horrified, he saw that they were cheering for *him*. He watched himself being sucked into the ventilator, and then blown upward to the surface. His body ached from being battered. But he had saved himself. He *had* survived, and that had been an actual experience. It was worth it for that, but poor Esme . . .

"You had one of the *most* exciting experiences," a woman said to him, as she touched his hand. He recoiled from her, and she shrugged, then moved on.

"I wish to register a complaint," said a stocky man dressed in period clothing to one of the *Titanic*'s officers, who was standing beside Stephen and sipping a cocktail.

"Yes?" asked the officer.

"I was saved against my wishes. I specifically took this voyage that I might pit myself against the elements."

"Did you sign one of our protection waivers?" asked the officer.

"I was not aware that we were required to sign any such thing."

"All such information was provided," the officer said, looking uninterested. "Those passengers who are truly committed to taking their chances sign, and we leave them to their own devices. Otherwise, we are responsible for every passenger's life."

"I might just as well have jumped into the ocean early and gotten pulled out," the passenger said sarcastically.

The officer smiled. "Most people want to test themselves out as long as they can. Of course, if you want to register a formal complaint, then . . ."

But the passenger stomped away.

"The man's trying to save face," the officer said to Stephen, who had been eavesdropping. "We see quite a bit of that. But *you* seemed to have an interesting ride. You gave us quite a start; we thought you were going to take a lifeboat with the others, but you disappeared belowdecks. It was a bit more difficult to monitor you, but we managed—that's the fun for *us*. You were never in any danger, of course. Well, maybe a *little*."

Stephen was shaken. He had felt that his experiences had been authentic, that he had really saved himself. But none of that had been *real*. Only Esme . . .

And then he saw her step into the room.

"Esme?" He couldn't believe it. "Esme?"

She walked over to him and smiled, as she had the first time they'd met. She was holding a water-damaged cedar box. "Hello, Stephen. Wasn't it exciting?"

Stephen threw his arms around her, but she didn't respond. She waited a proper time, then disengaged herself.

"And look," she said, "they've even found Poppa." She opened the box and held it up to him.

Poppa's eyes fluttered open. For a moment his eyes were vague and unfocused, then they fastened on Esme and sharpened. "Esme . . ." Poppa said uncertainly, and then he smiled. "Esme, I've had the strangest dream." He laughed. "I dreamed I was a head in a box. . . ."

Esme snapped the box closed. "Isn't he marvelous," she said. She patted the box and smiled. "He almost had me talked into going through with it this time."

Johnny Mnemonic

William Gibson

William Gibson writes that he had "the typical isolated geek childhood of SF writers. Thick glasses, crummy at sports, all that." After some years of roaming around the United States, Canada, and Europe, he settled in British Columbia.

"Johnny Mnemonic" is Gibson's second story. His first novel, Neuromancer, *set in this same haunting decadent future, was published by Ace in 1984.*

I put the shotgun in an Adidas bag and padded it out with four pairs of tennis socks, not my style at all, but that was what I was aiming for: If they think you're crude, go technical; if they think you're technical, go crude. I'm a very technical boy. So I decided to get as crude as possible. These days, though, you have to be pretty technical before you can even aspire to crudeness. I'd had to turn both those twelve-gauge shells from brass stock, on a lathe, and then load them myself; I'd had to dig up an old microfiche with instructions for hand-loading cartridges; I'd had to build a lever-action press to seat the primers—all very tricky. But I knew they'd work.

The meet was set for the Drome at 2300, but I rode the tube three stops past the closest platform and walked back. Immaculate procedure.

I checked myself out in the chrome siding of a coffee kiosk, your basic sharp-faced Caucasoid with a ruff of stiff, dark hair. The girls at Under the Knife were big on Sony Mao, and it was getting harder to keep them from adding the chic suggestion of epicanthic folds. It probably wouldn't fool Ralfi Face, but it might get me next to his table.

The Drome is a single narrow space with a bar down one side and tables along the other, thick with pimps and handlers and an arcane array of dealers. The Magnetic Dog Sisters were on the door that night, and I didn't relish trying to get out past them if things didn't work out. They were two meters tall and thin as greyhounds. One was black and the other white, but aside from that they were as nearly identical as cosmetic surgery could make them. They'd been lovers for years and were bad news in a tussle. I was never quite sure which one had originally been male.

Ralfi was sitting at his usual table. Owing me a lot of money. I had hundreds of megabytes stashed in my head on an idiot/savant basis, information I had no conscious access to. Ralfi had left it there. He hadn't, however, come back for it. Only Ralfi could retrieve the data, with a code phrase of his own invention. I'm not cheap to begin with, but my overtime on storage is astronomical. And Ralfi had been very scarce.

Then I'd heard that Ralfi Face wanted to put out a contract on me. So I'd arranged to meet him in the Drome, but I'd arranged it as Edward Bax, clandestine importer, late of Rio and Peking.

The Drome stank of biz, a metallic tang of nervous tension. Muscle-boys scattered through the crowd were flexing stock parts at one another and trying on thin, cold grins, some of them so lost under superstructures of muscle graft that their outlines weren't really human.

Pardon me. Pardon me, friends. Just Eddie Bax here, Fast Eddie the Importer, with his professionally nondescript gym bag, and please ignore this slit, just wide enough to admit his right hand.

Ralfi wasn't alone. Eighty kilos of blond California beef perched alertly in the chair next to his, martial arts written all over him.

Fast Eddie Bax was in the chair opposite them before the beef's hands were off the table. "You black belt?" I asked eagerly. He nodded, blue eyes running an automatic scanning pattern between my eyes and my hands. "Me, too," I said. "Got mine here in the bag." And I shoved my hand through the slit and thumbed the safety off. Click. "Double twelve-gauge with the triggers wired together."

"That's a gun," Ralfi said, putting a plump, restraining hand on his boy's taut blue nylon chest. "Johnny has an antique firearm in his bag." So much for Edward Bax.

I guess he'd always been Ralfi Something or Other, but he owed his acquired surname to a singular vanity. Built something like an overripe pear, he'd worn the once-famous face of Christian White for twenty years—Christian White of the Aryan Reggae Band, Sony Mao to his generation, and final champion of race rock. I'm a whiz at trivia.

Christian White: classic pop face with a singer's high-definition muscles, chiseled cheekbones. Angelic in one light, handsomely depraved in another. But Ralfi's eyes lived behind that face, and they were small and cold and black.

"Please," he said, "let's work this out like businessmen." His voice was marked by a horrible prehensile sincerity, and the corners of his beautiful Christian White mouth were always wet. "Lewis here," nodding in the beefboy's direction, "is a meatball." Lewis took this impassively, looking like something built from a kit. "You aren't a meatball, Johnny."

"Sure I am, Ralfi, a nice meatball chock-full of implants where you can store your dirty laundry while you go off shopping for people to kill me. From my end of this bag, Ralfi, it looks like you've got some explaining to do."

"It's this last batch of product, Johnny." He sighed deeply. "In my role as broker—"

"Fence," I corrected.

"As broker, I'm usually very careful as to sources."

"You buy only from those who steal the best. Got it."

He sighed again. "I try," he said wearily, "not to buy from fools. This time, I'm afraid, I've done that." Third sigh was the cue for Lewis to trigger the neural disruptor they'd taped under my side of the table.

I put everything I had into curling the index finger of my right hand, but I no longer seemed to be connected to it. I could feel the metal of the gun and the foam-padded tape I'd wrapped around the stubby grip, but my hands were cool wax, distant and inert. I was hoping Lewis was a true meatball, thick enough to go for the gym bag and snag my rigid trigger finger, but he wasn't.

"We've been very worried about you, Johnny. Very worried. You see, that's Yakuza property you have there. A fool took it from them, Johnny. A dead fool."

Lewis giggled.

It all made sense then, an ugly kind of sense, like bags of wet sand settling around my head. Killing wasn't Ralfi's style. Lewis wasn't even Ralfi's style. But he'd got himself stuck between the Sons of the Neon Chrysanthemum and something that belonged to them—or, more likely, something of theirs that belonged to someone else. Ralfi, of course, could use the code phrase to throw me into idiot/savant, and I'd spill their hot program without remembering a single quarter tone. For a fence like Ralfi, that would ordinarily have been enough. But not for the Yakuza. The Yakuza would know about Squids, for one thing, and they wouldn't want to worry about one lifting those dim and permanent traces of their program out of my head. I didn't know very much about Squids, but I'd heard stories, and I made it a point never to repeat them to my clients. No, the Yakuza wouldn't like that; it looked too much like evidence. They hadn't got where they were by leaving evidence around. Or alive.

Lewis was grinning. I think he was visualizing a point just behind my forehead and imagining how he could get there the hard way.

"Hey," said a low voice, feminine, from somewhere behind my right shoulder, "you cowboys sure aren't having too lively a time."

"Pack it, bitch," Lewis said, his tanned face very still. Ralfi looked blank.

"Lighten up. You want to buy some good free base?" She pulled up a chair and quickly sat before either of them could stop her. She was barely inside my fixed field of vision, a thin girl with mirrored glasses, her dark hair cut in a rough shag. She wore black leather, open over a T-shirt slashed diagonally with stripes of red and black. "Eight thou a gram weight."

Lewis snorted his exasperation and tried to slap her out of the chair. Somehow he didn't quite connect, and her hand came up and seemed to brush his wrist as it passed. Bright blood sprayed the table. He was clutching his wrist white-knuckle tight, blood trickling from between his fingers.

But hadn't her hand been empty?

He was going to need a tendon stapler. He stood up carefully, without bothering to push his chair back. The chair toppled backward, and he stepped out of my line of sight without a word.

"He better get a medic to look at that," she said. "That's a nasty cut."

"You have no idea," said Ralfi, suddenly sounding very tired, "the depths of shit you have just gotten yourself into."

"No kidding? Mystery. I get real excited by mysteries. Like why your friend here's so quiet. Frozen, like. Or what this thing here is for," and she held up the little control unit that she'd somehow taken from Lewis. Ralfi looked ill.

"You, ah, want maybe a quarter million to give me that and take a walk?" A fat hand came up to stroke his pale, lean face nervously.

"What I want," she said, snapping her fingers so that the

unit spun and glittered, "is work. A job. Your boy hurt his wrist. But a quarter'll do for a retainer."

Ralfi let his breath out explosively and began to laugh, exposing teeth that hadn't been kept up to the Christian White standard. Then she turned the disruptor off.

"Two million," I said.

"My kind of man," she said, and laughed. "What's in the bag?"

"A shotgun."

"Crude." It might have been a compliment.

Ralfi said nothing at all.

"Name's Millions. Molly Millions. You want to get out of here, boss? People are starting to stare." She stood up. She was wearing leather jeans the color of dried blood.

And I saw for the first time that the mirrored lenses were surgical inlays, the silver rising smoothly from her high cheekbones, sealing her eyes in their sockets. I saw my new face twinned there.

"I'm Johnny," I said. "We're taking Mr. Face with us."

He was outside, waiting. Looking like your standard tourist tech, in plastic zoris and a silly Hawaiian shirt printed with blowups of his firm's most popular microprocessor; a mild little guy, the kind most likely to wind up drunk on sake in a bar that puts out miniature rice crackers with seaweed garnish. He looked like the kind who sing the corporate anthem and cry, who shake hands endlessly with the bartender. And the pimps and the dealers would leave him alone, pegging him as innately conservative. Not up for much, and careful with his credit when he was.

The way I figured it later, they must have amputated part of his left thumb, somewhere behind the first joint, replacing it with a prosthetic tip, and cored the stump, fitting it with a spool and socket molded from one of the Ono-Sendai diamond analogs. Then they'd carefully wound the spool with three meters of monomolecular filament.

Molly got into some kind of exchange with the Magnetic
Dog Sisters, giving me a chance to usher Ralfi through the
door with the gym bag pressed lightly against the base of his
spine. She seemed to know them. I heard the black one laugh.

I glanced up, out of some passing reflex, maybe because
I've never got used to it, to the soaring arcs of light and the
shadows of the geodesics above them. Maybe that saved me.

Ralfi kept walking, but I don't think he was trying to
escape. I think he'd already given up. Probably he already had
an idea of what we were up against.

I looked back down in time to see him explode.

Playback on full recall shows Ralfi stepping forward as
the little tech sidles out of nowhere, smiling. Just a suggestion
of a bow, and his left thumb falls off. It's a conjuring trick.
The thumb hangs suspended. Mirrors? Wires? And Ralfi
stops, his back to us, dark crescents of sweat under the armpits
of his pale summer suit. He knows. He must have known. And
then the joke-shop thumbtip, heavy as lead, arcs out in a lightning yo-yo trick, and the invisible thread connecting it to the
killer's hand passes laterally through Ralfi's skull, just above
his eyebrows, whips up, and descends, slicing the pear-shaped
torso diagonally from shoulder to rib cage. Cuts so fine that no
blood flows until synapses misfire and the first tremors surrender the body to gravity.

Ralfi tumbled apart in a pink cloud of fluids, the three
mismatched sections rolling forward onto the tiled pavement.
In total silence.

I brought the gym bag up, and my hand convulsed. The
recoil nearly broke my wrist.

It must have been raining; ribbons of water cascaded from a
ruptured geodesic and spattered on the tile behind us. We
crouched in the narrow gap between a surgical boutique and
an antique shop. She'd just edged one mirrored eye around
the corner to report a single Volks module in front of the
Drome, red lights flashing. They were sweeping Ralfi up. Asking questions.

I was covered in scorched white fluff. The tennis socks. The gym bag was a ragged plastic cuff around my wrist. "I don't see how the hell I missed him."

"Cause he's fast, so fast." She hugged her knees and rocked back and forth on her bootheels. "His nervous system's jacked up. He's factory custom." She grinned and gave a little squeal of delight. "I'm gonna get that boy. Tonight. He's the best, number one, top dollar, state of the art."

"What you're going to get, for this boy's two million, is my ass out of here. Your boyfriend back there was mostly grown in a vat in Chiba City. He's a Yakuza assassin."

"Chiba. Yeah. See, Molly's been Chiba, too." And she showed me her hands, fingers slightly spread. Her fingers were slender, tapered, very white against the polished burgundy nails. Ten blades snicked straight out from their recesses beneath her nails, each one a narrow, double-edged scalpel in pale blue steel.

I'd never spent much time in Nighttown. Nobody there had anything to pay me to remember, and most of them had a lot they paid regularly to forget. Generations of sharpshooters had chipped away at the neon until the maintenance crews gave up. Even at noon the arcs were soot-black against faintest pearl.

Where do you go when the world's wealthiest criminal order is feeling for you with calm, distant fingers? Where do you hide from the Yakuza, so powerful that it owns comsats and at least three shuttles? The Yakuza is a true multinational, like ITT and Ono-Sendai. Fifty years before I was born the Yakuza had already absorbed the Triads, the Mafia, the Union Corse.

Molly had an answer: You hide in the Pit, in the lowest circle, where any outside influence generates swift, concentric ripples of raw menace. You hide in Nighttown. Better yet, you hide *above* Nighttown, because the Pit's inverted, and the bottom of its bowl touches the sky, the sky that Nighttown never sees, sweating under its own firmament of acrylic resin, up where the Lo Teks crouch in the dark like gargoyles, black-market cigarettes dangling from their lips.

She had another answer, too.

"So you're locked up good and tight, Johnny-san? No way to get that program without the password?" She led me into the shadows that waited beyond the bright tube platform. The concrete walls were overlaid with graffiti, years of them twisting into a single metascrawl of rage and frustration.

"The stored data are fed in through a modified series of microsurgical contraautism prostheses." I reeled off a numb version of my standard sales pitch. "Client's code is stored in a special chip; barring Squids, which we in the trade don't like to talk about, there's no way to recover your phrase. Can't drug it out, cut it out, torture it. I don't *know* it, never did."

"Squids? Crawly things with arms?" We emerged into a deserted street market. Shadowy figures watched us from across a makeshift square littered with fish heads and rotting fruit.

"Superconducting quantum interference detectors. Used them in the war to find submarines, suss out enemy cyber systems."

"Yeah? Navy stuff? From the war? Squid'll read that chip of yours?" She'd stopped walking, and I felt her eyes on me behind those twin mirrors.

"Even the primitive models could measure a magnetic field a billionth the strength of geomagnetic force; it's like pulling a whisper out of a cheering stadium."

"Cops can do that already, with parabolic microphones and lasers."

"But your data's still secure." Pride in profession. "No government'll let their cops have Squids, not even the security heavies. Too much chance of interdepartmental funnies; they're too likely to watergate you."

"Navy stuff," she said, and her grin gleamed in the shadows. "Navy stuff. I got a friend down here who was in the Navy, name's Jones. I think you'd better meet him. He's a junkie, though. So we'll have to take him something."

"A junkie?"

"A dolphin."

He was more than a dolphin, but from another dolphin's point of view he might have seemed like something less. I watched him swirling sluggishly in his galvanized tank. Water slopped over the side, wetting my shoes. He was surplus from the last war. A cyborg.

He rose out of the water, showing us the crusted plates along his sides, a kind of visual pun, his grace nearly lost under articulated armor, clumsy and prehistoric. Twin deformities on either side of his skull had been engineered to house sensor units. Silver lesions gleamed on exposed sections of his gray-white hide.

Molly whistled. Jones thrashed his tail, and more water cascaded down the side of the tank.

"What is this place?" I peered at vague shapes in the dark, rusting chainlink and things under tarps. Above the tank hung a clumsy wooden framework, crossed and recrossed by rows of dusty Christmas lights.

"Funland. Zoo and carnival rides. 'Talk with the War Whale.' All that. Some whale Jones is. . . ."

Jones reared again and fixed me with a sad and ancient eye.

"How's he talk?" Suddenly I was anxious to go.

"That's the catch. Say 'hi,' Jones."

And all the bulbs lit simultaneously. They were flashing red, white, and blue.

RWBRWBRWB
RWBRWBRWB
RWBRWBRWB
RWBRWBRWB
RWBRWBRWB

"Good with symbols, see, but the code's restricted. In the Navy they had him wired into an audiovisual display." She drew the narrow package from a jacket pocket. "Pure shit,

Jones. Want it?" He froze in the water and started to sink. I felt a strange panic, remembering that he wasn't a fish, that he could drown. "We want the key to Johnny's bank, Jones. We want it fast."

The lights flickered, died.

"Go for it, Jones!"

```
        B
   BBBBBBBBB
        B
        B
        B
```

Blue bulbs, cruciform.

Darkness.

"Pure! It's *clean.* Come on Jones."

```
   WWWWWWWWWW
   WWWWWWWWWW
   WWWWWWWWWW
   WWWWWWWWWW
   WWWWWWWWWW
```

White sodium glare washed her features, stark mono-chrome, shadows cleaving from her cheekbones.

```
   R     RRRRR
   R     R
   RRRRRRRRR
           R    R
   RRRRR        R
```

The arms of the red swastika were twisted in her silver glasses. "Give it to him," I said. "We've got it."

Ralfi Face. No imagination.

Jones heaved half his armored bulk over the edge of his tank, and I thought the metal would give way. Molly stabbed him overhand with the syrette, driving the needle between two plates. Propellant hissed. Patterns of light exploded, spasming across the frame and then fading to black.

We left him drifting, rolling languorously in the dark water. Maybe he was dreaming of his war in the Pacific, of the cyber mines he'd swept, nosing gently into their circuitry with the Squid he'd used to pick Ralfi's pathetic password from the chip buried in my head.

"I can see them slipping up when he was demobbed, letting him out of the Navy with that gear intact, but how does a cybernetic dolphin get wired to smack?"

"The war," she said. "They all were. Navy did it. How else you get 'em working for you?"

"I'm not sure this profiles as good business," the pirate said, angling for better money. "Target specs on a comsat that isn't in the book—"

"Waste my time and you won't profile at all," said Molly, leaning across his scarred plastic desk to prod him with her forefinger.

"So maybe you want to buy your microwaves somewhere else?" He was a tough kid, behind his Mao-job. A Nighttowner by birth, probably.

Her hand blurred down the front of his jacket, completely severing a lapel without even rumpling the fabric.

"So we got a deal or not?"

"Deal," he said, staring at his ruined lapel with what he must have hoped was only polite interest. "Deal."

While I checked the two recorders we'd bought, she extracted the slip of paper I'd given her from the zippered wrist pocket of her jacket. She unfolded it and read silently, moving her lips. She shrugged. "This is it?"

"Shoot," I said, punching the RECORD studs of the two decks simultaneously.

"Christian White," she recited, "and his Aryan Reggae Band."

Faithful Ralfi, a fan to his dying day.

Transition to idiot/savant mode is always less abrupt than I expect it to be. The pirate broadcaster's front was a failing travel agency in a pastel cube that boasted a desk, three chairs,

and a faded poster of a Swiss orbital spa. A pair of toy birds
with blown-glass bodies and tin legs were sipping monoto-
nously from a styrofoam cup of water on a ledge beside
Molly's shoulder. As I phased into mode, they accelerated
gradually until their Day-Glo-feathered crowns became solid
arcs of color. The LEDs that told seconds on the plastic wall
clock had become meaningless pulsing grids, and Molly and
the Mao-faced boy grew hazy, their arms blurring occasionally in insect-quick ghosts of gesture. And then it all faded to
cool gray static and an endless tone poem in an artificial
language.

I sat and sang dead Ralfi's stolen program for three hours.

The mall runs forty kilometers from end to end, a ragged
overlap of Fuller domes roofing what was once a suburban
artery. If they turn off the arcs on a clear day, a gray approx-
imation of sunlight filters through layers of acrylic, a view like
the prison sketches of Giovanni Piranesi. The three south-
ernmost kilometers roof Nighttown. Nighttown pays no taxes,
no utilities. The neon arcs are dead, and the geodesics have
been smoked black by decades of cooking fires. In the nearly
total darkness of a Nighttown noon who notices a few dozen
mad children lost in the rafters?

We'd been climbing for two hours, up concrete stairs and
steel ladders with perforated rungs, past abandoned gantries
and dust-covered tools. We'd started in what looked like a
disused maintenance yard, stacked with triangular roofing
segments. Everything there had been covered with that same
uniform layer of spraybomb graffiti: gang names, initials,
dates back to the turn of the century. The graffiti followed us
up, gradually thinning until a single name was repeated at
intervals. LO TEK. In dripping black capitals.

"Who's Lo Tek?"

"Not us, boss." She climbed a shivering aluminum ladder
and vanished through a hole in a sheet of corrugated plastic.

" 'Low technique, low technology.' " The plastic muffled her voice. I followed her up, nursing my aching wrist. "Lo Teks, they'd think that shotgun trick of yours was effete."

An hour later I dragged myself up through another hole, this one sawn crookedly in a sagging sheet of plywood, and met my first Lo Tek.

" 'S okay," Molly said, her hand brushing my shoulder. "It's just Dog. Hey, Dog."

In the narrow beam of her taped flash, he regarded us with his one eye and slowly extruded a thick length of grayish tongue, licking huge canines. I wondered how they wrote off tooth-bud transplants from Dobermans as low technology. Immunosuppressives don't exactly grow on trees.

"Moll." Dental augmentation impeded his speech. A string of saliva dangled from his twisted lower lip. "Heard ya comin'. Long time." He might have been fifteen, but the fangs and a bright mosaic of scars combined with the gaping socket to present a mask of total bestiality. It had taken time and a certain kind of creativity to assemble that face, and his posture told me he enjoyed living behind it. He wore a pair of decaying jeans, black with grime and shiny along the creases. His chest and feet were bare. He did something with his mouth that approximated a grin. "Bein' followed, you."

Far off, down in Nighttown, a water vendor cried his trade.

"Strings jumping, Dog?" She swung her flash to the side, and I saw thin cords tied to eyebolts, cords that ran to the edge and vanished.

"Kill the fuckin' light!"

She snapped it off.

"How come the one who's followin' you's got no light?"

"Doesn't need it. That one's bad news, Dog. Your sentries give him a tumble, they'll come home in easy-to-carry sections."

"This a *friend* friend, Moll?" He sounded uneasy. I heard his feet shift on the worn plywood.

"No. But he's mine. And this one," slapping my shoulder, "he's a friend. Got that?"

"Sure," he said, without much enthusiasm, padding to the platform's edge, where the eyebolts were. He began to pluck out some kind of message on the taut cords.

Nighttown spread beneath us like a toy village for rats; tiny windows showed candlelight, with only a few harsh, bright squares lit by battery lanterns and carbide lamps. I imagined the old men at their endless games of dominoes, under warm, fat drops of water that fell from wet wash hung out on poles between the plywood shanties. Then I tried to imagine him climbing patiently up through the darkness in his zoris and ugly tourist shirt, bland and unhurried. How was he tracking us?

"Good," said Molly. "He smells us."

"Smoke?" Dog dragged a crumpled pack from his pocket and prised out a flattened cigarette. I squinted at the trademark while he lit it for me with a kitchen match. Yiheyuan filters. Beijing Cigarette Factory. I decided that the Lo Teks were black marketeers. Dog and Molly went back to their argument, which seemed to revolve around Molly's desire to use some particular piece of Lo Tek real estate.

"I've done you a lot of favors, man. I want that floor. And I want the music."

"You're not Lo Tek . . ."

This must have been going on for the better part of a twisted kilometer, Dog leading us along swaying catwalks and up rope ladders. The Lo Teks leech their webs and huddling places to the city's fabric with thick gobs of epoxy and sleep above the abyss in mesh hammocks. Their country is so attenuated that in places it consists of little more than holds for hands and feet, sawn into geodesic struts.

The Killing Floor, she called it. Scrambling after her, my new Eddie Bax shoes slipping on worn metal and damp plywood, I wondered how it could be any more lethal than the rest of the territory. At the same time I sensed that Dog's protests were ritual and that she already expected to get whatever it was she wanted.

Somewhere beneath us, Jones would be circling his tank, feeling the first twinges of junk sickness. The police would be boring the Drome regulars with questions about Ralfi. What did he do? Who was he with before he stepped outside? And the Yakuza would be settling its ghostly bulk over the city's data banks, probing for faint images of me reflected in numbered accounts, securities transactions, bills for utilities. We're an information economy. They teach you that in school. What they don't tell you is that it's impossible to move, to live, to operate at any level without leaving traces, bits, seemingly meaningless fragments of personal information. Fragments that can be retrieved, amplified . . .

But by now the pirate would have shuttled our message into line for blackbox transmission to the Yakuza comsat. A simple message: Call off the dogs or we wideband your program.

The program. I had no idea what it contained. I still don't. I only sing the song, with zero comprehension. It was probably research data, the Yakuza being given to advanced forms of industrial espionage. A genteel business, stealing from Ono-Sendai as a matter of course and politely holding their data for ransom, threatening to blunt the conglomerate's research edge by making the product public.

But why couldn't any number play? Wouldn't they be happier with something to sell back to Ono-Sendai, happier than they'd be with one dead Johnny from Memory Lane?

Their program was on its way to an address in Sydney, to a place that held letters for clients and didn't ask questions once you'd paid a small retainer. Fourth-class surface mail. I'd erased most of the other copy and recorded our message in the resulting gap, leaving just enough of the program to identify it as the real thing.

My wrist hurt. I wanted to stop, to lie down, to sleep. I

knew that I'd lose my grip and fall soon, knew that the sharp black shoes I'd bought for my evening as Eddie Bax would lose their purchase and carry me down to Nighttown. But he rose in my mind like a cheap religious hologram, glowing, the enlarged chip on his Hawaiian shirt looming like a reconnaissance shot of some doomed urban nucleus.

So I followed Dog and Molly through Lo Tek heaven, jury-rigged and jerry-built from scraps that even Nighttown didn't want.

The Killing Floor was eight meters on a side. A giant had threaded steel cable back and forth through a junkyard and drawn it all taut. It creaked when it moved, and it moved constantly, swaying and bucking as the gathering Lo Teks arranged themselves on the shelf of plywood surrounding it. The wood was silver with age, polished with long use and deeply etched with initials, threats, declarations of passion. This was suspended from a separate set of cables, which lost themselves in darkness beyond the raw white glare of the two ancient floods suspended above the Floor.

A girl with teeth like Dog's hit the Floor on all fours. Her breasts were tattooed with indigo spirals. Then she was across the Floor, laughing, grappling with a boy who was drinking dark liquid from a liter flask.

Lo Tek fashion ran to scars and tattoos. And teeth. The electricity they were tapping to light the Killing Floor seemed to be an exception to their overall esthetic, made in the name of . . . ritual, sport, art? I didn't know, but I could see that the Floor was something special. It had the look of having been assembled over generations.

I held the useless shotgun under my jacket. Its hardness and heft were comforting, even though I had no more shells. And it came to me that I had no idea at all of what was really happening, or of what was supposed to happen. And that was the nature of my game, because I'd spent most of my life as a blind receptacle to be filled with other people's knowledge and then drained, spouting synthetic languages I'd never understand. A very technical boy. Sure.

And then I noticed just how quiet the Lo Teks had become.

He was there, at the edge of the light, taking in the Killing Floor and the gallery of silent Lo Teks with a tourist's calm. And as our eyes met for the first time with mutual recognition, a memory clicked into place for me, of Paris, and the long Mercedes electrics gliding through the rain to Notre Dame; mobile greenhouses, Japanese faces behind the glass, and a hundred Nikons rising in blind phototropism, flowers of steel and crystal. Behind his eyes, as they found me, those same shutters whirring.

I looked for Molly Millions, but she was gone.

The Lo Teks parted to let him step up onto the bench. He bowed, smiling, and stepped smoothly out of his sandals, leaving them side by side, perfectly aligned, and then he stepped down onto the Killing Floor. He came for me, across that shifting trampoline of scrap, as easily as any tourist padding across synthetic pile in any featureless hotel.

Molly hit the Floor, moving.

The Floor screamed.

It was miked and amplified, with pickups riding the four fat coil springs at the corners and contact mikes taped at random to rusting machine fragments. Somewhere the Lo Teks had an amp and a synthesizer, and now I made out the shapes of speakers overhead, above the cruel white floods.

A drumbeat began, electronic, like an amplified heart, steady as a metronome.

She'd removed her leather jacket and boots; her T-shirt was sleeveless, faint telltales of Chiba City circuitry traced along her thin arms. Her leather jeans gleamed under the floods. She began to dance.

She flexed her knees, white feet tensed on a flattened gas tank, and the Killing Floor began to heave in response. The sound it made was like a world ending, like the wires that hold heaven snapping and coiling across the sky.

He rode with it, for a few heartbeats, and then he moved, judging the movement of the Floor perfectly, like a man stepping from one flat stone to another in an ornamental garden.

He pulled the tip from his thumb with the grace of a man at ease with social gesture and flung it at her. Under the floods, the filament was a refracting thread of rainbow. She threw herself flat and rolled, jackknifing up as the molecule whipped past, steel claws snapping into the light in what must have been an automatic rictus of defense.

The drum pulse quickened, and she bounced with it, her dark hair wild around the blank silver lenses, her mouth thin, lips taut with concentration. The Killing Floor boomed and roared, and the Lo Teks were screaming their excitement.

He retracted the filament to a whirling meter-wide circle of ghostly polychrome and spun it in front of him, thumbless hand held level with his sternum. A shield.

And Molly seemed to let something go, something inside, and that was the real start of her mad-dog dance. She jumped, twisting, lunging sideways, landing with both feet on an alloy engine block wired directly to one of the coil springs. I cupped my hands over my ears and knelt in a vertigo of sound, thinking Floor and benches were on their way down, down to Nighttown, and I saw us tearing through the shanties, the wet wash, exploding on the tiles like rotten fruit. But the cables held, and the Killing Floor rose and fell like a crazy metal sea. And Molly danced on it.

And at the end, just before he made his final cast with the filament, I saw something in his face, an expression that didn't seem to belong there. It wasn't fear and it wasn't anger. I think it was disbelief, stunned incomprehension mingled with pure aesthetic revulsion at what he was seeing, hearing—at what was happening to him. He retracted the whirling filament, the ghost disc shrinking to the size of a dinner plate as he whipped his arm above his head and brought it down, the thumbtip curving out for Molly like a live thing.

The Floor carried her down, the molecule passing just above her head; the Floor whiplashed, lifting him into the path of the taut molecule. It should have passed harmlessly over his head and been withdrawn into its diamond-hard socket. It took his hand off just behind the wrist. There was a gap in the Floor in front of him, and he went through it like a diver, with a strange deliberate grace, a defeated kamikaze on his way down to Nighttown. Partly, I think, he took that dive to buy himself a few seconds of the dignity of silence. She'd killed him with culture shock.

The Lo Teks roared, but someone shut the amplifier off, and Molly rode the Killing Floor into silence, hanging on now, her face white and blank, until the pitching slowed and there was only a faint pinging of tortured metal and the grating of rust on rust.

We searched the Floor for the severed hand, but we never found it. All we found was a graceful curve in one piece of rusted steel, where the molecule went through. Its edge was bright as new chrome.

We never learned whether the Yakuza had accepted our terms, or even whether they got our message. As far as I know, their program is still waiting for Eddie Bax on a shelf in the back room of a gift shop on the third level of Sydney Central-5. Probably they sold the original back to Ono-Sendai months ago. But maybe they did get the pirate's broadcast, because nobody's come looking for me yet, and it's been nearly a year. If they do come, they'll have a long climb up through the dark, past Dog's sentries, and I don't look much like Eddie Bax these days. I let Molly take care of that, with a local anesthetic. And my new teeth have almost grown in.

I decided to stay up here. When I looked out across the Killing Floor, before he came, I saw how hollow I was. And I knew I was sick of being a bucket. So now I climb down and visit Jones, almost every night.

We're partners now, Jones and I, and Molly Millions, too. Molly handles our business in the Drome. Jones is still in Funland, but he has a bigger tank, with fresh seawater trucked in once a week. And he has his junk, when he needs it. He still talks to the kids with his frame of lights, but he talks to me on a new display unit in a shed that I rent there, a better unit than the one he used in the Navy.

And we're all making good money, better money than I made before, because Jones's Squid can read the traces of anything that anyone ever stored in me, and he gives it to me on the display unit in languages I can understand. So we're learning a lot about all my former clients. And one day I'll have a surgeon dig all the silicon out of my amygdalae, and I'll live with my own memories and nobody else's, the way other people do. But not for a while.

In the meantime it's really okay up here, way up in the dark, smoking a Chinese filtertip and listening to the condensation that drips from the geodesics. Real quiet up here—unless a pair of Lo Teks decide to dance on the Killing Floor.

It's educational, too. With Jones to help me figure things out, I'm getting to be the most technical boy in town.

Films and Television—1981

Baird Searles

The Science Fiction Shop, Baird Searles's Greenwich Village emporium, is a seductive and dangerous place, probably the most complete specialty store on the East Coast. My wallet goes into spasms at the mere thought of it. My credit cards squeal "Feed me!"

Searles does occasionally take time off from feeding the insatiable hunger of science fiction collectors, to write. He did the Cliff Notes guide to Robert Heinlein, and co-wrote A Reader's Guide to Science Fiction (with Michael Franklin, Beth Meacham, and Martin Last) and A Reader's Guide to Fantasy (with Michael Franklin and Beth Meacham). He writes a monthly column reviewing, and usually bemoaning, the state of science fiction cinema and television for Amazing magazine.

There have been worse years for the science fiction film, I guess. For instance, 1783 comes immediately to mind. In point of fact, there was exactly one film in 1981* that could be considered real SF and not some mass media idea of the field, or a bastard combo with some other genre. That one film was *Outland*, and as the sole representative of its kind, it's too bad it wasn't better.

But it was a serious effort. It was action-oriented, but not childishly so, and it was written and produced with comparative intelligence—at least to the degree that there were no blatant scientific bloopers and the word "intergalactic" was *not* used for "interstellar" or even "interplanetary." And it had the distinct advantage, not usually enjoyed by an SF film, of two excellent actors, Sean Connery and Francis Sternhagen.

But with all this, it so thoroughly violated one of the prime tenets of the field that it might legitimately be suspected of being as spurious as the rest of the year's lot. Practically the first thing the aspiring science fiction writer learns (one hopes) is that the plot must arise from the science-fictional elements; in other words, you can't just take a Western, transfer it to Mars, call the Indians and horses exotic names, and end up with a piece of valid SF. So what does *Outland* do? It takes the classic Western film *High Noon* and transfers it to Io. Yup, the bad guys are comin' in on the noon shuttle, and nobody's willin' to help the sheriff. Despite a lot of shooting, breakage, and general mayhem, it's pretty tedious, and it has about as much sense of wonder as *High Noon* itself. A Western doesn't need that sense of wonder, but despite the tiredness of the phrase, it's still a *sine qua non* for good SF and fantasy.

Probably the closest thing otherwise to a true science fiction film was *Heartbeeps,* going on the theory that it was close to anything definable at all. The universal reaction to this tale

---

* Note for nitpickers: it is sometimes difficult to pin a movie to an exact year, given the variables of distribution, opening dates in various locales, and so forth. For instance, *Flash Gordon* opened in my area in the pre-New Year's holiday season of 1980, but was seen by the majority of its audience in 1981. So the movies mentioned were for 1981—give or take a month or so at either end.

of star-crossed robots was utter bafflement, and as is so often the case when the mainstream starts fooling around with robots, the temptation toward allegory—and what's worse, whimsical allegory—was irresistible. The peculiar talents of Bernadette Peters, who sometimes manages an eerily fey quality that is indeed unearthly, didn't help in this case.

Heartbeeps closed the year, and closed itself, with remarkable rapidity. I think it played in my area for about half a day, and showed up on cable TV with great dispatch.

The year opened with *Flash Gordon*, the first of several entries from the comics with some relationship to SF. (I, unlike the French and a fair number of Anglo-American illiterates, do not believe science fiction and the comics to be one and the same.) The new Flash followed the original (comic and film) pretty closely in plot, tried to give a contemporary look with an expensive production and effects, and did indeed use the word "intergalactic" (or, even worse in this case, "intergalactical"—urgh) for "interplanetary." The new look turned out to be closely akin to *The Wizard of Oz*, which was made about the same time as the first *Flash Gordon*, and the recent version more or less fell between stools, not quite camp and not quite straight. Sam J. Jones wasn't macho enough for the football-hero Flash, and Melody Anderson as Dale came across like Gilda Radner playing Little Eva, simpering and abrasive at the same time. But all in all, it was harmless and sometimes handsome fun.

The year's pits were reached with the *Heavy Metal* movie, which advertised itself as "beyond science fiction." And just as well, too. Just so nobody confuses it with the real thing. An anthology of stories in the fashion of the magazine *Heavy Metal*, which were animated in its visual style, it ranged from horror to pseudoscience fiction, linked by a device of utter inanity. It was a tossup as to which was more tasteless and inept, the content or the graphics.

The third major comix opera of the year was, of course, *Superman II*. It was a worthy successor to *Superman*, which does not necessarily mean that it was particularly good. Or particularly bad, for that matter. Unlike most sequels, it gave the public what its predecessor had—a festival of special effects, razzle-dazzle photography, and nonstop action, all done with a lightness of touch that is creditable in a production so big it could have sunk of its own weight.

There is a fine distinction between comic fiction and pulp fiction, but it would take a lot more space to make that distinction than I have here. Two of the year's films harked back to pulp fiction in different ways; though superficially having nothing to do with SF, they are probably more closely related to it (given the pulp ancestry of the field) than are contemporary comics.

One was, of course, *Raiders of the Lost Ark*, which by some miracle recaptured the old pulp action-adventure spirit without missing a beat. It could well have been written by Robert E. Howard in his nonfantasy vein, and, in fact, whether it has any fantasy content at all depends on how one feels about Judeo-Christian mythology.

The other was yet another remake of *Tarzan*; it starred someone named Bo Derek, which sounds like a derelict oil rig. Despite that, most of the film's publicity and much of its footage was devoted to this person, who portrayed Jane. The result was a curious shift of balance, as if Fay Wray had suddenly become the size and weight of King Kong. And despite all the hoopla, the swimming scene between Johnny Weissmuller and Maureen O'Sullivan in an early Tarzan film had this one beat for eroticism.

It's only recently that the science fiction film has become separate from the horror film to any degree, and the combination is still a hardy cinematic perennial. A couple could be sorted out this year from the geek and splatter films as being of some serious intent. Nobody seemed to notice that *Altered States* was simply a retelling of *Dr. Jekyll and Mr. Hyde*, with the polarity of good and evil changed to the more contemporary *advanced* and *primitive*. It was, in fact, all of the mad scientists who had ventured where man was not meant to go, with untoward results. (I kept thinking particularly of a horrendous little number from 1958 called *Monster on the Campus*, wherein a staid professor is changed into a Neanderthalesque monster at awkward moments, thanks to a serum he has whipped up from some primitive fish ichor.)

Writer Paddy Chayevsky, known for realism and satire (*Marty, Network*), and director Ken Russell, with a reputation for extravagent dramatics (*Women in Love, The Devils*) were something of a Jekyll-and-Hyde act in themselves, and despite jazzy "trip" sequences, atmospheric photography, and some muscular special effects, they still weren't able to disguise the basic banality of their story.

Then there was *Wolfen*, in which something-or-other chomped up people in the more blighted sections of New York. The something-or-other turned out to be either supernaturally intelligent or naturally superintelligent wolves. Despite the ambiguity, which led some confused mainstream critics to refer to it as a werewolf movie, it was effective and not dumb by any means.

The most interesting development for the science fiction film in this year was not a science fiction film (as you might guess from the sad showing listed above), but the emergence of the fantasy film; 1981 could go down in history as the year when fantasy came into its cinematic own.

Not that fantasy had been lacking on screen until this year, but it had almost always been whimsical, cute, and if not for children, certainly childish. (The 1940s were big on this kind of thing.) The exceptions, such as Cocteau's *Beauty and the Beast*, were rare indeed. But suddenly budgets were being expended on special effects that were not science-fictional, and there was a spate of films that might be considered heroic or even adult fantasy.

The word *adult* is, of course, relative; there was nothing that came close to the maturity of such works of literature as *Titus Groan* and *Islandia* among the fantasy films of the year. In fact, *adolescent* might be a better word than *adult*—it was at least a step up from *childish*.

Excalibur gave us a comic-book look at the life of King Arthur from Uther to Avalon, rendered in a series of brightly colored panels with dialogue of about the quality that you find in comic balloons. It was relatively sophisticated about the sexual side of the saga (What Tennyson Never Told Us) and mixed in a lot of magic, often on the obvious side, such as Morgan's Magic Grotto, which looked like a Disneyland reject.

Dragonslayer was about, of all things, a person who slew a dragon. It was curiously low-keyed, and showed some sensibility. *Clash of the Titans* slid us back to childishness in an awkward (in writing *and* special effects) retelling of the story of Perseus, leaving out the shower of gold and wasting some masterful British actors as a group of squabbling Olympians. Less juvenile despite a child as protagonist, *Time Bandits* tried so hard for laughs that it undercut any coherence as fantasy, but there were good moments, in particular a trip to the Greece of the Heroic Age, with Sean Connery as a noble Menelaus.

The most interesting of fantasy films for the year premiered on television with little fanfare or recognition. *Fugitive from the Empire* was set in a created world of sorcery and inhuman beings. An evil Empire dominated things from afar; the story was set on its fringes, among barbarians and nomads. There was a quest, a witch girl, and a magic bow (the type that uses arrows); the special effects were small-scale but used with good sense and imagination. Good sense, in fact, was the key quality; I felt, here in a fantasy mode, as I had felt with *Star Wars* in a science-fictional mode, that at last I was seeing onscreen the kind of work I had read all my life, but had never before seen transferred to another medium. Naturally, since it received nothing like the hype that the big-screen features had, it was dismissed by the majority of fantasy aficionados.

The rest of what happened on TV during the year was nowhere near that level of originality. More mileage was gotten out of that other comics-derived space opera, *Buck*

Rogers. With its second season delayed to midseason by the directors' strike of '80, it reappeared with some new additions: a boldly going starship à la the *Enterprise*, complete with an "Admiral Asimov," a hoity-toity robot named Crichton, and a dear, dithering old scientist. What it had lost, though, was the combination of strong-jawed seriousness that didn't take itself too seriously, and camp (typified by the wicked princess's wardrobe), which some of us had found so endearing in the first season. There was no third season.

New series got nowhere. *Mr. Merlin* had the enchanter running a garage in contemporary San Francisco and trying to break in a new Arthur; there were some good sorcerer's-apprentice jokes, but they ran out rapidly. *Darkroom* tried to recapture the spirit of *The Twilight Zone*; most of the stories in its short run were ghastly in the wrong way. The several good ones showed what it might have been.

Not a good year for particular works, certainly. No *2001*, no *Star Wars*. And on the audience side of the screen, developments whose end we haven't seen. The science fiction and fantasy consumer was now as likely to be a viewer as a reader; the Trekkies of a decade ago had spawned a mass whose bodies and paraphernalia had practically taken over the conventions. They had their own magazines, which were, of course, mostly pictures, and the only writers they'd heard of—if they even knew what a writer was—were those who had written for the big or little screens.

Changing also was the manner of viewing and the access to and acquisition of things to be viewed. Cable stations and networks and videotape and video discs were fragmenting what had once been a mass audience into myriad specialty audiences; movies and shows moved closer to being marketed as books have been.

It is customary to end this sort of piece with some kind of thumping generality. But for the life of me, given the scene I've just described for 1981, I can draw no conclusions whatsoever. So no epic long shot to conclude—just a quiet fade. . . .

Zeke

Timothy Robert Sullivan

*I don't really know Tim Sullivan, but I've run into him a few
times at science fiction gatherings. Handsome, well-met fellow,
he seems awfully normal to have written this story about a freak
meeting a freak in a freak show. His biographical sheet, though,
reveals a writerly kind of checkered past: flower child, taxi
driver, construction worker, manager of liquor store and pinball
arcade. He even stooped to teaching English at a Florida
university.*

*He's settled down now to writing for a living, working on
a trilogy for Starblaze Press while selling fantasy stories to
magazines like* Twilight Zone, *where this one, appropriately,
appeared. His first novel, a tie-in to the series* V, *appeared
in 1984.*

Along Route 31, from the Georgia border to Key West, much
of the old Florida remains. There one can still spend the night
in a roach-infested "motor court," visit a roadside spiritualist,
or marvel at the lethargic denizens of an alligator farm. This
is the Florida of Indian-head coconuts, cracked swimming

pools, and concrete fountains claimed by their exhibitors to be the very ones for which Ponce de León searched.

It was the third time I had traversed old Highway 31, though I'd never done it alone before. After spending a childhood of miserable solitude, I had discovered in my teens that I could exploit my freakishness, that I could even use it to get girls. Down that sultry road I went, in a busload of freewheelin' hippie "freaks" back in the smoky days of Fall 1968. The "family" was smaller on my second trip down Route 31 in 1974; a blue Toyota carried me and Joannie, a girl who saw in me all the weird and wonderful things she'd never dared to do herself. The results of that romantic interlude were pregnancy, marriage, and a boy we named Danny. A real family.

So, for masochism's sake, I was heading a third time—all by myself, just like when I was a kid—down that seldom-traveled road before long-distance driving became too exorbitant. Besides, I had an expense account; I'd been attending an exporters' convention in Atlanta, and had left a day early, on a Thursday morning. That way I could make a leisurely, bittersweet trek down memory lane. I wasn't planning to get back to work until Monday morning, so I had called to clear it with my boss. Okay, he had said, take your time, George. Not a bad guy, Mr. Noloff, but twenty-five years of selling heavy road equipment to banana republics had instilled in him a certain dictatorial air. I often dreamed, when he was being particularly imperious, of telling him off and chucking my job at Coastal Trading, Inc. . . . but there was always the rent, the payments on my year-old Plymouth Horizon, the alimony, and of course the child support, at a time when the price of a loaf of bread approached a buck.

Through a loose tweeter, the grinding white blues guitar of Johnny Winter vibrated. I turned it up anyway, cruising over the rolling hills of central Florida, orange groves sliding by on either side of the potholed two-lane blacktop. A curved damask strip of late afternoon sunlight melted into the treetops as I passed a tattered sign announcing MONSTERS, BEASTS,

FREAKS OF NATURE, JUST AHEAD, SR 74, in pastel colors that had once been lurid.

"This," I said over Johnny's melodic growls, "has got to be the world's sleaziest roadside attraction."

My tank was almost empty, and there weren't any open gas stations in sight, but I wasn't worried. There hadn't been a lit neon NO in front of VACANCY on any of these fleabags' signs in years; they were all dying for business. I would spend the night in this next town—whatever town it was—and search for fuel in the morning.

The Horizon turned easily into the parking lot of the Azalea Motel, a low pink building with rust stains bleeding through the walls from the reinforcing steel rods beneath the concrete.

Such establishments rarely have lobbies, and the Azalea was no exception. Inside the cramped manager's office, a fat woman sat in the arctic gale of a Fedders air conditioner, watching "Hee-Haw." She couldn't hear me over the AC's ceaseless exhalations and the laugh track, but soon subdued strains of sweet country music replaced the canned yoks, making conversation barely possible. I negotiated a room key, but she didn't let it go at that.

"You look like the type might wanna see the freak show," she said.

It had been some time since an adult had made such a reference to my albinism. I always explain to children about the lack of pigmentation that makes my skin so white, but this woman was no child. I glared at her . . . and she glared right back until I lowered my eyes to the guest book.

"I'm Mrs. Nickerson," she said as I signed my name. "Bump—that's my husband—ain't here right now." She eyed my suitcase as if it were a dangerous animal.

"Oh." I assumed she was trying to tell me she wasn't taking my bag to my room for me. "Just point me in the right direction."

"Ain't but one direction." She gestured to her left.

"Uh . . . thank you, Mrs. Nickerson." I hefted my bag,

key dangling from my free hand, and went back out into the
still considerable heat like a good boy. Sunset had now created a peach-colored world, except for blood-red ixora, yellow
hibiscus, and purple bougainvillea, whose roots snaked into
the broken walk alongside the motel. I didn't see any azaleas.

The room wasn't as bad as I'd expected: plasterboard
walls; a reasonably unlumpy mattress sheathed in fresh linen;
a lampshade emblazoned with a horse's head, the animal's
sensitive eyes gazing longingly toward the alcove harboring
the sink (why don't motels ever have sinks in the bathrooms?);
clean white towels; a color TV with a sick tube, making the
actors look a little bilious; a slightly musty smell; and a
shower, which I promptly tried out.

After cleaning up, I decided to go for a walk. There were
three vehicles besides mine in the parking lot. One was a
green Ford pickup loaded with sacks of peat moss. A big man,
fat, fiftyish, and sunburned, was finishing the loading. He
wore a white undershirt, the kind with shoulder straps, and his
few remaining hairs were plastered to his creased skull with
hair cream. Once he noticed me and nodded, I asked him if he
was by any chance Bump Nickerson.

"None other," he replied, wiping sweat from his brow.
He shook my hand, and then leaned against the tailgate while
I asked him what went on in these parts.

"Florabella Tavern's closed for renovations. There's a
movie in Apopka, but that's twenty-five mile. Ain't much in
Boca Blanca nowadays."

"I guess there wouldn't be." So that was the name of this
burg: Boca Blanca, or White Mouth, if my rudimentary Spanish didn't fail me. Funny, I thought, Boca, or "mouth" always
refers to a bay or inlet, but this Boca is nowhere near the
Atlantic or Gulf coasts. . . .

"No, sir," Bump agreed. "No, sir."

"Apopka's got the closest entertainment, huh?" No place
to lose myself here, like there was in Miami when my loneliness became intolerable. "What about the freak show?"

" 'At's the on'y thing till the Florabella opens up agin."

Bump shrugged. "Course, it's a little off the beaten path."

"Oh, yeah?" I'd always had a penchant for the bizarre, and this seemed a sufficiently mysterious diversion to cure my melancholy. "How do I get there?"

"South two mile, then a left, jis past the canal bridge. She's down the jog road there another mile or so."

I thanked Bump and got into the Horizon. Smacked the gas gauge a couple of times and decided six miles wouldn't drain it dry. So off to see the Fat Lady, the Dog-faced Boy, or whatever exotic creatures might infest Boca Blanca's version of the Big Top. Odd that it was located off the main road, I thought. As the stars brightened over the darkening orange groves, I expected to hear the *pizzicato* guitar that used to preface "The Twilight Zone."

"George Hallahan," Rod Serling's gravelly voice intoned inside my skull, "thirty-two years old. A rather peculiar-looking idealist who once foolishly thought he could help fashion a better world out of a cloud of cannabis smoke. George found that he couldn't even hold his own life together, much less an ailing society. Now, driving on a back road in Florida, the disillusioned albino ex-hippie exporter is headed straight toward . . ." Straight toward a tacky freak show. Appropriate.

The stigma of albinism hadn't been quite so bad in the New England town where I spent the first eight years of my life. A bout of rheumatic fever had made me unable to tolerate the cold weather, however, and my father, a civil servant, took a job in Miami at my mom's instigation. So, for my sake, the family went south, and I grew up a ghostly exile among the bronzed gods and goddesses.

Then came the Summer of Love. I grew my white hair long, and wasted people thought I was far out. There wasn't a cynical bone in my body the first time I dropped acid, at a rock festival near Orlando—even after I recovered from the severe case of sun poisoning I got from dancing naked under the blazing sun—but reality soon reared its ugly head during my radical-college days. The tear gas and truncheons the cops wielded at the political conventions at Miami Beach in '72 taught me a valuable lesson about the way things *are*, as opposed to the way I thought they ought to be.

Then there had been the courtship of Joannie, culminating at the Saturn Motor Lodge on good ol' Route 31. Love? I don't know; looking back, I think I just had to have her because she was such a nice girl. Cute, brunette, upper-middle-class background; what more could I have asked for? Not that she was guiltless in this bizarre misalliance of woman and freak. How neat it must have seemed to her murky sense of developing social consciousness to miscegenate with a misfit. Danny's birth had shortly thereafter squelched that particular living fantasy, forcing my capitulation to the ogre of capitalism in the bargain.

Every single one of these misadventures had been a failure in some painfully essential way, each taking a bigger chunk of my soul than the last.

By the time I got to the canal bridge, I couldn't stop thinking of Danny. I hadn't wanted a child, judging the two of us far too immature for such a responsibility, but Joannie had refused to consider abortion. I never told her how scared I was that the child would be a freak like me. But when I saw that normal, beautiful baby, I was happy for the one and only time in my life. At first Danny was kind of a novelty, but when he got a little older and we started to get to know each other, I think we were more than father and son. We were friends.

Still, the bickering between Joannie and me got worse—and, oh, she always had a sharp tongue. When we finally decided to split, there was never any doubt about who was better suited to bring up Danny. I was an aging albino hippie earning a shaky income from the exporting trade. She, on the other hand, was solidly establishment; she'd never touched a drug, never even smoked a cigarette. I knew it was only right, and yet I resented her for the way things had turned out.

A year had passed since she took my son away from me. He was only five when his home fell apart. On Sunday he'd be celebrating his sixth birthday, and his father was too scared of a verbal whipping—"Why don't you get a job where you can make enough money to provide the things Danny needs?"—to be where he could help Danny blow out the candles. I'd have to mail him a present in the morning. Would it get to Miami in time?

The jog road was dusty and bumpy as the night descended. On the other side of the canal there were no orange groves, just palmetto clumps and Florida pines. Down the road was a house made of cinder blocks, one story high, with no windows in the front, like a porn parlor. The house was flanked by two sago palms in the terminal stages of "lethal yellowing disease," their drooping fronds like black spiders' legs in the deepening gloom.

I parked in front of the house, and the Horizon bogged down in the sugary sand. I wondered if its wheels would be able to spin free, and, if not, whether Boca Blanca had a wrecker. As I walked toward the house, I reflected that mine had not always been such a defeatist attitude.

"Whatever happened to the Woodstock Generation?" I muttered, recalling a more innocent time when I could toke up and consider obliterating war, racism, and injustice. Particularly the injustice that I suffered because I happened to be born a "whiter shade of pale," to borrow a phrase from the old Procol Harum song.

A light around the side of the little house threw a patch of amber on the sand. There was a screen door, and what looked like the kitchen on the other side of it. I took a whiff of jasmine-scented air and rapped.

From within came a stirring, a rustling of paper, the creaking of a chair sliding across the floor, footsteps; there was no television or radio to dilute these intimate sounds, only the chirruping of crickets. A shadow appeared on the screen, followed by a thin, stooped old man, wearing baggy pants and smiling.

"I've, uh, come to see the freak show," I said.

He nodded and unhooked the screen door. "Through here," he said, leading me through a room filled with books and magazines, literary and scientific journals in a state of disarray on tables, sofa, and floor. Curiouser and curiouser.

The back door opened into a dark shed, and the old man pulled a dangling string, illuminating a naked hundred-watt bulb that cast swinging shadows on four small cages and something draped with a greasy cloth. The cages were made of pine and chicken wire. In them were four unfortunate animals—not the usual circus freaks, but strange enough in their various ways.

How do you define a freak, anyway? The word is used to hurt more often than to inform or amuse. At least these creatures would never know what people called them.

The most striking of the animals was a two-headed calf. One of the heads was a shrunken, lolling appendage with dead eyes and flaccid lips, but the rest of the calf seemed healthy enough.

In spite of the terrible stench, I moved closer to the cages. Next to the calf, so help me, was a snake with legs. Spindly little useless things, but four limbs nonetheless. It was asleep on a pile of hay inside its two-foot-square prison.

Then there was a "giant lizard," as the old man called it—nothing but an iguana.

The fourth cage held a featherless chicken, its hideously pocked flesh a repulsive sight. In its nakedness, the fowl resembled a scrawny old man. It stared at me so murderously that it must have thought I plucked it myself.

"Donations appreciated," my affable host said as he shuffled toward the door.

"Uh, fine. But I don't think I've seen everything yet, have I?" I turned toward the thing under the greasy cloth, in a cage that appeared to be circular at the top, unlike the others.

Hitching up his trousers, the old man looked from me to the covered object and back again. "Well . . ."

I waited. The old man clearly didn't want to show me what was under that cloth, which naturally made me want to see it all the more.

"He's asleep, I think."

"He?"

The old man didn't seem to hear me. He lifted a corner of the cloth and peeked under it. "No, it's all right . . . if you're sure you want to see him."

"Yes."

Without ceremony, he undraped a large glass terrarium, standing back with the greasy cloth in his gnarled farmer's hands.

I don't know how long I stood there with my mouth open, staring at that incredible sight. I remember the old man speaking to me as if in a dream: "That's the way most folks act when they see him."

The thing was an albino monkey . . . no . . . the white fur was flesh . . . bald, like the chicken . . . arms and legs bent at ridiculous angles . . . as stooped as the old man. . . .

No, not stooped. The impossible thing stood erect on a bed of dark chips. Its joints suggested a Rube Goldberg cartoon in their complexity. With delicate, hinged hands much too large for its eighteen-inch body, it grasped the lip of the terrarium, gazing at me from between its pipestem arms with crimson eyes.

It was a mockery, an image from a funhouse mirror in a nightmare. As if to imitate my gape, the creature opened its mouth, revealing a ribbed whiteness inside, a furrowed snow-field here in the stifling Florida summer. No discernible sound came from that virginal cavity.

The chicken clucked, the sound bringing me a little closer to reality. Without taking my eyes off the creature, I whispered, "What is it?"

"He," the old man corrected me. "He's a person. Might look and act a little different, but he's folks. Just like me . . . just like you."

"What?" I glanced at him to see if he was goading me as Mrs. Nickerson had at the motel. But there was no malice in his weatherbeaten face. He nodded at the strange creature.

"Ain't he sum'p'n?"

"Where did you get him?"

"Well, he's been livin' with me since I was, let's see . . . twenty-six. Before that he stayed with ol' Bo Wadley till Bo passed away, and Bo told me his daddy kept him 'fore Bo was born. Claimed he was livin' around here 'fore white men ever come to Florida."

"Boca Blanca," I said. A revelation. The Spanish must have named their settlement for this creature perhaps four centuries ago. "But how could he have been around so long?"

The old man sucked on his false teeth. "Jis longer-lived than us, I guess."

"What does he eat?"

"Dead plants, rotten wood, peat moss. Takes a little water with it."

I could make out the baroque pattern of the ribs, a surrealist structure beneath striated bands of muscle and smooth, milky flesh. The physique was vaguely humanoid, and the gleaming red eyes were unfathomable. These features were grotesque enough, but that mouth twisted the ridged skull into a painful prognathous expression that opened like a funnel—a scream of silence that touched an empathic chord inside me.

"Why do you keep him in this shed with these deformed animals?" I demanded.

"Why, it was his idea," the old man said reproachfully. "We got to have money to git along on, so he come up with the idea of a freak show some years back. After a while, he got in the habit of sleepin' out here, sorta keepin' a eye on things."

"*His* idea? Did I hear you right?"

"Yup. He's smart as a whip. Showed me where to find these critters—cept for the lizard. Him we bought from a pet shop in Orlando."

"This is beyond belief." I shook my head. "He's . . ."

"Sum'p'n, ain't he?" It was Bump, carrying a sack of peat moss through the shed door.

"You're in on this, too?" I asked.

"In on what?" Bump said. "I run a garden s'ply ever since

the interstate highway and Disney World pulled the rug out from under the motel bidness. Oncet a week I bring Zeke out some peat moss."

"Zeke!" I laughed, remembering the old gospel song about Ezekiel's "dry bones," an image that perfectly suggested the creature in the terrarium.

"Got to call him sum'p'n," Bump said, and he laughed too. "Never did tell us what his right name is."

"Prob'ly where he come from," the old man said, "they don't have names same as we do."

"Where he comes from . . ." The thought inspired awe, wonder.

"A long ways away," Bump said softly. "A long ways."

"Another world," I said, even more quietly.

The old man was grave, and none of us spoke while we considered the implications of what we had just said.

After a while Bump tore open the sack, scooping out some peat moss with a meaty hand and dropping it into the snifter-shaped terrarium. Zeke's twiglike fingers, catching the offering, were nearly as long as Bump's. Instead of eating in front of us, Zeke set the peat moss chips among those already spread on the floor of his terrarium.

"Not ever'body knows what they seein' when they come in here," the old man said, frowning. "Bump's wife, now, she don't care for things that are . . . different."

"So I noticed," I said.

"She thinks to this day he's jis some kinda hairless monkey."

"Hell, Levon," Bump said, "she never stuck around long enough to see him read and write, and she never would believe me. Rayette can't hardly read, herself, and she don't want to nohow. It's all she can do to set in front of that damn TV all day long."

Having vented his spleen, Bump stuck his hand inside the terrarium. Grasping two fingers, Zeke allowed himself to be lifted out of the terrarium and set on the straw-covered shed floor. He was wearing a tiny pair of beige shorts.

It seemed wrong for Zeke to be here. My fitful sense of social morality awakened briefly as I considered our Duty to Mankind. "Kennedy Space Center's not far," I said. "Why don't you let somebody over there have a look at Zeke?"

"Let him 'splain about things hisself," Levon said.

The diminutive alien led us inside the house in a jerkily articulated walk, the calf lowing as Levon closed the shed door. The adjoining room was littered with reading material. Next to a battered old sofa, a slate leaned against one of the cinder-block walls. Zeke picked up a piece of chalk and wrote, "I have no desire to go anywhere."

"Maybe they could get you back home someday," I said.

"By the time your spacecraft are able to go that far," he wrote in carefully blocked-in letters, "I will no longer be living."

"But the things you must know!" I protested. "Don't you want to share them with us? Help us?"

Zeke bowed, showing two pinpricks on top of his snowy skull that I took to be his ears. The chalk squeaked in the still room as he wrote, "My technological expertise is limited, but even if it weren't, there would be difficulties."

"Difficulties?"

"In bypassing so many levels of technical sophistication."

"I see." I had skipped third grade. Adjusting to life in fourth grade was hell, intellectually and emotionally. At least the kids my age were used to "Whitey," as I came to be called. The bigger kids really put me through the meatgrinder, and I had trouble with my math, too. So you might say I had found it difficult to bypass only one level of sophistication.

Zeke wiped the slate clean with a chalkdust-caked eraser, and then wrote, "How well does the average human being understand the principle behind a machine he or she uses every day?"

"Like television?" I was amused to think of Rayette Nickerson contributing to our discussion.

"Yes, television," Zeke wrote, "or even an automobile? Our machines were autonomous. They built themselves, maintained themselves, but were still slaves to do our bidding. I couldn't begin to show you how to make even the simplest of them."

So much for saviors from the stars. Still, there was wonder enough here, even without miracles. "But how did you end up on Earth?" I asked. "Where did you come from?"

Instead of answering, Zeke beckoned for me to follow him through the kitchen. With both hands, he pushed open the groaning screen door and went outside. The stars gleamed like ice and the night breeze was cool, quickly drying the sweat on my forehead. It took me a moment to identify a pungent odor wafting over the jasmine as Zeke. I hadn't noticed his exotic smell inside the house because of the animals, whose odor persisted even into the living room. His aroma surprised me because I had already come to regard him as human, perhaps more like me than anyone I'd ever known. It wasn't unpleasant, it was just . . . different.

With a little flourish, Zeke indicated the heavens. Overhead were Venus and Mars, and in the west was brilliant Jupiter. The Pleiades were peripherally visible, hard to see when I looked directly at them. Just to the north were Perseus and Cassiopeia, frozen in an eternal marital spat, like Joannie and me. Happiness seemed as unattainable as Zeke's planet.

"He never tells how he come here," Levon said, "or why. And you can ask him till you're blue in the face. When he don't want to talk about sum'p'n, he jis don't talk."

We stood in the moonlight by two sickly palms. Zeke's unaccountably graceful figure was as immobile as his crimson eyes were dispassionate. Had my initial impression of anguish been nothing more than a distorted projection of my own pain?

Then Zeke's mouth jutted forward, widening once again into that terrible, silent scream. As though in sympathetic reaction, the night sounds of insects and hoot owls quieted. Zeke lifted a hand, opening his fingers as if to grasp the stars and pull them to Earth. His entire body trembled while he stretched onto the tips of his splayed feet. And then he slumped so close to the sand I thought he would fall. He managed to stay on his feet, though, staring down at the crabgrass.

My face felt flushed, and a drop of perspiration rolled down my forehead in spite of the cool breeze. I was embarrassed—this vision of pain was like a distorted reflection of my own soul—and had to look away.

So I said good-bye to Bump and Levon, their homely faces showing the depth of their emotion at their friend's anguish. Taking a five-dollar bill from my wallet, I slipped it to Levon as a donation.

"He gits tired," Levon said.

I nodded and, without turning back, walked the few yards to my car.

I felt, rather than heard, Zeke behind me. My hand on the open car door, I turned to him. I squatted so that we were more or less on the same eye level.

In the dim illumination shed by the car's dome light, Zeke raised his fragile hands to touch mine. I stretched out my fingers and their tips met his. His fingers were warm, and emotion seemed to emanate from them, entering me. Something went out of me, too. Something sour and ugly I had been carrying around for far too long. Zeke absorbed it like dirty water in a sponge.

I won't say that I was suddenly whole, like the laying on of hands is supposed to make you, I was just relieved. Not a revelation or a cleansing, but an exchange, a sharing. Zeke shared my pain . . . and I shared his.

It took only an instant, and then our fingertips parted. I stood, still transfixed by Zeke's ruby eyes. They no longer seemed dispassionate; I had, in a sense, seen with them. There was no sudden Fujicolor image of an alien world, only the feeling of a loss so great that acceptance had been the only alternative to death. My problems seemed so insignificant next to Zeke's that I felt ashamed of myself for wallowing in self-pity.

"So long, Zeke," I said, "and thanks." As I got in the car

and shut the door, the dome light winked out, leaving a vague, pale shape outside in place of Zeke. I started up the motor and backed out of the sand with no problem. As I headed back toward Route 31, there were three shrinking silhouettes in the rearview mirror, two men and the small figure of a being from another world. Was he an exile, a fugitive, a lost traveler? He would die on this planet, but even so, he had made the best of things.

Next morning, as I walked down to the office to pay my bill, I noticed that Bump's pickup wasn't in the parking lot. Maybe he had spent the night at Levon's, or maybe he was just out early, delivering garden supplies to some of his more conventional customers.

Mrs. Nickerson's manners hadn't improved. She was watching "Bowling for Dollars," but turned grudgingly away to take my money. While I signed my check, she asked, "So you seen the freak?"

I looked straight at her, masking my hostility. "Yes, I did. Don't you think we look a lot alike?"

The smirk vanished from her puffy face, and she turned stiffly back to her television program. I smiled. The question had freaked her out, but it wasn't really a joke. Especially for Zeke. Coming from so far away, living so long with no chance of getting home, he had to be Earth's greatest expert on alienation.

It was already sweltering and muggy at half past eight, but I walked out of that air-conditioned office whistling. After all, I still had plenty of time to make it back for Danny's birthday party.

The Saturn Game

Poul Anderson

One of the writing problems peculiar to science fiction is that science has a way of catching up with your imagining. Just as you finish writing a book about the poor folks who live on the perpetually dark side of Mercury, the damned Mariner flyby shows that there's no such thing as a dark side. Out the window with the manuscript (maybe followed by the typewriter and even the writer).

Poul Anderson was one of the dozen or so science fiction writers invited by the Jet Propulsion Laboratories to witness the first Saturn flyby at their headquarters in Pasadena. Most of us adjourned to the company cafeteria, getting out of the way of the working press and overworked scientists, watching the marvelous pictures come in as we sipped coffee and swapped tales. There was quite a feeling of suspense, since very little was known about any of the planet's satellites, so in effect we had a brand-new world being presented to us every few hours. Poul was the only one actually on the edge of his seat, though; he said he had just finished a story set on Iapetus. The background was perforce 95 percent imagination, since very little could be de-

duced about the satellite from earthbound observation. One clear picture could blow him out of the water. Fortunately for all of us, the Pioneer cooperated with Poul's imaginings. The story was "The Saturn Game," and it won the Nebula for best novella of the year.

No one but Poul Anderson could have written this story. That's true in a literal sense of any story, any author, because even a tired, trite rehash of boy-meets-girl will show some evidence of having been written by a particular boy or girl. But "The Saturn Game," besides being startlingly original in structure and plot, reveals a combination of special knowledge and special feeling that amounts to oblique autobiography. Poul is a consummate "hard science" writer, who not only sports a degree in physics (with honors) but, more important, reveals in books like Tau Zero *that he keeps up with the fast-changing science. He is also a swashbuckling romantic, with such titles as* Hrolf Kraki's Saga *and* The Last Viking *to his credit. The association with sword-and-sorcery derring-do percolates over into "real" life: Poul was one of the founders of the Society for Creative Anachronism, an outfit dedicated to the re-creation and celebration of medieval life through costumed fairs and tourneys, usually livened up with a certain amount of barely controlled mayhem as the participants duel with somewhat blunted weapons.*

In the man, these two worlds are well integrated, apparently; Poul is a soft-spoken charmer who wouldn't smite a fly. In the story, well, it's another story.

If we are to understand what happened, which is vital if we are to avoid repeated and worse tragedies in the future, we must begin by dismissing all accusations. Nobody was negligent; no action was foolish. For who could have predicted the eventuality, or recognized its nature, until too late? Rather should we appreciate the spirit with which those people struggled against disaster, inward and outward, after they knew. The fact is that thresholds exist throughout reality, and that things on their far sides are altogether different from things on their hither sides. The *Chronos* crossed more than an abyss, it crossed a threshold of human experience.

—Francis L. Minamoto, *Death
Under Saturn: A Dissenting View*
(Apollo University Communications, Leyburg, Luna, 2057)

I

"The City of Ice is now on my horizon," *Kendrick says. Its towers gleam blue.* "My griffin spreads his wings to glide." *Wind whistles among those great, rainbow-shimmering pinions. His cloak blows back from his shoulders; the air strikes through his ring-mail and sheathes him in cold.* "I lean over and peer after you." *The spear in his left hand counterbalances him. Its head flickers palely with the moonlight that Wayland Smith hammered into the steel.*

"Yes, I see the griffin," *Ricia tells him,* "high and far, like a comet above the courtyard walls. I run out from under the portico for a better look. A guard tries to stop me, grabs my sleeve, but I tear the spider silk apart and dash forth into the open." *The elven castle wavers as if its sculptured ice were turning to smoke. Passionately, she cries,* "Is it in truth you, my darling?"

"Hold, there!" *warns Alvarlan from his cave of arcana ten thousand leagues away.* "I send your mind the message that if the King suspects this is Sir Kendrick of the Isles, he will raise a dragon against him, or spirit you off beyond any chance of rescue. Go back, Princess of Maranoa. Pretend you decide that it is only an eagle. I will cast a belief-spell on your words."

"I stay far aloft," *Kendrick says.* "Save he use a scrying stone, the Elf King will not be aware this beast has a rider. From here I'll spy out city and castle." *And then—? He knows not. He knows simply that he must set her free or die in the quest. How long will it take him, how many more nights will she lie in the King's embrace?*

"I thought you were supposed to spy out Iapetus," Mark Danzig interrupted.

His dry tone startled the three others into alertness. Jean Broberg flushed with embarrassment, Colin Scobie with irritation; Luis Garcilaso shrugged, grinned, and turned his gaze to the pilot console before which he sat harnessed. For a moment silence filled the cabin, and shadows, and radiance from the universe.

To help observation, all lights were out except a few dim glows from the instruments. The sunward ports were lidded. Elsewhere thronged stars, so many and so brilliant that they well-nigh drowned the blackness which held them. The Milky Way was a torrent of silver. One port framed Saturn at half phase, dayside pale gold and rich bands amidst the jewelry of its rings, nightside wanly ashimmer with starlight upon clouds, as big to the sight as Earth over Luna.

Forward was Iapetus. The spacecraft rotated while orbiting the moon, to maintain a steady optical field. It had crossed the dawn line, presently at the middle of the inward-facing hemisphere. Thus it had left bare, crater-pocked land behind it in the dark, and was passing above sunlit glacier country. Whiteness dazzled, glittered in sparks and shards of color, reached fantastic shapes heavenward; cirques, crevasses, caverns brimmed with blue.

"I'm sorry," Jean Broberg whispered. "It's too beautiful, unbelievably beautiful, and . . . almost like the place where our game had brought us. Took us by surprise—"

"Huh!" Mark Danzig said. "You had a pretty good idea of what to expect, therefore you made your play go in the direction of something that resembled it. Don't tell me any different. I've watched these acts for eight years."

Colin Scobie made a savage gesture. Spin and gravity were too slight to give noticeable weight, and his movement sent him flying through the air, across the crowded cabin. He checked himself by a handhold just short of the chemist. "Are you calling Jean a liar?" he growled.

Most times he was cheerful, in a bluff fashion. Perhaps because of that, he suddenly appeared menacing. He was a big, sandy-haired man in his mid-thirties; a coverall did not disguise the muscles beneath, and the scowl on his face brought forth its ruggedness.

"Please!" Broberg exclaimed. "Not a quarrel, Colin."

The geologist glanced back at her. She was slender and fine-featured. At her age of forty-two, despite longevity treatment, the reddish-brown hair that fell to her shoulders was becoming streaked with white, and lines were engraved around large gray eyes.

"Mark is right," she sighed. "We're here to do science, not daydream." She reached forth to touch Scobie's arm, smiling shyly. "You're still full of your Kendrick persona, aren't you? Gallant, protective—" She stopped. Her voice had quickened with more than a hint of Ricia. She covered her lips and flushed again. A tear broke free and sparkled off on air currents. She forced a laugh. "But I'm just physicist Broberg, wife of astronomer Tom, mother of Johnnie and Billy."

Her glance went Saturnward, as if seeking the ship where her family waited. She might have spied it, too, as a star that moved among stars by the solar sail. However, that was now furled, and naked vision could not find even such huge hulls as *Chronos* possessed, across millions of kilometers.

Luis Garcilaso asked from his pilot's chair: "What harm if we carry on our little *commedia dell' arte*?" His Arizona drawl soothed the ear. "We won't be landin' for a while yet, and everything's on automatic till then." He was small, swarthy, and deft, still in his twenties.

Danzig twisted his leathery countenance into a frown. At sixty, thanks to his habits as well as to longevity, he kept springiness in a lank frame; he could joke about wrinkles and encroaching baldness. In this hour, he set humor aside.

"Do you mean you don't know what's the matter?" His beak of a nose pecked at a scanner screen which magnified the moonscape. "Almighty God! That's a new world we're about to touch down on—tiny, but a world, and strange in ways we can't guess. Nothing's been here before us except one un-manned flyby and one unmanned lander that soon quit send-ing. We can't rely on meters and cameras alone. We've got to use our eyes and brains."

He addressed Scobie. "You should realize that in your bones, Colin, if nobody else aboard does. You've worked on Luna as well as on Earth. In spite of all the settlements, in spite of all the study that's been done, did you never hit any nasty surprises?"

The burly man had recovered his temper. Into his own voice came a softness that recalled the serenity of the Idaho mountains from which he hailed. "True," he admitted. "There's no such thing as having too much information when you're off Earth, or enough information, for that matter." He paused. "Nevertheless, timidity can be as dangerous as rash-ness—not that you're timid, Mark," he added in haste. "Why, you and Rachel could've been in a nice O'Neill on a nice pension—"

Danzig relaxed and smiled. "This was a challenge, if I may sound pompous. Just the same, we want to get home when we're finished here. We should be in time for the Bar Mitzvah of a great-grandson or two. Which requires staying alive."

"My point is," Scobie said, "if you let yourself get buf-faloed, you may end up in a worse bind than— Oh, never mind. You're probably right, and we should not have begun fantasizing. The spectacle sort of grabbed us. It won't happen again."

Yet when Scobie's eyes looked anew on the glacier, they had not quite the dispassion of a scientist in them. Nor did Broberg's or Garcilaso's. Danzig slammed fist into palm. "The game, the damned childish game," he muttered, too low for his companions to hear. "Was nothing saner possible for them?"

II

Was nothing saner possible for them? Perhaps not.

If we are to answer the question, we should first review some history. When early industrial operations in space offered the hope of rescuing civilization, and Earth, from ruin, then greater knowledge of sister planets, prior to their development, became a clear necessity. The effort started with Mars, the least hostile. No natural law forbade sending small manned spacecraft yonder. What did was the absurdity of using as much fuel, time, and effort as were required, in order that three or four persons might spend a few days in a single locality.

Construction of the *J. Peter Vajk* took longer and cost more, but paid off when it, virtually a colony, spread its immense solar sail and took a thousand people to their goal in half a year and in comparative comfort. The payoff grew overwhelming when they, from orbit, launched Earthward the beneficiated minerals of Phobos that they did not need for their own purposes. Those purposes, of course, turned on the truly thorough, long-term study of Mars, and included landings of auxiliary craft, for ever lengthier stays, all over the surface.

Sufficient to remind you of this much; no need to detail the triumphs of the same basic concept throughout the inner Solar System, as far as Jupiter. The tragedy of the *Vladimir* became a reason to try again for Mercury, and, in a left-handed, political way, pushed the Britannic-American consortium into its *Chronos* project.

They named the ship better than they knew. Sailing time to Saturn was eight years.

Not only the scientists must be healthy, lively-minded people. Crewfolk, technicians, medics, constables, teachers, clergy, entertainers—every element of an entire community must be. Each must command more than a single skill, for emergency backup, and keep those skills alive by regular, tedious rehearsal. The environment was limited and austere; communication with home was soon a matter of beamcasts; cosmopolitans found themselves in what amounted to an isolated village. What were they to *do*?

Assigned tasks. Civic projects, especially work on improving the interior of the vessel. Research, or writing a book, or the study of a subject, or sports, or hobby clubs, or service and handicraft enterprises, or more private interactions, or— There was a wide choice of television tapes, but Central Control made sets usable for only three hours in twenty-four. You dared not get into the habit of passivity.

Individuals grumbled, squabbled, formed and dissolved cliques, formed and dissolved marriages or less explicit relationships, begot and raised occasional children, worshiped, mocked, learned, yearned, and for the most part found reasonable satisfaction in life. But for some, including a large proportion of the gifted, what made the difference between this and misery were their psychodramas.

—Minamoto

Dawn crept past the ice, out onto the rock. It was a light both dim and harsh, yet sufficient to give Garcilaso the last data he wanted for descent.

The hiss of the motor died away. A thump shivered through the hull, landing jacks leveled it, and stillness fell. The crew did not speak for a while. They were staring out at Iapetus.

Immediately around them was desolation like that which reigns in much of the Solar System. A darkling plain curved visibly away to a horizon that, at man-height, was a bare three kilometers distant; higher up in the cabin, you could see farther, but that only sharpened the sense of being on a minute ball awhirl among the stars. The ground was thinly covered with cosmic dust and gravel; here and there a minor crater or an upthrust mass lifted out of the regolith to cast long, knife-edged, utterly black shadows. Light reflections lessened the number of visible stars, turning heaven into a bowlful of night. Halfway between the zenith and the south, half-Saturn and its rings made the vista beautiful.

Likewise did the glacier—or the glaciers? Nobody was sure. The sole knowledge was that, seen from afar, Iapetus gleamed bright at the western end of its orbit and grew dull at the eastern end, because one side was covered with whitish material while the other side was not; the dividing line passed nearly beneath the planet which it eternally faced. The probes from *Chronos* had reported that the layer was thick, with puzzling spectra that varied from place to place, and little more about it.

In this hour, four humans gazed across pitted emptiness and saw wonder rear over the world-rim. From north to south went ramparts, battlements, spires, depths, peaks, cliffs, their shapes and shadings an infinity of fantasies. On the right Saturn cast soft amber, but that was nearly lost in the glare from the east, where a sun dwarfed almost to stellar size nonetheless blazed too fierce to look at, just above the summit. There the silvery sheen exploded in brilliance, diamond-glitter of shattered light, chill blues and greens; dazzled to tears, eyes saw the vision glimmer and waver, as if it bordered on dreamland, or on Faerie. But despite all delicate intricacies, underneath was a sense of chill and of brutal mass; here dwelt also the Frost Giants.

Broberg was the first to breathe forth a word. "The City of Ice."

"Magic," said Garcilaso as low. "My spirit could lose itself forever, wanderin' yonder. I'm not sure I'd mind. My cave is nothin' like this, nothin'—"

"Wait a minute!" snapped Danzig in alarm.

"Oh, yes. Curb the imagination, please." Though Scobie was quick to utter sobrieties, they sounded drier than needful. "We know from probe transmissions that the scarp is, well, Grand Canyon-like. Sure, it's more spectacular than we realized, which I suppose makes it still more of a mystery." He turned to Broberg. "I've never seen ice or snow as sculptured as this. Have you, Jean? You've mentioned visiting a lot of mountain and winter scenery when you were a girl in Canada."

The physicist shook her head. "No. Never. It doesn't seem possible. What could have done it? There's no weather here . . . is there?"

"Perhaps the same phenomenon is responsible that laid a hemisphere bare," Danzig suggested.

"Or that covered a hemisphere," Scobie said. "An object seventeen hundred kilometers across shouldn't have gases, frozen or otherwise. Unless it's a ball of such stuff clear through, like a comet, which we know it's not." As if to demonstrate, he unclipped a pair of pliers from a nearby tool rack, tossed it, and caught it on its slow way down. His own ninety kilos of mass weighed about seven. For that, the satellite must be essentially rocky.

Garcilaso registered impatience. "Let's stop tradin' facts and theories we already know about, and start findin' answers."

Rapture welled in Broberg. "Yes, let's get out. Over *there*."

"Hold on," protested Danzig as Garcilaso and Scobie nodded eagerly. "You can't be serious. Caution, step-by-step advance—"

"No, it's too wonderful for that." Broberg's tone shivered.

"Yeah, to hell with fiddlin' around," Garcilaso said. "We need at least a preliminary scout right away."

The furrows deepened in Danzig's visage. "You mean you too, Luis? But you're our pilot!"

"On the ground I'm general assistant, chief cook, and bottle washer to you scientists. Do you think I want to sit idle, with somethin' like that to explore?" Garcilaso clamed his voice. "Besides, if I should come to grief, any of you can fly back, given a bit of radio talk from *Chronos* and a final approach under remote control."

"It's quite reasonable, Mark," Scobie argued. "Contrary

to doctrine, true; but doctrine was made for us, not vice versa. A short distance, low gravity, and we'll be on the lookout for hazards. The point is, until we have some notion of what that ice is like, we don't know what the devil to pay attention to in this vicinity, either. No, first we'll take a quick jaunt. When we return, then we'll plan."

Danzig stiffened. "May I remind you, if anything goes wrong, help is at least a hundred hours away? An auxiliary like this can't boost any higher if it's to get back, and it'd take longer than that to disengage the big boats from Saturn and Titan."

Scobie reddened at the implied insult.

"And may I remind you, on the ground I am the captain. I say an immediate reconnaissance is safe and desirable. Stay behind if you want— In fact, yes, you must. Doctrine is right in saying the vessel mustn't be deserted."

Danzig studied him for several seconds before murmuring, "Luis goes, though, is that it?"

"Yes!" cried Garcilaso so that the cabin rang.

Broberg patted Danzig's limp hand. "It's okay, Mark," she said gently. "We'll bring back samples for you to study. After that, I wouldn't be surprised but what the best ideas about procedure will be yours."

He shook his head. Suddenly he looked very tired. "No," he replied in a monotone, "that won't happen. You see, I'm only a hardnosed industrial chemist who saw this expedition as a chance to do interesting research. The whole way through space, I kept myself busy with ordinary affairs, including, you remember, a couple of inventions I'd wanted the leisure to develop. You three, you're younger, you're romantics—"

"Aw, come off it, Mark." Scobie tried to laugh. "Maybe Jean and Luis are, a little, but me, I'm about as otherworldly as a plate of haggis."

"You played the game, year after year, until at last the game started playing you. That's what's going on this minute, no matter how you rationalize your motives." Danzig's gaze on the geologist, who was his friend, lost the defiance that had been in it and turned wistful. "You might try recalling Delia Ames."

Scobie bristled. "What about her? The business was hers and mine, nobody else's."

"Except afterward she cried on Rachel's shoulder, and Rachel doesn't keep secrets from me. Don't worry, I'm not about to blab. Anyhow, Delia got over it. But if you'd recollect objectively, you'd see what had happened to you already, three years ago."

Scobie set his jaw. Danzig smiled in the left corner of his mouth. "No, I suppose you can't," he went on. "I admit I had no idea either, till now, how far the process had gone. At least keep your fantasies in the background while you're outside, will you? Can you?"

In half a decade of travel, Scobie's apartment had become idiosyncratically his—perhaps more so than was usual, since he remained a bachelor who seldom had women visitors for longer than a few nightwatches at a time. Much of the furniture he had made himself; the agrosections of *Chronos* produced wood, hide, and fiber as well as food and fresh air. His handiwork ran to massiveness and archaic carved decorations. Most of what he wanted to read he screened from the data banks, of course, but a shelf held a few old books—Child's border ballads, an eighteenth-century family Bible (despite his agnosticism), a copy of *The Machinery of Freedom* which had nearly disintegrated but displayed the signature of the author, and other valued miscellany. Above them stood a model of a sailboat in which he had cruised northern European waters, and a trophy he had won in handball aboard this ship. On the bulkheads hung his fencing sabers and numerous pictures—of parents and siblings, of wilderness areas he had tramped on Earth, of castles and mountains and heaths in Scotland where he had often been, of his geological team on Luna, of Thomas Jefferson and, imagined, Robert the Bruce.

On a certain evenwatch he had, though, been seated before his telescreen. Lights were turned low in order that he might fully savor the image. Auxiliary craft were out in a joint exercise, and a couple of their personnel used the opportunity to beam back views of what they saw.

That was splendor. Starful space made a chalice for *Chronos*. The two huge, majestically counter-rotating cylinders, the entire complex of linkages, ports, locks, shields, collectors, transmitters, docks, all became Japanesely exquisite at a distance of several hundred kilometers. It was the solar sail which filled most of the screen, like a turning golden sunwheel; yet remote vision could also appreciate its spiderweb intricacy, soaring and subtle curvatures, even the less-than-gossamer thinness. A mightier work than the Pyramids, a finer work than a refashioned chromosome, the ship moved on toward a Saturn which had become the second brightest beacon in the firmament.

The doorchime hauled Scobie out of his exaltation. As he started across the deck, he stubbed his toe on a table leg. Coriolis force caused that. It was slight, when a hull this size spun to give a full gee of weight, and a thing to which he had long since adapted; but now and then he got so interested in something that Terrestrial habits returned. He swore at his absent-mindedness, good-naturedly, since he anticipated a pleasurable time.

When he opened the door, Delia Ames entered in a single stride. At once she closed it behind her and stood braced against it. She was a tall blond woman who did electronics maintenance and kept up a number of outside activities. "Hey!" Scobie said. "What's wrong? You look like"—he tried for levity—"something my cat would've dragged in, if we had any mice or beached fish aboard."

She drew a ragged breath. Her Australian accent thickened till he had trouble understanding: "I . . . today . . . I happened to be at the same cafeteria table as George Harding—"

Unease tingled through Scobie. Harding worked in Ames's department, but had much more in common with him. In the game group to which they both belonged, Harding likewise took a vaguely ancestral role, N'Kuma the Lionslayer.

"What happened?" Scobie asked.

Woe stared back at him. "He mentioned . . . you and he and the rest . . . you'd be taking your next holiday together . . . to carry on your, your bloody act uninterrupted."

"Well, yes. Work at the new park over in Starboard Hull will be suspended till enough metal's been recycled for the water pipes. The area will be vacant, and my gang has arranged to spend a week's worth of days—"

"But you and I were going to Lake Armstrong!"

"Uh, wait, that was just a notion we talked about, no definite plan yet, and this is such an unusual chance— Later, sweetheart, I'm sorry." He took her hands. They felt cold. He essayed a smile. "Now, c'mon, we were going to cook a festive dinner together and afterward spend a, shall we say, quiet evening at home. But for a start, this absolutely gorgeous presentation on the screen—"

She jerked free of him. The gesture seemed to calm her. "No, thanks," she said, flat-voiced. "Not when you'd rather be with that Broberg woman. I only came by to tell you in person I'm getting out of the way of you two."

"*Huh?*" He stepped back. "What the flaming hell do you mean?"

"You know jolly well."

"I don't! She, I, she's happily married, got two kids, she's older than me, we're friends, sure, but there's never been a thing between us that wasn't in the open and on the level—" Scobie swallowed. "You suppose maybe I'm in love with her?"

Ames looked away. Her fingers writhed together. "I'm not about to go on being a mere convenience to you, Colin. You have plenty of those. Myself, I'd hoped— But I was wrong, and I'm going to cut my losses before they get worse."

"But . . . Dee, I swear I haven't fallen for anybody else,

and I . . . I swear you're more than a body to me, you're a fine person—" She stood mute and withdrawn. Scobie gnawed his lip before he could tell her: "Okay, I admit it, the main reason I volunteered for this trip was I'd lost out in a love affair on Earth. Not that the project doesn't interest me, but I've come to realize what a big chunk out of my life it is. You, more than any other woman, Dee, you've gotten me to feel better about the situation."

She grimaced. "But not as much as your psychodrama has, right?"

"Hey, you must think I'm obsessed with the game. I'm not. It's fun and—oh, maybe 'fun' is too weak a word—but anyhow, it's just little bunches of people getting together fairly regularly to play. Like my fencing, or a chess club, or, or anything."

She squared her shoulders. "Well, then," she asked, "will you cancel the date you've made and spend your holiday with me?"

"I, uh, I can't do that. Not at this stage. Kendrick isn't off on the periphery of current events. He's closely involved with everybody else. If I didn't show, it'd spoil things for the rest."

Her glance steadied upon him. "Very well. A promise is a promise, or so I imagined. But afterward— Don't be afraid. I'm not trying to trap you. That would be no good, would it? However, if I maintain this liaison of ours, will you phase yourself out of your game?"

"I can't—" Anger seized him. "No, God damn it!" he roared.

"Then good-bye, Colin," she said, and departed. He stared for minutes at the door she had shut behind her.

Unlike the large Titan and Saturn-vicinity explorers, landers on the airless moons were simply modified Luna-to-space shuttles, reliable, but with limited capabilities. When the blocky shape had dropped below the horizon, Garcilaso said into his radio, "We've lost sight of the boat, Mark. I must say it improves the view." One of the relay microsatellites which had been sown in orbit passed his words on.

"Better start blazing your trail, then," Danzig reminded.

"My, my, you *are* a fussbudget, aren't you?" Nevertheless, Garcilaso unholstered the squirt gun at his hip and splashed a vividly fluorescent circle of paint on the ground. He would do it at eyeball intervals until his party reached the glacier. Except where dust lay thick over the regolith, footprints were faint under the feeble gravity, and absent when a walker crossed continuous rock.

Walker? No, leaper. The three bounded exultant, little hindered by spacesuits, life-support units, tool and ration packs. The naked land fled from their haste, and ever higher, ever clearer and more glorious to see, loomed the ice ahead of them.

There was no describing it, not really. You could speak of lower slopes and palisades above, to a mean height of perhaps a hundred meters, with spires towering farther still. You could speak of gracefully curved tiers going up those braes, of lacy parapets and fluted crags and arched openings to caves filled with wonders, of mysterious blues in the depths and greens where light streamed through translucencies, of gem-sparkle across whiteness where radiance and shadow wove mandalas—and none of it would convey anything more than Scobie's earlier, altogether inadequate comparison to the Grand Canyon.

"Stop," he said for the dozenth time. "I want to take a few pictures."

"Will anybody understand them who hasn't been here?" whispered Broberg.

"Probably not," said Garcilaso in the same hushed tone. "Maybe no one but us ever will."

"What do you mean by that?" demanded Danzig's voice.

"Never mind," snapped Scobie.

"I think I know," the chemist said. "Yes, it is a great piece of scenery, but you're letting it hypnotize you."

"If you don't cut out that drivel," Scobie warned, "we'll cut you out of the circuit. Damn it, we've got work to do. Get off our backs."

Danzig gusted a sigh. "Sorry. Uh, are you finding any clues to the nature of that—that thing?"

Scobie focused his camera. "Well," he said, partly mollified, "the different shades and textures, and no doubt the different shapes, seem to confirm what the reflection spectra from the flyby suggested. The composition is a mixture, or a jumble, or both, of several materials, and varies from place to place. Water ice is obvious, but I feel sure of carbon dioxide too, and I'd bet on ammonia, methane, and presumably lesser amounts of other stuff."

"Methane? Could that stay solid at ambient temperatures, in a vacuum?"

"We'll have to find out for sure. However, I'd guess that most of the time it's cold enough, at least for methane strata that occur down inside where there's pressure on them."

Within the vitryl globe of her helmet, Broberg's features showed delight. "Wait!" she cried. "I have an idea—about what happened to the probe that landed." She drew a breath. "It came down almost at the foot of the glacier, you recall. Our view of the site from space seemed to indicate that an avalanche buried it, but we couldn't understand how that might have been triggered. Well, suppose a methane layer at exactly the wrong location melted. Heat radiation from the jets may have warmed it, and later the radar beam used to map contours added the last few degrees necessary. The stratum flowed, and down came everything that had rested on top of it."

"Plausible," Scobie said. "Congratulations, Jean."

"Nobody thought of the possibility in advance?" Garcilaso scoffed. "What kind of scientists have we got along?"

"The kind who were being overwhelmed by work after we reached Saturn, and still more by data input," Scobie answered. "The universe is bigger than you or anybody can realize, hotshot."

"Oh. Sure. No offense." Garcilaso's glance returned to the ice. "Yes, we'll never run out of mysteries, will we?"

"Never." Broberg's eyes glowed enormous. "At the heart of things will always be magic. The Elf King rules—"

Scobie returned his camera to its pouch. "Stow the gab and move on," he ordered curtly.

His gaze locked for an instant with Broberg's. In the weird, mingled light, it could be seen that she went pale, then red, before she sprang off beside him.

Ricia had gone alone into Moonwood on Midsummer Eve. The King found her there and took her unto him as she had hoped. Ecstasy became terror when he afterward bore her off; yet her captivity in the City of Ice brought her many more such hours, and beauties and marvels unknown among mortals. Alvarlan, her mentor, sent his spirit in quest of her, and was himself beguiled by what he found. It was an effort of will for him to tell Sir Kendrick of the Isles where she was, albeit he pledged his help in freeing her.

N'Kuma the Lionslayer, Béla of Eastmarch, Karina Far West, Lady Aurelia, Olav Harpmaster had none of them been present when this happened.

The glacier (a wrong name for something that might have no counterpart in the Solar System) lifted off the plain as abruptly as a wall. Standing there, the three could no longer see the heights. They could, though, see that the slope which curved steeply upward to a filigree-topped edge was not smooth. Shadows lay blue in countless small craters. The sun had climbed just sufficiently high to beget them; a Iapetan day is more than seventy-nine of Earth's.

Danzig's question crackled in their earphones: "Now are you satisfied? Will you come back before a fresh landslide catches you?"

"It won't," Scobie replied. "We aren't a vehicle, and the local configuration has clearly been stable for centuries or better. Besides, what's the point of a manned expedition if nobody investigates anything?"

"I'll see if I can climb," Garcilaso offered.

"No, wait," Scobie commanded. "I've had experience with mountains and snowpacks, for whatever that may be worth. Let me work out a route for us first."

"You're going onto that stuff, the whole gaggle of you?" exploded Danzig. "Have you completely lost your minds?"

Scobie's brow and lips tightened. "Mark, I warn you again, if you don't get your emotions under control, we'll cut you off. We'll hike on a ways if I decide it's safe."

He paced back and forth, in floating low-weight fashion, while he surveyed the jökull. Layers and blocks of distinct substances were plain to see, like separate ashlars laid by an elvish mason—where they were not so huge that a giant must have been at work. The craterlets might be sentry posts on this lowest embankment of the City's defenses. . . .

Garcilaso, most vivacious of men, stood motionless and let his vision lose itself in the sight. Broberg knelt down to examine the ground, but her own gaze kept wandering aloft.

Finally she beckoned. "Colin, come over here, please," she said. "I believe I've made a discovery."

Scobie joined her. As she rose, she scooped a handful of fine black particles off the shards on which she stood and let it trickle from her glove. "I suspect this is the reason the boundary of the ice is sharp," she told him.

"What is?" Danzig inquired from afar. He got no answer.

"I noticed more and more dust as we went along," Broberg continued. "If it fell on patches and lumps of frozen stuff, isolated from the main mass, and covered them, it would absorb solar heat till they melted or, likelier, sublimed. Even water molecules would escape to space, in this weak gravity. The main mass was too big for that; square-cube law. Dust grains there would simply melt their way down a short distance, then be covered as surrounding material collapsed on them, and the process would stop."

"H'm." Scobie raised a hand to stroke his chin, encountered his helmet, and sketched a grin at himself. "Sounds reasonable. But where did so much dust come from—and the ice, for that matter?"

"I think—" Her voice dropped until he could barely hear, and her look went the way of Garcilaso's. His remained upon her face, profiled against stars. "I think this bears out your comet hypothesis, Colin. A comet struck Iapetus. It came from the direction it did because it got so near Saturn that it was forced to swing in a hairpin bend around the planet. It was enormous; the ice of it covered almost a hemisphere, in spite of much more being vaporized and lost. The dust is partly from it, partly generated by the impact."

He clasped her armored shoulder. "*Your* theory, Jean. I was not the first to propose a comet, but you're the first to corroborate with details."

She didn't appear to notice, except that she murmured further: "Dust can account for the erosion that made those lovely formations, too. It caused differential melting and sublimation on the surface, according to the patterns it happened to fall in and the mixes of ices it clung to, until it was washed away or encysted. The craters, these small ones and the major ones we've observed from above, they have a separate but similar origin. Meteorites—"

"Whoa, there," he objected. "Any sizable meteorite would release enough energy to steam off most of the entire field."

"I know. Which shows the comet collision was recent, less than a thousand years ago, or we wouldn't be seeing this miracle today. Nothing big has since happened to strike, yet. I'm thinking of little stones, cosmic sand, in prograde orbits around Saturn so that they hit with low relative speed. Most simply make dimples in the ice. Lying there, however, they collect solar heat because they're dark, and re-radiate it to melt away their surroundings, till they sink beneath. The concavities they leave reflect incident radiation from side to side, and thus continue to grow. The pothole effect. And again, because the different ices have different properties, you don't get perfectly smooth craters, but those fantastic bowls we saw before we landed."

"By God!" Scobie hugged her. "You're a genius."

Helmet against helmet, she smiled and said, "No. It's obvious, once you've seen for yourself." She was quiet for a bit while still they held each other. "Scientific intuition is a funny thing, I admit," she went on at last. "Considering the problem, I was hardly aware of my logical mind. What I thought was— the City of Ice, made with starstones out of that which a god called down from heaven—"

"Jesus Maria!" Garcilaso spun about to stare at them.

Scobie released the woman. "We'll go after confirmation," he said unsteadily. "To the large crater we spotted a few klicks inward. The surface appears quite safe to walk on."

"I called that crater the Elf King's Dance Hall," Broberg mused, as if a dream were coming back to her.

"Have a care." Garcilaso's laugh rattled. "Heap big medicine yonder. The King is only an inheritor; it was giants who built these walls, for the gods."

"Well, I've got to find a way in, don't I?" Scobie responded.

"Indeed," *Alvarlan says.* "I cannot guide you from this point. My spirit can only see through mortal eyes. I can but lend you my counsel, until we have neared the gates."

"Are you sleepwalking in that fairy tale of yours?" Danzig yelled. "Come back before you get yourselves killed!"

"Will you dry up?" Scobie snarled. "It's nothing but a style of talk we've got between us. If you can't understand that, you've got less use of your brain than we do."

"Listen, won't you? I didn't say you're crazy. You don't have delusions or anything like that. I do say you've steered your fantasies toward this kind of place, and now the reality has reinforced them till you're under a compulsion you don't recognize. Would you go ahead so recklessly anywhere else in the universe? Think!"

"That does it. We'll resume contact after you've had time to improve your manners." Scobie snapped off his main radio switch. The circuits that stayed active served for close-by communication but had no power to reach an orbital relay. His companions did likewise.

The three faced the awesomeness before them. "You can help me find the Princess when we are inside, Alvarlan," *Kendrick says.*

"That I can and will," *the sorcerer vows.*

"I wait for you, most steadfast of my lovers," *Ricia croons.*

Alone in the spacecraft, Danzig well-nigh sobbed, "Oh, damn that game forever!" The sound fell away into emptiness.

III

To condemn psychodrama, even in its enhanced form, would be to condemn human nature.

It begins in childhood. Play is necessary to an immature mammal, a means of learning to handle the body, the perceptions, and the outside world. The young human plays, must play, with its brain too. The more intelligent the child, the more its imagination needs exercise. There are degrees of activity, from the passive watching of a show on a screen, onward through reading, daydreaming, storytelling, and psychodrama . . . for which the child has no such fancy name.

We cannot give this behavior any single description, for the shape and course it takes depend on an endless number of variables. Sex, age, culture, and companions are only the most obvious. For example, in pre-electronic North America little girls would often play "house" while little boys played "cowboys and Indians" or "cops and robbers," whereas nowadays a mixed group of their descendants might play "dolphins" or "astronauts and aliens." In essence, a small band forms, and each individual makes up a character to portray or borrows one from fiction. Simple props may be employed, such as toy weapons; or a chance object—a stick, for instance—may be declared something else such as a metal detector; or a thing may be quite imaginary, as the scenery almost always is. The children then act out a drama which they compose as they go along. When they cannot physically perform a certain action, they describe it. ("I jump real high, like you can do on Mars, an' come out over the edge o' that ol' Valles Marineris, an' take that bandit by surprise.") A large cast of characters, especially villains, frequently comes into existence by fiat.

The most imaginative member of the troupe dominates the game and the evolution of the story line, though in a rather subtle fashion, through offering the most vivid possibilities. The rest, however, are brighter than average; psychodrama in this highly developed form does not appeal to everybody.

For those to whom it does, the effects are beneficial and lifelong. Besides increasing their creativity through use, it lets them try out a play version of different adult roles and experiences. Thereby they begin to acquire insight into adulthood.

Such play-acting ends when adolescence commences, if not earlier—but only in that form, and not necessarily forever in it. Grownups have many dream-games. This is plain to see in lodges, for example, with their titles, costumes, and ceremonies; but does it not likewise animate all pageantry, every ritual? To what extent are our heroisms, sacrifices, and self-aggrandizements the acting out of personae that we maintain? Some thinkers have attempted to trace this element through every aspect of society.

Here, though, we are concerned with overt psychodrama among adults. In Western civilization it first appeared on a noticeable scale during the middle twentieth century. Psychiatrists found it a powerful diagnostic and therapeutic technique. Among ordinary folk, war and fantasy games, many of which involved identification with imaginary or historical characters, became increasingly popular. In part this was doubtless a retreat from the restrictions and menaces of that unhappy period, but likely in larger part it was a revolt of the mind against the inactive entertainment, notably television, which had come to dominate recreation.

The Chaos ended those activities. Everybody knows about their revival in recent times—for healthier reasons, one hopes. By projecting three-dimensional scenes and appropriate sounds from a data bank—or, better yet, by having a computer produce them to order—players gained a sense of reality that intensified their mental and emotional commitment. Yet in those games that went on for episode after episode, year after real-time year, whenever two or more members of a group could get together to play, they found themselves less and less dependent on such appurtenances. It seemed that, through practice, they had regained the vivid imaginations of their childhoods, and could make anything, or airy nothing itself, into the objects and the worlds they desired.

I have deemed it necessary thus to repeat the obvious in order that we may see it in perspective. The news beamed from Saturn has brought widespread revulsion. (Why? What buried fears have been touched? This is subject matter for potentially important research.) Overnight, adult psychodrama has become unpopular; it may become extinct. That would, in many ways, be a worse tragedy than what has occurred yonder. There is no reason to suppose that the game ever harmed any mentally sound person on Earth; on the contrary. Beyond doubt, it has helped astronauts stay sane and alert on long, difficult missions. If it has no more medical use, that is because psychotherapy has become a branch of applied biochemistry.

And this last fact, the modern world's dearth of experience with madness, is at the root of what happened. Although he could not have foreseen the exact outcome, a twentieth-century psychiatrist might have warned against spending eight years, an unprecedented stretch of time, in as strange an environment as the *Chronos*. Strange it certainly has been, despite all efforts—limited, totally man-controlled, devoid of countless cues for which our evolution on Earth has fashioned us. Extraterrestrial colonists have, thus far, had available to them any number of simulations and compensations, of which close, full contact with home and frequent opportunities to visit there are probably the most significant. Sailing time to Jupiter was long, but half of that to Saturn. Moreover, because they were earlier, scientists in the *Zeus* had much research to occupy them en route, which it would be pointless for later travelers to duplicate; by then, the interplanetary medium between the two giants held few surprises.

Contemporary psychologists were aware of this. They understood that the persons most adversely affected would be the most intelligent, imaginative, and dynamic—those who were supposed to make the very discoveries at Saturn which were the purpose of the undertaking. Being less familiar than their predecessors with the labyrinth that lies, Minotaur-haunted, beneath every human consciousness, the psychologists expected purely benign consequences of whatever psychodramas the crew engendered.

—Minamoto

Assignments to teams had not been made in advance of departure. It was sensible to let professional capabilities reveal themselves and grow on the voyage, while personal relationships did the same. Eventually such factors would help in deciding what individuals should train for what tasks. Long-term participation in a group of players normally forged bonds of friendship that were desirable, if the members were otherwise qualified.

In real life, Scobie always observed strict propriety toward Broberg. She was attractive, but she was monogamous, and he had no wish to alienate her. Besides, he liked her husband. (Tom did not partake of the game. As an astronomer, he had plenty to keep his attention happily engaged.) They had played for a couple of years, and their group had acquired as many characters as it could accommodate in a narrative whose milieu and people were becoming complex, before Scobie and Broberg spoke of anything intimate.

By then, the story they enacted was doing so, and maybe it was not altogether by chance that they met when both had several idle hours. This was in the weightless recreation area at the spin axis. They tumbled through aerobatics, shouting and laughing, until they were pleasantly tired, went to the clubhouse, turned in their wingsuits, and showered. They had not seen each other nude before; neither commented, but he did not hide his enjoyment of the sight, while she colored and averted her glance as tactfully as she was able. Afterward, their clothes resumed, they decided on a drink before they went home, and sought the lounge.

Since evenwatch was approaching nightwatch, they had the place to themselves. At the bar, he thumbed a chit for Scotch, she for Pinot Chardonnay. The machine obliged them and they carried their refreshments out onto the balcony. Seated at a table, they looked across immensity. The clubhouse was built into the support frame on a Lunar gravity level. Above them they saw the sky wherein they had been as birds; its reach did not seem any more hemmed in by far-spaced, spidery girders than it was by a few drifting clouds. Beyond, and straight ahead, decks opposite were a commingling of masses and shapes which the scant illumination at this hour turned into mystery. Among those shadows the humans made out woods, brooks, pools, turned hoary or agleam by the light of stars which filled the skyview strips. Right and left, the hull stretched off beyond sight, a dark in which such lamps as there were appeared lost.

The air was cool, slightly jasmine-scented, drenched with silence. Underneath and throughout, subliminally, throbbed the myriad pulses of the ship.

"Magnificent," Broberg said low, gazing outward. "What a surprise."

"Eh?" asked Scobie.

"I've only been here before in daywatch. I didn't antici-pate that a simple rotation of the reflectors would make it wonderful."

"Oh, I wouldn't sneer at the daytime view. Mighty im-pressive."

"Yes, but—but then you see too plainly that everything is manmade, nothing is wild or unknown or free. The sun blots out the stars; it's as though no universe existed beyond this shell we're in. Tonight is like being in Maranoa," *the kingdom of which Ricia is Princess, a kingdom of ancient things and ways, wildernesses, enchantments.*

"H'm, yeah, sometimes I feel trapped myself," Scobie admitted. "I thought I had a journey's worth of geological data to study, but my project isn't going anywhere very interesting."

"Same for me." Broberg straightened where she sat, turned to him, and smiled a trifle. The dusk softened her features, made them look young. "Not that we're entitled to self-pity. Here we are, safe and comfortable till we reach Saturn. After that we should never lack for excitement, or for material to work with on the way home."

"True." Scobie raised his glass. "Well, skoal. Hope I'm not mispronouncing that."

"How should I know?" she laughed. "My maiden name was Almyer."

"That's right, you've adopted Tom's surname. I wasn't thinking. Though that is rather unusual these days, hey?"

She spread her hands. "My family was well-to-do, but they were—are—Jerusalem Catholics. Strict about certain things; archaistic, you might say." She lifted her wine and sipped. "Oh, yes, I've left the Church, but in several ways the Church will never leave me."

"I see. Not to pry, but, uh, this does account for some traits of yours I couldn't help wondering about."

She regarded him over the rim of her glass. "Like what?"

"Well, you've got a lot of life in you, vigor, a sense of fun, but you're also—what's the word?—uncommonly domestic. You've told me you were a quiet faculty member of Yukon University till you married Tom." Scobie grinned. "Since you two kindly invited me to your last anniversary party, and I know your present age, I deduced that you were thirty then." Unmentioned was the likelihood that she had still been a virgin. "Nevertheless—oh, forget it. I said I don't want to pry."

"Go ahead, Colin," she urged. "That line from Burns sticks in my mind, since you introduced me to his poetry. 'To see oursels as others see us!' Since it looks as if we may visit the same moon—"

Scobie took a hefty dollop of Scotch. "Aw, nothing much," he said, unwontedly diffident. "If you must know, well, I have the impression that being in love wasn't the single good reason you had for marrying Tom. He'd already been accepted for this expedition, and given your personal qualifications, that would get you in too. In short, you'd grown tired of routine respectability and here was how you could kick over the traces. Am I right?"

"Yes." Her gaze dwelt on him. "You're more perceptive than I supposed."

"No, not really. A roughneck rockhound. But Ricia's made it plain to see that you're more than a demure wife, mother, and scientist—" She parted her lips. He raised a palm. "No, please, let me finish. I know it's bad manners to claim that somebody's persona is a wish fulfillment, and I'm not doing that. Of course you don't want to be a free-roving, free-loving female scamp, any more than I want to ride around cutting down assorted enemies. Still, if you'd been born and raised in the world of our game, I feel sure you'd be a lot like Ricia. And that potential is part of you, Jean." He tossed off his drink. "If I've said too much, please excuse me. Want a refill?"

"I'd better not, but don't let me stop you."

"You won't." He rose and bounded off.

When he returned, he saw that she had been observing him through the vitryl door. As he sat down, she smiled, leaned a bit across the table, and told him softly: "I'm glad you said what you did. Now I can declare what a complicated man Kendrick reveals you to be."

"What?" Scobie asked in honest surprise. "Come on! He's a sword-and-shield tramp, a fellow who likes to travel, same as me; and in my teens I was a brawler, same as him."

"He may lack polish, but he's a chivalrous knight, a compassionate overlord, a knower of sagas and traditions, an appreciator of poetry and music, a bit of a bard. . . . Ricia misses him. When will he get back from his latest quest?"

"I'm bound home this minute. N'Kuma and I gave those pirates the slip and landed at Haverness two days ago. After we buried the swag, he wanted to visit Béla and Karina and join them in whatever they've been up to, so we bade goodbye for the time being." Scobie and Harding had lately taken a few hours to conclude that adventure of theirs. The rest of the group had been mundanely occupied for some while.

Broberg's eyes widened. "From Haverness to the Isles? But I'm in Castle Devaranda, right in between."

"I hoped you'd be."

"I can't wait to hear your story."

"I'm pushing on after dark. The moon is bright and I've got a pair of remounts I bought with a few gold pieces from the loot." *The dust rolls white beneath drumming hoofs. Where a horseshoe strikes a flint pebble, sparks fly ardent. Kendrick scowls.* "You, aren't you with . . . what's his name? . . . Joran the Red? I don't like him."

"I sent him packing a month ago. He got the idea that sharing my bed gave him authority over me. It was never anything but a romp. I stand alone on the Gerfalcon Tower, looking south over moonlit fields, and wonder how you fare. The road flows toward me like a gray river. Do I see a rider come at a gallop, far and far away?"

After many months of play, no image on a screen was necessary. *Pennons on the night wind stream athwart the stars.* "I arrive. I sound my horn to rouse the gatekeepers."

"How I do remember those merry notes—"

That same night, Kendrick and Ricia become lovers. Experienced in the game and careful of its etiquette, Scobie and Broberg uttered no details about the union; they did not touch each other and maintained only fleeting eye contact; the ultimate good-nights were very decorous. After all, this was a

story they composed about two fictitious characters in a world
that never was.

The lower slopes of the jökull rose in tiers which were themselves deeply concave; the humans walked around their rims
and admired the extravagant formations beneath. Names
sprang onto lips: the Frost Garden, the Ghost Bridge, the
Snow Queen's Throne, *while Kendrick advances into the City,
and Ricia awaits him at the Dance Hall, and the spirit of Alvarlan carries word between them so that it is as if already she
too travels beside her knight.* Nevertheless they proceeded war-
ily, vigilant for signs of danger, especially whenever a change
of texture or hue or anything else in the surface underfoot
betokened a change in its nature.

Above the highest ledge reared a cliff too sheer to scale,
Iapetan gravity or no, *the fortress wall.* However, from orbit
the crew had spied a gouge in the vicinity, forming a pass,
doubtless plowed by a small meteorite *in the war between the
gods and the magicians, when stones chanted down from the sky
wrought havoc so accursed that none dared afterward rebuild.*
That was an eerie climb, hemmed in by heights which glim-
mered in the blue twilight they cast, heaven narrowed to a belt
between them where stars seemed to blaze doubly brilliant.

"There must be guards at the opening," *Kendrick says.*

"A single guard," *answers the mind-whisper of Alvarlan,*
"but he is a dragon. If you did battle with him, the noise and
flame would bring every warrior here upon you. Fear not. I'll
slip into his burnin' brain and weave him such a dream that
he'll never see you."

"The King might sense the spell," *says Ricia through him.*
"Since you'll be parted from us anyway, while you ride the
soul of that beast, Alvarlan, I'll seek him out and distract
him."

*Kendrick grimaces, knowing full well what means are hers
to do that. She has told him how she longs for freedom and her
knight; she has also hinted that elven lovemaking transcends the
human. Does she wish for a final time before her rescue? . . .*

Well, Ricia and Kendrick have neither plighted nor practiced single troth. Assuredly, Colin Scobie had not. He jerked forth a grin and continued through the silence that had fallen on all three.

They came out on top of the glacial mass and looked around them. Scobie whistled. Garcilaso stammered, "J-J-Jesus Christ!" Broberg smote her hands together.

Below them the precipice fell to the ledges, whose sculpturing took on a wholly new, eldritch aspect, gleam and shadow, until it ended at the plain. Seen from here aloft, the curvature of the moon made toes strain downward in boots, as if to cling fast and not be spun off among the stars which surrounded, rather than shone above, its ball. The spacecraft stood minute on dark, pocked stone, like a cenotaph raised to loneliness.

Eastward the ice reached beyond an edge of sight which was much closer. ("Yonder could be the rim of the world," Garcilaso said, and *Ricia replies*, "Yes, the City is nigh to there.") Bowls of different sizes, hillocks, crags, no two of them eroded the same way, turned its otherwise level stretch into a surreal maze. An arabesque openwork ridge which stood at the explorers' goal overtopped the horizon. Everything that was illuminated lay gently aglow. Radiant though the sun was, it cast the light of only perhaps five thousand full Lunas upon Earth. Southward, Saturn's great semidisc gave about one-half more Lunar shining; but in that direction, the wilderness sheened pale amber.

Scobie shook himself. "Well, shall we go?" His prosaic question jarred the others; Garcilaso frowned and Broberg winced.

She recovered. "Yes, hasten," *Ricia says*. "I am by myself once more. Are you out of the dragon, Alvarlan?"

"Aye," *the wizard informs her.* "Kendrick is safely behind a ruined palace. Tell us how best to reach you."

"You are at the time-gnawed Crown House. Before you lies the Street of Shieldsmiths—"

Scobie's brows knitted. "It is noonday, when elves do not

fare abroad," *Kendrick says* remindingly, commandingly. "I do not wish to encounter any of them. No fights, no complications. We are going to fetch you and escape, without further trouble."

Broberg and Garcilaso showed disappointment, but understood him. A game broke down when a person refused to accept something that a fellow player tried to put in. Often the narrative threads were not mended and picked up for many days. Broberg sighed.

"Follow the street to its end at a forum where a snow fountain springs," *Ricia directs.* "Cross, and continue on Aleph Zain Boulevard. You will know it by a gateway in the form of a skull with open jaws. If anywhere you see a rainbow flicker in the air, stand motionless until it has gone by, for it will be an auroral wolf. . . ."

At a low-gravity lope, the distance took some thirty minutes to cover. In the later part, the three were forced to detour by great banks of an ice so fine-grained that it slid about under their bootsoles and tried to swallow them. Several of these lay at irregular intervals around their destination.

There the travelers stood again for a time in the grip of awe.

The bowl at their feet must reach down almost to bedrock, a hundred meters, and was twice as wide. On this rim lifted the wall they had seen from the cliff, an arc fifty meters long and high, nowhere thicker than five meters, pierced by intricate scrollwork, greenly agleam where it was not translucent. It was the uppermost edge of a stratum which made serrations down the crater. Other outcrops and ravines were more dreamlike yet . . . was that a unicorn's head, was that a colonnade of caryatids, was that an icicle bower. . . ? The depths were a lake of cold blue shadow.

"You have come, Kendrick, beloved!" *cries Ricia, and casts herself into his arms.*

"Quiet," *warns the sending of Alvarlan the wise.* "Rouse not our immortal enemies."

"Yes, we must get back." Scobie blinked. "Judas priest, what possessed us? Fun is fun, but we sure have come a lot farther and faster than was smart, haven't we"

"Let us stay for a little while," Broberg pleaded. "This is such a miracle—the Elf King's Dance Hall, which the Lord of the Dance built for him—"

"Remember, if we stay we'll be caught, and your captivity may be forever." Scobie thumbed his main radio switch. "Hello, Mark? Do you read me?"

Neither Broberg nor Garcilaso made that move. They did not hear Danzig's voice: "Oh, yes! I've been hunkered over the set gnawing my knuckles. How are you?"

"All right. We're at the big hole and will be heading back as soon I've gotten a few pictures."

"They haven't made words to tell how relieved I am. From a scientific standpoint, was it worth the risk?"

Scobie gasped. He stared before him.

"Colin?" Danzig called. "You still there?"

"Yes. Yes."

"I asked what observations of any importance you made."

"I don't know," Scobie mumbled. "I can't remember. None of it after we started climbing seems real."

"Better you return right away," Danzig said grimly. "Forget about photographs."

"Correct." Scobie addressed his companions: "Forward march."

"I can't," *Alvarlan answers.* "A wanderin' spell has caught my spirit in tendrils of smoke."

"I know where a fire dagger is kept," *Ricia says.* "I'll try to steal it."

Broberg moved ahead, as though to descend into the crater. Tiny ice grains trickled over the verge from beneath her boots. She could easily lose her footing and slide down.

"No, wait," *Kendrick shouts to her.* "No need. My spearhead is of moon alloy. It can cut—"

The glacier shuddered. The ridge cracked asunder and fell in shards. The area on which the humans stood split free and toppled into the bowl. An avalanche poured after. High-flung crystals caught sunlight, glittered prismatic in challenge to the stars, descended slowly and lay quiet.

Except for shock waves through solids, everything had happened in the absolute silence of space.

Heartbeat by heartbeat, Scobie crawled back to his senses. He found himself held down, immobilized, in darkness and pain. His armor had saved, was still saving his life; he had been stunned but escaped a real concussion. Yet every breath hurt abominably. A rib or two on the left side seemed broken; a monstrous impact must have dented metal. And he was buried under more weight than he could move.

"Hello," he coughed. "Does anybody read me?" The single reply was the throb of his blood. If his radio still worked—which it should, being built into the suit—the mass around him screened him off.

It also sucked heat at an unknown but appalling rate. He felt no cold because the electrical system drew energy from his fuel cell as fast as needed to keep him warm and to recycle his air chemically. As a normal thing, when he lost heat through the slow process of radiation—and a trifle through kerofoam-lined bootsoles—the latter demand was much the greater. Now conduction was at work on every square centimeter. He had spare unit in the equipment on his back, but no means of getting at it.

Unless— He barked forth a chuckle. Straining, he felt the stuff that entombed him yield the least bit under the pressure of arms and legs. And his helmet rang slightly with noise, rustle, a gurgle. This wasn't water ice that imprisoned him, but stuff with a much lower freezing point. He was melting it, subliming it, making room for himself.

If he lay passive, he would sink, while frozenness above slid down to keep him in his grave. He might evoke super new formations, but he would not see them. Instead, he must use the small capability given him to work his way upward, scrabble, get a purchase on matter that was not yet aflow, burrow to the stars.

He began.

Agony soon racked him. Breath rasped in and out of lungs aflame. His strength drained away and trembling took its place, and he could not tell whether he ascended or slipped back. Blind, half suffocated, Scobie made mole-claws of his hands and dug.

It was too much to endure. He fled from it—

His strong enchantments failing, the Elf King brought down his towers of fear in wreck. If the spirit of Alvarlan returned to its body, the wizard would brood upon things he had seen, and understand what they meant, and such knowledge would give mortals a terrible power against Faerie. Waking from the sleep, the King scried Kendrick about to release that fetch. There was no time to do more than break the spell which upheld the Dance Hall. It was largely built of mist and starshine, but enough blocks quarried from the cold side of Ginnungagap were in it that when they crashed they should kill the knight. Ricia would perish too, and in his quicksilver intellect the King regretted that. Nevertheless he spoke the necessary word.

He did not comprehend how much abuse flesh and bone can bear. Sir Kendrick fights his way clear of the ruins, to seek and save his lady. While he does, he heartens himself with thoughts of adventures past and future—

—and suddenly the blindness broke apart and Saturn stood lambent within rings.

Scobie belly-flopped onto the surface and lay shuddering.

He must rise, no matter how his injuries screamed, lest he melt himself a new burial place. He lurched to his feet and glared around.

Little but outcroppings and scars was left of the sculpture. For the most part, the crater had become a smooth-sided whiteness under heaven. Scarcity of shadows made distances hard to gauge, but Scobie guessed the new depth was about seventy-five meters. And empty, empty.

"Mark, do you hear?" he cried.

"That you, Colin?" rang in his earpieces. "Name of mercy, what's happened? I heard you call out, and saw a cloud rise and sink . . . then nothing for more than an hour. Are you okay?"

"I am, sort of. I don't see Jean or Luis. A landslide took us by surprise and buried us. Hold on while I search."

When he stood upright, Scobie's ribs hurt less. He could move about rather handily if he took care. The two types of standard analgesic in his kit were alike useless, one too weak to give noticeable relief, one so strong that it would turn him sluggish. Casting to and fro, he soon found what he expected, a concavity in the tumbled snowlike material, slightly aboil.

Also a standard part of his gear was a trenching tool. Scobie set pain aside and dug. A helmet appeared. Broberg's head was within it. She too had been tunneling out.

"Jean!"

"Kendrick!" She crept free and they embraced, suit to suit. "Oh, Colin."

"How are you?" rattled from him.

"Alive," she answered. "No serious harm done, I think. A lot to be said for low gravity. . . . You? Luis?" Blood was clotted in a streak beneath her nose, and a bruise on her forehead was turning purple, but she stood firmly and spoke clearly.

"I'm functional. Haven't found Luis yet. Help me look. First, though, we'd better check out our equipment."

She hugged arms around chest, as if that would do any good here. "I'm chilled," she admitted.

Scobie pointed at a telltale. "No wonder. Your fuel cell's down to its last couple of ergs. Mine isn't in a lot better shape. Let's change."

They didn't waste time removing their backpacks, but reached into each other's. Tossing the spent units to the ground, where vapors and holes immediately appeared and then froze, they plugged the fresh ones into their suits. "Turn your thermostat down," Scobie advised. "We won't find shelter soon. Physical activity will help us keep warm."

"And require faster air recycling," Broberg reminded.

"Yeah. But for the moment, at least, we can conserve the energy in the cells. Okay, next let's check for strains, potential leaks, any kind of damage or loss. Hurry. Luis is still down there."

Inspection was a routine made automatic by years of drill. While her fingers searched across the man's spacesuit, Broberg let her eyes wander. "The Dance Hall is gone," *Ricia murmurs.* "I think the King smashed it to prevent our escape."

"Me too. If he finds out we're alive, and seeking for Alvarlan's soul— Hey, wait! None of that!"

Danzig's voice quavered. "How're you doing?"

"We're in fair shape, seems like," Scobie replied. "My corselet took a beating but didn't split or anything. Now to find Luis . . . Jean, suppose you spiral right, I left, across the crater floor."

It took a while, for the seething which marked Garcilaso's burial was minuscule. Scobie started to dig. Broberg watched how he moved, heard how he breathed, and said, "Give me that tool. Just where are you bunged up, anyway?"

He admitted his condition and stepped back. Crusty chunks flew from Broberg's toil. She progressed fast, since whatever kind of ice lay at this point was, luckily, friable, and under Iapetan gravity she could cut a hole with almost vertical sides.

"I'll make myself useful," Scobie said, "namely, find us a way out."

When he started up the nearest slope, it shivered. All at once he was borne back in a tide that made rustly noises through his armor, while a fog of dry white motes blinded him. Painfully, he scratched himself free at the bottom and tried elsewhere. In the end he could report to Danzig: "I'm afraid there is no easy route. When the rim collapsed where we stood, it did more than produce a shock which wrecked the delicate formations throughout the crater. It let tons of stuff pour down from the surface—a particular sort of ice that, under local conditions, is like fine sand. The walls are covered by it. Most places, it lies meters deep over more stable material. We'd slide faster than we could climb, where the layer is thin; where it's thick, we'd sink."

Danzig sighed. "I guess I get to take a nice, healthy hike."

"I assume you've called for help."

"Of course. They'll have two boats here in about a hundred hours. The best they can manage. You knew that already."

"Uh-huh. And our fuel cells are good for perhaps fifty hours."

"Oh, well, not to worry about that. I'll bring extras and toss them to you, if you're stuck till the rescue party arrives. M-m-m . . . maybe I'd better rig a slingshot or something first."

"You might have a problem locating us. This isn't a true crater, it's a glorified pothole, the lip of it flush with the top of the glacier. The landmark we guided ourselves by, that fancy ridge, is gone."

"No big deal. I've got a bearing on you from the directional antenna, remember. A magnetic compass may be no use here, but I can keep myself oriented by the heavens. Saturn scarcely moves in this sky, and the sun and the stars don't move fast."

"Damn! You're right. I wasn't thinking. Got Luis on my mind, if nothing else." Scobie looked across the bleakness toward Broberg. Perforce she was taking a short rest, stoop-shouldered above her excavation. His earpieces brought him the harsh sound in her windpipe.

He must maintain what strength was left him, against later need. He sipped from his water nipple, pushed a bite of food through his chowlock, pretended an appetite. "I may as

well try reconstructing what happened," he said. "Okay,
Mark, you were right, we got crazy reckless. The game— Eight
years was too long to play the game, in an environment that
gave us too few reminders of reality. But who could have
foreseen it? My God, warn *Chronos!* I happen to know that
one of the Titan teams started playing an expedition to the
merfolk under the Crimson Ocean—on account of the red
mists—deliberately, like us, before they set off. . . ."

Scobie gulped. "Well," he slogged on, "I don't suppose
we'll ever know exactly what went wrong here. But plain to
see, the configuration was only metastable. On Earth, too, av-
alanches can be fatally easy to touch off. I'd guess at a methane layer underneath the surface. It turned a little slushy
when temperatures rose after dawn, but that didn't matter in
low gravity and vacuum—till we came along. Heat, vibration—
Anyhow, the stratum slid out from under us, which triggered a
general collapse. Does that guess seem reasonable?"

"Yes, to an amateur like me," Danzig said. "I admire how
you can stay academic under these circumstances."

"I'm being practical," Scobie retorted. "Luis may need
medical attention earlier than those boats can come for him. If
so, how do we get him to ours?"

Danzig's voice turned stark. "Any ideas?"

"I'm fumbling my way toward that. Look, the bowl still
has the same basic form. The whole shebang didn't cave in.
That implies hard material, water ice and actual rock. In fact,
I see a few remaining promontories, jutting out above the
sandlike stuff. As for what *it* is—maybe an ammonia-carbon
dioxide combination, maybe more exotic—that'll be for you to
discover later. Right now . . . my geological instruments
should help me trace where the solid masses are least deeply
covered. We all have trenching tools, so we can try to shovel a
path clear, along a zigzag of least effort. That may bring more
garbage slipping down on us from above, but that in turn may
expedite our progress. Where the uncovered shelves are too
steep or slippery to climb, we can chip footholds. Slow and

tough work; and we may run into a bluff higher than we can jump, or something like that."

"I can help," Danzig proposed. "While I waited to hear from you, I inventoried our stock of spare cable, cord, equipment I can cannibalize for wire, clothes and bedding I can cut into strips—whatever might be knotted together to make a rope. We won't need much tensile strength. Well, I estimate I can get about forty meters. According to your description, that's about half the slope length of that trap you're in. If you can climb halfway up while I trek there, I can haul you the rest of the way."

"Thanks, Mark," Scobie said, "although—"

"Luis!" shrieked in his helmet. "Colin, come fast, help me, this is dreadful!"

Regardless of the pain, except for a curse or two, Scobie sped to Broberg's aid.

Garcilaso was not quite unconscious. In that lay much of the horror. They heard him mumble, "—Hell, the King threw my soul into Hell. I can't find my way out. I'm lost. If only Hell weren't so cold—" They could not see his face; the inside of his helmet was crusted with frost. Deeper and longer buried than the others, badly hurt in addition, he would have died shortly after his fuel cell was exhausted. Broberg had uncovered him barely in time, if that.

Crouched in the shaft she had dug, she rolled him over onto his belly. His limbs flopped about and he babbled, "A demon attacks me. I'm blind here but I feel the wind of its wings," in a blurred monotone. She unplugged the energy unit and tossed it aloft, saying, "We should return this to the ship if we can."

Above, Scobie gave the object a morbid stare. It didn't even retain the warmth to make a little vapor, like his and hers, but lay quite inert. Its case was a metal box, thirty centimeters by fifteen by six, featureless except for two plug-in prongs on one of the broad sides. Controls built into the spacesuit circuits allowed you to start and stop the chemical reactions within and regulate their rate manually; but as a rule you left that chore to your thermostat and aerostat. Now those reactions had run their course. Until it was recharged, the cell was merely a lump.

Scobie leaned over to watch Broberg, some ten meters below him. She had extracted the reserve unit from Garcilaso's gear, inserted it properly at the small of his back, and secured it by clips on the bottom of his packframe. "Let's have your contribution, Colin," she said. Scobie dropped the meter of heavy-gauge insulated wire which was standard issue on extravehicular missions, in case you needed to make a special electrical connection or a repair. She joined it by Western Union splices to the two she already had, made a loop at the end, and, awkwardly reaching over her left shoulder, secured the opposite end by a hitch to the top of her packframe. The triple strand bobbed above her like an antenna.

Stooping, she gathered Garcilaso in her arms. The Iapetan weight of him and his apparatus was under ten kilos, of her and hers about the same. Theoretically she could jump straight out of the hole with her burden. In practice, her spacesuit was too hampering; constant-volume joints allowed considerable freedom of movement, but not as much as bare skin, especially when circum-Saturnian temperatures required extra insulation. Besides, if she could have reached the top, she could not have stayed. Soft ice would have crumbled beneath her fingers and she would have tumbled back down.

"Here goes," she said. "This had better be right the first time, Colin. I don't think Luis can take much jouncing."

"Kendrick, Ricia, where are you?" Garcilaso moaned. "Are you in Hell too?"

Scobie dug his heels into the ground near the edge and crouched ready. The loop in the wire rose to view. His right hand grabbed hold. He threw thimself backward, lest he slide forward, and felt the mass he had captured slam to a halt.

Anguish exploded in his rib cage. Somehow he dragged his burden to safety before he fainted.

He came out of that in a minute. "I'm okay," he rasped at the anxious voices of Broberg and Danzig. "Only let me rest awhile."

The physicist nodded and knelt to minister to the pilot. She stripped his packframe in order that he might lie flat on it, head and legs supported by the packs themselves. That would prevent significant heat loss by convection and cut loss by conduction. Still, his fuel cell would be drained faster than if he were on his feet, and first it had a terrible energy deficit to make up.

"The ice is clearing away inside his helmet," she reported. "Merciful Mary, the blood! Seems to be from the scalp, though; it isn't running anymore. His occiput must have been slammed against the vitryl. We ought to wear padded caps in these rigs. Yes, I know accidents like this haven't happened before, but—" She unclipped the flashlight at her waist, stooped, and shone it downward. "His eyes are open. The pupils—yes, a severe concussion, and likely a skull fracture, which may be hemorrhaging into the brain. I'm surprised he isn't vomiting. Did the cold prevent that? Will he start soon? He could choke on his own vomit, in there where nobody can lay a hand on him."

Scobie's pain had subsided to a bearable intensity. He rose, went over to look, whistled, and said, "I judge he's doomed unless we get him to the boat and give him proper care soon. Which isn't possible."

"Oh, Luis." Tears ran silently down Broberg's cheeks.

"You think he can't last till I bring my rope and we carry him back?" Danzig asked.

" 'Fraid not," Scobie replied. "I've taken paramedical courses, and in fact I've seen a case like this before. How come you know the symptoms, Jean?"

"I read a lot," she said dully.

"They weep, the dead children weep," Garcilaso muttered.

Danzig sighed. "Okay, then. I'll fly over to you."

"Huh?" burst from Scobie, and from Broberg: "Have you also gone insane?"

"No, listen," Danzig said fast. "I'm no skilled pilot, but I have the same basic training in this type of craft that everybody does who might ride in one. It's expendable: the rescue vessels can bring us back. There'd be no significant gain if I landed close to the glacier—I'd still have to make that rope and so forth—and we know from what happened to the probe that there would be a real hazard. Better I make straight for your crater."

"Coming down on a surface that the jets will vaporize out from under you?" Scobie snorted. "I bet Luis would consider that a hairy stunt. You, my friend, would crack up."

"Nu!" They could almost see the shrug. "A crash from low altitude, in this gravity, shouldn't do more than rattle my teeth. The blast will cut a hole clear to bedrock. True, the surrounding ice will collapse in around the hull and trap it. You may need to dig to reach the airlock, though I suspect thermal radiation from the cabin will keep the upper parts of the structure free. Even if the craft topples and strikes sidewise—in which case, it'll sink down into a deflating cushion—even if it did that on bare rock, it shouldn't be seriously damaged. It's designed to withstand heavier impacts." Danzig hesitated. "Of course, could be this would endanger you. I'm confident I won't fry you with the jets, assuming I descend near the middle and you're as far offside as you can get. Maybe, though, maybe I'd cause a . . . an ice quake that'll kill you. No sense in losing two more lives."

"Or three, Mark," Broberg said low. "In spite of your brave words, you could come to grief yourself."

"Oh, well, I'm an oldish man. I'm fond of living, yes, but you guys have a whole lot more years due you. Look, suppose the worst, suppose I don't just make a messy landing but wreck the boat utterly. Then Luis dies, but he would anyway. You two, however, would have access to the stores aboard, including those extra fuel cells. I'm willing to run what I consider to be a small risk of my own neck, for the sake of giving Luis a chance at survival."

"Um-m-m," went Scobie, deep in his throat. A hand strayed in search of his chin, while his gaze roved around the glimmer of the bowl.

"I repeat," Danzig proceeded, "if you think this might jeopardize you in any way, we scrub it. No heroics, please. Luis would surely agree, better three people safe and one dead than four stuck with a high probability of death."

"Let me think." Scobie was mute for minutes before he said: "No, I don't believe we'd get in too much trouble here. As I remarked earlier, the vicinity has had its avalanche and must be in a reasonably stable configuration. True, ice will volatilize. In the case of deposits with low boiling points, that could happen explosively and cause tremors. But the vapor will carry heat away so fast that only material in your immediate area should change state. I daresay that the fine-grained stuff will get shaken down the slopes, but it's got too low a density to do serious harm; for the most part, it should simply act like a brief snowstorm. The floor will make adjustments, of course, which may be rather violent. However, we can be above it—do you see that shelf of rock over yonder, Jean, at jumping height? It has to be part of a buried hill; solid. That's our place to wait. . . . Okay, Mark, it's go as far as we're concerned. I can't be absolutely certain, but who ever is about anything? It seems like a good bet."

"What are we overlooking?" Broberg wondered. She glanced down at Luis, who lay at her feet. "While we considered all the possibilities, Luis might die. Yes, fly if you want to, Mark, and God bless you."

But when she and Scobie had brought Garcilaso to the ledge, she gestured from Saturn to Polaris and: "I will sing a spell, I will cast what small magic is mine, in aid of the Dragon Lord, that he may deliver Alvarlan's soul from Hell," *says Ricia.*

IV

No reasonable person will blame any interplanetary explorer for miscalculations about the actual environment, especially when *some* decision has to be made, in haste and under stress. Occasional errors are inevitable. If we knew exactly what to expect throughout the Solar System, we would have no reason to explore it.

—Minamoto

The boat lifted. Cosmic dust smoked away from its jets. A hundred and fifty meters aloft, thrust lessened and it stood still on a pillar of fire.

Within the cabin was little noise, a low hiss and a bone-deep but nearly inaudible rumble. Sweat studded Danzig's features, clung glistening to his beard stubble, soaked his coverall and made it reek. He was about to undertake a maneuver as difficult as a rendezvous, and without guidance.

Gingerly, he advanced a vernier. A side jet woke. The boat lurched toward a nosedive. Danzig's hands jerked across the console. He must adjust the forces that held his vessel on high and those that pushed it horizontally, to get a resultant that would carry him eastward at a slow, steady pace. The vectors would change instant by instant, as they do when a human walks. The control computer, linked to the sensors, handled much of the balancing act, but not the crucial part. He must tell it what he wanted it to do.

His handling was inexpert. He had realized it would be. More altitude would have given him more margin for error, but deprived him of cues that his eyes found on the terrain beneath and the horizon ahead. Besides, when he reached the glacier he would perforce fly low to find his goal. He would be too busy for the precise celestial navigation he could have practiced afoot.

Seeking to correct his error, he overcompensated, and the

boat pitched in a different direction. He punched for "hold
steady" and the computer took over. Motionless again, he
took a minute to catch his breath, regain his nerve, rehearse in
his mind. Biting his lip, he tried afresh. This time he did not
quite approach disaster. Jets aflicker, the boat staggered
drunkenly over the moonscape.

The ice cliff loomed nearer and nearer. He saw its fragile
loveliness and regretted that he must cut a swathe of ruin. Yet
what did any natural wonder mean unless a conscious mind
was there to know it? He passed the lowest slope. It vanished
in billows of steam.

Onward. Beyond the boiling, right and left and ahead,
the Faerie architecture crumbled. He crossed the palisade.
Now he was a bare fifty meters above the surface, and the
clouds reached vengefully close before they disappeared into
vacuum. He squinted through the port and made the scanner
sweep a magnified overview across its screen, a search for his
destination.

A white volcano erupted. The outburst engulfed him.
Suddenly he was flying blind. Shocks belled through the hull
when upflung stones hit. Frost sheathed the craft; the scanner
screen went as blank as the ports. Danzig should have ordered
ascent, but he was inexperienced. A human in danger has less
of an instinct to jump than to run. He tried to scuttle sideways.
Without exterior vision to aid him, he sent the vessel tumbling
end over end. By the time he saw his mistake, less than a
second, it was too late. He was out of control. The computer
might have retrieved the situation after a while, but the glacier
was too close. The boat crashed.

"Hello, Mark?" Scobie cried. "Mark, do you read me? Where
are you, for Christ's sake?"

Silence replied. He gave Broberg a look which lingered.
"Everything seemed to be in order," he said, "till we heard a
shout, and a lot of racket, and nothing. He should've reached

us by now. Instead, he's run into trouble. I hope it wasn't lethal."

"What can we do?" she asked as redundantly. They needed talk, any talk, for Garcilaso lay beside them and his delirious voice was dwindling fast.

"If we don't get fresh fuel cells within the next forty or fifty hours, we'll be at the end of our particular trail. The boat should be someplace near. We'll have to get out of this hole under our own power, seems like. Wait here with Luis and I'll scratch around for a possible route."

Scobie started downward. Broberg crouched by the pilot.

"—alone forever in the dark—" she heard.

"No, Alvarlan." She embraced him. Most likely he could not feel that, but she could. "Alvarlan, hearken to me. This is Ricia. I hear in my mind how your spirit calls. Let me help. Let me lead you back to the light."

"Have a care," advised Scobie. "We're too damn close to rehypnotizing ourselves as it is."

"But I might, I just might get through to Luis and . . . comfort him. . . . Alvarlan, Kendrick and I escaped. He's seeking a way home for us. I'm seeking you. Alvarlan, here is my hand, come take it."

On the crater floor, Scobie shook his head, clicked his tongue, and unlimbered his equipment. Binoculars would help him locate the most promising areas. Devices that ranged from a metal rod to a portable geosonar would give him a more exact idea of what sort of footing lay buried under what depth of unclimbable sand-ice. Admittedly, the scope of such probes was very limited. He did not have time to shovel tons of material aside so that he could mount higher and test further. He would simply have to get some preliminary results, make an educated guess at which path up the side of the bowl would prove negotiable, and trust he was right.

He shut Broberg and Garcilaso out of his consciousness as much as he was able, and commenced work.

An hour later he was ignoring pain while clearing a strip

across a layer of rock. He thought a berg of good, hard frozen water lay ahead, but wanted to make sure.

"Jean! Colin! Do you read?"

Scobie straightened and stood rigid. Dimly he heard Broberg: "If I can't do anything else, Alvarlan, let me pray for your soul's repose."

"Mark!" ripped from Scobie. "You okay? What the hell happened?"

"Yeah, I wasn't too badly knocked around," Danzig said, "and the boat's habitable, though I'm afraid it'll never fly again. How are you? Luis?"

"Sinking fast. All right, let's hear the news."

Danzig described his misfortune. "I wobbled off in an unknown direction for an unknown distance. It can't have been extremely far, since the time was short before I hit. Evidently I plowed into a large, um, snowbank, which softened the impact but blocked radio transmission. It's evaporated from the cabin area now. I see tumbled whiteness around, and formations in the offing. . . . I'm not sure what damage the jacks and the stern jets suffered. The boat's on its side at about a forty-five-degree angle, presumably with rock beneath. But the after part is still buried in less whiffable stuff—water and CO_2 ices, I think—that's reached temperature equilibrium. The jets must be clogged with it. If I tried to blast, I'd destroy the whole works."

Scobie nodded. "You would, for sure."

Danzig's voice broke. "Oh, God, Colin! What have I done? I wanted to help Luis, but I may have killed you and Jean."

Scobie's lips tightened. "Let's not start crying before we're hurt. True, this has been quite a run of bad luck. But neither you nor I nor anybody could have known that you'd touch off a bomb underneath yourself."

"What was it? Have you any notion? Nothing of the sort ever occurred at rendezvous with a comet. And you believe the glacier is a wrecked comet, don't you?"

"Uh-huh, except that conditions have obviously modified it. The impact produced heat, shock, turbulence. Molecules got scrambled. Plasmas must have been momentarily present. Mixtures, compounds, clathrates, alloys—stuff formed that never existed in free space. We can learn a lot of chemistry here."

"That's why I came along. . . . Well, then, I crossed a deposit of some substance or substances that the jets caused to sublime with tremendous force. A certain kind of vapor refroze when it encountered the hull. I had to defrost the ports from inside after the snow had cooked off them."

"Where are you in relation to us?"

"I told you, I don't know. And I'm not sure I can determine it. The crash crumpled the direction-finding antenna. Let me go outside for a better look."

"Do that," Scobie said. "I'll keep busy meanwhile."

He did, until a ghastly rattling noise and Broberg's wail brought him at full speed back to the rock.

Scobie switched off Garcilaso's fuel cell. "This may make the difference that carries us through," he said low. "Think of it as a gift. Thanks, Luis."

Broberg let go of the pilot and rose from her knees. She straightened the limbs that had threshed about in the death struggle and crossed his hands on his breast. There was nothing she could do about the fallen jaw or the eyes that glared at heaven. Taking him out of this suit, here, would have worsened his appearance. Nor could she wipe the tears off her own face. She could merely try to stop their flow. "Goodbye, Luis," she whispered.

Turning to Scobie, she asked, "Can you give me a new job? Please."

"Come along," he directed. "I'll explain what I have in mind about making our way to the surface."

They were midway across the bowl when Danzig called. He had not let his comrade's dying slow his efforts, nor said much while it happened. Once, most softly, he had offered Kaddish.

"No luck," he reported like a machine. "I've traversed the largest circle I could while keeping the boat in sight, and found only weird, frozen shapes. I can't be a huge distance from you, or I'd seen an identifiably different sky, on this miserable little ball. You're probably within a twenty- or thirty-kilometer radius of me. But that covers a bunch of territory."

"Right," Scobie said. "Chances are you can't find us in the time we've got. Return to the boat."

"Hey, wait," Danzig protested. "I can spiral onward, marking my trail. I might come across you."

"It'll be more useful if you return," Scobie told him. "Assuming we climb out, we should be able to hike to you, but we'll need a beacon. What occurs to me is the ice itself. A small energy release, if it's concentrated, should release a large plume of methane or something similarly volatile. The gas will cool as it expands, recondense around dust particles that have been carried along—it'll steam—and the cloud ought to get high enough, before it evaporates again, to be visible from here."

"Gotcha!" A tinge of excitement livened Danzig's words. "I'll go straight to it. Make tests, find a spot where I can get the showiest result, and . . . how about I rig a thermite bomb? No, that might be too hot. Well, I'll develop a gadget."

"Keep us posted."

"But I, I don't think we'll care to chatter idly," Broberg ventured.

"No, we'll be working our tails off, you and I," Scobie agreed.

"Uh, wait," said Danzig. "What if you find you can't get clear to the top? You implied that's a distinct possibility."

"Well, then it'll be time for more radical procedures whatever they turn out to be," Scobie responded. "Frankly, at this moment my head is too full of . . . of Luis, and of choosing an optimum escape route, for much thought about anything else."

"M-m, yeah, I guess we've got an ample supply of trouble without borrowing more. Tell you what, though. After my beacon's ready to fire off, I'll make that rope we talked of. You might find you prefer having it to clean clothes and sheets when you arrive." Danzig was silent for seconds before he ended: "God damn it, you *will* arrive."

Scobie chose a point on the north side for his and Broberg's attempt. Two rock shelves jutted forth, near the floor and several meters higher, indicating that stone reached at least that far. Beyond, in a staggered pattern, were similar outcroppings of hard ices. Between them, and onward from the uppermost, which was scarcely more than halfway to the rim, was nothing but the featureless, footingless slope of powder crystals. Its angle of repose gave a steepness that made the surface doubly treacherous. The question, unanswerable save by experience, was how deeply it covered layers on which humans could climb, and whether such layers extended the entire distance aloft.

At the spot, Scobie signaled a halt. "Take it easy, Jean," he said. "I'll go ahead and commence digging."

"Why don't we go together? I have my own tool, you know."

"Because I can't tell how so large a bank of that pseudo-quicksand will behave. It might react to the disturbance by causing a gigantic slide."

She bridled. Her haggard countenance registered mutiny. "Why not me first, then? Do you suppose I always wait passive for Kendrick to save me?"

"As a matter of fact," he rapped, "I'll begin because my rib is giving me billy hell, which is eating away what strength I've got left. If we run into trouble, you can better come to my help than I to yours."

Broberg bent her neck. "Oh, I'm sorry. I must be in a

fairly bad state myself, I let false pride interfere with our business." Her look went toward Saturn, around which *Chronos* orbited, bearing her husband and children.

"You're forgiven." Scobie bunched his legs and sprang the five meters to the lower ledge. The next one up was slightly too far for such a jump, when he had no room for a running start.

Stooping, he scraped his trenching tool against the bottom of the declivity that sparkled before him, and shoveled. Grains poured from above, a billionfold, to cover what he cleared. He worked like a robot possessed. Each spadeful was nearly weightless, but the number of spadefuls was nearly endless. He did not bring the entire bowlside down on himself as he had half feared, half hoped. (If that didn't kill him, it would save a lot of toil.) A dry torrent went right and left over his ankles. Yet at last somewhat more of the underlying rock began to show.

From beneath, Broberg listened to him breathe. It sounded rough, often broken by a gasp or a curse. In his spacesuit, in the raw, wan sunshine, he resembled a knight who, in despite of wounds, did battle against a monster.

"All right," he called at last. "I think I've learned what to expect and how we should operate. It'll take the two of us."

"Yes . . . oh, yes, my Kendrick."

The hours passed. Ever so slowly, the sun climbed and the stars wheeled and Saturn waned.

Most places, the humans labored side by side. They did not require more than the narrowest of lanes, but unless they cut it wide to begin with, the banks to right and left would promptly slip down and bury it. Sometimes the conformation underneath allowed a single person at a time to work. Then the other could rest. Soon it was Scobie who must oftenest take advantage of that. Sometimes they both stopped briefly for food and drink and reclining on their packs.

Rock yielded to water ice. Where this rose very sharply

the couple knew it, because the sand-ice that they undercut would come down in a mass. After the first such incident, when they were nearly swept away, Scobie always drove his geologist's hammer into each new stratum. At any sign of danger, he would seize its handle and Broberg would cast an arm around his waist. Their other hands clutched their trenching tools. Anchored, but forced to strain every muscle, they would stand while the flood poured around them, knee-high, once even chest-high, seeking to bury them irretrievably deep in its quasi-fluid substance. Afterward they would confront a bare stretch. It was generally too steep to climb unaided, and they chipped footholds.

Weariness was another tide to which they dared not yield. At best, their progress was dismayingly slow. They needed little heat input to keep warm, except when they took a rest, but their lungs put a furious demand on air recyclers. Garcilaso's fuel cell, which they had brought along, could give a single person extra hours of life, though depleted as it was after coping with his hypothermia, the time would be insufficient for rescue by the teams from *Chronos*. Unspoken was the idea of taking turns with it. That would put them in wretched shape, chilled and stifling, but at least they would leave the universe together.

Thus it was hardly a surprise that their minds fled from pain, soreness, exhaustion, stench, despair. Without that respite, they could not have gone on as long as they did.

At ease for a few minutes, their backs against a blue-shimmering parapet which they must scale, they gazed across the bowl, where Garcilaso's suited body gleamed like a remote pyre, and up the curve opposite to Saturn. The planet shone lambent amber, softly banded, the rings a coronet which a shadow band across their arc seemed to make all the brighter. That radiance overcame sight of most nearby stars, but elsewhere they arrayed themselves multitudinous, in splendor, around the silver road which the galaxy clove between them.

"How right a tomb for Alvarlan," *Ricia says in a dreamer's murmur.*

"Has he died, then?" *Kendrick asks.*

"You do not know?"

"I have been too busied. After we won free of the ruins and I left you to recover while I went scouting, I encountered a troop of warriors. I escaped, but must needs return to you by devious, hidden ways." *Kendrick strokes Ricia's sunny hair.* "Besides, dearest dear, it has ever been you, not I, who had the gift of hearing spirits."

"Brave darling . . . yes, it is a glory to me that I was able to call his soul out of Hell. It sought his body, but that was old and frail and could not survive the knowledge it now had. Yet Alvarlan passed peacefully, and before he did, for his last magic he made himself a tomb from whose ceiling starlight will eternally shine."

"May he sleep well. But for us there is no sleep. Not yet. We have far to travel."

"Aye. But already we have left the wreckage behind. Look! Everywhere around in this meadow, anemones peep through the grass. A lark sings above."

"These lands are not always calm. We may well have more adventures ahead of us. But we shall meet them with high hearts."

Kendrick and Ricia rise to continue their journey.

Cramped on a meager ledge, Scobie and Broberg shoveled for an hour without broadening it much. The sand-ice slid from above as fast as they could cast it down. "We'd better quit this as a bad job," the man finally decided. "The best we've done is flatten the slope ahead of us a tiny bit. No telling how far inward the shelf goes before there's a solid layer on top. Maybe there isn't any."

"What shall we do instead?" Broberg asked in the same worn tone.

He jerked a thumb. "Scramble back to the level beneath and try a different direction. But first we absolutely require a break."

They spread kerofoam pads and sat. After a while during which they merely stared, stunned by fatigue, Broberg spoke.

"I go to the brook," *Ricia relates.* "It chimes under arches of green boughs. Light falls between them to sparkle on it. I kneel and drink. The water is cold, pure, sweet. When I raise my eyes, I see the figure of a young woman, naked, her tresses the color of leaves. A wood nymph. She smiles."

"Yes, I see her too," *Kendrick joins in.* "I approach carefully, not to frighten her off. She asks our names and errands. We explain that we are lost. She tells us how to find an oracle which may give us counsel."

They depart to find it.

Flesh could no longer stave off sleep. "Give us a yell in an hour, will you, Mark?" Scobie requested.

"Sure," Danzig said, "but will that be enough?"

"It's the most we can afford, after the setbacks we've had. We've come less than a third of the way."

"If I haven't talked to you," Danzig said slowly, "it's not because I've been hard at work, though I have been. It's that I figured you two were having a plenty bad time without me nagging you. However—do you think it's wise to fantasize the way you have been?"

A flush crept across Broberg's cheeks and down toward her bosom. "You listened, Mark?"

"Well, yes, of course. You might have an urgent word for me at any minute—"

"Why? What could you do? A game is a personal affair."

"Uh, yes, yes—"

Ricia and Kendrick have made love whenever they could. The accounts were never explicit, but the words were often passionate.

"We'll keep you tuned in when we need you, like for an alarm clock," Broberg clipped. "Otherwise we'll cut the circuit."

"But—look, I never meant to—"

"I know," Scobie sighed. "You're a nice guy, and I daresay we're overreacting. Still, that's the way it's got to be. Call us when I told you."

Deep within the grotto, the Pythoness sways on her throne, in the ebb and flow of her oracular dream. As nearly as Ricia and Kendrick can understand what she chants, she tells them to fare westward on the Stag Path until they meet a one-eyed graybeard who will give them further guidance; but they must be wary in his presence, for he is easily angered. They make obeisance and depart. On their way out, they pass the offering they brought. Since they had little with them other than garments and his weapons, the Princess gave the shrine her golden hair. The knight insists that, close-cropped, she remains beautiful.

"Hey, whoops, we've cleared us an easy twenty meters," Scobie said, albeit in a voice which weariness had hammered flat. *At first, the journey through the land of Nacre is a delight.*

His oath afterward had no more life in it. "Another blind alley, seems like." *The old man in the blue cloak and wide-brimmed hat was indeed wrathful when Ricia refused him her favors and Kendrick's spear struck his own aside. Cunningly, he has pretended to make peace and told them what road they should next take. But at the end of it are trolls. The wayfarers elude them and double back.*

"My brain's stumbling around in a fog," Scobie groaned. "My busted rib isn't exactly helping, either. If I don't get another nap I'll keep on making misjudgments till we run out of time."

"By all means, Colin," Broberg said. "I'll stand watch and rouse you in an hour."

"What?" he asked in dim surprise. "Why not join me and have Mark call us as he did before?"

She grimaced. "No need to bother him. I'm tired, yes, but not sleepy."

He lacked wit or strength to argue. "Okay," he said. He stretched his insulating pad on the ice, and toppled out of awareness.

Broberg settled herself next to him. They were halfway to the heights, but they had been struggling, with occasional breaks, for more than twenty hours, and progress grew harder and trickier even as they themselves grew weaker and more stupefied. If ever they reached the top and spied Danzig's signal, they would have something like a couple of hours' stiff travel to shelter.

Saturn, sun, stars shone through vitryl. Broberg smiled down at Scobie's face. He was no Greek god. Sweat, grime, unshavenness, the manifold marks of exhaustion were upon him, but— For that matter, she was scarcely an image of glamour herself.

Princess Ricia sits by her knight, where he slumbers in the dwarf's cottage, and strums a harp the dwarf lent her before he went off to his mine, and sings a lullaby to sweeten the dreams of Kendrick. When it is done, she passes her lips lightly across his, and drifts into the same gentle sleep.

Scobie woke a piece at a time. "Ricia, beloved," *Kendrick whispers, and feels after her. He will summon her up with kisses—*

He scrambled to his feet. "Judas priest!" She lay unmoving. He heard her breath in his earplugs, before the roaring of his pulse drowned it. The sun glared farther aloft, he could see it had moved, and Saturn's crescent had thinned more, forming sharp horns at its ends. He forced his eyes toward the watch on his left wrist.

"Ten hours," he choked.

He knelt and shook his companion. "Come, for Christ's sake!" Her lashes fluttered. When she saw the horror on his visage, drowsiness fled from her.

"Oh, no," she said. "Please, no."

Scobie climbed stiffly erect and flicked his main radio switch. "Mark, do you receive?"

"Colin!" Danzig chattered. "Thank God! I was going out of my head from worry."

"You're not off that hook, my friend. We just finished a ten-hour snooze."

"What? How far did you get first?"

"To about forty meters elevation. The going looks tougher ahead than in back. I'm afraid we won't make it."

"Don't *say* that, Colin," Danzig begged.

"My fault," Broberg declared. She stood rigid, fists doubled, her features a mask. Her tone was steely. "He was worn out, had to have a nap. I offered to wake him, but fell asleep myself."

"Not your fault, Jean," Scobie began.

She interrupted: "Yes. Mine. Perhaps I can make it good. Take my fuel cell. I'll still have deprived you of my help, of course, but you might survive and reach the boat anyway."

He seized her hands. They did not unclench. "If you imagine I could do that—"

"If you don't, we're both finished," she said unbendingly. "I'd rather go out with a clear conscience."

"And what about my conscience?" he shouted. Checking himself, he wet his lips and said fast: "Besides, you're not to blame. Sleep slugged you. If I'd been thinking, I'd have realized it was bound to do so, and contacted Mark. The fact that you didn't either shows how far gone you were yourself. And . . . you've got Tom and the kids waiting for you. Take my cell." He paused. "And my blessing."

"Shall Ricia forsake her true knight?"

"Wait, hold on, listen," Danzig called. "Look, this is terrible, but—oh, hell, excuse me, but I've got to remind you that dramatics only clutter the action. From what descriptions you've sent, I don't see how either of you can possibly proceed solo. Together, you might yet. At least you're rested—sore in

the muscles, no doubt, but clearer in the head. The climb
before you may prove easier than you think. Try!"

Scobie and Broberg regarded each other for a whole minute. A thawing went through her, and warmed him. Finally
they smiled and embraced. "Yeah, right," he growled. "We're
off. But first a bite to eat. I'm plain, old-fashioned hungry.
Aren't you?" She nodded.

"That's the spirit," Danzig encouraged them. "Uh, may I
make another suggestion? I am just a spectator, which is pretty
hellish but does give me an overall view. Drop that game of
yours."

Scobie and Broberg tautened.

"It's the real culprit," Danzig pleaded. "Weariness alone
wouldn't have clouded your judgment. You'd never have cut
me off, and— But weariness and shock and grief did lower
your defenses to the point where the damned game took
you over. You weren't yourselves when you feel asleep. You
were those dreamworld characters. They had no reason not to
cork off!"

Broberg shook her head violently. "Mark," said Scobie,
"you are correct about being a spectator. That means there are
some things you don't understand. Why subject yourself to the
torture of listening in, hour after hour? We'll call you back
from time to time, naturally. Take care." He broke the circuit.

"He's wrong," Broberg insisted.

Scobie shrugged. "Right or wrong, what difference? We
won't pass out again in the time we have left. The game didn't
handicap us as we traveled. In fact, it helped, by making the
situation feel less gruesome."

"Aye. Let us break our fast and set forth anew on our
pilgrimage."

The struggle grew stiffer. "Belike the White Witch has cast a
spell on this road," *says Ricia.*

"She shall not daunt us," *vows Kendrick.*

"No, never while we fare side by side, you and I, noblest of men."

A slide overcame them and swept them back a dozen meters. They lodged against a crag. After the flow had passed by, they lifted their bruised bodies and limped in search of a different approach. The place where the geologist's hammer lay was no longer accessible.

"What shattered the bridge?" *asks Ricia.*

"A giant," *answers Kendrick.* "I saw him as I fell into the river. He lunged at me, and we fought in the shallows until he fled. He bore away my sword in his thigh."

"You have your spear that Wayland forged," *Ricia says,* "and always you have my heart."

They stopped on the last small outcrop they uncovered. It proved to be not a shelf but a pinnacle of water ice. Around it glittered sand-ice, again quiescent. Ahead was a slope thirty meters in length, and then the rim, and stars.

The distance might as well have been thirty light-years. Whoever tried to cross would immediately sink to an unknown depth.

There was no point in crawling back down the bared side of the pinnacle. Broberg had clung to it for an hour while she chipped niches to climb by with her knife. Scobie's condition had not allowed him to help. If they sought to return, they could easily slip, fall, and be engulfed. If they avoided that, they would never find a new path. Less than two hours' worth of energy was left in their fuel cells. Attempting to push onward while swapping Garcilaso's back and forth would be an exercise in futility.

They settled themselves, legs dangling over the abyss, and held hands.

"I do not think the orcs can burst the iron door of this tower," *Kendrick says,* "but they will besiege us until we starve to death."

"You never yielded up your hope ere now, my knight," *replies Ricia, and kisses his temple.* "Shall we search about? These walls are unutterably ancient. Who knows what relics of wizardry lie forgotten within? A pair of phoenix-feather cloaks, that will bear us laughing through the sky to our home—?"

"I fear not, my darling. Our weird is upon us." *Kendrick touches the spear that leans agleam against the battlement.* "Sad and gray will the world be without you. We can but meet our doom bravely."

"Happily, since we are together." *Ricia's gamin smile breaks forth.* "I did notice that a certain room holds a bed. Shall we try it?"

Kendrick frowns. "Rather should we seek to set our minds and souls in order."

She tugs his elbow. "Later, yes. Besides—who knows?— when we dust off the blanket, we may find it is a Tarnkappe that will take us invisible through the enemy."

"You dream."

Fear stirs behind her eyes. "What if I do?" *Her words tremble.* "I can dream us free if you will help."

Scobie's fist smote the ice. "No!" he croaked. "I'll die in the world that is."

Ricia shrinks from him. He sees terror invade her. "You, you rave, beloved," *she stammers.*

He twisted about and caught her by the arms. "Don't you want to remember Tom and your boys?"

"Who—?"

Kendrick slumps. "I don't know. I have forgotten too."

She leans against him, there on the windy height. A hawk circles above. "The residuum of an evil enchantment, surely. Oh, my heart, my life, cast it from you! Help me find the means to save us." *Yet her entreaty is uneven, and through it speaks dread.*

Kendrick straightens. He lays hand on Wayland's spear, and it is as though strength flows thence, into him. "A spell in truth," *he says. His tone gathers force.* "I will not abide in its darkness, nor suffer it to blind and deafen you, my lady." *His gaze takes hold of hers, which cannot break away.* "There is but a single road to our freedom. It goes through the gates of death."

She waits, mute and shuddering.

"Whatever we do, we must die, Ricia. Let us fare hence as our own folk."

"I—no—I won't—I will—"

"You see before you the means of your deliverance. It is sharp, I am strong, you will feel no pain."

She bares her bosom. "Then quickly, Kendrick, before I am lost!"

He drives the weapon home. "I love you," *he says. She sinks at his feet.* "I follow you, my darling," *he says, withdrawing the steel, bracing the shaft against stone, and lunging forward. He falls beside her.* "Now we are free."

"That was . . . a nightmare." Broberg sounded barely awake.

Scobie's voice shook. "Necessary, I think, for both of us." He gazed straight before him, letting Saturn fill his eyes with dazzle. "Else we'd have stayed . . . insane? Maybe not, by definition. But we'd not have been in reality either."

"It would have been easier," she mumbled. "We'd never have known we were dying."

"Would you have preferred that?"

Broberg shivered. The slackness in her countenance gave place to the same tension that was in his. "Oh, no," she said, quite softly but in the manner of full consciousness. "No, you were right, of course. Thank you for your courage."

"You've always had as much guts as anybody, Jean. You must have more imagination than me." Scobie's hand chopped empty space in a gesture of dismissal. "Okay, we should call poor Mark and let him know. But first—" His words lost the cadence he had laid on them. "First—"

Her glove clasped his. "What, Colin?"

"Let's decide about that third unit—Luis's," he said with difficulty, still confronting the great ringed planet. "Your decision, actually, though we can discuss the matter if you want. I will not hog it for the sake of a few more hours. Nor will I share it; that would be a nasty way for us both to go out. However, I suggest you use it."

"To sit beside your frozen corpse?" she replied. "No. I wouldn't even feel the warmth, not in my bones—"

She turned toward him so fast that she nearly fell off the pinnacle. He caught her. *"Warmth!"* she screamed, shrill as the cry of a hawk on the wing. "Colin, we'll take our bones home!"

"In point of fact," said Danzig. "I've climbed onto the hull. That's high enough for me to see over those ridges and needles. I've got a view of the entire horizon."

"Good," grunted Scobie. "Be prepared to survey a complete circle quick. This depends on a lot of factors we can't predict. The beacon will certainly not be anything like as big as what you had arranged. It may be thin and short-lived. And, of course, it may rise too low for sighting at your distance." He cleared his throat. "In that case, we two have bought the farm. But we'll have made a hell of a try, which feels great by itself."

He hefted the fuel cell, Garcilaso's gift. A piece of heavy wire, insulation stripped off, joined the prongs. Without a regulator, the unit poured its maximum power through the short circuit. Already the strand glowed.

"Are you sure you don't want me to do it, Colin?" Broberg asked. "Your rib—"

He made a lopsided grin. "I'm nonetheless better designed by nature for throwing things," he said. "Allow me that much male arrogance. The bright idea was yours."

"It should have been obvious from the first," she said. "I think it would have been, if we weren't bewildered in our dream."

"M-m, often the simple answers are the hardest to find. Besides, we had to get this far or it wouldn't have worked, and the game helped mightily. . . . Are you set, Mark? Heave-ho!"

Scobie cast the cell as if it were a baseball, hard and far through the Iapetan gravity field. Spinning, its incandescent wire wove a sorcerous web across vision. It landed somewhere beyond the rim, on the glacier's back.

Frozen gases vaporized, whirled aloft, briefly recondensed before they were lost. A geyser stood white against the stars.

"I see you!" Danzig yelped. "I see your beacon, I've got my bearing, I'll be on my way! With rope and extra energy units and everything!"

Scobie sagged to the ground and clutched at his left side. Broberg knelt and held him, as if either of them could lay hand on his pain. No large matter. He would not hurt much longer.

"How high would you guess the plume goes?" Danzig inquired, calmer.

"About a hundred meters," Broberg replied after study.

"Oh, damn, these gloves do make it awkward punching the calculator. . . . Well, to judge by what I observe of it, I'm between ten and fifteen klicks off. Give me an hour or a tad more to get there and find your exact location. Okay?"

Broberg checked gauges. "Yes, by a hair. We'll turn our thermostats down and sit very quietly to reduce oxygen demand. We'll get cold, but we'll survive."

"I may be quicker," Danzig said. "That was a worst-case estimate. All right, I'm off. No more conversation till we meet. I won't take any foolish chances, but I will need my wind for making speed."

Faintly, those who waited heard him breathe, heard his hastening footfalls. The geyser died.

They sat, arms around waists, and regarded the glory which encompassed them. After a silence, the man said, "Well, I suppose this means the end of the game. For everybody."

"It must certainly be brought under strict control," the woman answered. "I wonder, though, if they will abandon it altogether—out here."

"If they must, they can."

"Yes. We did, you and I, didn't we?"

They turned face to face, beneath that star-beswarmed, Saturn-ruled sky. Nothing tempered the sunlight that revealed them to each other, she a middle-aged wife, he a man ordinary except for his aloneness. They would never play again. They could not.

A puzzled compassion was in her smile. "Dear friend—" she began.

His uplifted palm warded her from further speech. "Best we don't talk unless it's essential," he said. "That'll save a little oxygen, and we can stay a little warmer. Shall we try to sleep?"

Her eyes widened and darkened. "I dare not," she confessed. "Not till enough time has gone past. Now, I might dream."

Disciples

Gardner Dozois

I was roaming the post-midnight halls of a science fiction convention hotel not long ago, trying to find a party still functional, when I heard great waves of laughter filtering through a locked door. I knocked and was informed that I had stumbled on the "bad joke" party; to gain admission you had to tell a joke bad enough to elicit universal groans. I did dredge one out of childhood memories, and entered to find—of course—Gardner Dozois, the party's perpetrator, surrounded by dozens of adoring science fiction fans. The party turned out to be one of the most entertaining times I've ever had, because although the rest of us did tell a joke now and then, it was mainly The Gardner Dozois Show, tale after hilarious tale emerging from the shaggy heap enthroned in the corner.

Gardner is a natural-born storyteller, with great gifts of gesture, accent, timing. He can hypnotize a crowd in seconds and keep them laughing for hours. But the aforementioned Buchwald Paradox is very much at work here: Gardner's writing is anything but jolly; his work is predominantly concerned with the dark face of life, with tragedy and pathos. His writing is a unique brand of gritty naturalism, done with terrible accuracy but also compassion and grace. As witness this tale of Nicky the Horse.

Nicky the Horse was a thin, weasely-looking man with long, dirty black hair that hung down either side of his face in greasy ropes, like inkmarks against the pallor of his skin. He was clean-shaven and hollow-cheeked, and had a thin but rubbery lower lip upon which his small yellowed teeth were forever biting, seizing the lip suddenly and worrying it, like a terrier seizing a rat. He wore a grimy purple sweater under a torn tan jacket enough sizes too small to look like something an organ grinder's monkey might wear, one pocket torn nearly off and both elbows worn through. Thrift-store jeans and a ratty pair of sneakers he'd once found in a garbage can behind the YMCA completed his wardrobe. No underwear. A crucifix gleamed around his neck, stainless steel coated to look like silver. Track marks, fading now, ran down both his arms, across his stomach, down his thighs, but he'd been off the junk for months; he was down to an occasional Red Devil, supplemented by the nightly quart of cheap chianti he consumed as he lay in the dark on his bare mattress at the Lordhouse, a third-floor loft in a converted industrial warehouse squeezed between a package store and a Rite-Aid.

He had just scavenged some two-day-old doughnuts from a pile of boxes behind a doughnut store on Broad Street, and bought a paper container of coffee from a Greek delicatessen where the counterman (another aging hippie, faded flower tattos still visible under the bristly black hair on his arms) usually knocked a nickel or two off the price for old times' sake. Now he was sitting on the white marble steps of an old brownstone row house, eating his breakfast. His breath steamed in the chill morning air. Even sitting still, he was in constant motion: his fingers drumming, his feet shuffling, his eyes flicking nervously back and forth as one thing or another—a car, some windblown trash, pigeons taking to the air—arrested and briefly held his attention; at such times his shoulders would momentarily hunch, as if he expected something to leap out at him.

Across the street, a work crew was renovating another old brownstone, swarming over the building's partially stripped skeleton like carrion beetles; sometimes a cloud of plaster powder and brick dust would puff from the building's broken doorway, like foul air from a dying mouth. Winos and pimps and whores congregated on the corner, outside a flophouse hotel, their voices coming to Nicky thin and shrill over the rumbling and farting of traffic. Occasionally a group of med students would go by, or a girl with a dog, or a couple of Society Hill faggots in designer jeans and expensive turtlenecks, and Nicky would call out "Jesus loves you, man," usually to no more response than a nervous sideways glance. One faggot smirked knowingly at him, and a collegiate-jock type got a laugh out of his buddies by shouting back "You bet your ass he does, honey." A small, intense-looking woman with short-cropped hair gave him the finger. Another diesel dyke, Nicky thought resignedly. "Jesus loves *you*, man," he called after her, but she didn't look back.

When his butt began to feel as if it had turned to stone, he got up from the cold stoop and started walking again, pausing only long enough to put a flyer for the Lordhouse on a lamppost, next to a sticker that said EAT THE RICH. He walked on, past a disco, a gay bookstore, a go-go bar, a boarded-up storefront with a sign that read LIVE NUDE MODELS, a pizza stand, slanting south and east now, through a trash-littered concrete park full of sleeping derelicts and arrogantly strutting pigeons—stopping now and then to panhandle and pass out leaflets, drifting on again.

He'd been up to Reading Terminal early that morning, hoping to catch the shoppers who came in from the suburbs on commuter trains, but the Hairy Krishnaites had been there already, out in force in front of the station, and he didn't like to compete with other panhandlers, particularly fucking *groups* of them with fucking *bongos*. The Krishnaites made him nervous anyway—with their razor-shaved pates and their air of panting, puppyish eagerness, they always reminded him of ROTC second lieutenants, fresh out of basic training. Once, in front of the Bellevue-Stratford, he'd seen a fight between a Krishnaite and a Moonie, the two of them arguing louder and louder, toe to toe, until suddenly they were beating each other over the head with thick packets of devotional literature, the leaflets swirling loose around them like flocks of startled birds. He'd had to grin at that one, but some of the panhandling groups were *mean*, particularly the political groups, particularly the niggers. They'd kick your ass up between your shoulder blades if they caught you poaching on their turf; they'd have your balls for garters.

No, you scored better if you worked alone. Always alone.

He ended up on South Street, down toward the Two-Street end, taking up a position between the laundromat and the plant store. It was much too early for the trendy people to be out, the "artists," the night people, but they weren't such hot prospects anyway. It was Saturday, and that meant there were tourists out, in spite of the early hour, in spite of the fact that it had been threatening to snow all day; it was cold, yes, but not as cold as it had been the rest of the week, the sun was peeking sporadically out from behind banks of dirty gray clouds, and maybe this would be the only halfway decent day left before winter really set in. No, they were here all right, the tourists, strolling up and down through this hick Greenwich Village, peering into the quaint little stores, the *boutiques*, the head shops full of tourist-trap junk, the artsy bookstores, staring at the resident freaks as though they were on display at the zoo, relishing the occasional dangerous whiff of illicit smoke in the air, the loud blare of music that they wouldn't have tolerated for a moment at home.

Of course, he wasn't the only one feeding on this rich stream of marks: there was a juggler outside of the steak-sandwich shop in the next block, a small jazz band—a xylophone, a bass, and an electric piano—in front of the Communist coffeehouse across the street, and, next to the upholsterer's, a fat man in a fur-lined parka who was tonelessly chanting "incense sticks check it out one dollar incense sticks check it out one dollar" without break or intonation. Such competition Nicky could deal with; in fact, he was contemptuous of it.

"Do you have your house in *order*?" he said in a conversational but carrying voice, starting his own spiel, pushing leaflets at a businessman who ignored him, at a strolling young married couple who smiled but shook their heads, at a middle-aged housewife in clogs and a polka-dot kerchief, who took a flyer reflexively and then, a few paces away, stopped to peek at it surreptitiously. "Did you know the Lord is coming, man? The Lord is *coming*. Spare some change for the Lord's work?" This last remark shot at the housewife, who looked uneasily around and then suddenly thrust a quarter at him. She hurried away, clutching her Lordhouse flyer to her chest as if it were a baby the gypsies were after.

Panhandling was an art, man, an *art*—and so, of course, of *course*, was the more important task of spreading the Lord's word. That was what *really* counted. Of course. Nevertheless, he brought more fucking change into the Lordhouse than any of the other converts who were out pounding the pavement every day, fucking-A, you better believe it. He'd always been a good panhandler, even before he'd seen the light, and what did it was making maximum use of your time. Knowing who to ask and who not to waste time on was the secret. College students, professional people, and young white male businessmen made the best marks—later, when the businessmen had aged into senior executives, the chances of their coming across went way down. Touristy types were good, straight suburbanites in the twenty-five-to-fifty age bracket, particularly a man out strolling with his wife. A man walking by himself was much more likely to give you something than a man walking in company with another man—faggots were sometimes an exception here. Conversely, women in pairs—especially prosperous *hausfraus*, although groups of teenage girls were pretty good too—were much more likely to give you change than were women walking by themselves; the housewife of a moment before had been an exception, but she had all the earmarks of someone who was just religious enough to feel guilty about not being more so. Brisk woman-executive types almost never gave you anything, or even took a leaflet. Servicemen in uniform were easy touches. Old people never gave you diddly-shit, except sometimes a well-heeled little old white lady would, especially a W.H.L.O.W.L. who had religion herself, although they could also be more trouble than their money was worth. There were a lot of punkers in this neighborhood, with their fifties crewcuts and greasy motercycle jackets, but Nicky usually left them alone; the punks were more violent and less gullible than the hippies had been back in the late sixties, the Golden Age of Panhandling. The few remaining hippies—and the college kids who passed for hippies these days—came across often enough that Nicky made a point of hitting on them, although he gritted his teeth each time he did; they were by far the most likely to be wiseasses—once he'd told one, "Jesus is coming to our town," and the kid had replied, "I hope he's got a reservation, then—the hotels are booked *solid*." Wiseasses. Those were also the types who would occasionally quote Scripture to him, coming up with some goddamn verse or other to refute anything he said. That made him uneasy. Nicky had never really actually *read* the Bible that much, although he'd meant to; he had the knowledge *intuitively*, because the Spirit was in him. At that, the hippie wiseasses were easier to take than the Puerto Ricans, who would pretend they didn't understand what he wanted and give him only tight bursts of superfast Spanish. The Vietnamese, now, being seen on the street with increasing frequency these days, the Vietnamese quite often *did* give something, perhaps because they felt that they were required to. Nicky wasn't terribly fond of Jews, either, but it was amazing how often they'd come across, even for a pitch about *Jesus*—all that guilt they imbibed with their mother's milk, he guessed. On the other hand, he mostly stayed clear of niggers; sometimes you could score off a middle-aged tom in a business suit or some graying workman, but the young street dudes were impossible, and there was always the chance that some coked-up young stud would turn mean on you and maybe pull a knife. Occasionally you could get money out of a member of that endless, seemingly cloned legion of short, fat, cone-shaped black women, but that had its special dangers too, particularly if they turned out to be devout Baptists, or snake-handlers, or whatever the fuck they were; one woman had screamed at him, "Don't talk to me about Jesus! Don't talk to *me* about Jesus! Don't talk to me about *Jesus*!" Then she'd hit him with her purse.

"The Last Days are at hand!" Nicky called. "The Last Days are *coming*, man. The Lord is coming to our town, and the wicked will be left *behind*, man. The *Lord* is coming." Nicky shoved a leaflet into someone's hand and the someone shoved it right back. Nicky shrugged. "Come to the Lordhouse tonight, brothers and sisters! Come and get your soul *together*." Someone paused, hesitated, took a leaflet. "Spare change? Spare change for the Lord's work? Every *penny* does the Lord's work. . . ."

The morning passed, and it grew colder. About half of Nicky's leaflets were gone, although many of them littered the sidewalk a few paces away, where people had discarded them once they thought that they were far enough from Nicky not to be noticed doing so. The sun had been swallowed by clouds, and once again it looked like it was going to snow, although once again it did not. Nicky's coat was too small to button, but he turned his collar up and put his hands in his pockets. The stream of tourists had pretty much run dry for the moment, and he was just thinking about getting some lunch, about going down to the hotdog stand on the corner where the black dudes stood jiving and handslapping, their giant radios blaring on their shoulders, he was just *thinking* about it when, at that very moment, as though conjured up by the thought, Saul Edelmann stepped out of the stand and walked briskly toward him.

"Shit in my hat," Nicky muttered to himself. He'd collected more than enough to buy lunch, but, because of the cold, not that *much* more. And Father Delardi, the unfrocked priest—the *unfairly* unfrocked priest—who had founded their order and who ran it with both love and, yessir, an iron hand— Father Delardi didn't *like* it when they came in off the streets at the end of the day with less than a certain amount of dough. Nicky had been hoping that he could con Saul into giving him a free hotdog, as he sometimes could, as Saul sometimes *had*, and now here was Saul himself, off on some dumbshit errand, bopping down the street as fat and happy as a clam (although how happy *were* clams anyway, come to think about it?), which meant that he, Nicky, was fucked.

"Nicky! My main man!" said Saul, who prided himself on an ability to speak jivey street patois that he definitely did not possess. He was a plump-cheeked man with modish-length gray-streaked hair, cheap black plastic-framed glasses, and a neatly trimmed mustache. Jews were supposed to have big noses, or so Nicky had always heard, but Saul's nose was small and upturned, as if there were an Irishman in the wood-pile somewhere.

"Hey, man," Nicky mumbled listlessly. Bad *enough* that he wasn't going to get his free hotdog—now he'd have to make friendly small talk with this dipshit in order to protect his investment in free hotdogs yet to come. Nicky sighed and un-limbered his shit-eating grin. "Hey, man! How you been, Saul? What's *happenin'*, man?"

"What's happening?" Saul said jovially, responding to Nicky as if he were really asking a question instead of emit-ting ritual noise. "Now how can I even begin to tell you what's happening, Nicky?" He was radiant today, Saul was, full of bouncy energy, rocking back and forth as he talked, unable to stand still, smiling a smile that revealed teeth some Yiddish momma had sunk a lot of dough into over the years. "I'm glad you came by today, though. I wanted to be sure to say good-bye if I could."

"Good-bye?"

Saul's smile became broader and broader. "Yes, good-bye! This is it, *boychick*. I'm off! You won't see me again after today."

Nicky peered at him suspiciously. "You goin' away?"

"You bet your ass I am, kid," Saul said, and then laughed. "Today I turned my half of the business over to Carlos, signed all the papers, took care of everything nice and legal. And now I'm free and clear, free as a damn bird, kid."

"You sold your half of the stand to *Carlos*?"

"Not sold, *boychick*—gave. I *gave* it to him. Not one red cent did I take."

Nicky gaped at him. "You *gave your business away*, man?"

Saul beamed. "Kid—I gave *everything* away. The car: I gave that to old Ben Miller, who washes dishes at the Green Onion. I gave up the lease on my apartment, gave away my furniture, gave away my savings—if you'd've been here yesterday, Nicky, I would've given you something too."

"Shit!" Nicky said harshly. "You go crazy, man, or what?" He choked back an outburst of bitter profanity. Missed out again! Screwed out of getting *his* yet *again*!

"I don't *need* any of that stuff anymore, Nicky," Saul said. He tapped the side of his nose, smiled. "Nicky—He's come."

"Who?"

"The *Messiah*. He's come! He's finally come! Today's the day the Messiah comes, after all those thousands of years—think of it, Nicky!"

Nicky's eyes narrowed. "What the fuck you talkin' about, man?"

"Don't you *ever* read the paper, Nicky, or listen to the

radio? The Messiah has come. His name is Murray Kupferberg, He was born in Pittsburgh—"

"*Pittsburgh?*" Nicky gasped.

"—and He used to be a plumber there. But He *is* the Messiah. Most of the scholars and the rabbis deny Him, but He really *is*. The Messiah has really come, at last!"

Nicky gave that snorting bray of laughter, blowing out his rubbery lips, that was one reason—but *only* one reason—why he was sometimes called Nicky the Horse. "*Jesus* is the Messiah, man," he said scornfully.

Saul smiled good-naturedly, shrugged, spread his hands. "For you, maybe he *is*. For you people, the *goyim*, maybe he *is*. But *we've* been waiting for more than five thousand years—and at last He's come."

"Murray Kupferberg? From *Pittsburgh?*"

"Murray Kupferberg," Saul repeated firmly, calmly. "From Pittsburgh. He's coming *here*, *today*. Jews are gathering here today from all over the country, from all over the world, and *today*—right *here*—He's going to gather His people to Him—"

"You stupid fucking kike!" Nicky screamed, his anger breaking free at last. "You're crazy in the head, man. You've been *conned.* Some fucking con man has taken you for *everything*, and you're too fucking dumb to see it! All that *stuff*, man, all that good stuff *gone*—" He ran out of steam, at a loss for words. All that good stuff gone, and he hadn't gotten *any* of it. After kissing up to this dipshit for all those years . . . "Oh, you dumb kike," he whispered.

Saul seemed unoffended. "You're wrong, Nicky—but I haven't got time to argue with you. *Shalom.*" He stuck out his hand, but Nicky refused to shake it. Saul shrugged, smiled again, and then walked briskly away, turning the corner onto Sixth Street.

Nicky sullenly watched him go, still shaking with rage. Screwed again! There went his free hotdogs, flying away into the blue on fucking gossamer wings. Carlos was a hard dude, a streetwise dude—Carlos wasn't going to *give* him anything, Carlos wouldn't stop to piss on Nicky's head if Nicky's *hair* was on fire. Nicky stared at the tattered and overlapping posters on the laundromat wall, and the faces of long-dead politicians stared back at him from among the notices for lost cats and the ads for Czech films and karate classes. Suddenly he was cold, and he shivered.

The rest of the day was a total loss. Nicky's sullen mood threw his judgment and his timing off, and the tourists were thinning out again anyway. The free-form jazz of the Communist coffeehouse band was getting on his nerves—the fucking xylophone player was chopping away as if he were making sukiyaki at Benihana of Tokyo—and the smell of sauerkraut would float over from the hotdog stand every now and then to torment him. And it kept getting colder and colder. Still, some obscure, self-punishing instinct kept him from moving on.

Late in the afternoon, what amounted to a little unofficial parade went by—a few hundred people walking in the street, heading west against the traffic, many of them barefoot in spite of the bitter cold. If they were all Jews on their way to the Big Meeting, as Nicky suspected, then some of them must have been black Jews, East Indian Jews, even *Chinese* Jews.

Smaller groups of people straggled by for the next hour or so, all headed uptown. The traffic seemed to have stopped completely, even the crosstown buses; this rally must be *big*, for the city to've done that.

The last of the pilgrims to go by was a stout, fiftyish Society Hill matron with bleached blue hair, walking calmly in the very center of the street. She was wearing an expensive ermine stole, although she was barefoot and her feet were bleeding. As she passed Nicky, she suddenly laughed, unwrapped the stole from around her neck, and threw it into the air, walking on without looking back. The stole landed across the shoulders of the Communist xylophone player, who goggled blankly for a moment, then stared wildly around him—his eyes widening comically—and then bolted, clutching the stole tightly in his hands; he disappeared down an alleyway.

"You bitch!" Nicky screamed. "Why not *me*? Why didn't you give it to *me*?"

But she was gone, the street was empty, and the gray afternoon sky was darkening toward evening.

"The Last Days are coming," Nicky told the last few strolling tourists and window shoppers. "The strait gate is narrow, sayeth the Lord, and few will fit *in*, man." But his heart wasn't in it anymore. Nicky waited, freezing, his breath puffing out in steaming clouds, stamping his feet to restore circulation, slapping his arms, doing a kind of shuffling jig that—along with his too-small jacket—made him look more than ever like an organ grinder's monkey performing for some unlikely kind of alms. He didn't understand why he didn't just give up and go back to the Lordhouse. He was beginning to think yearningly of the hot stew they would be served there after they had turned the day's take in to Father Delardi, the hymn-singing later, and after that the bottle of strong raw wine, his mattress in the rustling, fart-smelling communal darkness, oblivion. . . .

There was . . . a sound, a note, a chord, an upswelling of something that the mind interpreted as music, as blaring iron trumpets, only because it had no other referents by which to understand it. The noise, the music, the *something*—it swelled until it shook the empty street, the buildings, the world, shook the bones in the flesh and the very marrow in the bones, until it filled every inch of the universe like hot wax being poured into a mold.

Nicky looked up.

As he watched, a crack appeared in the dull gray sky. The sky split open, and behind the sky was nothingness, a wedge of darkness so terrible and absolute that it hurt the eyes to look at it. The crack widened, the wedge of darkness grew. Light began to pour through the crack in the sky, blinding white light more intense and frightening than the darkness had been. Squinting against that terrible radiance, his eyes watering, Nicky saw tiny figures rising into the air far away, thousands upon thousands of human figures floating up into

the sky, falling *up* while the iron music shook the firmament
around them, people falling up and into and through the
crack in the sky, merging into that wondrous and awful river
of light, fading, disappearing, until the last one was gone.

The crack in the sky closed. The music grumbled and
rumbled away into silence.

Everything was still.

Snowflakes began to squeeze like slow tears from the
slate-gray sky.

Nicky stayed there for hours, staring upward until his
neck was aching and the last of the light was gone, but after
that nothing else happened at all.

The Quickening

Michael Bishop

Michael Bishop seems to be that rare creature, a modest writer. In response to a request for biographical information, he responds only that this Nebula is the first fiction award he has won, though he has been on the final ballot for both Nebula and Hugo awards in the past, and that his most recent books are No Enemy but Time, *from Timescape,* One Winter in Eden, *a short-story collection, and* What Made Stevie Crye? *his first horror novel, both from Arkham House.*

I

Lawson came out of his sleep feeling drugged and disoriented. Instead of the susurrus of traffic on Rivermont and the early-morning barking of dogs, he heard running feet and an unsettling orchestration of moans and cries. No curtains screened or softened the sun that beat down on his face, and an incandescent blueness had replaced their ceiling. "Marlena," Lawson said doubtfully. He wondered if one of the children was sick and told himself that he ought to get up to help.

But when he tried to rise, scraping the back of his hand on a stone set firmly in mortar, he found that his bed had become a parapet beside a river flowing through an unfamiliar city. He was wearing, instead of the green Chinese-peasant pajamas that Marlena had given him for Christmas, a suit of khaki 1505s from his days in the Air Force and a pair of ragged Converse sneakers. Clumsily, as if deserting a mortuary slab, Lawson leapt away from the wall. In his sleep, the world had turned over. The forms of a bewildered anarchy had begun to assert themselves.

The city—and Lawson knew that it sure as hell wasn't Lynchburg, that the river running through it wasn't the James—was full of people. A few, their expressions terrified and their postures defensive, were padding past Lawson on the boulevard beside the parapet. Many shrieked or babbled as they ran. Other human shapes, dressed not even remotely alike, were lifting themselves bemusedly from paving stones, or riverside benches, or the gutter beyond the sidewalk. Their grogginess and their swiftly congealing fear, Lawson realized, mirrored his own: like him, these people were awakening to nightmare.

Because the terrible fact of his displacement seemed more important than the myriad physical details confronting him, it was hard to take in everything at once—but Lawson tried to balance and integrate what he saw.

The city was foreign. Its architecture was a clash of the Gothic and the sterile, pseudo-adobe Modern, one style to either side of the river. On this side, palm trees waved their dreamy fronds at precise intervals along the boulevard, and toward the city's interior an intricate cathedral tower defined by its great height nearly everything beneath it. Already the sun crackled off the rose-colored tower with an arid fierceness that struck Lawson, who had never been abroad, as Mediterranean. . . . Off to his left was a bridge leading into a more modern quarter of the city, where beige and brick-red highrises clustered like tombstones. On both sides of the bridge buses, taxicabs, and other sorts of motorized vehicles were stalled or abandoned in the thoroughfares.

Unfamiliar, Lawson reflected, but not unearthly—he recognized things, saw the imprint of a culture somewhat akin to his own. And, for a moment, he let the inanimate bulk of the city and the languor of its palms and bougainvillea crowd out of his vision the human horror show taking place in the streets.

A dark woman in a sari hurried past. Lawson lifted his hand to her. Dredging up a remnant of a high-school language course, he shouted, *"¿Habla Español?"* The woman quickened her pace, crossed the street, recrossed it, crossed it again; her movements were random, motivated, it seemed, by panic and the complicated need to *do* something.

At a black man in a loincloth farther down the parapet, Lawson shouted, "This is Spain! We're somewhere in Spain! That's all I know! Do you speak English? Spanish? Do you know what's happened to us?"

The black man, grimacing so that his skin went taut across his cheekbones, flattened himself atop the wall like a lizard. His elbows jutted, his eyes narrowed to slits. Watching him, Lawson perceived that the man was listening intently to a sound that had been steadily rising in volume ever since Lawson had opened his eyes: the city was wailing. From courtyards, apartment buildings, taverns, and plazas, an eerie and discordant wail was rising into the bland blue indifference of the day. It consisted of many strains. The Negro in the loincloth seemed determined to separate these and pick out the ones that spoke most directly to him. He tilted his head.

"Spain!" Lawson yelled against this uproar. *"¡España!"*

The black man looked at Lawson, but the hieroglyph of recognition was not among those that glinted in his eyes. As if to dislodge the wailing of the city, he shook his head. Then, still crouching lizard-fashion on the wall, he began methodically banging his head against its stones. Lawson, helplessly

aghast, watched him until he had knocked himself insensible
in a sickening, repetitive spattering of blood.

But Lawson was the only one who watched. When he
approached the man to see if he had killed himself, Lawson's
eyes were seduced away from the African by a movement in
the river. A bundle of some sort was floating in the greasy
waters below the wall—an infant, clad only in a shirt. The tie-
strings on the shirt trailed out behind the child like the severed, wavering legs of a water-walker. Lawson wondered if, in
Spain, they even had water-walkers. . . .

Meanwhile, still growing in volume, there crooned above
the highrises and Moorish gardens the impotent air-raid siren
of 400,000 human voices. Lawson cursed the sound. Then he
covered his face and wept.

II

The city was Seville. The river was the Guadalquivir. Lynchburg and the James River, around which Lawson had grown
up as the eldest child of an itinerant fundamentalist preacher,
were several thousand miles and one helluva big ocean away.
You couldn't get there by swimming, and if you imagined that
your loved ones would be waiting for you when you got back,
you were probably fantasizing the nature of the world's
changed reality. No one was where he or she belonged anymore, and Lawson knew himself lucky even to realize where
he was. Most of the dispossessed, displaced people inhabiting
Seville today *didn't* know that much; all they knew was the
intolerable cruelty of their uprooting, the pain of separation
from husbands, wives, children, lovers, friends. These things,
and fear.

The bodies of infants floated in the Guadalquivir; and
Lawson, from his early reconnoiterings of the city on a motor
scooter that he had found near the Jardines de Cristina park,
knew that thousands of adults already lay dead on streets and
in apartment buildings—victims of panic-inspired beatings on

their own traumatized hearts. Who knew exactly what was going on in the morning's chaos? Babel had come again and with it, as part of the package, the utter dissolution of all family and societal ties. You couldn't go around a corner without encountering a child of some exotic ethnic caste, her face snot-glazed, sobbing loudly or maybe running through a crush of bodies calling out names in an alien tongue.

What were you supposed to do? Wheeling by on his motor scooter, Lawson either ignored these children or searched their faces to see how much they resembled his daughters.

Where was Marlena now? Where were Karen and Hannah? Just as he played deaf to the cries of the children in the boulevards, Lawson had to harden himself against the implications of these questions. As dialects of German, Chinese, Bantu, Russian, Celtic, and a hundred other languages rattled in his ears, his scooter rattled past a host of cars and buses with uncertain-seeming drivers at their wheels. Probably he too should have chosen an enclosed vehicle. If these frustrated and angry drivers, raging in polyglot defiance, decided to run over him, they could do so with impunity. Who would stop them?

Maybe—in Istanbul, or La Paz, or Mangalore, or Jönköping, or Boise City, or Kaesŏng—his own wife and children had already lost their lives to people made murderous by fear or the absence of helmeted men with pistols and billy sticks. Maybe Marlena and his children were dead. . . .

I'm in Seville, Lawson told himself, cruising. He had determined the name of the city soon after mounting the motor scooter and going by a sign that said *Plaza de Toros de Sevilla.* A circular stadium of considerable size near the river. The bullring. Lawson's Spanish was just good enough to decipher the signs and posters plastered on its walls. *Corrida a las cinco de la tarde.* (García Lorca, he thought, unsure of where the name had come from.) *Sombra y sol.* That morning, then, he took the scooter around the stadium three or four times and then shot off toward the center of the city.

Lawson wanted nothing to do with the nondescript high-rises across the Guadalquivir, but had no real idea what he was going to do on the Moorish and Gothic side of the river, either. All he knew was that the empty bullring, with its dormant potential for death, frightened him. On the other hand, how did you go about establishing order in a city whose population had not willingly chosen to be there?

Seville's population, Lawson felt sure, had been redistributed across the face of the globe, like chess pieces flung from a height. The population of every other human community on Earth had undergone similar displacements. The result, as if by malevolent design, was chaos and suffering. Your ears eventually tried to shut out the audible manifestations of this pain, but your eyes held you accountable and you hated yourself for ignoring the wailing Arab child, the assaulted Polynesian woman, the blue-eyed old man bleeding from the palms as he prayed in the shadow of a department-store awning. Very nearly, you hated yourself for surviving.

Early in the afternoon, at the entrance to the Calle de las Sierpes, Lawson got off his scooter and propped it against a wall. Then he waded into the crowd and lifted his right arm above his head.

"I speak English!" he called. *"¡ Y hablo un poco Español!* Any who speak English or Spanish please come to me!"

A man who might have been Vietnamese or Kampuchean, or even Malaysian, stole Lawson's motor scooter and rode it in a wobbling zigzag down the Street of the Serpents. A heavyset blond woman with red cheeks glared at Lawson from a doorway, and a twelve- or thirteen-year-old boy who appeared to be Italian clutched hungrily at Lawson's belt, seeking purchase on an adult, hoping for commiseration. Although he did not try to brush the boy's hand away, Lawson avoided his eyes.

"English! English here! *¡ Un poco Español también!"*

Farther down Sierpes, Lawson saw another man with his hand in the air; he was calling aloud in a crisp but melodic

Slavic dialect, and already he had succeeded in attracting two or three other people to him. In fact, pockets of like-speaking people seemed to be forming in the crowded commercial avenue, causing Lawson to fear that he had put up his hand too late to end his own isolation. What if those who spoke either English or Spanish had already gathered into survival-conscious groups? What if they had already made their way into the countryside, where the competition for food and drink might be a little less predatory? If they had, he would be a lost, solitary Virginian in this Babel. Reduced to sign language and guttural noises to make his wants known, he would die a cipher. . . .

"*Signore,*" the boy hanging on his belt cried. "*Signore.*"

Lawson let his eyes drift to the boy's face. "*Ciao,*" he said. It was the only word of Italian he knew, or the only word that came immediately to mind, and he spoke it much louder than he meant.

The boy shook his head vehemently, pulled harder on Lawson's belt. His words tumbled out like the contents of an unburdened closet into a darkened room, not a single one of them distinct or recognizable.

"English!" Lawson shouted. "English here!"

"English here too, man!" a voice responded from the milling crush of people at the mouth of Sierpes. "Hang on a minute, I'm coming to you!"

A small muscular man with a large head and not much chin stepped daintily through an opening in the crowd and put out his hand to Lawson. His grip was firm. As he shook hands, he placed his left arm over the shoulder of the Italian boy hanging on to Lawson's belt. The boy stopped talking and gaped at the newcomer.

"Dai Secombe," the man said. "I went to bed in Aberystwyth, where I teach philosophy, and I woke up in Spain. Pleased to meet you, Mr.—"

"Lawson," Lawson said.

The boy began babbling again, his hand shifting from

Lawson's belt to the Welshman's flannel shirt facing. Secombe took the boy's hands in his own. "I've got you, lad. There's a ragged crew of your compatriots in a pool-hall pub right down this lane. Come on, then, I'll take you." He glanced at Lawson. "Wait for me, sir. I'll be right back."

Secombe and the boy disappeared, but in less than five minutes the Welshman had returned. He introduced himself all over again. "To go to bed in Aberystwyth and to wake up in Seville," he said, "is pretty damn harrowing. I'm glad to be alive, sir."

"Do you have a family?"

"Only my father. He's eighty-four."

"You're lucky. Not to have anyone else to worry about, I mean."

"Perhaps," Dai Secombe said, a sudden trace of sharpness in his voice. "Yesterday I would not've thought so."

The two men stared at each other as the wail of the city modulated into a less hysterical but still inhuman drone. People surged around them, scrutinized them from foyers and balconies, took their measure. Out of the corner of his eye Lawson was aware of a moonfaced woman in summer deerskins slumping abruptly and probably painfully to the street. An Eskimo woman—the conceit was almost comic, but the woman herself was dying and a child with a Swedish-steel switchblade was already freeing a necklace of teeth and shells from her throat.

Lawson turned away from Secombe to watch the plundering of the Eskimo woman's body. Enraged, he took off his wristwatch and threw it at the boy's head, scoring a glancing sort of hit on his ear.

"You little jackal, get away from there!"

The red-cheeked woman who had been glaring at Lawson applied her foot to the rump of the boy with the switchblade and pushed him over. Then she retrieved the thrown watch, hoisted her skirts, and retreated into the dim interior of the café whose door she had been haunting.

"In this climate, in this environment," Dai Secombe told Lawson, "an Eskimo is doomed. It's as much psychological and emotional as it is physical. There may be a few others who've already died for similar reasons. Not much we can do, sir."

Lawson turned back to the Welshman with a mixture of awe and disdain. How had this curly-haired lump of a man, in the space of no more than three or four hours, come to respond so lackadaisically to the deaths of his fellows? Was it merely because the sky was still blue and the edifices of another age still stood?

Pointedly, Secombe said, "That was a needless forfeiture of your watch, Lawson."

"How the hell did that poor woman get here?" Lawson demanded, his gesture taking in the entire city. "How the hell did any of us get here?" The stench of open wounds and the first sweet hints of decomposition mocked the luxury of his ardor.

"Good questions," the Welshman responded, taking Lawson's arm and leading him out of the Calle de las Sierpes. "It's a pity I can't answer 'em."

III

That night they ate fried fish and drank beer together in a dirty little apartment over a shop whose glass display cases were filled with a variety of latex contraceptives. They had obtained the fish from a *pescaderia* voluntarily tended by men and women of Greek and Yugoslavian citizenship, people who had run similar shops in their own countries. The beer they had taken from one of the classier bars on the Street of the Serpents. Both the fish and the beer were at room temperature, but tasted none the worse for that.

With the fall of evening, however, the wail that during the day had subsided into a whine began to reverberate again with its first full burden of grief. If the noise was not quite so loud as it had been that morning, Lawson thought, it was probably because the city contained fewer people. Many had died, and a great many more, unmindful of the distances involved, had set out to return to their homelands.

Lawson chewed a piece of *adobo* and washed this down with a swig of the vaguely bitter *Cruz del Campo* beer.

"Isn't this fine?" Secombe said, his butt on the tiles of the room's one windowsill. "Dinner over a rubber shop. And this a Catholic country, too."

"I was raised a Baptist," Lawson said, realizing at once that his confession was a non sequitur.

"Oh," Secombe put in immediately. "Then I imagine you could get all the rubbers you wanted."

"Sure. For a quarter. In almost any gas-station restroom."

"Sorry," Secombe said.

They ate for a while in silence. Lawson's back was to a cool plaster wall; he leaned his head against it, too, and released a sharp moan from his chest. Then, sustaining the sound, he moaned again, adding his own strand of grief to the cacophonous harmonies already afloat over the city. He was no different from all the bereaved others who shared his pain by concentrating on their own.

"What did you do in . . . in Lynchburg?" Secombe suddenly asked.

"Campus liaison for the Veterans Administration. I traveled to four different colleges in the area, straightening out people's problems with the GI Bill. I tried to see to it that—Sweet Jesus, Secombe, who cares? I miss my wife. I'm afraid my girls are dead."

"Karen and Hannah?"

"They're three and five. I've taught them to play chess. Karen's good enough to beat me occasionally if I spot her my queen. Hannah knows the moves, but she hasn't got her sister's patience—she's only three, you know. Yeah. Sometimes she sweeps the pieces off the board and folds her arms, and we play hell trying to find them all. There'll be pawns under the sofa, horsemen upside down in the shag—" Lawson stopped.

"She levels them," Secombe said. "As we've all been leveled. The knight's no more than the pawn, the king no more than the bishop."

Lawson could tell that the Welshman was trying to turn aside the ruinous thrust of his grief. But he brushed the metaphor aside: "I don't think we've been 'leveled,' Secombe."

"Certainly we have. Guess who I saw this morning near the cathedral when I first woke up."

"God only knows."

"God and Dai Secombe, sir. I saw the Marxist dictator of . . . oh, you know, that little African country where there's just been a coup. I recognized the bastard from the telly broadcasts during the purge trials there. There he was, though, in white ducks and a ribbed T-shirt—terrified, Lawson, and as powerless as you or I. He'd been quite decidedly leveled; you'd better believe he had."

"I'll bet he's alive tonight, Secombe."

The Welshman's eyes flickered with a sudden insight. He extended the greasy cone of newspaper from the *pescadería*. "Another piece of fish, Lawson? Come on, then, there's only one more."

"To be leveled, Secombe, is to be put on a par with everyone else. Your dictator, even deprived of office, is a grown man. What about infant children? Toddlers and preadolescents? And what about people like that Eskimo woman who haven't got a chance in an unfamiliar environment, even if its inhabitants don't happen to be hostile? I saw a man knock his brains out on a stone wall this morning because he took a look around and knew he couldn't make it here. Maybe he thought he was in Hell, Secombe. I don't know. But his chance certainly wasn't ours."

"He knew he couldn't adjust."

"Of course he couldn't adjust. Don't give me that bullshit about leveling!"

Secombe turned the cone of newspaper around and withdrew the last piece of fish. "I'm going to eat this myself, if you don't mind." He ate. As he was chewing, he said, "I didn't think that Virginia Baptists were so free with their tongues, Lawson. Tsk, tsk. Undercuts my preconceptions."

"I've fallen away."

"Haven't we all."

Lawson took a final swig of warm beer. Then he hurled the bottle across the room. Fragments of amber glass went everywhere. "God!" he cried. "God, God, God!" Weeping, he was no different from three quarters of Seville's new citizens-by-chance. Why, then, as he sobbed, did he shoot such guilty and threatening glances at the Welshman?

"Go ahead," Secombe advised him, waving the empty cone of newspaper. "I feel a little that way myself."

IV

In the morning an oddly blithe woman of forty-five or so accosted them in the alley outside the contraceptive shop. A military pistol in a patent-leather holster was strapped about her skirt. Her seeming airiness, Lawson quickly realized, was a function of her appearance and her movements; her eyes were as grim and frightened as everyone else's. But, as soon as they came out of the shop onto the cobblestones, she approached them fearlessly, hailing Secombe almost as if he were an old friend.

"You left us yesterday, Mr. Secombe. Why?"

"I saw everything dissolving into cliques."

"Dissolving? Coming together, don't you mean?"

Secombe smiled noncommittally, then introduced the woman to Lawson as Mrs. Alexander. "She's one of your own, Lawson. She's from Wyoming or some such place. I met her outside the cathedral yesterday morning when the first self-appointed muezzins started calling their language-mates together. She didn't have a pistol then."

"I got it from one of the Guardia Civil stations," Mrs.

Alexander said. "And I feel lots better just having it, let me tell you." She looked at Lawson. "Are you in the Air Force?"

"Not anymore. These are the clothes I woke up in."

"My husband's in the Air Force. Or was. We were stationed at Warren in Cheyenne. I'm originally from upstate New York. And these are the clothes *I* woke up in." A riding skirt, a blouse, low-cut rubber-soled shoes. "I think they tried to give us the most serviceable clothes we had in our wardrobes—but they succeeded better in some cases than in others."

" 'They'?" Secombe asked.

"Whoever's done this. It's just a manner of speaking."

"What do you want?" Secombe asked Mrs. Alexander. His brusqueness of tone surprised Lawson.

Smiling, she replied, "The word for today is Exportadora. We're trying to get as many English-speaking people as we can to Exportadora. That's where the commercial center for American servicemen and their families in Seville is located, and it's just off one of the major boulevards to the south of here."

On a piece of paper sack Mrs. Alexander drew them a crude map and explained that her husband had once been stationed in Zaragoza in the north of Spain. Yesterday she had recalled that Seville was one of the four Spanish cities supporting the American military presence, and with persistence and a little luck a pair of carefully briefed English-speaking DPs (the abbreviation was Mrs. Alexander's) had discovered the site of the American PX and commissary just before nightfall. Looting the place when they arrived had been an impossibly mixed crew of foreigners, busily hauling American merchandise out of the ancient buildings. But Mrs. Alexander's DPs had run off the looters by the simple expedient of revving the engine of their commandeered taxicab and blowing its horn as if to announce Armageddon. In ten minutes the little American enclave had emptied of all human beings but the two men in the cab. After that, as English-speaking DPs all over the city learned of Exportadora's existence and sought to reach it, the place had begun to fill up again.

"Is there an airbase in Seville?" Lawson asked the woman.

"No, not really. The base itself is near Morón de la Frontera, about thirty miles away, but Seville is where the real action is." After a brief pause, lifting her eyebrows, she corrected herself: "Was."

She thrust her map into Secombe's hands. "Here. Go on out to Exportadora. I'm going to look around for more of us. You're the first people I've found this morning. Others are looking too, though. Maybe things'll soon start making some sense."

Secombe shook his head. "Us. Them. There isn't anybody now who isn't a 'DP,' you know. This regrouping on the basis of tired cultural affiliations is probably a mistake. I don't like it."

"You took up with Mr. Lawson, didn't you?"

"Out of pity only, I assure you. He looked lost. Moreover, you've got to have companionship of *some* sort—especially when you're in a strange place."

"Sure. That's why the word for today is Exportadora."

"It's a mistake, Mrs. Alexander."

"Why?"

"For the same reason your mysterious 'they' saw fit to displace us to begin with, I'd venture. It's a feeling I have."

"Old cultural affiliations are a source of stability," Mrs. Alexander said earnestly. As she talked, Lawson took the rumpled map out of Secombe's fingers. "This chaos around us won't go away until people have settled themselves into units—it's a natural process, it's beginning already. Why, walking along the river this morning, I saw several groups of like-speaking people burying yesterday's dead. The city's churches and chapels have begun to fill up, too. You can still hear the frightened and the heartbroken keening in solitary rooms, of course—but it can't go on forever. They'll either make connection or die. I'm not one of those who wish to die, Mr. Secombe."

"Who wishes that?" Lawson put in, annoyed by the shallow metaphysical drift of this exchange and by Secombe's irrationality. Although Mrs. Alexander was right, she didn't have to defend her position at such length. The map was her most important contribution to the return of order in their lives, and Lawson wanted her to let them use that map.

"Come on, Secombe," he said. "Let's get out to this Exportadora. It's probably the only chance we have of making it home."

"I don't think there's any chance of our making it home again, Lawson. Ever."

Perceiving that Mrs. Alexander was about to ask the Welshman why, Lawson turned on his heel and took several steps down the alley. "Come on, Secombe. We have to try. What the hell are you going to do in this flip-flopped city all by yourself?"

"Look for somebody else to talk to, I suppose."

But in a moment Secombe was at Lawson's side helping him decipher the smudged geometries of Mrs. Alexander's map, and the woman herself, before heading back to Sierpes to look for more of her own kind, called out, "It'll only take you twenty or so minutes, walking. Good luck. See you later."

Walking, they passed a white-skinned child lying in an alley doorway opening on to a courtyard festooned with two-day-old washing and populated by a pack of orphaned dogs. The child's head was covered by a coat, but she did appear to be breathing. Lawson was not even tempted to examine her more closely, however. He kept his eyes resolutely on the map.

V

The newsstand in the small American enclave had not been looted. On Lawson's second day at Exportadora it still contained quality paperbacks, the most recent American news and entertainment magazines, and a variety of tabloids, including the military paper *Stars and Stripes*. No one knew how old these publications were, because no one knew over what length of time the redistribution of the world's population had taken place. How long had everyone slept? And what about the discrepancies among time zones and the differences among people's waking hours within the same time zones? These questions were academic now, it seemed to Lawson, because the agency of transfer had apparently encompassed every single human being alive on Earth.

Thumbing desultorily through a copy of *Stars and Stripes*, he encountered an article on the problems of military hospitals and wondered how many of the world's sick had awakened in the open, doomed to immediate death because the care they required was nowhere at hand. The smell of spilled tobacco and melted Life Savers made the newsstand a pleasant place to contemplate these horrors; and even as his conscience nagged and a contingent of impatient DPs awaited him, Lawson perversely continued to flip through the newspaper.

Secombe's squat form appeared in the doorway. "I thought you were looking for a local roadmap."

"Found it already, just skimmin' the news."

"Come on, if you would. The folks're ready to be off."

Reluctantly, Lawson followed Secombe outside, where the raw Andalusian sunlight broke like invisible surf against the pavement and the fragile-seeming shell of the Air Force bus. It was of the Bluebird shuttle variety, and Lawson remembered summer camp at Eglin Air Force Base in Florida and bus rides from his squadron's minimum-maintenance ROTC barracks to the survival-training camps near the swamp. That had been a long time ago, but this Bluebird might have hailed from an even more distant era. It was as boxy and sheepish-looking as if it had come off a 1954 assembly line, and it appeared to be made out of warped tin rather than steel. The people inside the bus had opened all its windows, and many of those on the driver's side were watching Secombe and Lawson approach.

"Move your asses!" a man shouted at them. "Let's get some wind blowing through this thing before we all suffo-damn-cate."

"Just keep talking," Secombe advised him. "That should do fine."

Aboard the bus was a motley lot of Americans, Britishers, and Australians, with two or three English-speaking Europeans and an Oxford-educated native of India to lend the group ballast. Lawson took up a window seat over the hump of one of the bus's rear tires, and Secombe squeezed in beside him. A few people introduced themselves; others, lost in fitful reveries, ignored them altogether. To Lawson, the most unsettling thing about the contingent was the absence of children. Although about equally divided between men and women, the group contained no boys or girls any younger than their early teens.

Lawson opened the map of southern Spain he had found in the newsstand and traced his finger along a highway route leading out of Seville to two small American enclaves outside the city, Santa Clara and San Pablo. Farther to the south were Jerez and the port city of Cádiz. Lawson's heart misgave him; the names were all so foreign, so formidable in what they evoked, and he felt this entire enterprise to be hopeless. . . .

About midway along the right-hand side of the bus, a black woman was sobbing into the hem of her blouse, and a man perched on the Bluebird's long rear seat had his hands clasped to his ears and his head canted forward to touch his knees. Lawson folded up the map and stuck it into the crevice between the seat and the side of the bus.

"The bottom-line common denominator here isn't our all speaking English," Secombe whispered. "It's what we're suffering."

Driven by one of Mrs. Alexander's original explorers, a doctor from Ivanhoe, New South Wales, the Bluebird shuddered and lurched forward. In a moment it had left Exportadora and begun banging along one of the wide avenues that would lead it out of town.

"And our suffering," Secombe went on, still whispering, "unites us with all those poor souls raving in the streets and sleeping facedown in their own vomit. You felt that the other night above the condom shop, Lawson. I know you did, talking of your daughters. So why are you so quick to go looking for what you aren't likely to find? Why are you so ready to unite yourself with this artificial family born out of catastrophe? Do you really think you're going to catch a flight home to Lynchburg? Do you really think the bird driving this sardine can—who ought to be out in the streets plying his trade instead of running a shuttle service—d'you really think he's ever going to get back to Australia?"

"Secombe—"

"Do you, Lawson?"

Lawson clapped a hand over the Welshman's knee and wobbled it back and forth. "You wouldn't be badgering me like this if you had a family of your own. What the hell do you want us to do? Stay here forever?"

"I don't know, exactly." He removed Lawson's hand from his knee. "But I do have a father, sir, and I happen to be fond of him. . . . All I know for certain is that things are *supposed* to be different now. We shouldn't be rushing to restore what we already had."

"Shit," Lawson murmured. He leaned his head against the bottom edge of the open window beside him.

From deep within the city came the brittle noise of gunshots. The Bluebird's driver, in response to this sound and to the vegetable carts and automobiles that had been moved into the streets as obstacles, began wheeling and cornering like a stock-car jockey. The bus clanked and stuttered alarmingly. It growled through an intersection below a stone bridge, leapt over that bridge like something living, and roared down into a semi-industrial suburb of Seville, where a Coca-Cola bottling factory and a local brewery lifted huge competing signs.

On top of one of these buildings Lawson saw a man with a rifle taking unhurried potshots at anyone who came into his sights. Several people already lay dead.

And a moment later the Bluebird's windshield shattered, another bullet ricocheted off its flank, and everyone in the bus was either shouting or weeping. The next time Lawson looked, the bus's windshield appeared to have woven inside it a large and exceedingly intricate spider's web.

The Bluebird careened madly, but the doctor from Ivanhoe kept it upright and turned it with considerable skill onto the highway to San Pablo. Here the bus eased into a quiet and rhythmic cruising that made this final incident in Seville—except for the evidence of the windshield—seem only the cottony aftertaste of nightmare. At last they were on their way. Maybe.

"Another good reason for trying to get home," Lawson said.

"What makes you think it's going to be different there?"

Irritably, Lawson turned on the Welshman. "I thought your idea was that this change was some kind of *improvement.*"

"Perhaps it will be. Eventually."

Lawson made a dismissive noise and looked at the olive orchard spinning by on his left. Who would harvest the crop? Who would set the aircraft factories, the distilleries, the chemical and textile plants running again? Who would see to it that seed was sown in the empty fields?

Maybe Secombe had something. Maybe, when you ran for home, you ran from the new reality at hand. The effects of this new reality's advent were not going to go away very soon, no matter what you did—but seeking to reestablish yesterday's order would probably create an even nastier entropic pattern than would accepting the present chaos and working to rein it in. How, though, did you best rein it in? Maybe by trying to get back home . . .

Lawson shook his head and thought of Marlena, Karen, Hannah; of the distant, mist-softened cradle of the Blue

Ridge. Lord. That was country much easier to get in tune with than the harsh, white-sky bleakness of this Andalusian valley. If you stay here, Lawson told himself, the pain will *never* go away.

They passed Santa Clara, which was a housing area for the officers and senior NCOs who had been stationed at Morón. With its neatly trimmed hedgerows, tall aluminum streetlamps, and low-roofed houses with carports and picture windows, Santa Clara resembled a middle-class exurbia in New Jersey or Ohio. Black smoke was curling over the area, however, and the people on the streets and lawns were definitely not Americans—they were transplanted Dutch South Africans, Amazonian tribesmen, Poles, Ethiopians, God only knew what. All Lawson could accurately deduce was that a few of these people had moved into the vacant houses— maybe they had awakened in them—and that others had aimlessly set bonfires about the area's neighborhoods. These fires, because there was no wind, burned with a maddening slowness and lack of urgency.

"Little America," Secombe said aloud.

"That's in Antarctica," Lawson responded sarcastically.

"Right. No matter where it happens to be."

"Up yours."

Their destination was now San Pablo, where the Americans had hospital facilities, a library, a movie theater, a snackbar, a commissary, and, in conjunction with the Spaniards, a small commercial and military airfield. San Pablo lay only a few more miles down the road, and Lawson contemplated the idea of a flight to Portugal. What would be the chances, supposing you actually reached Lisbon, of crossing the Atlantic, either by sea or air, and reaching one of the United States' coastal cities? One in a hundred? One in a thousand? Less than that?

A couple of seats behind the driver, an Englishman with a crisp-looking mustache and an American woman with a distinct Southwestern accent were arguing the merits of bypassing San Pablo and heading on to Gibraltar, a British possession. The Englishman seemed to feel that Gibraltar would have escaped the upheaval to which the remainder of the world had fallen victim, whereas the American woman thought he was crazy. A shouting match involving five or six other passengers ensued. Finally, his patience at an end, the Bluebird's driver put his elbow on the horn and held it there until everyone had shut up.

"It's San Pablo," he announced. "Not Gibraltar or anywhere else. There'll be a plane waitin' for us when we get there."

VI

Two aircraft were waiting, a pair of patched-up DC-7s that had once belonged to the Spanish airline known as Iberia. Mrs. Alexander had recruited one of her pilots from the DPs who had shown up at Exportadora; the other, a retired TWA veteran from Riverside, California, had made it by himself to the airfield by virtue of a prior acquaintance with Seville and its American military installations. Both men were eager to carry passengers home, one via a stopover in Lisbon and the other by using Madrid as a steppingstone to the British Isles. The hope was that they could transfer their passengers to jet aircraft at these cities' more cosmopolitan airports, but no one spoke very much about the real obstacles to success that had already begun stalking them: civil chaos, delay, inadequate communications, fuel shortages, mechanical hangups, doubt and ignorance, a thousand other things.

At twilight, then, Lawson stood next to Dai Secombe at the chainlink fence fronting San Pablo's pothole-riven runway and watched the evening light glimmer off the wings of the DC-7s. Bathed in a muted dazzle, the two old airplanes were almost beautiful. Even though Mrs. Alexander had informed the DPs that they must spend the night in the installation's movie theater, so that the Bluebird could make several more

shuttle runs to Exportadora, Lawson truly believed that he
was bound for home.

"Good-bye," Secombe told him.

"Good-bye? . . . Oh, because you'll be on the other
flight?"

"No, I'm telling you good-bye, Lawson, because I'm leaving. Right now, you see. This very minute."

"Where are you going?"

"Back into the city."

"How? What for?"

"I'll walk, I suppose. As for why, it has something to do
with wanting to appease Mrs. Alexander's 'they,' also with
finding out what's to become of us all. Seville's the place for
that, I think."

"Then why'd you even come out here?"

"To say good-bye, you bloody imbecile." Secombe
laughed, grabbed Lawson's hand, shook it heartily. "Since I
couldn't manage to change your mind."

With that, he turned and walked along the chainlink
fence until he had found the roadway past the installation's
commissary. Lawson watched him disappear behind that
building's complicated system of loading ramps. After a time
the Welshman reappeared on the other side, but against the
vast Spanish sky, his compact, striding form rapidly dwindled
to an imperceptible smudge. A smudge on the darkness.

"Good-bye," Lawson said.

That night, slumped in a lumpy theater chair, he slept
with nearly sixty other people in San Pablo's movie house. A
teenage boy, over only a few objections, insisted on showing
all the old movies still in tins in the projection room. As a
result, Lawson awoke once in the middle of *Apocalypse Now*
and another time near the end of Kubrick's *The Left Hand of
Darkness*. The ice on the screen, dunelike *sastrugi*, ranged
from horizon to horizon, chilled him, touching a sensitive spot
in his memory. "Little America," he murmured. Then he went
back to sleep.

VII

With the passengers bound for Lisbon, Lawson stood at the fence where he had stood with Secombe, and watched the silver pinwheeling of propellers as the aircraft's engines engaged. The DC-7 flying to Madrid would not leave until much later that day, primarily because it still had several vacant seats and Mrs. Alexander felt sure that more English-speaking DPs could still be found in the city.

The people at the gate with Lawson shifted uneasily and whispered among themselves. The engines of their savior airplane whined deafeningly, and the runway seemed to tremble. What woebegone eyes the women had, Lawson thought, and the men were as scraggly as railroad hoboes. Feeling his jaw, he understood that he was no more handsome or well groomed than any of those he waited with. And, like them, he was impatient for the signal to board, for the thumbs-up sign indicating that their airplane had passed its latest rudimentary ground tests.

At least, he consoled himself, you're not eating potato chips at ten-thirty in the morning. Disgustedly, he turned aside from a jut-eared man who was doing just that.

"There're more people here than our plane's supposed to carry," the potato-chip cruncher said. "That could be dangerous."

"But it isn't really that far to Lisbon, is it?" a woman replied. "And none of us has any luggage."

"Yeah, but—" The man gagged on a chip, coughed, tried to speak again. Facing deliberately away, Lawson felt that the man's words would acquire eloquence only if he suddenly volunteered to ride in the DC-7's unpressurized baggage compartment.

As it was, the signal came to board and the jut-eared man had no chance to finish his remarks. He threw his cellophane sack to the ground, and Lawson heard it crackling underfoot as people crowded through the gate onto the grassy verge of the runway.

In order to fix the anomaly of San Pablo in his memory, Lawson turned around and walked backward across the field. He saw that bringing up the rear were four men with automatic weapons—weapons procured, most likely, from the installation's Air Police station. These men, like Lawson, were walking backward, but with their guns as well as their eyes trained on the weirdly constituted band of people who had just appeared, seemingly out of nowhere, along the airfield's fence.

One of these people wore nothing but a ragged pair of shorts, another an ankle-length burnoose, another a pair of trousers belted with a rope. One of their number was a doe-eyed young woman with an exposed torso and a circlet of bright coral on her wrist. But there were others too, and they all seemed to have been drawn to the runway by the airplane's engine whine; they moved along the fence like desperate ghosts. As the first members of Lawson's group mounted into the plane, even more of these people appeared—an assembly of nomads, hunters, hod-carriers, fishers, herdspeople. Apparently they all understood what an airplane was for, and one of the swarthiest men among them ventured out onto the runway with his arms thrown out imploringly.

"Where you go?" he shouted. "Where you go?"

"There's no more room!" responded a blue-jeans-clad man with a machine gun. "Get back! You'll have to wait for another flight!"

Oh, sure, Lawson thought, the one to Madrid. He was at the base of the airplane's mobile stairway. The jut-eared man who had been eating potato chips nodded brusquely at him.

"You'd better get on up there," he shouted over the robust hiccoughing of the airplane's engines, "before we have unwanted company breathing down our necks!"

"After you." Lawson stepped aside.

Behind the swarthy man importuning the armed guards for a seat on the airplane, there clamored thirty or more insistent people, their only real resemblance to one another being their longing for a way out. "Where you go? Where you go?" the bravest and most desperate among them yelled, but they all wanted to board the airplane that Mrs. Alexander's charges had already laid claim to; and most of them could see that it was too late to accomplish their purpose without some kind of risk-taking. The man who had been shouting in English, along with four or five others, broke into an assertive dogtrot toward the plane. Although their cries continued to be modestly beseeching, Lawson could tell that the passengers' guards now believed themselves under direct attack.

A burst of machine-gun fire sounded above the field and echoed away like rain drumming on a tin roof. The man who had been asking "Where you go?" pitched forward on his face. Others fell beside him, including the woman with the coral bracelet. Panicked or prodded by this evidence of their assailants' mortality, one of the guards raked the chainlink fence with his weapon, bringing down some of those who had already begun to retreat and summoning forth both screams and the distressingly incongruous sound of popping wire. Then, eerily, it was quiet again.

"Get on that airplane!" a guard shouted at Lawson. He was the only passenger still left on the ground, and everyone wanted him inside the plane so that the mobile stairway could be rolled away.

"I don't think so," Lawson said to himself.

Hunching forward like a man under fire, he ran toward the gate and the crude mandala of bodies partially blocking it. The slaughter he had just witnessed struck him as abysmally repetitive of a great deal of recent history, and he did not wish to belong to that history anymore. Further, the airplane behind him was a gross iron-plated emblem of the burden he no longer cared to bear—even if it also seemed to represent the promise of passage home.

"Hey, where the hell you think you're goin'?"

Lawson did not answer. He stepped gingerly through the corpses on the runway's margin, halted on the other side of the fence, and, his eyes misted with glare and poignant bewilderment, turned to watch the DC-7 taxi down the scrub-lined length of concrete to the very end of the field. There the airplane negotiated a turn and started back the way it had come. Soon it was hurtling along like a colossal metal dragonfly, building speed. When it lifted from the ground, its tires screaming shrilly with the last series of bumps before takeoff, Lawson held his breath.

Then the airplane's right wing dipped, dipped again, struck the ground, and broke off like a piece of balsa wood, splintering brilliantly. After that, the airplane went flipping, cartwheeling, across the end of the tarmac and into the desolate open field beyond, where its shell and remaining wing were suddenly engulfed in flames. You could hear people frying in that inferno; you could smell gasoline and burnt flesh.

"Jesus," Lawson said.

He loped away from the airfield's fence, hurried through the short grass behind the San Pablo library, and joined a group of those who had just fled the English-speaking guards' automatic-weapon fire. He met them on the highway going back to Seville and walked among them as merely another of their number. Although several people viewed his 1505 trousers with suspicion, no one argued that he did not belong, and no one threatened to cut his throat for him.

As hangdog and exotically nondescript as most of his companions, Lawson watched his tennis shoes track the pavement like the feet of a mechanical toy. He wondered what he was going to do back in Seville. Successfully dodge bullets and eat fried fish, if he was lucky. Talk with Secombe again, if he could find the man. And, if he had any sense, try to organize his life around some purpose other than the insane and hopeless one of returning to Lynchburg. What purpose, though? What purpose beyond the basic, animal purpose of staying alive?

"Are any of you hungry?" Lawson asked.

He was regarded with suspicious curiosity.

"Hungry," he repeated. *"¿Tiene hambre?"*

English? Spanish? Neither worked. What languages did they have, these refugees from an enigma? It looked as if they had all tried to speak together before and found the task impossible—because, moving along the asphalt under the hot Andalusian sun, they now relied on gestures and easily interpretable noises to express themselves.

Perceiving this, Lawson brought the fingers of his right hand to his mouth and clacked his teeth to indicate chewing.

He was understood. A thin barefoot man in a capacious linen shirt and trousers led Lawson off the highway into an orchard of orange trees. The fruit was not yet completely ripe, and was sour because of its greenness, but all twelve or thirteen of Lawson's crew ate, letting the juice run down their arms. When they again took up the trek to Seville, Lawson's mind was almost absolutely blank with satiety. The only thing rattling about in it now was the fear that he would not know what to do once they arrived. He never did find out if the day's other scheduled flight, the one to Madrid, made it safely to its destination, but the matter struck him now as of little import. He wiped his sticky mouth and trudged along numbly.

VIII

He lived above the contraceptive shop. In the mornings he walked through the alley to a bakery that a woman with calm Mongolian features had taken over. In return for a daily allotment of bread and a percentage of the goods brought in for barter, Lawson swept the bakery's floor, washed the utensils that were dirtied each day, and kept the shop's front counter. His most rewarding skill, in fact, was communicating with those who entered to buy something. He had an uncanny grasp of several varieties of sign language, and on occasion he found himself speaking a monosyllabic patois whose derivation was a complete mystery to him. Sometimes he thought that he had invented it himself; sometimes he believed that he had learned it from the transplanted Sevillanos among whom he now lived.

English, on the other hand, seemed to leak slowly out of his mind, a thick, unrecoverable fluid.

The first three or four weeks of chaos following The Change had by this time run their course, a circumstance that surprised Lawson. Still, it was true. Now you could lie down at night on your pallet without hearing pistol reports or fearing that some benighted freak was going to set fire to your staircase. Most of the city's essential services—electricity, water, and sewerage—were working again, albeit uncertainly, and agricultural goods were coming in from the countryside. People had gone back to doing what they knew best, while those whose previous jobs had had little to do with the basics of day-to-day survival were now apprenticing as bricklayers, carpenters, bakers, fishers, and water and power technicians. That men and women chose to live separately, and that children were as rare as sapphires, no one seemed to find disturbing or unnatural. A new pattern was evolving. You lived among your fellows without tension or quarrel, and you formed no dangerously intimate relationships.

One night, standing at his window, Lawson's knee struck a loose tile below the casement. He removed the tile and set it on the floor. Every night for nearly two months he pried away at least one tile and, careful not to chip or break it, stacked it near an inner wall with those he had already removed.

After completing this task, as he lay on his pallet, he would often hear a man or a woman somewhere in the city singing a high, sweet song whose words had no significance for him. Sometimes a pair of voices would answer each other, always in different languages. Then, near the end of the summer, as Lawson stood staring at the lathing and the wall beams he had methodically exposed, he was moved to sing a melancholy song of his own. And he sang it without knowing what it meant.

The days grew cooler. Lawson took to leaving the bakery during its midafternoon closing and proceeding by way of the Calle de las Sierpes to a bodega across from the bullring. A crew of silent laborers, who worked very purposively in spite of their seeming to have no single boss, was dismantling the Plaza de Toros, and Lawson liked to watch as he drank his wine and ate the breadsticks he had brought with him.

Other crews about the city were carefully taking down the government buildings, banks, and barrio chapels that no one frequented anymore, preserving the bricks, tiles, and beams as if in the hope of some still unspecified future construction. By this time Lawson himself had knocked out the rear wall of his room over the contraceptive shop, and he felt a strong sense of identification with the laborers craftily gutting the bullring of its railings and barricades. Eventually, of course, everything would have to come down. Everything.

The rainy season began. The wind and the cold. Lawson continued to visit the sidewalk café near the ruins of the stadium; and because the bullring's destruction went forward even in wet weather, he wore an overcoat he had recently acquired and staked out a nicely sheltered table under the bodega's awning. This was where he customarily sat.

One particularly gusty day, rain pouring down, he shook out his umbrella and sat down at this table only to find another man sitting across from him. Upon the table was a wooden game board of some kind, divided into squares.

"Hello, Lawson," the interloper said.

Lawson blinked and licked his lips thoughtfully. Although he had not called his family to mind in some time, and wondered now if he had ever really married and fathered children, Dai Secombe's face had occasionally floated up before him in the dark of his room. But now Lawson could not remember the Welshman's name, or his nationality, and he had no notion of what to say to him. The first words he spoke, therefore, came out sounding like dream babble, or a voice played backward on the phonograph. In order to say hello he was forced to the indignity, almost comic, of making a childlike motion with his hand.

Secombe, pointing to the game board, indicated that they should play. From a carved wooden box with a velvet lining he emptied the pieces onto the table, then arranged them on both sides of the board. Chess, Lawson thought vaguely, but he really did not recognize the pieces—they seemed changed from what he believed they should look like. And when it came his turn to move, Secombe had to demonstrate the capabilities of all the major pieces before he, Lawson, could essay even the most timid advance. The piece that most reminded him of a knight had to be moved according to two distinct sets of criteria, depending on whether it started from a black square or a white one; the "rooks," on the other hand, were able, at certain times, to *jump* an opponent's intervening pieces. The game boggled Lawson's understanding. After ten or twelve moves he pushed his chair back and took a long, bittersweet taste of wine. The rain continued to pour down like an endless curtain of deliquescent beads.

"That's all right," Secombe said. "I haven't got it all down yet myself, quite. A Bhutanese fellow near where I live made the pieces, you see, and just recently taught me how to play."

With difficulty, Lawson managed to frame a question: "What work have you been doing?"

"I'm in demolition. As we all will be soon. It's the only really constructive occupation going." The Welshman chuckled mildly, finished his own wine, and rose. Lifting his umbrella, he bid Lawson farewell with a word that, when Lawson later tried to repeat and intellectually encompass it, had no meaning at all.

Every afternoon of that dismal, rainy winter, Lawson came back to the same table, but Secombe never showed up there again. Nor did Lawson miss him terribly. He had grown accustomed to the strange richness of his own company. Besides, if he wanted people to talk to, all he needed to do was remain behind the counter at the bakery.

IX

Spring came again. All of his room's interior walls were down, and it amused him to be able to see the porcelain chalice of the commode as he came up the stairs from the contraceptive shop.

The plaster that he had sledgehammered down would never be of use to anybody again, of course, but he had saved from the debris whatever was worth the salvage. With the return of good weather, men driving oxcarts were coming through the city's backstreets and alleys to collect these items. You never saw anyone trying to drive a motorized vehicle nowadays, probably because, over winter, most of them had been hauled away. The scarcity of gasoline and replacement parts might well have been a factor too—but, in truth, people seemed no longer to want to mess with internal-combustion engines. Ending pollution and noise had nothing to do with it, either. A person with dung on his shoes or front stoop was not very likely to be convinced of a vast improvement in the environment, and the clattering of wooden carts—the ringing of metal-rimmed wheels on cobblestone—could be as ear-wrenching as the hum and blare of motorized traffic. Still, Lawson liked to hear the oxcarts turn into his alley. More than once, called out by the noise, he had helped their drivers load them with masonry, doors, window sashes, even ornate carven mantels.

At the bakery, the Mongolian woman with whom Lawson worked, and had worked for almost a year, caught the handle of his broom one day and told him her name. Speaking the odd, quicksilver monosyllables of the dialect that nearly everyone in Seville had by now mastered, she asked him to call her Tij. Lawson did not know whether this was her name from before The Change or one she had recently invented for herself. Pleased in either case, he responded by telling her his own Christian name. He stumbled saying it, and when Tij also had trouble pronouncing the name, they laughed together about its uncommon awkwardness on our tongues.

A week later he had moved into the tenement building where Tij lived. They slept in the same "room" three flights up from a courtyard filled with clambering wisteria. Because all but the supporting walls on this floor had been knocked out, Lawson often felt that he was living in an open-bay barracks. People stepped over his pallet to get to the stairwell, and dressed in front of him as if he were not even there. Always a quick study, he emulated their casual behavior.

And when the ice in his loins finally began to thaw, he turned in the darkness to Tij—without in the least worrying about propriety. Their coupling was invariably silent, and the release Lawson experienced was always a serene rather than a shuddering one. Afterward, in the wisteria fragrance pervading their building, Tij and he lay beside each other like a pair of larval bumblebees as the moon rolled shadows over their naked, sweat-gleaming bodies.

Each day after they had finished making and trading away their bread, Tij and Lawson closed the bakery and took long walks. Often they strolled among the hedge-enclosed pathways and the small wrought-iron fences at the base of the city's cathedral. From these paths, so overwhelmed were they by buttresses of stones and arcaded balconies, they could not even see the bronze weathervane of Faith atop the Giralda. But, evening after evening, Lawson insisted on returning to that place, and at last his persistence and his sense of expectation were rewarded by the sound of jackhammers biting into marble in each one of the cathedral's five tremendous naves. He and Tij, holding hands, entered.

Inside, men and women were at work removing the altar screens, the metalwork grilles, the oil paintings, sections of stained-glass windows, religious relics. Twelve or more oxcarts were parked beneath the vault of the cathedral, and the noise of the jackhammers echoed shatteringly from nave to nave, from floor to cavernous ceiling. The oxen stood so complacently in their traces that Lawson wondered if the drivers of the carts had somehow contrived to deafen the animals. Tij released Lawson's hand to cover her ears. He covered his own ears. It did no good. You could remain in the cathedral only if you accepted the noise and resolved to be a participant in the building's destruction. Many people had already made that decision. They were swarming through its chambered stone belly like a spectacularly efficient variety of stone-eating termite.

An albino man of indeterminate race—a man as pale as a termite—thrust his pickax at Lawson. Lawson uncovered his ears and took the pickax by its handle. Tij, a moment later, found a crowbar hanging precariously from the side of one of the oxcarts. With these tools the pair of them crossed the nave they had entered and halted in front of an imposing mausoleum. Straining against the cathedral's poor light and the strange linguistic static in his head, Lawson painstakingly deciphered the plaque near the tomb.

"Christopher Columbus is buried here," he said.

Tij did not hear him. He made a motion indicating that this was the place where they should start. Tij nodded her understanding. Together, Lawson thought, they would dismantle the mausoleum of the discoverer of the New World and bring his corrupt remains out into the street. After all these centuries they would free the man.

Then the bronze statue of Faith atop the belltower would come down, followed by the lovely belltower itself. After that, the flying buttresses, the balconies, the walls; every beautiful, tainted stone.

It would hurt like hell to destroy the cathedral, and it would take a long, long time—but, considering everything, it was the only meaningful option they had. Lawson raised his pickax.

The Pusher

John Varley

John Varley didn't send any biographical information with his manuscript; when I called him he said he didn't believe in that sort of thing. Just make something up. Oh, the temptation. For the sake of the publisher's legal department, though, I won't yield to it.

Varley is generally considered to have been one of the two or three most important writers to emerge in the 1970s. His novella "The Persistence of Vision" won both Hugo and Nebula awards, and provides the title for his collection of short stories. His latest novel, Demon, *completes the trilogy started with* Titan *and* Wizard. *He lives in a land where the river runs backwards and he is named after an herb.*

Things change. Ian Haise expected that. Yet there are certain constants, dictated by function and use. Ian looked for those and he seldom went wrong.

The playground was not much like the ones he had known as a child. But playgrounds are built to entertain chil-

dren. They will always have something to swing on, something
to slide down, something to climb. This one had all those
things, and more. Part of it was thickly wooded. There was a
swimming hole. The stationary apparatus was combined with
dazzling light sculptures that darted in and out of reality.
There were animals too: pygmy rhinoceros and elegant ga-
zelles no taller than your knee. They seemed unnaturally gentle and unafraid.

But most of all, the playground had children.

Ian liked children.

He sat on a wooden park bench at the edge of the trees,
in the shadows, and watched them. They came in all colors
and all sizes, in both sexes. There were black ones like animated licorice jellybeans and white ones like bunny rabbits,
and brown ones with curly hair and more brown ones with
slanted eyes and straight black hair and some who had been
white but were now toasted browner than some of the
brown ones.

Ian concentrated on the girls. He had tried with boys
before, long ago, but it had not worked out.

He watched one black child for a time, trying to estimate
her age. He thought it was around eight or nine. Too young.
Another one was more like thirteen, judging from her shirt. A
possibility, but he'd prefer something younger. Somebody less
sophisticated, less suspicious.

Finally he found a girl he liked. She was brown, but with
startling blond hair. Ten? Possibly eleven. Young enough, at
any rate.

He concentrated on her and did the strange thing he did
when he had selected the right one. He didn't know what it
was, but it usually worked. Mostly it was just a matter of
looking at her, keeping his eyes fixed on her no matter where
she went or what she did, not allowing himself to be distracted
by anything. And sure enough, in a few minutes she looked
up, looked around, and her eyes locked with his. She held his
gaze for a moment, then went back to her play.

He relaxed. Possibly what he did was nothing at all. He had noticed, with adult women, that if one really caught his eye so he found himself staring at her, she would usually look up from what she was doing and catch him. It never seemed to fail. Talking to other men, he had found it to be a common experience. It was almost as if they could feel his gaze. Women had told him it was nonsense, or if not, it was just reaction to things seen peripherally by people trained to alertness for sexual signals. Merely an unconscious observation penetrating to the awareness; nothing mysterious, like ESP.

Perhaps. Still, Ian was very good at this sort of eye contact. Several times he had noticed the girls rubbing the backs of their necks while he observed them, or hunching their shoulders. Maybe they'd developed some kind of ESP and just didn't recognize it as such.

Now he merely watched her. He was smiling, so that every time she looked up to see him—which she did with increasing frequency—she saw a friendly, slightly graying man with a broken nose and powerful shoulders. His hands were strong too. He kept them clasped in his lap.

Presently she began to wander in his direction.

No one watching her would have thought she was coming toward him. She probably didn't know it herself. On her way, she found reasons to stop and tumble, jump on the soft rubber mats, or chase a flock of noisy geese. But she was coming toward him, and she would end up on the park bench beside him.

He glanced around quickly. As before, there were few adults in this playground. It had surprised him when he arrived. Apparently the new conditioning techniques had reduced the numbers of the violent and twisted to the point that parents felt it safe to allow their children to run without supervision. The adults present were involved with each other. No one had given him a second glance when he arrived.

That was fine with Ian. It made what he planned to do

much easier. He had his excuses ready, of course, but it could be embarrassing to be confronted with the questions representatives of the law ask single, middle-aged men who hang around playgrounds.

For a moment he considered, with real concern, how the parents of these children could feel so confident, even with mental conditioning. After all, no one was conditioned until he had first done something. New maniacs were presumably being produced every day. Typically, they looked just like everyone else until they proved their difference by some demented act.

Somebody ought to give those parents a stern lecture, he thought.

"Who are you?"

Ian frowned. Not eleven, surely, not seen up this close. Maybe not even ten. She might be as young as eight.

Would eight be all right? He tasted the idea with his usual caution, looked around again for curious eyes. He saw none.

"My name is Ian. What's yours?"

"*No.* Not your *name.* Who are *you*?"

"You mean what do I do?"

"Yes."

"I'm a pusher."

She thought that over, then smiled. She had her permanent teeth, crowded into a small jaw.

"You give away pills?"

He laughed. "Very good," he said. "You must do a lot of reading." She said nothing, but her manner indicated she was pleased.

"No," he said. "That's an old kind of pusher. I'm the other kind. But you knew that, didn't you?" When he smiled, she broke into giggles. She was doing the pointless things with her hands that little girls do. He thought she had a pretty good idea of how cute she was, but no inkling of her forbidden eroticism. She was a ripe seed with sexuality ready to burst to the surface. Her body was a bony sketch, a framework on which to build a woman.

"How old are you?" he asked.

"That's a secret. What happened to your nose?"

"I broke it a long time ago. I'll bet you're twelve."

She giggled, then nodded. Eleven, then. And just barely.

"Do you want some candy?" He reached into his pocket and pulled out the pink-and-white-striped paper bag.

She shook her head solemnly. "My mother says not to take candy from strangers."

"But we're not strangers. I'm Ian, the pusher."

She thought that over. While she hesitated, he reached into the bag and picked out a chocolate thing so thick and gooey it was almost obscene. He bit into it, forcing himself to chew. He hated sweets.

"Okay," she said, and reached toward the bag. He pulled it away. She looked at him in innocent surprise.

"I just thought of something," he said. "I don't know your name. So I guess we *are* strangers."

She caught on to the game when she saw the twinkle in his eye. He'd practiced that. It was a good twinkle.

"My name is Radiant. Radiant Shiningstar Smith."

"A very fancy name," he said, thinking how names had changed. "For a very pretty girl." He paused, and cocked his head. "No. I don't think so. You're Radiant . . . Starr. With two *r*'s. . . . *Captain* Radiant Starr, of the Star Patrol."

She was dubious for a moment. He wondered if he'd judged her wrong. Perhaps she was really Miz Radiant Faintingheart Belle, or Mrs. Radiant Motherhood. But her fingernails were a bit dirty for that.

She pointed a finger at him and made a Donald Duck sound as her thumb worked back and forth. He put his hand to his heart and fell over sideways, and she dissolved in laughter. She was careful, however, to keep her weapon firmly trained on him.

"And you'd better give me that candy or I'll shoot you again."

The playground was darker now, and not so crowded. She sat beside him on the bench, swinging her legs. Her bare feet did not quite touch the dirt.

. She was going to be quite beautiful. He could see it clearly in her face. As for the body . . . who could tell?

Not that he really gave a damn.

She was dressed in a little of this and a little of that, worn here and there without much regard for his concepts of modesty. Many of the children wore nothing. It had been something of a shock when he arrived. Now he was almost used to it, but he still thought it incautious on the part of her parents. Did they really think the world was that safe, to let an eleven-year-old girl go practically naked in a public place?

He sat there listening to her prattle about her friends—the ones she hated and the one or two she simply adored—with only part of his attention.

He inserted *um*'s and *uh-huh*'s in the right places.

She was cute, there was no denying it. She seemed as sweet as a child that age ever gets, which can be very sweet and as poisonous as a rattlesnake, almost at the same moment. She had the capacity to be warm, but it was on the surface. Underneath, she cared mostly about herself. Her loyalty would be a transitory thing, bestowed easily, just as easily forgotten.

And why not? She was young. It was perfectly healthy for her to be that way.

But did he dare try to touch her?

It was crazy. It was as insane as they all told him it was. It worked so seldom. Why would it work with her? He felt a weight of defeat.

"Are you okay?"

"Huh? Me? Oh, sure, I'm all right. Isn't your mother going to be worried about you?"

"I don't have to be in for hours, and hours yet." For a moment she looked so grown-up he almost believed the lie.

"Well, I'm getting tired of sitting here. And the candy's all gone." He looked at her face. Most of the chocolate had

ended up in a big circle around her mouth, except where she
had wiped it daintily on her shoulder or forearm. "What's
back there?"

She turned.

"That? That's the swimming hole."

"Why don't we go over there? I'll tell you a story."

The promise of a story was not enough to keep her out of the
water. He didn't know if that was good or bad. He knew she
was smart, a reader, and she had an imagination. But she was
also active. That pull was too strong for him. He sat far from
the water, under some bushes, and watched her swim with the
three other children still in the park this late in the evening.

Maybe she would come back to him, and maybe she
wouldn't. It wouldn't change his life either way, but it might
change hers.

She emerged dripping and infinitely cleaner from the
murky water. She dressed again in her random scraps, for
whatever good it did her, and came to him, shivering.

"I'm cold," she said.

"Here." He took off his jacket. She looked at his hands as
he wrapped it around her, and she reached out and touched
the hardness of his shoulder.

"You sure must be strong," she commented.

"Pretty strong. I work hard, being a pusher."

"Just what *is* a pusher?" she said, and stifled a yawn.

"Come sit on my lap, and I'll tell you."

He did tell her, and it was a very good story that no adven-
turous child could resist. He had practiced that story, refined
it, told it many times into a recorder until he had the rhythms
and cadences just right, until he found just the right words—
not too difficult words, but words with some fire and juice
in them.

And once more he grew encouraged. She had been tired
when he started, but he gradually caught her attention. It was

possible no one had ever told her a story in quite that way. She was used to sitting before the screen and having a story shoved into her eyes and ears. It was something new to be able to interrupt with questions and get answers. Even reading was not like that. It was the oral tradition of storytelling, and it could still mesmerize the nth generation of the electronic age.

"That sounds great," she said, when she was sure he was through.

"You liked it?"

"I really truly did. I think I want to be a pusher when I grow up. That was a really neat story."

"Well, that's not actually the story I was going to tell you. That's just what it's like to be a pusher."

"You mean you have another story?"

"Sure." He looked at his watch. "But I'm afraid it's getting late. It's almost dark, and everybody's gone home. You'd probably better go too."

She was in agony, torn between what she was supposed to do and what she wanted. It really should be no contest, if she was who he thought she was.

"Well . . . but—but I'll come back here tomorrow and you—"

He was shaking his head.

"My ship leaves in the morning," he said. "There's no time."

"Then tell me now! I can stay out. Tell me now. Please please please?"

He coyly resisted, harrumphed, protested, but in the end allowed himself to be seduced. He felt very good. He had her like a five-pound trout on a twenty-pound line. It wasn't sporting. But, then, he wasn't playing a game.

So at last he got to his specialty.

He sometimes wished he could claim the story for his own, but the fact was he could not make up stories. He no longer tried to. Instead, he cribbed from every fairy tale and fantasy story he could find. If he had a genius, it was in adapting some of the elements to fit the world she knew—while keeping it strange enough to enthrall her—and in ad-libbing the end to personalize it.

It was a wonderful tale he told. It had enchanted castles sitting on mountains of glass, moist caverns beneath the sea, fleets of starships, and shining riders astride horses that flew the galaxy. There were evil alien creatures, and others with much good in them. There were drugged potions. Scaled beasts roared out of hyperspace to devour planets.

Amid all the turmoil strode the Prince and Princess. They got into frightful jams and helped each other out of them.

The story was never quite the same. He watched her eyes. When they wandered, he threw away whole chunks of story. When they widened, he knew what parts to plug in later. He tailored it to her reactions.

The child was sleepy. Sooner or later she would surrender. He needed her in a trance state, neither awake nor asleep. That was when the story would end.

". . . and though the healers labored long and hard, they could not save the Princess. She died that night, far from her Prince."

Her mouth was a little round *o*. Stories were not supposed to end that way.

"Is that *all*? She died and she never saw the Prince again?"

"Well, not quite all. But the rest of it probably isn't true, and I shouldn't tell it to you." Ian felt pleasantly tired. His throat was a little raw, making him hoarse. Radiant was a warm weight on his lap.

"You *have* to tell me, you know," she said reasonably. He supposed she was right. He took a deep breath.

"All right. At the funeral, all the greatest people from that part of the galaxy were in attendance. Among them was the greatest Sorcerer who ever lived. His name . . . but I really shouldn't tell you his name. I'm sure he'd be very cross if I did.

"This Sorcerer passed by the Princess's bier . . . that's a—"

"I know, I *know*, Ian. Go on!"

"Suddenly he frowned and leaned over her pale form. 'What is this?' he thundered. 'Why was I not told?' Everyone was very concerned. This Sorcerer was a dangerous man. One time when someone insulted him he made a spell that turned everyone's heads backwards so they had to walk around with rearview mirrors. No one knew what he would do if he got really angry.

" 'This Princess is wearing the Starstone,' he said, and drew himself up and frowned all around as if he were surrounded by idiots. I'm sure he thought he was and maybe he was right. Because he went on to tell them just what the Starstone was, and what it did, something no one there had ever heard before. And this is the part I'm not sure of. Because, though everyone new the Sorcerer was a wise and powerful man, he was also known as a great liar.

"He said that the Starstone was capable of capturing the essence of a person at the moment of her death. All her wisdom, all her power, all her knowledge and beauty and strength would flow into the stone and be held there, timelessly."

"In suspended animation," Radiant breathed.

"Precisely. When they heard this, the people were amazed. They buffeted the Sorcerer with questions, to which he gave few answers, and those only grudgingly. Finally he left in a huff. When he was gone, everyone talked long into the night about the things he had said. Some felt the Sorcerer had held out hope that the Princess might yet live on. That if her body was frozen, the Prince, upon his return, might somehow infuse her essence back within her. Others thought the Sorcerer had said that was impossible, that the Princess was doomed to a half-life, locked in the stone.

"But the opinion that prevailed was this:

"The Princess would probably never come fully back to life. But her essence might flow from the Starstone and into another, if the right person could be found. All agreed this person must be a young maiden. She must be beautiful, very smart, swift of foot, loving, kind . . . oh, my, the list was very long. Everyone doubted such a person could be found. Many did not even want to try.

"But at last it was decided the Starstone should be given to a faithful friend of the Prince. He would search the galaxy for this maiden. If she existed, he would find her.

"So he departed with the blessings of many worlds behind him, vowing to find the maiden and give her the Starstone."

He stopped again, cleared his throat, and let the silence grow.

"Is that all?" she said at last, in a whisper.

"Not quite all," he admitted. "I'm afraid I tricked you."

"Tricked me?"

He opened the front of his coat, which was still draped around her shoulders. He reached in past her bony chest and down into an inner pocket of the coat. He came up with the crystal. It was oval, with one side flat. It pulsed ruby light as it sat in the palm of his hand.

"It shines," she said, looking at it wide-eyed and open-mouthed.

"Yes, it does. And that means you're the one."

"Me?"

"Yes. Take it." He handed it to her, and as he did so, he nicked it with his thumbnail. Red light spilled into her hands, flowed between her fingers, seemed to soak into her skin. When it was over, the crystal still pulsed, but dimmed. Her hands were trembling.

"It felt very, very hot," she said.

"That was the essence of the Princess."

"And the Prince? Is he still looking for her?"

"No one knows. I think he's still out there, and someday he will come back for her."

"And what then?"

He looked away from her. "I can't say. I think, even though you are lovely, and even though you have the Starstone, that he will just pine away. He loved her very much."

"I'd take care of him," she promised.

"Maybe that would help. But I have a problem now. I don't have the heart to tell the Prince that she is dead. Yet I feel that the Starstone will draw him to it one day. If he comes and finds you, I fear for him. I think perhaps I should take the stone to a far part of the galaxy, someplace he could never find it. Then at least he would never know. It might be better that way."

"But I'd help him," she said earnestly. "I promise. I'd wait for him, and when he came, I'd take her place. You'll see."

He studied her. Perhaps she would. He looked into her eyes for a long time, and at last let her see his satisfaction.

"Very well. You can keep it, then."

"I'll wait for him," she said. "You'll see."

She was very tired, almost asleep.

"You should go home now," he suggested.

"Maybe I could just lie down for a moment," she said.

"All right." He lifted her gently and placed her supine on the ground. He stood looking at her, then knelt beside her and began to stroke her forehead gently. She opened her eyes with no alarm, then closed them again. He continued to stroke her.

Twenty minutes later he left the playground, alone.

He was always depressed afterwards. It was worse than usual this time. She had been much nicer than he had imagined at first. Who could have guessed such a romantic heart beat beneath all that dirt?

He found a phone booth several blocks away. Punching her name into information yielded a fifteen-digit number, which he called. He held his hand over the camera eye.

A woman's face appeared on his screen.

"Your daughter is in the playground, at the south end by the pool, under the bushes," he said. He gave the address of the playground.

"We were so worried! What . . . is she . . . who is—"

He hung up and hurried away.

Most of the other pushers thought he was sick. Not that it mattered. Pushers were a tolerant group when it came to other pushers, and especially when it came to anything a pusher might care to do to a puller. He wished he had never told anyone how he spent his leave time, but he had, and now he had to live with it.

So, while they didn't care if he amused himef by pulling the legs and arms off infant puller pups, they were all just back from ground leave and couldn't pass up an opportunity to get on each other's nerves. They ragged him mercilessly.

"How were the swing-sets this trip, Ian?"

"Did you bring me those dirty knickers I asked for?"

"Was it good for you, honey? Did she pant and slobber?"

"My ten-year-old baby, she's a-pullin' me back home. . . ."

Ian bore it stoically. It was in extremely bad taste, and he was the brunt of it, but it really didn't matter. It would end as soon as they lifted again. They would never understand what he sought, but he felt he understood them. They hated coming to Earth. There was nothing for them there, and perhaps they wished there were.

And he was a pusher himself. He didn't care for pullers. He agreed with the sentiment expressed by Marian, shortly after lift-off. Marian had just finished her first ground leave after her first voyage. So naturally she was the drunkest of them all.

"Gravity sucks," she said, and threw up.

It was three months to Amity, and three months back. He hadn't the foggiest idea how far it was in miles; after the tenth or eleventh zero his mind clicked off.

Amity. Shit City. He didn't even get off the ship. Why bother? The planet was peopled with things that looked a little like ten-ton caterpillars and a little like sentient green turds. Toilets were a revolutionary idea to the Amiti; so were ice cream bars, sherbets, sugar donuts, and peppermint. Plumbing had never caught on, but sweets had, and fancy desserts from every nation on Earth. In addition, there was a pouch of reassuring mail for the forlorn human embassy. The cargo for the return trip was some grayish sludge that Ian supposed someone on Earth found tremendously valuable, and a packet of desperate mail for the folks back home. Ian didn't need to read the letters to know what was in them. They could all be summed up as "Get me *out* of here!"

He sat at the viewport and watched an Amiti family lumbering and farting its way down the spaceport road. They paused every so often to do something that looked like an alien cluster-fuck. The road was brown. The land around it was brown, and in the distance were brown, unremarkable hills. There was a brown haze in the air, and the sun was yellow-brown.

He thought of castles perched on mountains of glass, of Princes and Princesses, of shining white horses galloping among the stars.

He spent the return trip just as he had on the way out: sweating down in the gargantuan pipes of the stardrive. Just beyond the metal walls, unimaginable energies pulsed. And on the walls themselves, tiny plasmoids grew into bigger plasmoids. The process was too slow to see, but if left unchecked the encrustations would soon impair the engines. His job was to scrape them off.

Not everyone was cut out to be an astrogator.

And what of it? It was honest work. He had made his choices long ago. You spent your life either pulling gees or pushing *c*. And when you got tired, you grabbed some *z*'s. If there was a pushers' code, that was it.

The plasmoids were red and crystalline, teardrop-shaped.
When he broke them free of the walls, they had one flat side.
They were full of a liquid light that felt as hot as the center of
the sun.

It was always hard to get off the ship. A lot of pushers never
did. One day, he wouldn't either.

He stood for a few moments looking at it all. It was necessary to soak it in passively at first, get used to the changes.
Big changes didn't bother him. Buildings were just the world's
furniture, and he didn't care how it was arranged. Small
changes worried the shit out of him. Ears, for instance. Very
few of the people he saw had earlobes. Each time he returned,
he felt a little more like an ape who has fallen from his tree.
One day he'd return to find that everybody had three eyes or
six fingers, or that little girls no longer cared to hear stories of
adventure.

He stood there dithering, getting used to the way people
were painting their faces, listening to what sounded like Spanish being spoken all around him. Occasional English or Ara-
bic words seasoned it. He grabbed a crewmate's arm and
asked him where they were. The man didn't know. So he
asked the captain, and she said it was Argentina, or it had
been when they left.

The phone booths were smaller. He wondered why.

There were four names in his book. He sat there facing
the phone, wondering which name to call first. His eyes were
drawn to Radiant Shiningstar Smith, so he punched that name
into the phone. He got a number and an address in Novo-
sibirsk.

Checking the timetable he had picked—putting off making the call—he found the antipodean shuttle left on the hour.
Then he wiped his hands on his pants and took a deep breath
and looked up to see her standing outside the phone booth.
They regarded each other silently for a moment. She saw a

man much shorter than she remembered, but powerfully built, with big hands and shoulders and a pitted face that would have been forbidding but for the gentle eyes. He saw a tall woman around forty years old who was fully as beautiful as he had expected she would be. The hand of age had just begun to touch her. He thought she was fighting that waistline and fretting about those wrinkles, but none of that mattered to him. Only one thing mattered, and he would know it soon enough.

"You *are* Ian Haise, aren't you?" she said at last.

"It was sheer luck I remembered you again," she was saying. He noted the choice of words. She could have said *coincidence*.

"It was two years ago. We were moving again and I was sorting through some things and I came across that plasmoid. I hadn't thought about you in . . . oh, it must have been fifteen years."

He said something noncommittal. They were in a restaurant, away from most of the other patrons, at a booth near a glass wall beyond which spaceships were being trundled to and from the blast pits.

"I hope I didn't get you into trouble," he said.

She shrugged it away.

"You did, some, but that was so long ago. I certainly wouldn't bear a grudge that long. And the fact is, I thought it was all worth it at the time."

She went on to tell him of the uproar he had caused in her family, of the visits by the police, the interrogation, puzzlement, and final helplessness. No one knew quite what to make of her story. They had identified him quickly enough, only to find he had left Earth, not to return for a long, long time.

"I didn't break any laws," he pointed out.

"That's what no one could understand. I told them you had talked to me and told me a long story, and then I went to sleep. None of them seemed interested in what the story was about. So I didn't tell them. And I didn't tell them about the . . . the Starstone." She smiled. "Actually, I was relieved they hadn't asked. I was determined not to tell them, but I was a little afraid of holding it all back. I thought they were agents of the . . . who were the villains in your story? I've forgotten."

"It's not important."

"I guess not. But something is."

"Yes."

"Maybe you should tell me what it is. Maybe you can answer the question that's been in the back of my mind for twenty-five years, ever since I found out that thing you gave me was just the scrapings from a starship engine."

"Was it?" he said, looking into her eyes. "Don't get me wrong. I'm not saying it *was* more than that. I'm asking *you* if it wasn't more."

"Yes, I guess it was more," she said at last.

"I'm glad."

"I believed in that story passionately for . . . oh, years and years. Then I stopped believing it."

"All at once?"

"No. Gradually. It didn't hurt much. Part of growing up, I guess."

"And you remembered me."

"Well, that took some work. I went to a hypnotist when I was twenty-five and recovered your name and the name of your ship. Did you know—"

"Yes. I mentioned them on purpose."

She nodded, and they fell silent again. When she looked at him now, he saw more sympathy, less defensiveness. But there was still a question.

"Why?" she said.

He nodded, then looked away from her, out to the starships. He wished he was on one of them, pushing *c*. It wasn't working. He knew it wasn't. He was a weird problem to her, something to get straightened out, a loose end in her life that would irritate until it was made to fit in, then be forgotten.

To hell with it.

"Hoping to get laid," he said. When he looked up, she was slowly shaking her head back and forth.

"Don't trifle with me, Haise. You're not as stupid as you look. You knew I'd be married, leading my own life. You knew I wouldn't drop it all because of some half-remembered fairy tale thirty years ago. *Why?*"

And how could he explain the strangeness of it all to her?

"What do you do?" He recalled something, and rephrased it. "Who *are* you?"

She looked startled. "I'm a mysteliologist."

He spread his hands. "I don't even know what that is."

"Come to think of it, there was no such thing when you left."

"That's it, in a way," he said. He felt helpless again. "Obviously, I had no way of knowing what you'd do, what you'd become, what would happen to you that you had no control over. All I was gambling on was that you'd remember me. Because that way . . ." He saw the planet Earth looming once more out the viewport. So many, many years and only six months later. A planet full of strangers. It didn't matter that Amity was full of strangers. But Earth was home, if that word still had any meaning for him.

"I wanted somebody my own age I could talk to," he said. "That's all. All I want is a friend."

He could see her trying to understand what it was like. She wouldn't, but maybe she'd come close enough to think she did.

"Maybe you've found one," she said, and smiled. "At least I'm willing to get to know you, considering the effort you've put into this."

"It wasn't much effort. It seems so long-term to you, but it wasn't to me. I held you on my lap six months ago."

"How long is your leave?" she asked.

"Two months."

"Would you like to come stay with us for a while? We have room in our house."

"Will your husband mind?"

"Neither my husband nor my wife. That's them sitting over there, pretending to ignore us." Ian looked, caught the eye of a woman in her late twenties. She was sitting across from a man Ian's age, who now turned and looked at Ian with some suspicion but no active animosity. The woman smiled; the man reserved judgment.

Radiant had a wife. Well, times change.

"Those two in the red skirts are police," Radiant was saying. "So is that man over by the wall, and the one at the end of the bar."

"I spotted two of them," Ian said. When she looked surprised, he said, "Cops always have a look about them. That's one of the things that don't change."

"You go back quite a ways, don't you? I'll bet you have some good stories."

Ian thought about it, and nodded. "Some, I suppose."

"I should tell the police they can go home. I hope you don't mind that we brought them in."

"Of course not."

"I'll do that, and then we can go. Oh, and I guess I should call the children and tell them we'll be home soon." She laughed, reached across the table, and touched his hand. "See what can happen in six months? I have three children, and Gillian has two."

He looked up, interested.

"Are any of them girls?"

The Claw
of the Conciliator

Gene Wolfe

I think Gene Wolfe is the best writer working in science fiction today, and I have a lot of company. For some years he has been saddled with the epithet "writer's writer," which is not false—no one who does it for a living can read his work without being constantly amazed and envious—but the term usually carries a connotation of inaccessibility, which does not apply at all here. Gene's work is concrete and vivid and up-front. Like most good art, it does work on various levels, but unlike much deliberately "artistic" writing, it is not academic or obscure, not difficult.

The Book of the New Sun, of which this Nebula-winning novel is the second volume, will be a four-book series about Severian, by trade a torturer and executioner. What sort of man would write a half-million-word epic about such a character? Obviously a morose, ascetic sort of fellow, a cadaverous, hollow-cheeked Poe type, given to wearing dark suits and cold stares.

But Gene is more roly-poly than cadaverous, a dead ringer for Phil Silvers. He seems disgustingly well balanced for a writer: family man, raconteur, solid citizen. He has a scalpel wit and a huge fund of knowledge; talking with him for an hour is

both a tonic and a bracing duel. He manages to turn out a vol-
ume of work that would be respectable for a full-time writer,
while simultaneously raising a large family and holding down a
nine-to-five job as senior editor of an engineering journal. You
can't help liking the guy, but you sort of wistfully hope he has
some deep, dark flaw hidden somewhere.

If this sample from The Claw of the Conciliator *does make*
you want more, you'll also enjoy reading the first volume of the
series, The Shadow of the Torturer; *both of them are available*
from Pocket Books, as are volumes three and four, The Sword
of the Lictor *and* The Citadel of the Autarch.

Before this excerpt begins, Severian has received a message
from Thecla, the only woman he has ever loved; a woman he
believed long dead. Armed with Terminus Est, *his formidable*
executioner's sword, he goes with his friend Jonas to meet the
woman, who waits for him hidden inside a long-disused mine.
We begin in the middle of Chapter Five, "The Bourne."

At last we entered a vale smaller and narrower than any of the
others; and at the end of it, a chain or so off where the moonlight spilled upon a sheer elevation, I saw a dark opening. The
brook had its origin there, flooding out like saliva from the
lips of a petrified titan. I found a patch of ground beside
the water sufficiently level for my mount to stand and contrived to tie him there, knotting what remained of his reins
around a dwarfish tree.

Once, no doubt, a timber trestle had provided access to
the mine, but it had rotted away long ago. Though the climb
looked impossible in the moonlight, I was able to find a few
footholds in the ancient wall, and scaled it to one side of the
descending jet.

I had my hands inside the opening when I heard, or
thought I heard, some sound from the vale behind me. I
paused, and turned my head to look back. The rush of the
water would have drowned any noise less commanding than a

bugle call or an explosion, and it had drowned this, yet still I had sensed something—the note of stone falling upon stone, perhaps, or the splash of something plunging into the water.

The vale seemed peaceful and silent. Then I saw my destrier shift his stance, his proud head and forward-cocked ears coming for an instant into the light. I decided that what I had heard was nothing more than the striking of his steel-shod feet against the rock as he stamped in discontent at being so closely tethered. I drew my body into the mine entrance, and by doing so, as I later learned, saved my life.

A man of any wit, setting out as I had and knowing he must enter such a place, would have brought a lantern and a plentiful supply of candles. I had been so wild at the thought that Thecla still lived that I had none. Thus I crept forward in the dark, and had not taken a dozen steps before the moonlight of the vale had vanished behind me. My boots were in the stream, so I walked as I had when I had led the destrier up it. *Terminus Est* was slung over my left shoulder, and I had no fear that the tip of her sheath might be wet by the stream, for the ceiling of the tunnel was so low that I walked bent double. So I proceeded for a long time, fearing always that I had come wrong, and that Thecla waited for me elsewhere, and would wait in vain.

I grew so accustomed to the sound of the icy water that had you asked me I should have said I walked in silence; but it was not so, and when, most suddenly, the constricted tunnel opened into a large chamber equally dark, I knew it at once from the change in the music of the stream. I took another step, and then another, and raised my head. There was no ragged stone now to strike it. I lifted my arms. Nothing. I grasped *Terminus Est* by her onyx hilt and waved her blade, still in the protection of its sheath. Nothing still.

Then I did something that you, reading this record, will find foolish indeed, though you must recall that I had been

told that such guards as might be in the mine had been
warned of my arrival and instructed to do me no harm. I
called Thecla's name.

And the echoes answered: "*Thecla . . . Thecla . . .
Thecla . . .*"

Then silence again.

I remembered that I was to have followed the water until
it welled from a rock, and that I had not done so. Possibly it
trickled through as many galleries here beneath the hill as it
had through dells outside it. I began to wade again, feeling my
way at each step for fear I might plunge over my head with
the next.

I had not taken five strides when I heard something, far
off yet distinct, above the whispering of the now smoothly
flowing water. I had not taken five more when I saw light.

It was not the emerald reflection of the fabled forests of
the moon, nor was it such a light as guards might carry with
them—the scarlet flame of a torch, the golden radiance of a
candle, or even the piercing white beam I had sometimes
glimpsed by night when the fliers of the Autarch soared over
the Citadel. Rather, it was a luminous mist, sometimes seeming of no color, sometimes of an impure yellowish green. It
was impossible to say how far it was, and it seemed to possess
no shape. For a time it shimmered before my sight; and I, still
following the stream, splashed toward it. Then it was joined
by another.

It is difficult for me to concentrate on the events of the
next few minutes. Perhaps everyone holds in his subconscious
certain moments of horror, as our oubliette held, in its lowest
inhabited level, those clients whose minds had long ago been
destroyed or transformed into consciousness no longer human. Like them, these memories shriek and lash the walls
with their chains, but are seldom brought high enough to see
the light.

What I experienced under the hill remains with me as
they remained with us, something I endeavor to lock within

the furthest recesses of my mind but am from time to time made conscious of. (Not long ago, when the *Samru* was still near the mouth of Gyoll, I looked over the stern rail by night; there I saw each dipping of the oars appear as a spot of phosphorescent fire, and for a moment imagined that those from under the hill had come for me at last. They are mine to command now, but I have small comfort in that.)

The light I had seen was joined by a second, as I have described, then the first two by a third, and the first three by a a fourth, and still I went on. Soon there were too many of the lights to count; but not knowing what they were, I was actually comforted and encouraged by the sight of them, imagining each perhaps to be a spark from a torch of some kind not known to me, a torch held by one of the guards mentioned in the letter. When I had taken a dozen more steps, I saw that these flecks of light were coalescing into a pattern, and that the pattern was a dart or arrowhead pointed toward myself. Then I heard, very faintly, such a roaring as I used to hear from the tower called the Bear when the beasts were given their food. Even then, I think, I might have escaped if I had turned and fled.

I did not. The roaring grew—not quite any noise of animals, yet not the shouting of the most frenzied human mob. I saw that the flecks of light were not shapeless, as I had imagined before. Rather, each was of that figure called in art a star, having five unequal points.

It was then, much too late, that I halted.

By this time the uncertain, hueless light these stars shed had increased enough for me to see as looming shadows the shapes about me. To either side were masses whose angular sides suggested that they were works of men—it seemed I walked in the buried city (here not collapsed under the weight of the overlaying soil) from which the miners of Saltus delved their treasures. Among these masses stood squat pillars of an ordered irregularity such as I have sometimes noticed in ricks of firewood, from which every stick protrudes yet goes to

make the whole. These glinted softly, throwing back the
corpse light of the moving stars as something less sinister, or at
least more beautiful, than they had received.

For a moment I wondered at these pillars; then I looked
at the star-shapes again, and for the first time saw them. Have
you ever toiled by night toward what seemed a cottage window, and found it to be the balefire of a great fortress? Or
climbing, slipped, and caught yourself, and looked below, and
seen the fall a hundred times greater than you had believed?
If you have, you will have some notion of what I felt. The stars
were not sparks of light, but shapes like men, small only because the cavern in which I stood was more vast than I had
ever conceived that such a place could be. And the men, who
seemed not men, being thicker of shoulder and more twisted
than men, were rushing toward me. The roar I heard was the
sound of their voices.

I turned, and when I found I could not run through the
water, mounted the bank where the dark structures stood. By
that time they were almost upon me, and some were moving
wide to my right and left and cut me off from the outer world.

They were terrible in a fashion I am not certain I can
explain—like apes in that they had hairy, crooked bodies,
long-armed, short-legged, and thick-necked. Their teeth were
like the fangs of smilodons, curved and saw-edged, extending
a finger's length below their massive jaws. Yet it was not any
of these things, nor the noctilucent light that clung to their fur,
that brought the horror I felt. It was something in their faces,
perhaps in the huge, pale-irised eyes. It told me they were as
human as I. As the old are imprisoned in rotting bodies, as
women are locked in weak bodies that make them prey for the
filthy desires of thousands, so these men were wrapped in the
guise of lurid apes, and knew it. As they ringed me, I could see
that knowledge, and it was the worse because those eyes were
the only part of them that did not glow.

I gulped air to shout "Thecla" once more. Then I knew,
and closed my lips, and drew *Terminus Est.*

One, larger or at least bolder than the rest, advanced on me. He carried a short-hafted mace whose shaft had once been a thigh bone. Just out of sword reach he threatened me with it, roaring and slapping the metal head of his weapon in a long hand.

Something disturbed the water behind me, and I turned in time to see one of the glowing man-apes fording the stream. He leaped backward as I slashed at him, but the square blade-tip caught him below the armpit. So fine was that blade, so magnificently tempered and perfectly edged, that it cut its way out through the breastbone.

He fell and the water carried his corpse away, but before the stroke went home I had seen that he waded in the stream with distaste, and that it had slowed his movements at least as much as it had slowed mine. Turning to keep all my attackers in view, I backed into it and began slowly to move toward the point where it ran to the outside world. I felt that if I could once reach the constricted tunnel I would be safe; but I knew too that they would never permit me to do so.

They gathered more thickly around me until there must have been several hundred. The light they gave was so great then that I could see that the squared masses I had glimpsed earlier were indeed buildings, apparently of the most ancient construction, built of seamless gray stone and soiled everywhere by the dung of bats.

The irregular pillars were stacks of ingots in which each layer was laid across the last. From their color I judged them to be silver. There were a hundred in each stack, and surely many hundreds of stacks in the buried city.

All this I saw while taking a half-dozen steps. At the seventh they came for me, twenty at least, and from all sides. There was no time for clean strokes through the neck. I swung my blade in circles, and its singing filled that underground world and echoed from the stony walls and ceiling, audible over the bellowing and the screams.

One's sense of time goes mad at such moments. I recall

the rush of the attack and my own frantic blows, but in retro-spect everything seems to have happened in a breath. Two and five and ten were down, until the water around me was blood-black in the corpse light, choked with dying and dead; but still they came. A blow on my shoulder was like the smash of a giant's fist. *Terminus Est* slipped out of my hand, and the weight of the bodies bore me down until I was grappling blind underwater. My enemy's fangs slashed my arm as two spikes might, but he feared drowning too much, I think, to fight as he would have otherwise. I thrust fingers into his wide nostrils and snapped his neck, though it seemed tougher than a man's.

If I could have held my breath then until I worked my way to the tunnel, I might have escaped. The man-apes seemed to have lost sight of me, and I drifted underwater some small distance downstream. By then my lungs were bursting; I lifted my face to the surface, and they were upon me.

No doubt there comes a time for every man when by rights he should die. This, I have always felt, was mine. I have counted all the life I have held since as pure profit, an undeserved gift. I had no weapon, and my right arm was numbed and torn. The man-apes were bold now. That bold-ness gave me a moment more of life, for so many crowded forward to kill me that they obstructed one another. I kicked one in the face. A second grasped my boot; there was a flash of light, and I (moved by what instinct or inspiration I do not know) snatched at it. I held the Claw.

As though it gathered to itself all the corpse light and dyed it with the color of life, it streamed forth a clear azure that filled the cavern. For one heartbeat the man-apes halted as though at the stroke of a gong, and I lifted the gem over-head; what frenzy of terror I hoped for (if I really hoped at all) I cannot say now.

What happened was quite different. The man-apes nei-ther fled shrieking nor resumed their attack. Instead they re-treated until the nearest were perhaps three strides off, and squatted with their faces pressed against the floor of the mine. There was silence again as there had been when I had first entered it, with no sound but the whispering of the stream; but now I could see everything, from the stacks of tarnished silver ingots near to which I stood, to the very end where the man-apes had descended a ruined wall, appearing to my sight then like flecks of pale fire.

I began to back away. The man-apes looked up at that, and their faces were the faces of human beings. When I saw them thus, I knew of the eons of struggles in the dark from which their fangs and saucer eyes and flap ears had come to be. We, so the mages say, were apes once, happy apes in forests swallowed by deserts so long ago they have no names. Old men return to childish ways when at last the years becloud their minds. May it not be that mankind will return (as an old man does) to the decayed image of what once was, if at last the old sun dies and we are left scuffling over bones in the dark? I saw our future—one future at least—and I felt more sorrow for those who had triumphed in the dark battles than for those who had poured out their blood in that endless night.

I took a step backward (as I have said), and then another, and still none of the man-apes moved to stop me. Then I remembered *Terminus Est*. Were I to have made my escape from the most frantic battle, I would have despised myself if I had left her behind. To walk out unmolested without her was more than I could bear. I began to advance again, watching by the light of the Claw for her gleaming blade.

At this the faces of those strange, twisted men seemed to brighten, and I saw by their looks that they hoped I meant to remain with them, so that the Claw and its blue radiance would be theirs always. How terrible it seems now when I set the words on paper; yet it would not, I think, have been terrible in fact. Bestial though they appeared, I could see adoration on every brute face, so that I thought (as I think now) that if they are worse in many ways than we are, these people of

the hidden cities beneath Urth are better in others, blessed
with an ugly innocence.

From side to side I searched, from bank to bank; but I
saw nothing, though it seemed to me that the light shone from
the Claw more brightly, and more brightly still, until at last
each tooth of stone that hung from the ceiling of that cavernous space cast behind it a sharp-sided shadow of pitch black.
At last I called out to the crouching men, "My sword . . .
Where is my sword? Did one of you take her?"

I would not have spoken to them if I had not been half
frantic with the fear of losing her; but it seemed they understood. They began to mutter among themselves and to me,
and to make signs to me—without rising—to show they would
fight no more, extending their bludgeons and spears of
pointed bone for me to take.

Then, above the murmuring of the water and the mutter-
ing of the man-apes, I heard a new sound, and at once they
fell silent. If an ogre were to eat of the very legs of the world,
the grinding of his teeth would make just such a noise. The
bed of the stream (where I still stood) trembled under me, and
the water, which had been so clear, received a fine burden of
silt, so that it looked as though a ribbon of smoke wound
through it. From far below I heard a step that might have
been the walking of a tower on the Final Day, when it is said
all the cities of Urth will stride forth to meet the dawn of the
New Sun.

And then another.

At once the man-apes rose and, crouching low, fled
toward the farther end of the gallery, silent now and swift as
so many flitting bats. The light went with them, for it seemed,
as I had somehow feared, that the Claw had flamed for them
and not for me.

A third step came from underground, and with it the last
gleam winked out; but at that instant, in that final gleam, I
saw *Terminus Est* lying in the deepest water. In the dark I bent
and, putting the Claw back into the top of my boot, took up
my sword; and in so doing I discovered that the numbness

had left my arm, which now seemed as strong as it had before the fight.

A fourth step sounded and I turned and fled, groping before me with the blade. What creature it was we had called from the roots of the continent I think I now know. But I did not know then, and I did not know whether it was the roaring of the man-apes, or the light of the Claw, or some other cause that had waked it. I only knew that there was something far beneath us before which the man-apes, with all the terror of their apearance and their numbers, scattered like sparks before a wind.

When I recall my second passage through the tunnel that led to the outer world, I feel it occupied a watch or more. My nerves have never, I supposed, been fully sound, tormented as they have always been by a relentless memory. Then they were keyed to the highest pitch, so that to take three strides seemed to exhaust a lifetime. I was frightened, of course. I have never been called a coward since I was a small boy, and on certain occasions various persons have commented on my courage. I have performed my duties as a member of the guild without flinching, fought both privately and in war, climbed crags, and several times nearly drowned. But I believe there is no other difference between those who are called courageous and those who are branded craven than that the second are fearful before the danger and the first after it.

No one can be much frightened, certainly, during a period of great and imminent peril—the mind is too much concentrated on the thing itself, and on the actions necessary to meet or avoid it. The coward is a coward, then, because he has brought his fear with him; persons we think cowardly will sometimes amaze us by their bravery, if they have had no forewarning of their danger.

Master Gurloes, whom I had supposed to be of the most dauntless courage when I was a boy, was unquestionably a coward. During the period when Drotte was captain of apprentices, Roche and I used to alternate, turn and turn

about, in serving Master Gurloes and Master Palaemon; and
one night, when Master Gurloes had retired to his cabin but
instructed me to stay to fill his cup for him, he began to con-
fide in me.

"Lad, do you know the client Ia? An armiger's daughter
and quite good-looking."

As an apprentice I had few dealings with clients; I shook
my head.

"She is to be abused."

I had no idea what he meant, so I said, "Yes, Master."

"That's the greatest disgrace that can befall a woman. Or
a man either. To be abused. By the torturer." He touched his
chest and threw back his head to look at me. He had a re-
markably small head for so large a man; if he had worn a shirt
or jacket (which of course he never did), one would have been
tempted to believe it padded.

"Yes, Master."

"Aren't you going to offer to do it for me? A young fellow
like you, full of juice. Don't tell me you're not hairy yet."

At last I understood what he meant, and I told him that I
had not realized it would be permissible, since I was still
an apprentice; but that if he gave the order, I would certainly obey.

"I imagine you would. She's not bad, you know. But tall,
and I don't like them tall. There's an exultant's bastard in that
family a generation or so back, you may be sure. Blood will
confess itself, as they say, though only we know what all that
means. Want to do it?"

He held out his cup and I poured. "If you wish me to,
Master." The truth was that I was excited at the thought. I had
never possessed a woman.

"You can't. I must. What if I were to be questioned? Then
too, I must certify it—sign the papers. A master of the guild for
twenty years, and I've never falsified papers. I suppose you
think I can't do it."

The thought had never crossed my mind, just as the opposite thought (that he might still retain some potency) had

never occurred to me with regard to Master Palaemon, whose white hair, stooped shoulders, and peering lens made him seem like one who had been decrepit always.

"Well, look here," Master Gurloes said, and heaved himself out of his chair.

He was one of those who can walk well and speak clearly even when they are very drunk, and he strode over to a cabinet quite confidently, though I thought for a moment that he was going to drop the blue porcelain jar he took down.

"This is a rare and potent drug." He took the lid off and showed me a dark brown powder. "It never fails. You'll have to use it someday, so you ought to know about it. Just take as much as you could get under your fingernail on the end of a knife, you follow me? If you take too much, you won't be able to appear in public for a couple of days."

I said, "I'll remember, Master."

"Of course it's a poison. They all are, and this is the best—a little more than *that* would kill you. And you mustn't take it again until the moon changes, understand?"

"Perhaps you'd better have Brother Corbinian weigh the dose, Master." Corbinian was our apothecary; I was terrified that Master Gurloes might swallow a spoonful before my eyes.

"Me? I don't need it." Contemptuously, he put the lid on the jar again and banged it down on its shelf in the cabinet.

"That's well, Master."

"Besides" (he winked at me), "I'll have this." From his sabretache he took an iron phallus. It was about a span and a half long and had a leather thong through the end opposite the tip.

It must seem idiotic to you who read this, but for an instant I could not imagine what the thing was for, despite the somewhat exaggerated realism of its design. I had a wild notion that the wine had rendered him childish, as a little boy is who supposes there is no essential difference between his wooden mount and a real animal. I wanted to laugh.

"'Abuse,' that's their word. That, you see, is where

they've left us an out." He had slapped the iron phallus against his palm—the same gesture, now that I think of it, that the man-ape who had threatened me had made with his mace. Then I had understood and had been gripped by revulsion.

But even that revulsion was not the emotion I would feel now in the same situation. I did not sympathize with the client, because I did not think of her at all; it was only a sort of repugnance for Master Gurloes, who with all his bulk and great strength was forced to rely on the brown powder and, still worse, on the iron phallus I had seen, an object that might have been sawed from a statue, and perhaps had been. Yet I saw him on another occasion, when the thing had to be done immediately for fear the order could not otherwise be carried out before the client died, act at once, and without powder or phallus, and without difficulty.

Master Gurloes was a coward then. Still, perhaps his cowardice was better than the courage I would have possessed in his position, for courage is not always a virtue. I had been courageous (as such things are counted) when I had fought the man-apes, but my courage was no more than a mixture of foolhardiness, surprise, and desperation; now, in the tunnel, when there was no longer any cause for fear, I was afraid and nearly dashed my brains out against the low ceiling; but I did not pause or even slacken speed before I saw the opening before me, made visible by the blessed sheen of moonlight. Then, indeed, I halted and, considering myself safe, wiped my sword as well as I might with the ragged edge of my cloak, and sheathed her.

That done, I slung her over my shoulder and swung myself out and down, feeling with the toes of my sodden boots for the ledges that had supported me in the ascent. I had just gained the third when two quarrels struck the rock near my head. One must have wedged its point in some flaw in the ancient work, for it remained in place, blazing with white fire. I recall how astonished I was, and also how I hoped, in the few moments before the next struck nearer still and nearly blinded me, that the arbalests were not of the kind that bring a new projectile to the string when cocked, and thus are so swift to shoot again.

When the third exploded against the stone, I knew they were, and dropped before the marksmen who had missed could fire yet again.

There was, as I ought to have known there would be, a deep pool where the stream fell from the mouth of the mine. I got another ducking, but since I was already wet it did no harm, and in fact quenched the flecks of fire that had clung to my face and arms.

There could be no question here of cannily remaining below the surface. The water seized me as if I were a stick and flung me to the top where it willed. This, by the greatest good luck, was some distance from the rock face, and I was able to watch my attackers from behind as I clambered onto the bank. They and the woman who stood between them were staring at the place where the cascade fell.

As I drew *Terminus Est* for the final time that night, I called, "Over here, Agia."

I had guessed earlier that it was she, but as she turned (more swiftly than either of the men with her) I glimpsed her face in the moonlight. It was a terrible face to me (though for all her self-depreciation so lovely) because the sight of it meant that Thecla was surely dead.

The man nearest me was fool enough to try to bring his arbalest to his shoulder before he pulled the trigger. I ducked and cut his legs from under him, while the other's quarrel whizzed over my head like a meteor.

By the time I had straightened up again, the second man had dropped his arbalest and was drawing his hanger. Agia was quicker, making a cut at my neck with an athame before his weapon was free of the scabbard. I dodged her first stroke and parried her second, though *Terminus Est*'s blade was not made for fencing. My own attack made her bound back.

"Get behind him," she called to the second arbalestier. "I can front him."

He did not answer. Instead, his mouth swung open and

his point swung wide. Before I realized that it was not at me that he was looking, something feverishly gleaming bounded past me. I heard the ugly sound of a breaking skull. Agia turned as gracefully as any cat and would have spitted the man-ape, but I struck the poisoned blade from her hand and sent it skittering into the pool. She tried to flee then; I caught her by the hair and jerked her off her feet.

The man-ape was mumbling over the body of the arbalestier he had killed—whether he sought to loot it or was merely curious about its appearance I have never known. I set my foot on Agia's neck, and the man-ape straightened and turned to face me, then dropped in the crouching posture I had seen in the mine and held up his arms. One hand was gone; I recognized the clean cut of *Terminus Est.* The man-ape mumbled something I could not understand.

I tried to reply. "Yes, I did that. I am sorry. We are at peace now."

The beseeching look remained, and he spoke again. Blood still seeped from the stump, though his kind must possess a mechanism for pinching shut the veins, as thylacodons are said to do; without the attentions of a surgeon, a man would have bled to death from that wound.

"I cut it," I said. "But it was while we were still fighting, before you people saw the Claw of the Conciliator." Then it came to me that he must have followed me outside for another glimpse of the gem, braving the fear engendered by whatever we had waked below the hill. I thrust my hand into the top of my boot and pulled out the Claw, and the instant I had done so realized what a fool I had been to put the boot and its precious cargo so close to Agia's reach, for her eyes went wide with cupidity at the moment that the man-ape abased himself further and stretched forth his piteous stump.

For a moment we were posed, all three, and a strange group we must have looked in that eerie light. An astonished voice—Jonas's—called "Severian!" from the heights above. Like the trumpet note in a shadow play that dissolves all feigning, that shout ended our tableau. I lowered the Claw and concealed it in my palm. The man-ape bolted for the rock face, and Agia began to struggle and curse beneath my foot.

A rap with the flat of my blade quieted her, but I kept my boot on her until Jonas had joined me and there were two of us to prevent her escape.

"I thought you might need help," he said. "I perceive I was mistaken." He was looking at the corpses of the men who had been with Agia.

I said, "This wasn't the real fight."

Agia was sitting up, rubbing her neck and shoulders. "There were four, and we would have had you, but the bodies of those things, those firefly tiger-men, started pitching out of the hole, and two were afraid and slipped away."

Jonas scratched his head with his steel hand, a sound like the currying of a charger. "I saw what I thought I saw, then. I had begun to wonder."

I asked what he thought he had seen.

"A glowing being in a fur robe making an obeisance to you. You were holding up a cup of burning brandy, I think. Or was it incense? What's this?" He bent and picked up something from the edge of the bank, where the man-ape had crouched.

"A bludgeon."

"Yes, I see that." There was a loop of sinew at the end of the bone handle, and Jonas slipped it over his wrist. "Who are these people who tried to kill you?"

"We would have," Agia said, "if it hadn't been for that cloak. We saw him coming out of the hole, but it covered him when he started to climb down, and my men couldn't see the target, only the skin of his arms."

I explained as briefly as I could how I had become involved with Agia and her twin, and described the death of Agilus.

"So now she's come to join him." Jonas looked from her to the crimson length of *Terminus Est* and gave a little shrug.

"I left my merychip up there, and perhaps I ought to go and look after her. That way I can say afterward that I saw nothing. Was this woman the one who sent the letter?"

"I should have known. I had told her about Thecla. You don't know about Thecla, but she did, and that was what the letter was about. I told her while we were going through the Botanic Gardens in Nessus. There were mistakes in the letter and things Thecla would never have said, but I didn't stop to think of them when I read it."

I stepped away and replaced the Claw in my boot, thrusting it deep. "Maybe you had better attend to your animal, as you say. My own seems to have broken loose, and we may have to take turns riding yours."

Jonas nodded and began to climb back the way he had come.

"You were waiting for me, weren't you?" I asked Agia. "I heard something, and the destrier cocked his ears at the sound. That was you. Why didn't you kill me then?"

"We were up there." She gestured toward the heights. "And I wanted the men I'd hired to shoot you when you came wading up the brook. They were stupid and stubborn as men always are, and said they wouldn't waste their quarrels—that the creatures inside would kill you. I rolled down a stone, the biggest I could move, but by then it was too late."

"They had told you about the mine?"

Agia shrugged, and the moonlight turned her bare shoulders to something more precious and more beautiful than flesh. "You're going to kill me now, so what does it matter? All the local people tell stories about this place. They say those things come out at night during storms and take animals from the cowsheds, and sometimes break into the houses for children. There's also a legend that they guard treasure inside, so I put that in the letter too. I thought if you wouldn't come for your Thecla, you might for that. Can I stand with my back to you, Severian? If it's all the same, I don't want to see it coming."

When she said that, I felt as though a weight had been lifted from my heart: I had not been certain I could strike her if I had to look into her face.

I raised my own iron phallus, and as I did so felt there was one more thing I wanted to ask Agia; but I could not recall what it might be.

"Strike," she said. "I am ready."

I sought good footing, and my fingers found the woman's head at one end of the guard, the head that marked the female edge.

And a little later, again, "Strike!"

But by that time I had climbed out of the vale.

Two Poems

No Nebula Award is given for poetry (thank God, some say) but
the poets among us have their own award: the Rhysling, named
after the blind poet of Heinlein's immortal story "The Green
Hills of Earth." The Science Fiction Poetry Association gives
two annual Rhyslings, for best short poem and best long poem.
Here are this year's winners.

Meeting Place
Ken Duffin

Not in my lifetime, nor that of my sun;
but beyond the final collapse when
the last static ashes and
clinkered proteins bleed
slowly, from the microcracks of the next
cosmic egg—then
and there will spin

the tiny helix, eternally
recurring, lapped by pale
and teeming future seas.
Perhaps we'll meet?
Say yes;
say . . . an eon from now,
beside the gently sloping banks
of the gene pool. Come
as you were,
and I'll bring the wine.

On Science Fiction
Tom Disch

We are all cripples. First admit that
And it follows we incur no uncommon shame
By lying in our beds telling such tales
As will serve to cheer those who share our condition.

It is a painful business. Time does not fly
For paraplegics. Even those who find employment
Manipulating numbers and answering phones
Are afflicted with the rictus of sustained
Disappointment. We would all rather be whole.

There is another world we all imagine where
Our handicaps become the means of grace,
Where acne vanishes from every face,
And the slug-white bodies rise from wrinkled sheets
With cries of joy. Within each twisted this-world smile
Bubbles the subconscious slobber of a cover by Frazetta.

Of course we are proud of our ability to move
At high velocity among our many self-delusions.

We invalids, because we share the terrible
Monotony of childhood, preserve the childlike knack
Of crossing the border into the Luna of our dreams.

Many cannot. Look deep in the glazed eyes of the normative
And you will discern that genteel poverty of the imagination
Which is our scorn, our torment, our sordid delight.
Why, we ask ourselves, can't they *learn* to be crippled?

Some do—but only as a father may enter
The house inhabited by his daughter's dolls.
And then only for the interval of a smile, only to visit.
He cannot know what it is to live
Completely in the imagination, never to leave it.

To live, that is, imprisoned in a wheelchair,
In limbs that can no longer suffer pains
Of growth. There is a story we love to hear told
About a man who comes to our utopia
And is initiated to our ways. We teach him
A special form of basketball. He sees our rodeo.

His normal fingers touch our withered legs.
His mouth makes love. He's soundly whipped
For the careless enjoyment of his health, and then—
This is the part we relish most—he sees us
As we really are, transfigured, transcendent, gods.

We form our wheelchairs in a perfect circle. We
close our eyes, we wish with all our might, and
Suddenly, zap, thanks to the secret psychic powers
We handicapped, so called, possess, we disappear!

Where to? Never ask. Believe, as the hero of that tale
Believed, that we were switched by the flick of a wish
Into that lovely Otherwhere beloved by every visitor

To Lourdes. Suppose, for the sake of story
We were lifted up into the fresco's glory. Believe.

Do we deceive ourselves? Assuredly.
How else sustain the years of pain, the sneers
And hasty aversions of those who recognize
In our deformities the mirror image of their own
Intolerable irregularities? The antidote
To shame is arrogance; to prison, an escape.

To be a cripple, however, is to know
That all attempts must fail. We open our eyes
And at once Barsoom dissolves. We're back within
Our irremediable skin in that familiar cruel
World where every doorknob's out of reach.

You are welcome, therefore, Stranger, to join
Our confraternity. But please observe the rules.
Always display a cheerful disposition. Do not refer
To our infirmities. Help us to conquer the galaxy.

Appendixes

NEBULA NOMINEES FOR 1981

For the record, here is a list of the stories that made the final ballot for the Nebula Awards.

Novel

Winner:	*The Claw of the Conciliator* by Gene Wolfe
Runners-up:	*The Many-Colored Land* by Julian May
	Little, Big by John Crowley
	The Vampire Tapestry by Suzy McKee Charnas
	Radix by A. A. Attanasio

Novella

Winner:	"The Saturn Game" by Poul Anderson
Runners-up:	"Swarmer, Skimmer" by Gregory Benford
	"Amnesia" by Jack Dann
	"In the Western Tradition" by Phyllis Eisenstein

"True Names" by Vernor Vinge

"The Winter Beach" by Kate Wilhelm

Novelette

Winner: "The Quickening" by Michael Bishop

Runners-up: "Sea Changeling" by Mildred Downey Broxon

"The Thermals of August" by Edward Bryant

"The Fire When It Comes" by Parke Godwin

"Mummer Kiss" by Michael Swanwick

"Lirios: A Tale of the Quintana Roo" by James Tiptree, Jr.

Short Story

Winner: "The Bone Flute" by Lisa Tuttle

Runners-up: "Going Under" by Jack Dann

"Disciples" by Gardner Dozois

"The Quiet" by George Florance-Guthridge

"Johnny Mnemonic" by William Gibson

"Venice Drowned" by Kim Stanley Robinson

"Zeke" by Timothy Robert Sullivan

"The Pusher" by John Varley

As mentioned in the Introduction, the selection of stories for this anthology is an example of "democracy in action"; only Nebula winners and nominees can be included. Literary taste is a quirky thing, though, and it would be a remarkable coincidence if any editor of this volume agreed one hundred percent with the judgment of his peers.

Being on the Nebula jury gave me the obligation and pleasure of reading almost all of the short science fiction published during the year and, inevitably, many of my personal favorites didn't go on the final ballot. If this were a plain best-of-the-year anthology, I would include some of the following:

"Exposures" by Gregory Benford
"A Day at the Fair" by Neal Barret, Jr.
"The Rosfo Gate" or "Eligible for Parole After Three Hours"
    by Coleman Brax
"Walk the Ice" by Mildred Downey Broxon
"The Coming of the Dolls" by Pat Cadigan
"Executive Clemency" by Gardner Dozois and Jack C.
Haldeman II
"I Have a Winter Reason" by Melissa Michaels
"Emergence" by David Palmer
"Serpent's Teeth" by Spider Robinson
"The Sleepwalkers" by Scott Sanders

THE NEBULA AWARD WINNERS

1965
Best Novel: *Dune* by Frank Herbert
Best Novella: "The Saliva Tree" by Brian W. Aldiss
                       "He Who Shapes" by Roger Zelazny (tie)
Best Novelette: · "The Doors of His Face, the Lamps of
                       His Mouth" by Roger Zelazny
Best Short Story: " 'Repent, Harlequin!' Said the Ticktock-
                       man" by Harlan Ellison

1966
Best Novel: *Flowers for Algernon* by Daniel Keyes
                       Babel-17 by Samuel R. Delany (tie)
Best Novella: "The Last Castle" by Jack Vance
Best Novelette: "Call Him Lord" by Gordon R. Dickson
Best Short Story: "The Secret Place" by Richard McKenna

1967
Best Novel: *The Einstein Intersection* by Samuel R.
                       Delany

Best Novella:	"Behold the Man" by Michael Moorcock
Best Novelette:	"Gonna Roll the Bones" by Fritz Leiber
Best Short Story:	"Aye, and Gomorrah" by Samuel R. Delany

1968

Best Novel:	*Rite of Passage* by Alexei Panshin
Best Novella:	"Dragonrider" by Anne McCaffrey
Best Novelette:	"Mother to the World" by Richard Wilson
Best Short Story:	"The Planners" by Kate Wilhelm

1969

Best Novel:	*The Left Hand of Darkness* by Ursula K. Le Guin
Best Novella:	"A Boy and His Dog" by Harlan Ellison
Best Novelette:	"Time Considered as a Helix of Semi-Precious Stones" by Samuel R. Delany
Best Short Story:	"Passengers" by Robert Silverberg

1970

Best Novel:	*Ringworld* by Larry Niven
Best Novella:	"Ill Met in Lankhmar" by Fritz Leiber
Best Novelette:	"Slow Sculpture" by Theodore Sturgeon
Best Short Story:	No Award

1971

Best Novel:	*A Time of Changes* by Robert Silverberg
Best Novella:	"The Missing Man" by Katherine MacLean
Best Novelette:	"The Queen of Air and Darkness" by Poul Anderson
Best Short Story:	"Good News from the Vatican" by Robert Silverberg

1972

Best Novel:	*The Gods Themselves* by Isaac Asimov
Best Novella:	"A Meeting with Medusa" by Arthur C. Clarke
Best Novelette:	"Goat Song" by Poul Anderson
Best Short Story:	"When It Changed" by Joanna Russ

1973
Best Novel: *Rendezvous with Rama* by Arthur C. Clarke

Best Novella: "The Death of Doctor Island" by Gene Wolfe

Best Novelette: "Of Mist, and Grass, and Sand" by Vonda N. McIntyre

Best Short Story: "Love Is the Plan, the Plan Is Death" by James Tiptree, Jr.

1974
Best Novel: *The Dispossessed* by Ursula K. Le Guin

Best Novella: "Born with the Dead" by Robert Silverberg

Best Novelette: "If the Stars Are Gods" by Gordon Eklund and Gregory Benford

Best Short Story: "The Day Before the Revolution" by Ursula K. Le Guin

Best Dramatic Presentation: *Sleeper*

Grand Master Award: Robert A. Heinlein

1975
Best Novel: *The Forever War* by Joe Haldeman

Best Novella: "Home Is the Hangman" by Roger Zelazny

Best Novelette: "San Diego Lightfoot Sue" by Tom Reamy

Best Short Story: "Catch That Zeppelin!" by Fritz Leiber

Best Dramatic Presentation: *Young Frankenstein*

Grand Master: Jack Williamson

1976
Best Novel: *Man Plus* by Frederik Pohl

Best Novella: "Houston, Houston, Do You Read?" by James Tiptree, Jr.

Best Novelette: "The Bicentennial Man" by Isaac Asimov

Best Short Story: "A Crowd of Shadows" by Charles L. Grant

Grand Master: Clifford D. Simak

1977

Best Novel: *Gateway* by Frederik Pohl
Best Novella: "Stardance" by Spider and Jeanne Robinson
Best Novelette: "The Screwfly Solution" by Raccoona Sheldon
Best Short Story: "Jeffty Is Five" by Harlan Ellison
Grand Master: Jack Williamson
Special Award: *Star Wars*

1978

Best Novel: *Dreamsnake* by Vonda N. McIntyre
Best Novella: "The Persistence of Vision" by John Varley
Best Novelette: "A Glow of Candles, a Unicorn's Eye" by Charles L. Grant
Best Short Story: "Stone" by Edward Bryant
Grand Master: L. Sprague de Camp

1979

Best Novel: *The Fountains of Paradise* by Arthur C. Clarke
Best Novella: "Enemy Mine" by Barry Longyear
Best Novelette: "Sandkings" by George R. R. Martin
Best Short Story: "giANTS" by Edward Bryant

1980

Best Novel: *Timescape* by Gregory Benford
Best Novella: "The Unicorn Tapestry" by Suzy McKee Charnas
Best Novelette: "The Ugly Chickens" by Howard Waldrop
Best Short Story: "Grotto of the Dancing Deer" by Clifford D. Simak

This list was compiled with the help of *A History of the Hugo, Nebula, and International Fantasy Awards*, by Donald Franson and Howard Devore. (Copyright © 1981 by Misfit Press. Available from Misfit Press, 4705 Wedel, Dearborn, MI 48125.)

AWARD-WINNING
Science Fiction!

The following titles are winners of the prestigious Nebula or Hugo Award for excellence in Science Fiction. A must for lovers of good science fiction everywhere!

☐ 77421-0	**SOLDIER ASK NOT,** Gordon R. Dickson	$2.95
☐ 47810-7	**THE LEFT HAND OF DARKNESS,** Ursula K. Le Guin	$2.95
☐ 16651-2	**THE DRAGON MASTERS,** Jack Vance	$1.95
☐ 16706-3	**THE DREAM MASTER,** Roger Zelazny	$2.25
☐ 24905-1	**FOUR FOR TOMORROW,** Roger Zelazny	$2.25
☐ 80698-8	**THIS IMMORTAL,** Roger Zelazny	$2.75

Prices may be slightly higher in Canada.

Available at your local bookstore or return this form to:

ACE SCIENCE FICTION
Book Mailing Service
P.O. Box 690, Rockville Centre, NY 11571

Please send me the titles checked above. I enclose _____. Include 75¢ for postage and handling if one book is ordered; 25¢ per book for two or more not to exceed $1.75. California, Illinois, New York and Tennessee residents please add sales tax.

NAME_____

ADDRESS_____

CITY_____STATE/ZIP_____

(allow six weeks for delivery)   **SF-3**

MORE *SCIENCE FICTION* ADVENTURE!